Anna

Anna

Heather Ingman

POOLBEG

Published 1995 by
Poolbeg Press Ltd,
Knocksedan House,
123 Baldoyle Industrial Estate,
Dublin 13, Ireland

© Heather Ingman 1995

The moral right of the author has been asserted.

A catalogue record for this book is available from the British Library.

ISBN 1 85371 450 X

Cover painting *Kerry Reading* by Stephen Darbishire
Courtesy of Richard Hagen Ltd, Yew Tree House,
Broadway Worcestershire WR12 7DT
Cover design by Poolbeg Group Services Ltd
Set by Poolbeg Group Services Ltd in Garamond 10/12.5
Printed by The Guernsey Press Ltd,
Vale, Guernsey, Channel Islands.

The Publishers gratefully acknowledge the support of

The Arts Council / An Chomhairle Ealaíon.

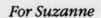

For Suzanne

CHAPTER ONE

LAST NIGHT I DREAMED OF MAKING love with Richard. He moved around the room setting the scene, lighting the candles, putting on music, scattering cushions across the floor. Gently he undressed me, lay down beside me on the cushions and began kissing my body, starting with my toes, moving his mouth gently all the way up the inside of my legs, licking and sucking my clitoris then slipping softly inside, whispering, "I love you, Anna. Do you love me?" Yes, Richard, yes. I love you. I'll always love you. Till the end of time.

Leaving safety behind, Anna woke to find her cheeks damp with tears. It had been, then, only a dream. Panic rose inside her, kicking her stomach like a restless foetus. She stretched out one arm across the desert of a bed. "My love, my love," she murmured. "My love is gone." The words pressed against her chest like a stone. For a few moments she lay quite still, trying to catch her breath.

The panic attack passed. The dream had woken her early. There was no sound from the children. The soothing effect on her nerves of an unexpected few minutes of peace made her decide that today she would be a really good mother. A 1950s Hollywood film mother. Swirling skirts, painted face and low sweet tones . . . she pictured herself crawling around on the floor after Sam – no, maybe not swirling skirts. Hearing sounds of stirring next door, she thrust back the duvet and reached for her jeans. On second thoughts, she wouldn't bother with the make-up either. It had been months since she'd worn any and a sweaty tussle with the baby in the bath would soon make short work of it. Perhaps she could manage the low sweet tones?

Averting her eyes from the empty space on the other side of the bed, she twitched the thin Indian bedspread over the duvet and gave it a final pull before strolling into the room next door where Toby was chatting away to himself in a language of his own invention. Seeing her, he rolled over onto his back and held out his arms. He was a large blond baby. As she drew back the curtains, his sparse fair hair glinted red in the sunlight. Like Richard's.

"Hello, darling," she murmured. Deborah Kerr incarnate. She lifted him out of his cot and brought his face close to hers. "Bathtime, old fellow?"

He smiled in ecstatic bliss.

Bit of a doddle, this mothering business. It all depends on your frame of mind. Stay cool and everything falls into place. Passing the bathroom mirror with Toby in her arms, Anna took the opportunity of throwing herself quite a smug little smile. Considering her lack of a role model . . .

She ran the bath water, tested it, tossed in a plastic duck or two, then gently lowered Toby into it. She tried to persuade him to sit down. He insisted, as usual, on remaining upright. I will not blame myself for my child's eccentricities, she thought, supporting him with one hand and soaping him with the other. Probably hundreds of children take their bath standing up. It's simply that childcare manuals omit to mention this extremely well-known fact.

She was congratulating herself on her healthy state of mind this morning when an injured wail reached her ears from the floor below. But this was Hollywood. Mothers didn't panic. Calmly, she lifted Toby out of the bath onto the mat and began to dry him. He started to whimper. She took a deep breath and hurried him into nappy, shorts and T-shirt. Together, they ran down to the first floor. All this running surprised Toby out of his fretfulness. Anna entered Sam's bedroom feeling for once remarkably in control of things.

"Morning, sweetheart," she whispered into Sam's ear.

Sam sat bolt upright in his bed and stared at her. Such wide-eyed astonishment was not flattering. It's hard to play the perfect

Hollywood Mum under the sceptical gaze of a knowing three-year-old. Still she persevered, obediently kissing each one of his bears good morning, and merely saying, when he pulled thick winter trousers and a sweater from his drawer, "Won't you be rather hot in those, Sam?" Giving her an odd look, Sam scrambled into the shorts and Thomas the Tank Engine T-shirt that were lying on a chair and ran through into the kitchen.

Anna, Sam and Toby lived in a tall narrow eighteenth-century house in a narrow cobbled street in the centre of Hull. Anna felt that the peculiarities of her house somehow symbolised the peculiarities of her life. It was a crazy house for children. The sitting-room, originally a shop, was on the ground floor and the kitchen was on the first. Anna was up and down the stairs between the two rooms a hundred times a day. By evening her back ached and there was a pain all the way down her left leg (Toby's birth had left her with a bad case of sciatica). The house had, though, other advantages: it was in a secluded part of the city, yet within walking distance of the shops. Besides, it was where she'd lived with Richard. She had no wish to move.

Arriving in the kitchen with Toby, she found Sam standing in front of an open cupboard pointing urgently at something out of reach.

"Er, er, er."

"What is it, Sam? What do you want? A biscuit?"

He shook his head.

"Juice?"

He shook his head more vigorously.

"Coco Pops?"

"No." He struggled to frame the word. Anna could see what an effort it was costing him just to control the muscles of his mouth. She set Toby down on his activitymat and waited. "Dish," he said at last. It was his word for "this," the nearest he could come to it. "Dish! Dish! Dish!" He pointed up at the shelves.

"Chocolate?" suggested Anna, abandoning all standards.

"No!" He stamped his foot. "Dish! Dish!"

She looked down at the small dark-haired figure whose features so strongly resembled her own. "Sam, I can't understand you. What is it, sweetheart?"

His body became tense with frustration. He began pummelling her on the leg. She bent down.

"Try to say the word, Sam."

He started to cry. Praying she wouldn't put out whatever it was in her back that kept going wrong, Anna lifted him up. "Now, Sam. Look quickly. See what it is you want."

His hand ranged indecisively over the packets of biscuits, cartons of juice, beakers and plates. She felt a twinge in her back.

"Sam! Hurry up! I can't hold you much longer."

By her feet, Toby started wailing, the sort that was liable to go on for hours. He wanted his bottle.

"Sam, whatever it is you want, it can't be there."

"Er, er," he grunted.

"No, that's it, Sam. Finished. I'm putting you down now."

"No!" He twisted round in her arms and whacked her hard across the nose. The force of the blow made her eyes water. She set him down on the floor and gripped his shoulders.

"Sam, it's not my fault," she said, racked with guilt and pain and frustration. "I can't understand what you're saying." Against her principles, she gave him a little shake. "Why can't you learn to speak? Why can't you?" She shook him once more, then forced herself to let him go. She felt as if she'd like to go on shaking him for a long time, till his teeth rattled, till he learned to speak.

She turned away, trying to gain control over herself by putting some physical space between them. She picked up Toby, red in the face and roaring by now, and switched on the kettle for his bottle. Sam stood beside the cupboard weeping. Before she could calm him down she had to calm herself. She forced herself to go through the mechanics of filling and warming Toby's bottle. The familiar routine was comforting. Her breathing returned to normal, her rage subsided. She put the bottle to Toby's lips. The roaring stopped. As he sucked on the bottle his eyes gradually closed. He fell asleep. She set the bottle down. Still holding Toby she knelt beside Sam and put an arm around him.

"I'm sorry, Sam. I'm sorry." Tears rolled down her cheeks. "I couldn't understand you. I'm sorry."

He rested his dark head on her shoulder and sobbed his heart out. He was three years old and could barely say two words. His speech which had seemed to be coming along fine had suddenly got blocked around the time of Richard's death. Now he uttered at most one or two monosyllables at a time. Anna read to him, sang songs, invented language games. Nothing seemed to work. It was her private fear that he'd never learn to speak but remain wrapped in his secret silent world for ever.

"Sam, Sam, what is going to become of you? How are we going to manage?" With her free hand, she wiped his tear-stained face and blew his nose.

In return, Sam dabbed clumsily at her wet cheeks with his fingers. Then he gave her a radiant grin. It was over.

"Would you like some juice?" she asked tentatively.

He nodded.

Thankful that at last there was something she could do for him, she laid the sleeping Toby down on his mat and rushed over to pour Ribena into Sam's beaker.

Watching her son contentedly drinking his juice, Anna reflected that her resolution to be the perfect Hollywood mother had lasted less than half an hour. Things had returned to normal. But should this be normal? She turned on the taps and began to wash up last night's supper things. *Was* there such a thing as normal family life? If so, what was it? She had yet to come across it. Richard had died too soon.

She gazed down at her hands in the water, at the plain gold band still on the third finger of her left hand. Richard, why did you have to go and die when we need you so much here? Why? Not a day had gone by in the six months since his death without her missing him. The smell, the touch, the feel of him. Her whole body ached for him. Felt angry at him too, for leaving her like this to bring up their children on her own. "I knew you'd never be able to keep a man," said her mother's voice in her head, as if it had been Anna herself who'd poured gallons of beer down that motorist's throat.

Rousing herself, she dried her hands, seated Sam at the table in front of a bowl of Rice Krispies, tied up the ears of the bunny-bag and told Sam to stay at the table till she got back. Shutting the kitchen door tightly behind her, she went down the stairs, out the back door and across the courtyard to the wheelie-bin. Wheelie-bins and bunny-bags. If a race from outer space were to invade would they find us up to much? She lingered to smell the yellow wind-blown roses clinging to the wall. Then she heard Toby's screams. Seized with panic, she ran back across the courtyard and up the stairs two at a time, her mother's voice drumming in her head, "You should never have left those children alone. What kind of a mother are you?"

She shot across the room to where Toby, having woken up, had begun to fiddle with the plug on the electric heater and was being soundly spanked by Sam. She dragged Toby away from the plug and yanked Sam off Toby.

Sam looked indignant. "Bo!" He pointed a finger at Toby. It was his word for "bad."

"I know he's bad, but you mustn't hit him. He's only tiny. Besides," she added hurriedly, seeing her faulty logic, "we don't hit people in this house, do we?" Only shake them, she added mentally.

"Bo!" repeated Sam as Toby, with the instincts of a homing pigeon, began to crawl back towards the heater. Sam darted forward and slapped him across the back of his legs.

"Don't do that!" roared Anna in vain.

Toby began to shriek.

The phone rang. She snatched up the receiver with one hand and Toby with the other. Out of the corner of her eye she saw Sam give her a look then wander off to play with his trains.

"Yes?"

"Anna? It's Penelope. Are you all right? You sound a bit odd."

"I'm fine."

Penelope was Richard's mother and had become, since his death, her best friend. But there are some things (like being unable to cope with your children) you don't tell your best friends.

"Anna, I was wondering – would you be able to pop over some time today?"

"Sure. We could come on after gym club. We've nothing else planned for this morning. The children will love to see you."

"I . . . I meant without the children."

"Oh?"

This was unusual. Penelope adored her grandsons. Couldn't get enough of them usually.

"Something's come up. I need to speak to you. Not over the phone."

Some unfinished business to do with Richard's will, probably. For a barrister he'd left his affairs in an extraordinary muddle. He hadn't expected to die. No one does at thirty-six.

Anna set Toby down on his mat and did some calculating. "I've got to see Professor Fry in the department at four and after that there's a meeting of the women's group. Donna was coming in anyway. I'll check if she can come early."

Anna put down the receiver and looked at Sam.

"Sam, how would you like to play with Donna this afternoon?"

His face lit up. Anna had to remind herself that it wasn't that he preferred Donna to herself – it was just that, like everyone else, he enjoyed a change from time to time. They lived too much on their own, the three of them. Anna leant back against the kitchen cupboards watching Toby happily browse through his squeaking book and Sam push his train across the carpet. Love for them tugged at her heart.

Lottie, a friend at the women's group, was always on at her to employ Donna full-time and return to work. Until Richard's death Anna had lectured part-time in the English Department at Hull University. Then she'd applied for extended leave of absence saying she owed it to her sons to provide them with a full!-time mother now they no longer had a father. That was six

7

months ago. Money was running short and her department was getting impatient, but she kept putting off the decision to return to work. Somehow she couldn't bear to go out and leave them in someone else's care all day. They were all of Richard she had left.

No, she couldn't leave them and go out to work. Everything must remain exactly the same for them, just as the house had remained the same after Richard's death. Even his toothbrush still stood in the mug beside hers in the bathroom. If he were to walk through the front door right now he'd have no difficulty finding anything. But he never would walk through that door, or any other, ever again.

A wail from Sam roused her. His train had crashed into the leg of a chair. She bent down to put it back together again for him. They keep me alive, she thought. They prevent me from thinking too much. There's always something to be done when they're around.

When the train had been successfully put back together she stood up and braced herself to phone Donna. Since she was the employer and Donna the employee in need of money, Anna should have been in a strong position. Theoretically. Very theoretically. Donna, though good with children and earning her living looking after them, in fact disapproved of mothers who went out and left their children with someone else. Which made her rather an awkward child-minder.

Anna grasped the receiver tightly. "Hello, Donna. It's Anna."

"Yes?"

The monosyllable had never sounded so unpromising.

"I'm awfully sorry to bother you."

Silence at the other end. No little pleasantries about it being no bother, she hadn't been doing anything in particular.

"The thing is, Donna," Anna plunged on recklessly, "I wondered if you'd be able to come round a little earlier? Say, about one? Some business has come up."

"All right then."

The phone went dead at the other end.

I'll sack her, I swear I will, thought Anna.

"Now, boys, time for gym club."

Sam looked glum. He loathed gym but she'd read somewhere that improving a child's physical co-ordination could help speech development so off they went every Tuesday to gym club.

"Quick, Sam. To the toilet."

He dragged his heels.

"Quick, or we'll be late! Oh Toby, not another dirty nappy!"

Hurriedly she changed him, hauled Sam off to the toilet, then bundled them downstairs and out of the door. Toby was wailing in his buggy, Sam was dragging his feet and scowling. She felt grubby and tear stained. She hadn't had time to comb her hair and there were bits of biscuit stuck to her T-shirt. She hoped they wouldn't meet anyone they knew.

The first person they met was their next-door neighbour, Julia. Anna began to feel persecuted. Julia's thick dark hair was cut in a bob, the sides curving neatly up her rosy cheeks. Dressed in a navy corduroy skirt and a brightly patterned jumper, with extremely white ruffles peeking out at her collar and cuffs, Julia looked like a Laura Ashley advert – clean, healthy and well balanced. Shining. Her baby was shining too. She lay placidly in her Silver Cross pram cooing up at the row of plastic teddy bears above her head, in the way babies are supposed to do, the way Anna's never had. But then Sam and Toby hadn't had a Silver Cross pram, or bears to coo at. Was that where the problems had started? Was that the reason why Toby cried such a lot and Sam didn't speak? Meetings with Julia always had this effect on Anna – her mind spiralled off into endless cycles of guilt and self-punishment.

"What's the matter, little Toby? Come on now. There's nothing to cry about, is there?" Julia beamed down at the buggy. Toby stopped crying.

Little hypocrite, thought Anna.

Julia straightened up. "Isn't Toby growing? Aren't our children wonderful? Aren't we lucky?"

"Yes," replied Anna dutifully. She attempted a smile, then gave it up. She thought she probably looked grotesque. "How's India?"

"Marvellous. She's so good. Sleeps right through the night now, from seven o'clock in the evening till seven in the morning, don't you, my poppet?"

Anna had heard this before. It didn't make her feel less depressed and inferior. Toby, seven months older than India, still woke up on average three or four times a night. Even Sam woke up sometimes, indicating he wanted juice or his bedclothes rearranged. Anna was sure she hadn't had an unbroken night's sleep since Sam was born. It felt like it, anyhow. What did Julia do to her children, bang them on the head?

"How are the twins?" she asked, hoping to hear some bad news. Well, not bad news exactly, but perhaps Julian and Dorian might have failed just one week to be top of their class in something.

"Splendid, thank you. Loving school, of course."

Of course.

"Have you put the boys' names down yet?"

Anna coughed. "Er, not yet, Julia."

The twins, aged four-and-a-half, didn't go to the friendly local school round the corner but to a small private one over the other side of Hull. Frank, their father, dropped them off each morning on his way to work. All three males emerged from the house next door at precisely eight each morning dressed in suits and ties and very white shirts. Anna had strong objections to private schools but didn't know how to put this to Julia without sounding as if it was forking out for the fees she objected to.

"You'd better hurry up, Anna. Places are like gold-dust. You may already have left it too late for Sam."

"I'll see about it," said Anna in cowardly fashion. "We've got to go now, I'm afraid. Gym club."

Julia smiled. "Isn't it lovely for them? The twins are very keen."

"Yes," said Anna. Sam kicked moodily at a stone. Anna yanked him away.

Why did meetings with Julia leave her feeling she was, and always would be, a failure as a mother? What made someone a good mother? She trudged along the street, pushing the buggy with one hand, pulling Sam with the other. She frowned, remembering another morning and her mother's voice exclaiming, "This girl makes me so furious I could hit her!" She hadn't been hit. Sometimes she wished she had. It would have been something to go on, something definite to have laid at her mother's door. As it was, she had nothing. A relationship that had declined from open hostility into frozen silence.

She reached back into memory and pictured the scene at the breakfast table. Her father pretending to be alone with his newspaper. Brian stolidly munching on his toast. No help there. Then Georgia came into the room. She must have been about ten years old. *She* wasn't talking of leaving home. *She* wasn't going through puberty. *She* didn't have strange awkward bumps on her chest or sweat glands or acne. Her body was still that of a young girl, fresh and slim in her pink summer frock. Their mother's face relaxed into the special smile she reserved for her youngest child. Yes, Georgia had rescued her.

Beside her, Sam gave a moan. They'd arrived at the place where the gym club was held. It was an ugly yellow brick building in the centre of the city, only five minutes walk away from their house. At least it would have been five minutes if Sam hadn't dragged his heels all the way there.

Anna bent down. "It'll be all right, Sam. Really it will."

Sam looked doubtful about this.

And of course it wasn't.

The other children had already changed out of their shoes and she discovered they'd forgotten to bring their star. Sam hopped around looking distressed.

"Never mind," she whispered. "Perhaps they'll have some spares."

A worried frown appeared on Sam's face. His confidence was ebbing away. Any minute now he'd be pleading to be taken home. She cursed her disorganisation. She could see the blue paper star they'd spent hours making yesterday, lying at home on the sitting-room carpet.

"We've a spare star, if you'd like one," said the mother next to her.

Swallowing her pride, Anna humbly accepted the pink plastic star. "Thanks. Thank you very much." Was she always then going to be the kind of mother who comes unprovided and has to be lent things?

With a struggle, she got Sam's shoes and socks off. The music started up. Gill, the instructor, demonstrated some simple dance movements. Then she clapped her hands and the children ran into the centre of the room. Sam remained firmly glued to his seat.

"Come on, Sam!"

A small blonde-haired girl ran up to him and tugged at his hand. She was Kylie, the niece of Carol, a member of the women's group. Already, at four, she knew how to twist younger males round her little finger. Sam adored her. But even Kylie's charms failed to work today. After a moment, she ran off back to the others.

"Go on, Sam," whispered Anna. "You like dancing."

He made a face and wriggled in his chair.

She gave up on the dancing.

Next, the children had to pick up bean-bags and throw them into a barrel. She set Sam on his feet and gave him a little push. "Go on now." Reluctantly he moved in towards the others and made a half-hearted attempt to join in.

Anna sighed. "I don't know why I bother. He hates it."

Her neighbour on the chair next to hers, the woman who'd given them the star, glanced at her. "It's excellent for them," she said bracingly. "Children nowadays don't get enough physical exercise – chauffeured here and there in cars. And it's good for them to mix with children of their own age."

"I know, but . . ."

How could she explain that Sam much preferred to be on his own playing with his trains? Young as he was, the death of his father had left a great unfilled gap in his life. She felt it. He didn't want to mix with other children, he didn't want to have to speak to them. He wanted to be left on his own. As she did. The three of them, in their own private world. They had a perfect right to be like that.

12

She watched him now, standing in the middle of the circle, refusing to hold hands with the other children. Her heart turned over in fear. How would he get through life? The other children were dancing around him and he looked so sad and puzzled and out of it all that she thought, he'll remember this all his life.

In panic, she started up from her seat, Toby under her arm. Ignoring the protests of the children and Gill's frowns, she broke through the circle and rescued him. She brought him back to her chair. He burst into tears. The other mothers stared. She bent down to fasten his shoes. Why put him through this agony? He was happy at home. He wasn't handicapped. He wasn't emotionally disturbed. He was missing his father, that was all. He needed space to grieve before he was forced out into the world; she must give him that. Even if it meant he never went out into the world at all.

"Sam, we won't come here again if you don't want to."

He looked up at her, his face shining with happiness. She bent down and hugged him.

"We'll manage on our own, won't we? Just the three of us."

On the steps outside they met Tessa, clasping her two daughters by the hand.

"Hello, Tess."

Tessa's freckled face creased into a grimace. "Am I late? Oh crikey, I haven't got the time wrong *again*, have I?"

Anna smiled. "They're probably about half-way through. If you hurry, you'll be in time for the apparatus."

"Thanks. Come on you two, we'll have to be quick, Mummy's got things wrong again. Coming to the meeting this evening?" she called out over her shoulder.

"Yes."

"Good. See you there then."

Anna walked on feeling happier. Meetings with Tessa, unlike those with Julia, always cheered her up. Tessa, tall, with pale freckled skin and masses of faded red hair, was the wife of a colleague of Richard's. Former colleague. They'd been in the same chambers. Anna had met Bill and Tessa through Richard but it was only since his death that she'd become friendly with

13

Tessa. They'd both begun attending meetings at the women's centre at around the same time. Tessa's daughters were four and two and her life seemed, like Anna's, always on the verge of chaos. She was a useful antidote to Julia.

They trudged back home. Turning into their street and seeing Donna's car parked outside the house, Anna felt herself tense up. If she looks grumpy or says anything about latchkey children, I'll sack her, she resolved. The door opened. Donna stood on the step. Plump, with cropped blonde hair, her normally rather sour face (why did plump people have the reputation of being cheerful?) was wreathed in smiles.

"Hello, Sam, love. How was gym club? Hello, Toby. Have you a kiss for me?"

Anna's shoulders relaxed in relief. It was going to be all right. Donna was in a good mood. She wasn't going to have to feel guilty.

"Don't worry about anything. I'll give them their lunch. Just slip off when you're ready," whispered Donna, helping her carry the buggy into the hall.

Skipping upstairs to change into a skirt, Anna felt almost light-hearted. Everything was going to be all right. Sam would stay at home and he'd learn to speak eventually.

"Anna!"

Penelope opened the door, gave her a swift embrace, then stood back resting her hands on Anna's shoulders and looking into her face.

"How are you, my dear?"

"Coping."

Penelope nodded and released her. Her motherly gestures were never overdone. Anna had liked Penelope from the beginning. Richard had rung his mother up from London to say they were going to get married and Penelope had insisted on speaking to Anna. Her voice on the phone had been gentle and low. When Anna had tried to imagine what the owner of such a voice would look like, she'd pictured someone tall and elegant and still youthful-looking. Coming face to face with a short dumpy woman with grey hair, for a second she'd been disappointed. The last thing she wanted was another mother in her life. But Penelope defied the stereotypes. She was well read, sharing Anna's fondness for detective stories, and far from being an overpowering Northern mother, she'd brought Richard up to iron his own shirts and get his own supper. She was – had been – the ideal mother-in-law.

"The children send lots of kisses and Sam's drawn a picture for you." Anna produced it from her bag. "It's a train. I think. You've got visitors," she added, hearing voices from the kitchen. An elderly woman scolding what sounded, from the high-pitched whine, like a young girl. Nanny at it again with, presumably, some neighbour's child.

"Visitors?" Penelope glanced over her shoulder at something invisible and then ushered Anna swiftly into the living-room. "Yes. Douglas is home from Oxford."

Douglas was Richard's younger brother, younger by sixteen years. The brothers were not at all alike. Douglas was as dark and stocky as Richard had been tall and fair. And Douglas had been brought up by Nanny.

"Is he? But that wasn't what I meant. I heard a girl's voice."

Penelope hesitated. "I – I've someone staying with me."

It occurred to Anna that Penelope was on edge this afternoon. She'd begun prowling round the room in a most un-Penelope-like way.

"Pen, is anything the . . . ?"

"Mother!" Douglas burst into the room. "What are those men doing with our lawn?"

Penelope glanced unhappily towards the French window. "I'm not quite sure, darling. I didn't like to ask. They seemed happy digging holes. They're from Kingston Communications. I expect it's their job."

Penelope's self-possession seemed definitely to have deserted her today. Anna wondered why.

"Mother!"

Exasperated, Douglas strode purposefully over the deep pile carpet to the French window and undid the catch.

The two women watched as he marched across the lawn to the workmen.

"With his father in the Lebanon, Douglas has decided to be head of the household," murmured Penelope. "I've been wondering how I'm going to cope."

Anna smiled. "Does he think the household needs a head?"

"Apparently."

"Richard never thought like that." She sat down on the sofa, averting her eyes from the bright bold painting opposite. It was one of her sister's, one of Georgia's last before her death.

"No. Richard didn't think like that. But Douglas was brought up by Nanny, remember."

"I always wondered why you allowed that."

"After Douglas's birth I was sick for a year. Henry's solution was to call up his old Nanny. By the time I got my strength back here she was, ensconced, bringing with her all her plain-speaking Yorkshire habits."

Anna grinned, thinking of Donna. "Still, you succeeded in rearing one non-sexist male."

"Let's not idealise Richard, shall we?" said Penelope, a little sharply. "He had his faults."

"You know, I can hardly remember what they were. He seems to me to have been perfect."

"Anna, I . . ."

"Well!" Douglas strode back in through the French window rubbing his hands. "That's settled their hash. I told them to go and dig their holes somewhere else. All it needed was someone to take a firm hand with them."

"Yes, dear."

"When I think of the hours father's spent fertilising that lawn . . ."

The two women stared at him. Neither could remember Henry Vale taking the slightest interest in the garden. A busy man, he'd always employed others to do the gardening for him. Penelope was less surprised than Anna. She'd got used to the expansion of Henry in Douglas's mind since his absence, the unexpected new talents his father had developed.

"You're too easygoing, Mother." He glanced around the

room, as if looking for something else to criticise.

Before he could find anything Penelope, with a gesture towards the sofa, said, "Douglas, Anna's here."

"Anna." He extended a hand. "Sorry. Didn't see you sitting there. Too taken up with sorting out those fellows." He took a step backwards and eyed Anna in a perplexed sort of way, which was the manner he'd adopted towards her since Richard's death. Having fitted her into his life as Richard's wife, it was as if he didn't now know what to do with her. However, in the last six months she'd got used to people looking at her like this – as if she was mildly embarrassing.

Douglas glanced shiftily at his mother. "Have you told her?"

"Not yet, dear."

Panic appeared on Douglas's face. "Er, I – I'll be in my, er, room working if anyone needs me. Bye for now, Anna." He rushed out of the room.

Puzzled, Anna turned to Penelope. "Told me what?"

"Oh." Penelope sighed, raised an arm and let it fall. She moved over to the French window and stood with her back to Anna. "He's so young still. Nanny rather ruined him, I'm afraid." She played with the curtain-cord for a moment, then turned to face Anna. "How are the boys?"

"Fine. We've done that bit already, Pen. Told me what?"

"Anna, I can't think how to say this."

Penelope stood in the middle of her elegant living-room, hand to her forehead, half-shielding her eyes.

Anna felt a little shock run through her. Then fear. Then the fear subsided. The boys were safe at home with Donna and Richard was dead. The worst had already happened. What was the matter then with Penelope this afternoon?

"What is it, Penelope?"

"I – " Penelope sat down on the sofa and took Anna's hand in hers. "Anna, do you remember the girlfriend Richard had before he met you?"

Anna frowned. "Let's see. Her name began with a C, I think. Charlotte, Camilla – something classy anyway. No, I remember. It was Claudia. Why on earth are you asking about her?"

"He told you they'd lived together?"

"Of course. We didn't have secrets. It was in London, wasn't it, while he was studying for the Bar? They split up just before he got called to the Bar, didn't they? I never met her. I was working in Ireland at the time. She was some kind of actress, wasn't she?"

"Mostly unemployed – or bit parts in soft porn movies. Actress was Richard's respectable gloss, I came to the conclusion." Penelope sighed and glanced away. "I never liked her."

Anna suppressed a smile. "So Richard said."

"I thought she was selfish and irresponsible . . . Is that all he told you about her?"

"Well, he sometimes mentioned some of the things they'd done together. You know, in passing, like I told him about my boyfriends, if it happened to come up . . . We didn't have any secrets, Pen. Richard wasn't that kind of person. You know how out in the open he always was."

Penelope gave a short laugh. Rather hard. Rather unlike her. "I thought I knew."

"Penelope, what is it?"

"Two days ago, Claudia turned up."

"What? Here?"

"Yes, she didn't have any other address for Richard. Didn't know he'd married you. Didn't even know he was dead."

"Poor thing! That must have come as a shock."

"I don't think much registers with Claudia outside her own immediate concerns. She certainly wasn't thinking of anybody else when she came here."

The undertone of anger in Penelope's voice surprised Anna. Penelope rarely got angry. "Why? What do you mean? Is she still here?" Perhaps Claudia was out of work and wanting to sponge off the Vales for a while?

"No, she left yesterday. She's gone to live in Africa with her latest lover." Penelope paused. "The thing is, she . . . she has a daughter. She's left her with me."

"With you? Why?"

"She couldn't take her with her – the climate's unsuitable. Or so she said. It's my belief she simply wanted rid of the child."

"But what on earth has it got to do with you?"

"Not me, Richard."

"Richard?"

"Yes. Oh, Anna, I can't think of any kind way of putting this."

She paused, evidently hoping Anna would say something. Anna stared at her blankly.

"She's his daughter."

"Daughter? I didn't know he had one." Anna's response was automatic. Then Penelope's words sank in. "You mean this child, whose voice I heard just now in the kitchen, is Richard's daughter? But how can she be? I mean . . . " She frowned. It wasn't possible. A daughter. Richard didn't have a daughter. He had sons.

Penelope looked down at her lap. "I never knew about this, believe me, Anna. By the time Claudia realised a baby was on the way, Richard and she had split up and she was involved with somebody else. Apparently, she was too far gone for an abortion – she's always been incredibly vague about the realities of life. They agreed between them that she'd bring up the child. Richard was struggling with his pupillage. You know yourself the long hours he worked. I suppose he felt he couldn't take on responsibility for a child." She glanced at Anna. "Mind you, I'm not excusing him. What he did was terrible – cutting himself off from his own child like that." She sighed. It was almost a groan. "It seems he gave her money. A lump sum for the child's upbringing. He must have taken out a loan or something. I don't know how he found the money. Anyway, now it seems it's all gone. The money, I mean. I'm sorry, Anna, I'm telling this terribly badly. It's just I'm so . . ." She reached for Anna's hand again. "I don't know what to say. Did he never tell you anything about this?"

Anna shook her head dumbly.

"You and he were so close. All I can think is he must have got himself into such a state that he couldn't think how to tell you."

"Why? Did he think I'd judge him? I'm not that sort of

person. I thought he knew that." Anna covered her face with her hands. "This is horrible! Horrible!"

"Anna, I . . . "

Anna looked up, struck by a thought. "Is it certain? I mean, about Richard being the father?"

"Yes. Quite certain. She brought a letter with her. From Richard. *He* was in no doubt. I can show it to you if you like." Penelope half rose from the sofa.

"No! Please don't! I couldn't bear it!" She burst into tears.

"Anna." Penelope took her in her arms. "Anna, I'd have spared you this if I could."

"How could he? How could he do this to me?"

"I expect he thought you'd never find out."

"This is like him dying all over again. I want him here, Pen."

"I know, love, I know."

"I want him to explain. Richard!"

Anna broke out of Penelope's arms. She fled over to the window and stood banging her fists against the glass, like a bird trying to escape.

"Why did you do this to me, you bastard!"

She swung round.

"What's her name?" Did she want to know? No, she didn't. Yes, she did. "What's her name?"

"Beatrice."

"How old?"

"Ten."

Seven years older than Sam. His half-sister. She turned back and rested her forehead against the glass. "He was so good with the boys. How could he have done it? How could he father a child and have nothing more to do with her? It's against all we believed in, all you brought him up to believe in."

She turned round, her eyes pleading with the older woman to tell her it wasn't true.

"I know."

Anna leaned back against the window. There's something in our society that militates against men becoming full human beings, she thought. Even the best of them. Even Richard.

"So. You have another grandchild."

Penelope shifted her glance.

"It doesn't feel like that. All I feel at the moment is ordinary human duty. Claudia's found that a ten-year-old cramps her lifestyle. And the other grandmother, Claudia's mother, is an alcoholic as far as I can make out. Or perhaps that's an excuse. Anyway, there seems nowhere else for the child to be."

Anna ran a hand over her eyes. "What are you going to do with her?"

"I – I don't know yet."

"Does she look like Richard?"

There was a moment's pause.

"Yes."

Anna swallowed. "I suppose Nanny will look after her. Or she could go away to school."

"Boarding-school's one solution, certainly. Nanny, I'm afraid, is past looking after children. I feel a bit like that myself. Too impatient, too irritable, too old for a child."

"Irritable?" said Anna, in surprise. "You're never irritable."

Penelope sighed. "The thing is, Anna, she's a girl who needs a proper family – with other children around. She's never had that. It would be an unnatural kind of life for her here with just Henry and me. Of course, we'd provide the money for her upbringing . . . "

The two women faced each other. All those lengthy vigils into the night, grieving for Richard, had forged a bond between them. Without a word being spoken, Anna knew what Penelope was hoping.

"No!" she shouted, taking a step forward. "No! No! No!"

"Not even for Richard's sake? She's a child who badly needs a home. She's been shunted from pillar to post since the day she was born. She's older than her years. Half grown up already. But she desperately needs some affection and a loving stable family."

"Stable? What's stable about us?" Anna screamed. "Since Richard died, I've been hanging on by the tips of my fingernails. Pen, I'm making a mess of it. I've one son who doesn't speak and another who wakes up three or four times a night!"

"You're a good mother, Anna. I've always thought so."

"No. Not a girl. I couldn't do it. I could never bring up a girl."

Penelope glanced at her sharply. "Who told you that?"

"I've nothing to give a daughter. Look how badly I got on with my own mother. I couldn't face going through all that again. Pen, you don't know how relieved I was to have sons. Besides, having her around – she'd be a permanent reminder that Richard and I – that we weren't as close as I thought."

The door opened. They both turned, expecting Douglas. A tall fair-haired girl stood angrily on the threshold. She was dressed in striped shorts and a T-shirt.

"Mrs Vale, Nanny says – " She stopped, noticing Anna.

Anna stood rooted to the spot as the girl turned Richard's eyes on her. This wasn't a child. This was some ghastly spectre come back from the past to haunt her. With a muttered exclamation, Anna fled the room.

She drove like a madwoman out of Swanland, blind with tears, overtaking every car in sight. Then she remembered her sons and forced herself to slow down. She took several deep breaths and stopped the car near the Humber Estuary. Numb, feeling life would never be the same again, she sat looking out over the flat still water which glittered grey and silver in the sun. For the second time in a year she felt as though she'd stepped through a door and into an elevator shaft.

"How could he not tell me?" The question kept going over and over in her mind. "How could he keep a child secret from me?"

If he'd loved me, he would have told me. Her hands clenched the steering wheel. He must never have been sure of me. He must never have known me. I've never been properly loved in my life then. Not for me, as I am. Never. Mother was always hostile and father was always too busy. When I found Richard I thought that at last I'd found someone who loved me for myself. What happens to people who're never loved? Do their souls dry up? Do they become non-persons?

That girl back there had no one either, no father and now no mother. For a fraction of a second, Anna felt pity for her, this little girl, this bit of Richard, abandoned, without a home. Then she thought, I owe him nothing, I owe his child nothing. He didn't tell me about her. If I'd known about her before, I might have done something for her, brought her into our family . . . No, I wouldn't. Not a girl. I can do nothing for a girl. The women in our family are all mad. We devour one another. She must find some other family.

She looked at her watch. Christ! That meeting with Cornelius Fry. She couldn't put it off, she'd postponed it twice already. For a moment, she was filled with panic. I can't, I can't. Not feeling like this. I want to go home to my children. I want my children around me.

But at home there'd be Donna. There would have to be explanations. Sour faces. Donna didn't like plans being changed. Besides, much better leave the children with her. However much she tried to hide it, they'd sense something was wrong and get upset. She got out of the car, locked it and walked a couple of hundred yards down the road to the pub. In this state, sober, she could face neither Cornelius Fry nor the women's meeting.

"Are you drunk?"

Professor Fry's sharp eyes fixed on her. His colleagues complained he was absent-minded, but Anna had always found him remarkably acute about the things that interested him; they just weren't the same things that interested most other people.

"Drunk? Good gracious, no." She looked down at her lap. "I did have a glass of wine. I've had bad news."

"Anything you want to talk about?" ◄◄

She shook her head.

"I'll get you some black coffee. You look as though you could do with it."

He disappeared. She glanced around his office trying to collect her thoughts. The carpet was covered with books and papers. "A tidy office is the sign of a sick mind," Cornelius was fond of declaring. By her feet was a pile of unmarked essays.

She looked at the title of the first one: *"Could the imaginative writing of the Elizabethan period seriously entertain the idea of a godless world?"* She felt a moment's fright. Could it? What did godless mean, exactly? Who were the imaginative writers of the period? How much she'd forgotten in six months.

Cornelius returned with her coffee.

"Thanks." She gulped down a mouthful. Her head began to clear. "How's the department?" she asked conversationally.

He groaned. "Don't ask. We're about to have the external assessors in. My colleagues keep battering my ear about good teaching practice. I never know what people mean by that. I start a tutorial with a vague idea and we go on from there."

"That's probably why they work so well."

"Humph!" He perched on the edge of his cluttered desk, swinging his glasses in his hand. He was a small man, in his mid-fifties. Anna had first met him in Ireland. He'd been Professor at University College, Dublin when she'd been working in Trinity. "Anna, you know why you're here?"

"I expect you're going to tell me you're going to advertise my post," she mumbled over the rim of her coffee cup.

He smiled. "Not quite. But I can't hold off the baying hordes, i.e. our colleagues, much longer. It's only a part-time post, I know, but in these straitened times we can't keep it vacant for ever. It's now June. If I'm to get someone to start in October, I'll need to advertise pretty soon."

She sighed. "I don't know, Cornelius. I sat down in the sitting-room the other evening and found I couldn't remember when *The Faerie Queene* was published. I feel so out of it all now."

He took a grubby handkerchief from his trouser pocket and polished his glasses. "It'll come back. We need you here, Anna. I need someone in that post I can trust."

In the past, Anna had assisted Cornelius in the teaching of Elizabethan literature. Anna taught poetry and gender – what Cornelius called the fashionable end of the syllabus. This had left Cornelius free to concentrate on the topics that really interested him, like witchcraft and magic and peculiar religious

24

sects. They'd built up a good working partnership. Anna had enjoyed the teaching. But Richard's death had torn a hole through all that.

She put down her cup. "You see there's Sam. He hardly speaks yet. He needs me at home to help him. How will he manage in life without language?"

"Language is a devilish invention." Cornelius finished polishing his glasses and put them on. "The entire Elizabethan age was an optical illusion based on language. Look at their myths – the Virgin Queen, the Golden Age, Astraea. Poets like Spenser and Raleigh, they really believed in them – and when the myths began to disintegrate, they were devastated. Mark my words, Anna, language is a dangerous thing. People can be controlled by it. Whole ideologies can be founded on it. Think of Mao's China. Believe me, Sam's much better off without it."

"Cornelius! You know perfectly well we can't function without language. Lacan says it's how we get our identity and power over the world. It's the world of words that creates the world of things. Sam needs words. Without them he'll be powerless."

"Lacan!" snorted Cornelius. "Why you let yourself get involved in all that psychoanalytic claptrap beats me, Anna. Why can't you be a straightforward literary historian like myself?"

"It's the cutting edge, Cornelius."

"That's one way of describing it. I could think of others."

"Such as?"

"Unprovable theories wrapped up in meaningless jargon. Take Lacan's mirror stage. My six-month-old grandson doesn't appear to have heard of it. I keep pointing him at the mirror to see if it will give him a sense of identity. He seems remarkably indifferent, I must say. No, I'll be a humanist till I die. I prefer to talk about people not signifiers. I believe in conversation not discourse."

Anna smiled.

"At last!"

"What?"

"A smile. The first since you came through that door. You

know, you used to have a sense of humour, Anna. What happened to it?"

"Life. Death. The children."

He leaned forward. "Leave them, Anna. You've too good a brain to waste. They'll be all right without you. Who knows? They might even benefit from a change of carer. Children are remarkably resilient."

"You're not really as chauvinistic as they say, are you?"

"As who says?"

"Lottie for one." She could still hear Lottie's indignant exclamation: "Honestly! When I asked him what women writers he taught he said he didn't. There weren't any women writers in the Elizabethan period. Only witches. Anna, he needs working on!"

Cornelius chuckled, much as he had during his one and only encounter with Lottie. "Someone forgot to provide your friend Lottie with an irony button. You're not still going to that dreadful women's group, are you? No wonder you've lost your sense of humour."

"You see – you say things like that and people like Lottie believe you. But you don't really mean them, do you?"

He grinned. "I have to give people something to gossip about behind my back." He took his glasses off and sighed. "Ach! This is a dreadfully dull country. Elizabeth and I go to dinner parties and all people chat about is mortgages and foreign holidays and their children's schools. I haven't had a decent political argument for months. Don't you miss Ireland, Anna?"

"Sometimes. Nearly all the time. What's the matter with the English, do you think?"

"You have the Queen."

"Come on, Cornelius!"

"Seriously, it's very hampering for you. She prevents you from growing up. You think that, in the last resort, she'll take care of you. In reality, she's surrounded, as kings and queens have always been, by a self-perpetuating coterie of more or less corrupt courtiers."

Anna thought of what Julia would have to say to that. Julia

26

thought, quite seriously, that the Queen had been badly let down by the younger generation of royals.

"And then the English have so much to distract their attention from political issues – football, the garden, washing the car on Sundays. They understand nothing about politics, even less about their own culture. Did I tell you about the time I helped a friend of mine bring his sculptures down from Belfast to Dublin? We were stopped by the security forces outside Craigavon. 'What have you got there?' the soldier asked. He had a thick Geordie accent. 'Sculptures,' replied my friend. 'Don't you get funny with me,' said the squaddie. So there we were on a dark road in the middle of the Irish countryside explaining two hundred years of civilisation to a lad from Newcastle. He knew nothing. Nothing."

The phone rang.

"Anna, I've got to go," he said, after a brief exchange. "That was Elspeth reminding me I've got a lecture to give. Think about what I've said. We need you here. I need you here. If you were to go, God knows who I'd get in your place – some raging Marxist feminist I suppose. Take pity on me, Anna."

She rose. "I'll see. I can't promise."

"I'll give you another month to make up your mind."

"Thanks, Cornelius. Thanks for everything." Goodness knows how many battles he'd fought on her behalf to keep her post open for her. It was more than she deserved.

But he only said, waving away her thanks, "1590."

"What?"

"The date of publication of the first three books of *The Faerie Queene*."

"Oh yes. And books IV to VI were published in 1596."

"See? It'll all come back. Don't stay away, Anna."

She stood outside his office, her head reeling from wine, strong coffee and Cornelius's conversation. For a moment in there her worries had disappeared. She could have that all the time if she went back to work. She would become clear-headed again, able to think rationally. She'd get less disturbed by every little thing that happened to them – like Sam and gym club.

27

Perhaps it would be better for the children if she put some distance between herself and them? But could she bear to be apart from them? They were the only people who loved her. Really loved her. After what Penelope had told her, she could no longer trust her memories of Richard. No, she'd never be able to leave them. Never. Cornelius had better advertise her post.

She glanced at her watch. There was just time before the women's meeting to make another call. She retrieved her car from the university car park.

She drove for less than five minutes, then turned into a street where the corner shop had bars on the windows and several of the houses were boarded up. She pulled up outside the church. It wasn't an imposing stone edifice like the parish church where her parents had been married. St Hilda's had been built some time in the fifties. A redbrick oblong, its windows were covered with wire mesh. The notice advertising Sunday Mass was half torn away. Her cousin Adam worked in a rough tough environment. She opened the gate of the small detached house next door to the church, took two steps up the garden path and rang the bell.

Adam came to the door, looking tall and lean in shabby jeans and sweatshirt. Behind his spectacles, his gaunt face brightened when he saw who it was.

"Anna! Come in!"

He held open the door and then led the way across the threadbare hall carpet to a tiny room on the right. His study.

She wondered what she was going to say to him.

"I was in the area and thought I'd drop by," she began.

"Anna, surely not!" He grinned.

They had a running joke about Anna belonging to the richer branch of the family. Adam's father had owned a greengrocer's shop in Scunthorpe. The two branches were barely on speaking terms, but Anna had always had a soft spot for Adam. He'd been her refuge in times of trouble. It was Adam she'd asked to perform Richard's funeral service.

She glanced at his desk. "I'm disturbing you."

"I'm glad to be disturbed, quite frankly. Sit down. I was in the middle of totting up my accounts. Whichever way I add them up I still seem to come out in the red. Will you have a coffee?"

"I'd love one. Can I . . . ?" She half rose from her chair.

"No, no." He waved a hand. "You stay there. Read Augustine's *Confessions* or something."

"Ho! Ho!"

Left alone she glanced around the room. If Cornelius's saying about tidy offices and sick minds was true, then her cousin Adam must be very well balanced indeed. The carpet was a minefield of books and papers. Bank accounts lay strewn across his desk. There seemed an awful lot of red about them. She didn't want to pry but it was difficult not to in such a small room. She stood up hurriedly, negotiated her way over a heap of toys in the hall and went down into the kitchen.

"Oh."

Adam's face as she came into the kitchen was a mixture of dismay and embarrassment. The room was in utter confusion. Even Anna, who rated her own capacity for being sluttish pretty highly, had never seen anything like it. Filthy pots littered every available surface, a heap of dirty clothes lay on the floor in front of the washing-machine, the rubbish bin was overflowing and six or seven empty wine bottles stood beside it. Anna decided to pretend she'd noticed nothing. Absolutely nothing.

"How are the children?" she enquired. Adam had two, Peter who was eleven and Rachel who was nine.

"Thriving." He rinsed a couple of mugs under the cold water tap and then poured boiling water over them. "We don't switch on the immersion during the day," he explained.

"And Sue?" she asked tentatively.

Sue, a speech therapist, was subject to bouts of depression which she tried to cure by drinking her way through them. By the look of the kitchen she was going through one now.

"Oh. You know. The same." A shadow passed over his narrow sensitive face. He changed the subject quickly. "What about your two? How's Sam's talking coming along?"

"Not too well."

"Have you thought any more about speech therapy? It might help, you know. Sue deals with cases like his all the time."

A stab of irritation ran through her. "He's not a case," she snapped. "It's not that bad. I can understand him. Most of the time."

"Yes, but . . ." He hesitated, seemed about to say something, then handed her a mug of coffee instead.

"He'll learn to speak soon, Adam, I'm sure he will. One day, he'll open his mouth and it'll all come tumbling out, all the thoughts and questions he's been storing up for months, ever since Richard died."

Adam nodded.

Carrying their mugs, they went back down the narrow hall, skirting round the toys.

"Adam, I seem to recognise some of these."

"Yes. Your mother called by the other day and brought us some things for the children – clothes and so on."

"Did she?"

This was an unwelcome new light on her mother. Or was she just enjoying playing Lady Bountiful? Averting her eyes from a doll of Georgia's, Anna hurried into the study and sat down in an armchair.

Adam sat down opposite. "I suppose there's still no contact between you?"

Anna shook her head. "None."

He sighed. "Pity. They are family, after all."

"What a family!"

"She's had a hard life, Anna."

"I know. Nana and then Georgia."

"Your grandmother and Georgia and . . . and other things."

Anna frowned. What other things? What was he talking about? Wasn't her mother one of the lucky ones? Living in that great old house, three children, a husband ready to give her anything she asked for? She could have had everything, if only she hadn't insisted on trying to mould them all to her will. For the first time in her life, Anna felt irritated with Adam. Then she remembered his kitchen. You couldn't be angry with someone who had a kitchen like that.

"It would be too difficult, Adam. After all this time. To be honest, I'd be scared to meet her again."

There were few enough people she could have admitted that to. But she'd seen his kitchen. She didn't want him to feel she was above all that.

"I'm sorry I keep sounding cross," she added. "I can hardly think straight at the moment."

Adam scrutinised her carefully from behind his spectacles.

"Anna, why are you here?"

"Does there have to be a reason? I told you, I was in the area."

His silence was heavy with disbelief.

"All right then." She put down her mug and told him about Richard and Richard's daughter. "I'm so angry with him. Why didn't he tell me? It's as if he didn't trust me, didn't trust my reactions."

Adam was silent for a moment. She could feel all his attention focused on her problem. Now she knew why his parishioners adored him. "Don't you think perhaps he may have felt ashamed?" he said, at last.

"Ashamed?"

"Yes." He leaned forward and clasped his long pale hands over one knee. "And afraid you'd despise him for not keeping in touch with his daughter."

"Me despise him! He was the one with the high standards."

"Yes, but . . . " He hesitated again. "When you're in love with someone the way he was, you're afraid of displeasing them."

"You make me sound like some terrible god or something."

"Not exactly. But Richard didn't have God, did he? He put you in His place. The romantic myth. Men *are* afraid of women, you know. I'm afraid of Sue, though she never believes me when I say so. She thinks I secretly condemn her because of her . . . depressions and so on. But I don't. I admire her because of them, the way she manages to pull herself through every time." He fell silent. "I expect you're wondering about the state the house is in."

"Not at all," said Anna quickly. Too quickly to be convincing.

He half smiled at her transparency. "She's been more than

31

usually depressed lately. You see, we've found out she's pregnant again. It's been rather a blow. The state our finances are in. Also, she'd thought she'd got free of all that – nappies and teething and so on. And now we're going to have to start all over again."

"Adam, if there's anything I can do . . . ever?" It was difficult offering Adam help. He was used to being the one who gave. It was his profession. No, more than his profession – his vocation; it was burned into him.

"Keep coming to church." He smiled. "I like to have my family there and you lower the average age of the congregation quite considerably. Besides, I like to think there's someone out there who's on my side. Apart from Sue of course," he added hastily.

"I am on your side, Adam. I'll always be on your side." She rose and went over and kissed him on the cheek.

His pale face reddened. "Try to forgive Richard. I'm sure he never meant to hurt you. He thought the world of you."

"I – I'll try."

He accompanied her to the door. As they stood there, they saw a youngish man, unshaven and with holes in his trousers, walk unsteadily down the middle of the road.

Adam winced. "Jimmy. He's mildly schizophrenic. They call this 'care in the community'."

He went over and gently guided the man onto the pavement. The last Anna saw of her cousin he was bringing Jimmy into his house.

The Hull Women's Support Group (to give it its official title) held their fortnightly meetings in the women's centre, three tiny rooms at the top of the building in which Sam's gym club had taken place earlier that day. To Anna, once more crossing the square towards the ugly yellow building, it was as though the morning's fiasco at the gym club was a lifetime away. The news that Richard had a daughter had torn a gash through her day. Nothing would ever be the same again. How secure she'd been before in her memories of Richard. Now it felt as though there was no safety anywhere.

She ran the usual gauntlet of people standing around outside the building holding up banners. They were a group of Pro-lifers who'd somehow got it into their heads that the women's centre was a hotbed of information on abortion.

"Don't kill our children!" yelled one man after her.

She vaguely recognised him. A small, thin man in a brown suit, he always seemed to be there. The rest of the group were mostly middle-aged women in their fifties and sixties. Having reared their own children, no doubt they felt they had the authority to pronounce on other people's lives. Anna felt that, one way or another, she'd had enough well-meaning advice from older women on how to bring up her children to last her a lifetime.

The other members of the group were already seated in a circle ready to hear Clara deliver her paper when Anna entered the room in a rush and slid into the chair nearest the door. They were used to her arriving late. Even Tessa generally managed to get there on time. She waved to Anna from across the room. Lottie, notionally the chairperson (since such things are necessary, even in women's groups), gave her a nod. Lottie was short, with bubbly blonde curls and the type of temperament novelists used to call vivacious. Anna sometimes felt tired just looking at her. Lottie and Clara lived together.

"What is Clara's paper on?" whispered Anna to her neighbour Jennifer, a tall striking-looking woman, a deacon in the Church of England.

"Gender and Identity," Jennifer whispered back.

Anna bit a nail. In theory, the topic should be familiar to her. She'd used material on it often enough in her teaching. It would be interesting, though perhaps demoralising, to see how much of it she could actually remember.

There was a pause while Clara set her papers in order. Anna glanced around the room. There were about twenty women present. A good turn-out. She knew quite a few of them by now – Tessa of course, Lottie, Clara, Jennifer, Gill, Carol, Angela . . . The group had been founded by Lottie to promote women's causes in the city. The idea was that women would meet socially in what Lottie called "a non-threatening environment", i.e. no males over the age of seven were allowed on the premises. At these early evening meetings papers were read. During the day the place was a drop-in centre where women could come for coffee, leave their children in the crèche for an hour or so, consult the jobs vacant noticeboard or use the word processor. The group had been going for about a year and had already been successful in forming a women's network around the city. Lottie was its unpaid administrator, squeezing the job in between her work in the University of Humberside's drama department.

Anna had been attending the meetings for over two months. It got her out of the house, allowed her to have some adult conversation with people like Tessa and, unlike those dinner parties to which Richard's barrister colleagues still felt obliged to ask her, she wasn't made to feel uncomfortable because she had no man to bring along. It was the only thing she did in which memories of Richard played no part. Usually she felt guilty about this, as if she was already starting on a new life, putting him behind her. Today, for the first time, she did not. How could he do this to me? The question had been spinning round in her head since she'd fled Penelope's house. How could he have left me to find out in this way? He surely must have known I'd find out one day? He couldn't have kept her secret for ever, could he?

She let out a low moan. Jennifer half turned towards her in concern. Anna shook her head. She clenched her hands and forced herself to attend to the meeting.

"You all know the format," Lottie was saying. "Clara reads her paper. We have a brief discussion, then break for coffee. After that, business. Have you all got a copy of the agenda? If you have any extra items, bring them up under AOB. Clara."

"I'm going to talk this evening about how our identity is formed." Clara peered shyly around at them all from beneath her fringe, then raised her papers to form a barrier between herself and her audience. She was a nursery-school teacher and any kind of public speaking was an ordeal for her. But Lottie was strict in making sure every member of the group got a chance to research a topic and report back their findings. Since she was a relatively new member Anna's turn hadn't yet come round, which was, she felt, just as well. She doubted whether she'd be up to giving a paper at the moment. She sometimes thought she must have mislaid half her brain cells – she'd never really got going again after Toby's birth.

"The fact," continued Clara, "that most children in our society are still raised almost exclusively by mothers, or by a variety of female caretakers, continues to influence the child's view of the world. From the very beginning, women are associated in the child's mind with life in the home, the private, messy life of the emotions. Whereas the father is identified with the wider world outside, which the child longs to join. Maturity for both sexes involves, therefore, a rejection of the mother, and the world of the mother, in favour of the father. In the case of the girl . . . "

The girl. A girl with Richard's hair and Richard's eyes. A ghost from the past. If I had a daughter, I'd have to be strong and free for her, teach her to be the woman I'd like to have been. I'm not that strong. She might grow up to hate me. Sons are easier. I can do nothing for her.

Switching her attention back to Clara, Anna realised she'd missed some vital connection.

"Why is our sexual identity so important to us?" Clara was asking. "Because it's the only way we have left of defining ourselves, now that class distinctions have all but disappeared and the races are becoming mixed up . . . "

Anna sat up straight in her chair. She'd heard this argument many times before. It was beginning to fail to convince her. Did she, when it came down to it, get her identity from being a woman? No. Her identity came from defining herself against her family. All they were she didn't want to be. Neither solid East Riding farming folk like her mother's family (meat three times a day and smug unchanging certainties about life), nor nervy, high-strung businesspeople like her father's family. I'm some sort of throwback, she thought. Descendant of an earlier ancestor, a younger son perhaps, languishing in some rural parsonage or schoolroom and yearning for a wider life. Like Adam, she'd failed to fit into the family pattern.

She remembered that photograph of her parents' wedding day, a formal group photo of both families standing on the steps of Holy Trinity Church. Her mother, small and dark, stared solemnly into the camera; her father, tall, painfully thin, his bushy dark hair rearing up in a quiff from his forehead, leaned nervously on her arm. The Holdens' confidence and solid sense of self-worth showed up in her mother's stance, planted there firmly like a young oak. It would take more than a gust of wind to uproot her.

Her father's family were townspeople. They lived on their wits, starting up new businesses when the old ones failed. Perhaps this accounted for their twitchiness. They were slightly shady – one ancestor had gone bankrupt and been drummed out of Hull. Whereas Stella, her mother, stared limpidly into the camera, her father's gaze, beneath heavy black brows, slid sideways.

The photograph had lied. The fatal flaw wasn't on her father's side but her mother's. Over the years, the Holden women had all gone mad and killed themselves or had to be put away, like old Aunt Gertie. All except her mother and herself. And God knows, these days, Anna felt she was hanging onto her sanity only by the tips of her fingernails. She moved restlessly in her chair. As usual, thoughts of her family had aroused all sorts of uncomfortable and haunting emotions. Far better not to think of them. In fact, never to think of them.

She wrenched her attention back to the meeting and became aware of some disagreement in the circle.

"I don't get my identity from being a woman," Carol was objecting. "It's my class I identify with. What a typical middle-class assumption it is to assume class distinctions are dead and everyone is just like everyone else."

Clara went red.

"We're not. Playing out on the streets of East Hull was what gave me *my* identity. We bonded together, all the kids on our street." Carol was in full flight now. "We were a gang, girls and boys. Gender didn't come into it. When I think back to what I was, it's those kids I remember. That kind of upbringing marks you for life. It gave us our identity. We knew we were different from the grammar school kids. There were things we wanted and couldn't have. Clothes. Books. Sometimes we didn't have enough to eat. Poverty gave me my identity – "

"But you weren't exactly starving, were you?" Jennifer's judicious tones cut in. "I mean not like in the Sudan."

"Excuse me?"

"I mean it wasn't like the Sudan."

"How do you know? How do you know it wasn't?"

Jennifer, on an inter-church committee for Third World affairs, looked exasperated.

The women in the circle glanced from Carol, dressed in patched jeans and home-knitted jumper, to Jennifer in her smart blue suit and deacon's collar. Consternation appeared on their faces. Which was the more politically correct line to take – support for the Third World or support for the working classes? The meetings were always throwing up awkward questions like this.

Carol glared round at them all. "How would any of you know what it's like to be a working-class kid in East Hull?"

The women squirmed and looked uneasy. None of them dared challenge Carol. Her credentials were impeccable. She lived in a high-rise block of flats on the edge of Hull in a curious ménage made up of her boyfriend, her mother, her sister and her sister's daughter, Kylie. At least it seemed curious to Anna. Carol claimed they were carrying on the working-class tradition of the extended family. One short conversation with Carol had seen Anna written off as irretrievably middle class in Carol's eyes.

She became aware of movement around the room. In an effort to calm the meeting down – the emotional temperature was still high after Carol's attack – Lottie had suggested a break for coffee.

"It got quite sticky there for a moment," said Tessa's voice beside her.

"What? Oh yes." She hoped Tessa wasn't going to expect her

to make any intelligent comments on Clara's paper. But Tessa didn't seem taken aback by Anna's vagueness. Perhaps I'm always like this, thought Anna. I wouldn't be surprised.

"Penelope babysitting?"

"No, Donna." Would Penelope be able to babysit for her ever again? After all, she had a granddaughter now to look after. "What about you? Is Bill in charge?"

Tessa nodded. "And he'll get them off to bed with hands washed and teeth brushed quicker than I ever manage to." She pushed back her mop of red hair. "Gruesome thought, isn't it? That my husband's turned out to be a better mother than I am."

"Perhaps not better," said Jennifer, smiling. "Just different from you?" She was used to counselling couples with marital difficulties.

Tessa looked doubtful.

Anna was never quite sure how seriously to take Tessa's comments about Bill. They were always said as a joke, but there was an edge of bitterness to them which sometimes made Anna wonder whether things were really all right between them. She'd met Bill once, long ago, in Richard's company. He'd seemed a quiet unassuming man. A plodder, rather than a high-flyer like Richard.

"How's the battle going to get your parish to accept women priests?" asked Tessa, changing the subject and looking at Jennifer.

Jennifer grimaced. "The usual arguments – can a woman celebrate Communion and still be home in time to cook her family Sunday lunch? Some people have apparently never heard of microwaves."

"Nor of husbands like Bill who're better cooks than their wives," added Tessa. "And what about you, Anna. How's things?"

"Fine," said Anna as all mothers of young children are tempted to. Then she thought, no, that's Julia's trick. "Pretty gruesome, actually."

"Toby still waking up four times a night?"

"'Fraid so. I found myself in the doctor's surgery last Thursday afternoon, complaining about existential anguish and the general pointlessness of life. He took one look at me, enquired if the baby was sleeping through, then prescribed sleeping-tablets."

"You're not taking them, are you?" asked Jennifer, concerned.

"No. I did get them from the chemists. Then I thought this is the slippery slope, it'll be tranquillisers next. So I flushed them down the loo."

"Good for you."

"I regret it every time Toby wakes up crying."

"There's a local group which helps mothers of young children who have problems sleeping. I can give you the details if you like," Jennifer offered.

"No, it's all right. I'll manage. Thanks," replied Anna determined, as always, to prove she could get by without help.

"It'll get better, Anna, believe me." Jennifer squeezed her arm and moved off to join the queue for coffee.

"It's all right for her," muttered Tessa darkly. "Her children have reached a civilised age. I do find myself envying women whose children are school age, don't you? Actually I envy practically everyone at the moment – mothers like your Julia who look as if they've stepped out of a fashion page, businessmen who think they have the right to be let off all the messes of domestic life, pensioners – especially pensioners, idling into town to spend all morning drinking coffee. How are you getting on with Donna?"

"Better, I think. She hasn't told me off about anything for over a week."

"It's amazing your children don't make a fuss about being left with her if she's such a gorgon as you make out."

"The children aren't afraid of her. I am. Has your Hungarian au pair arrived yet?"

Tessa groaned. "Don't speak to me about her! Here we were thinking we were going to get some rosy-cheeked jolly countrygirl who'd sweep in, take over the children and cook us all ravishing goulashes in her spare time. Instead she arrives off the plane at Manchester looking nervous and haunted. The last thing we want in this household is another intellectual, I thought. In the kitchen her first words were, pointing to the washing-machine, 'Is that the cooker?' I think she may be anorexic. At any rate, she never seems to eat enough. It's now got to the stage where I have to pin up lists above the fridge – *'What We Can Eat Without Getting Fat.'* Honestly there's more work than before she came because now I have her to look after as well. However, the children are fond of her. Look, are you staying? We'd better get into the queue for coffee before it runs out."

Anna glanced down at the agenda in her hand. Under business Lottie had put Fundraising, Professor West's lecture, Appointment of Crèche Worker, George Mitchell Case. She particularly didn't want to stay to hear about that.

"Er, no, I don't think I can stay. I'd like to get back in time to put Sam to bed."

"Are you coming to Gloria West's lecture?"

Professor Gloria West was due to come over from the University of the South Riding to give a talk to the group. She was their prestige speaker for this term.

"I expect so. Lottie's got a three-line whip out."

"See you there then. Take care."

"And you."

Anna hurried down the narrow scuffed stairs and out of the building feeling guilty that she'd used Sam as an excuse to avoid Lottie's agenda. She turned left and crossed the square towards the Marina. At Prince's Quay she paused, rested her arms on the railing and looked down into the black water.

She thought of her father. His trouble was he thought he was John Wayne. You could tell by the way he bounced into a room and took charge. Like Wayne riding into town you knew Someone had arrived. The John Wayne approach to business. The John Wayne approach to personal relations. The John Wayne approach to women.

Take his story of how he'd met her mother. They'd been introduced to one another, casually, by a mutual acquaintance, on the top of a number 49 bus. He'd pestered her for her address (only someone who'd met her mother would know how much courage that took). By the time it was his stop, he'd got it. The following Sunday he'd put on a tie, borrowed a car and charged round to her house expecting Mrs Holden to invite him to tea. She hadn't. Nana was distrustful of strangers. She came from a large farming family. They had a habit of intermarrying. Her father had invited Mabel Holden out, got rid of the competition (a slow-witted youth called Joe, due to inherit a family farm), and changed her name from Mabel to Stella. Mabel was a name that was going nowhere, he declared.

What their mother had thought of this, no one knew. They'd never heard the tale from her side. Her mother would sit tight-lipped through their father's recital, refusing to give her version, even when pressed. It was as if she disclaimed all responsibility for the marriage.

Anna tapped the side of the railing and walked on. She turned down the cobbled street, let herself into the house and went straight up to the kitchen where she found Donna on the phone.

"And you'll never *believe* what she gives them for lunch when I'm not . . . "

Anna coughed.

Donna half turned. "Oh. She's back. Got to go. Ring you tomorrow."

Anna decided that she'd think about that phone call later. "Are the children all right?" Try as she might, the question always came tumbling out with an urgency that seemed to cast doubt on Donna's abilities.

As usual, Donna paused before replying. On purpose, Anna thought, to pay her back by keeping her in suspense a moment longer. "They're fine. Toby's asleep and Sam's in his pyjamas watching a video downstairs."

Anna felt her shoulders relax. "Thanks awfully. Here's your money." She'd sorted it out beforehand. Donna's eagle eye always made her flustered to the point of being unable to count up properly.

Donna received the money with her usual air of it not being *quite* enough. "Will you be wanting me tomorrow? Only I've got to look after Hugo and Jeremy in the morning."

"No, it's all right, Donna. I've no meetings or anything."

Donna put on her coat. "I hope you won't mind me saying this . . . "

Anna braced herself.

"But it's about time Sam had something to play with outside. A swing or a climbing-frame or something. Now that the weather's bucking up. We got awfully bored this afternoon."

Ever heard of imagination? thought Anna, remembering those games in the garden her father had invented for the three of them on his rare moments off work. Aloud, she said, "I'll look into it. The thing is, swings are awfully expensive, aren't they?"

"Hugo and Jeremy have two swings and a sandpit and a climbing-frame."

And a father, Anna mentally added.

"However, if you can't afford it . . . "

Sam will have to be deprived, Anna finished the sentence in her head. "I'll take a look at the Mothercare catalogue and order something," she promised, wondering how it was that a twenty-two-year-old had come to wield such authority over her life. Sheer spinelessness, her mother would have said. She followed Donna downstairs and heard the front door close with relief.

She went into the sitting-room.

"Hello, darling. Have you had a lovely afternoon?"

Sam turned to her, nodding.

"Did you play outside?"

He nodded.

"Did you eat tea?"

He nodded.

"What did you eat?"

He made an effort to move his mouth. "Chush."

"Juice?"

He nodded.

"And what else? Fish fingers?"

He shook his head.

"A boiled egg?"

He shook his head.

"Thomas Pasta?"

He shook his head and looked cross. Anna sensed a scene coming on any minute now. She racked her brains.

"Soup?" she said desperately.

He nodded.

42

"And toast?"

He nodded.

They smiled at one another in relief.

She sat down beside him on the floor and he lay back with his head in her lap, watching the video till it was time for him to go to bed. Before he went to sleep, she sat on his bed and explained several things to him which she thought he might like to know, such as what summer was and where heaven was and where God was. Just because he hadn't the language didn't mean he didn't wonder about these questions like any other three-year-old, she reasoned. Not that she was awfully sure about God herself now, since Richard had died.

The moment she'd got Sam off to sleep, Toby woke up. She took him downstairs, changed him and gave him a bottle. When he too was safely asleep, she went down to the kitchen, kicked off her shoes and poured herself a whiskey. She had one every night. It was her alternative to sleeping-pills and she was always hoping the taste would grow on her. She switched on the radio and settled down to listen to *Book at Bedtime*. But, try as she might, her thoughts would keep straying to the fridge. It needed defrosting. It hadn't been defrosted in months. Richard liked it to be defrosted regularly. He said it kept it working longer. Should she be sitting here so very idly?

The guilty feeling grew. In the end she hauled herself out of her chair, opened the door and began clearing out old cartons of Flora, odds and ends of rotting vegetables, lumps of cheese which had passed their expiry date. Halfway through she stopped and gave the fridge a kick.

"You bastard!" she muttered to herself. "You let me down. You lied to me. You hid your daughter from me. What the hell am I doing here trying to live up to your standards? Sod it! I don't have to do everything right any more."

She poured herself another whiskey, drank it and went to bed leaving the fridge frosted.

In the night, in-between getting up for Toby, she had dreams. A girl with Richard's eyes stared at her, pleading with her. Then the girl turned into Anna's mother and the eyes changed to witch's eyes.

CHAPTER TWO

IT WAS A BAD AWAKENING. Both the children were crying. The noise devoured her, played on her nerves till she felt like sitting down and crying herself. Their crying like this, early on a morning, always had the trick of awakening the small frightened child in herself and she had no one, now, to turn to for comfort.

She stumbled around in her woolly dressing-gown dressing and feeding Sam; bathing, dressing and feeding Toby. She caught sight of herself in the mirror looking pale-faced and tense.

Richard had held back on her. The thought went round and round in her head. There must have been times, sitting beside her on the sofa or lying in bed, when he'd thought of his daughter. Even worse, times when he played with the boys and wished he was with their half-sister instead.

She got dressed and made herself a cup of coffee. Had there been any hint in Richard's behaviour, any clue he'd given her that she'd failed to pick up on? She rested her aching head on her hands. She wanted to have it out with him. Hear him explain, if he could, just why it was he'd never told her a thing about the daughter he'd fathered and then abandoned. Adam had said she should forgive him. But it wasn't that easy. She had a frightening feeling the past was slipping out of her control. Things had not been as they'd seemed. The picture was distorted.

You bastard! Her hands clenched round her coffee cup. You've fucked off and left me here stranded. I'll never know now why you didn't tell me about Beatrice.

She got up to put on some music. Strains of Clannad drifted around the kitchen, wafting her back to Ireland and the days when she'd been free, a single woman living without ties or responsibilities in Dublin. Staying up late, going to parties or the pub. It seemed a lifetime away.

She'd given it all up to live with Richard in England. Here at last, she'd thought, was someone she could make happy. But their love had been a lie. Richard hadn't been happy with her. He hadn't trusted her with his past. All her memories were built on sand.

The phone rang. She got up to answer it. It was Penelope.

"Anna, my dear. I rang because, well, you know – "

Penelope had still not recovered her self-possession. Richard's lies had been a blow for her too. But Anna felt she didn't have much sympathy to spare this morning. "Yes," she said, not helping Penelope out.

"How are you feeling this morning? Lousy, I expect."

"Yes. Lousy."

"Anna, I'm so sorry about this."

"It's not your fault," replied Anna dully.

"No. I suppose it's not anybody's fault, but . . . "

Yes it was. It was Richard's fault. He should have told us. He should have come clean.

"Where is she?" She could not say her name. She could not.

"With Nanny. They've gone out to the park." Penelope sighed. "Nanny's in her element. She's spied a new victim. But I'm afraid it won't last. Nanny's no longer the woman she was. The child is running rings round her. Can I see my grandsons soon, Anna? I'd like to be reminded of the old Richard, the Richard I thought I knew."

"Yes, of course," said Anna quickly. Penelope sounded at the end of her tether. "Drop in here whenever you like. The children will love to see you." She was never going back to Penelope's house, not while that girl was in it. It was haunted.

Sam nudged her knee.

"Sorry, Pen. Got to go."

"Take care," said Penelope, sounding very far away.

Anna replaced the receiver and looked down at Sam. He was standing in front of her, holding out one of Richard's ties. There was a puzzled expression on his face.

"Da?" he said, frowning.

Not again. She bent down. In the early days after Richard's death, Sam had kept looking for his father. In the evenings, especially. And Anna had kept on having to explain all over again that Daddy was never coming back. Sam had gone off his food, had nightmares, refused to play with his toys and was often to be found standing in front of the open wardrobe in her bedroom, staring at Richard's suits in a puzzled sort of way. He'd come out of that period speaking only in monosyllables.

She reached out and took hold of one end of the tie. It was navy blue with a thin red stripe and there was a food stain on it. Some dinner Richard had attended. When? Had she been with him? She couldn't remember. Yesterday, that would have seemed like heresy. Today? She didn't know what she felt.

"Yes, that was Daddy's."

"Gone?"

"Yes, he's gone."

He struggled to put his mouth into the right shape. "Da co ba?"

"No, Sam. I told you." She put an arm round his shoulders. "Daddy's never coming back."

"Oh."

"Sam, Daddy's in a lovely place now and even if we can't see him, he can see us. He still loves you, you know. One day you will see him again, I promise."

"Soon?"

"No, not soon."

He wriggled out of her embrace, snatched the tie from her hand and marched over to the plastic Winnie-the-Pooh box where he kept his most treasured possessions. He put the tie inside, shut the lid and stared at her defiantly.

"It's all right, Sam. You can keep it."

His defiance collapsed. He crept up beside her. "Ma go?"

Anna saw the panic in his eyes. She lifted him up, carried him over to a chair and sat him down on her knee. "No, Sam, Mummy's never going away. Mummy will never leave you."

She rocked him to and fro in her arms, forgetting her pain in soothing his. She owed him her life for, in those terrible first weeks after Richard's death, it had been the children who'd saved her. The routine of feeding, dressing and bathing that had to be mindlessly gone through. Penelope had offered to look after them but after one morning on her own, Anna had gone and fetched them home again, knowing there was now no life for her apart from them.

She kissed Sam's cheek and smoothed back his dark hair. Toby sat in the middle of the kitchen floor and watched, and presently he crawled up for a cuddle too.

The doorbell rang. Surprised, Anna set the boys gently down on the floor and hurried downstairs to answer it. She glanced at her watch on the way. Eight thirty. Bit early in the day for callers, wasn't it?

On the doorstep she found Lottie, full of suppressed excitement. The excitement was nothing new. Several times a day, Lottie found things to get excited about. Anna looked at her and yawned. What was new, though, was Lottie on her doorstep. Why was she here?

"Hello, Lottie," she said uncertainly. "Well. You'd better come in." She stood back against the wall to let Lottie past into the narrow hallway. "Come upstairs. We're in the kitchen."

"I should be at work but I had to come as soon as I heard," panted Lottie, following Anna up the stairs and into the kitchen.

"Heard what?"

"The news."

"What news?"

Lottie stared at her. "You mean you haven't heard?"

"Heard what?" asked Anna, with a sense of going round in circles. What *was* Lottie doing here? It was miles out of her way and since, with the exception of Tessa, Anna wasn't in the habit of socialising with members of the women's group outside their meetings, Lottie would have had to have gone to the trouble of looking up her address in the members' book. Whatever it was that had brought Lottie here must be urgent.

Out of the corner of her eye she saw that Sam had begun laying out his train track. He was absorbed in his task. Toby was squatting over his activity-ball, shaking it this way and that to make the beads rattle. They were all right. She glanced at Lottie standing in her kitchen, bobbing her blonde curls and looking mysterious and important. With a sigh of resignation she filled the kettle.

"Take a seat."

Lottie pulled out a chair and sat on it. "It's about George Mitchell," she began.

Anna frowned. She didn't want to hear about this. The women's group had supported one of their members, Angela Smith, in a case of unfair dismissal she'd brought against George Mitchell, a prominent local businessman. Angela had lost her case. The women felt they had a grievance against Mitchell and were thinking of lodging an appeal. But the case had been lost before Anna had even joined the group. It was nothing to do with her.

"It's nothing to do with me," she said out loud. "George Mitchell's nothing to do with me."

She turned her back on Lottie, put a tea bag into a mug, poured boiling water over it and felt guilty. Richard had always made tea with real leaves claiming, probably with justification, that tea bags were full of sawdust and odds and ends swept up off the floor. Then she remembered Richard had a daughter he hadn't told her about. What *was* she doing feeling guilty? She handed the mug to Lottie and held out the milk carton.

"Thanks. No. No sugar." Lottie bounced around on her chair looking as if she might explode at any moment. "Directly we heard the news, I said to Clara, and she agreed with me, I must go and see Anna."

Anna frowned again. "Why? I've never taken an interest in the Mitchell case. It was lost before I joined the group."

She sat down on a chair and glanced at the unpolished, badly chewed fingernails that had been, until she'd stopped caring, her mother's despair.

"I said to Clara, and she agreed with me, Anna's the only one who can do this."

"Do what?" asked Anna, completely at sea.

"Go and see . . . heavens! What's that?"

Sam was pinching Toby and Toby was giving vent to the high-pitched police siren wail he'd perfected over recent weeks.

"Sam!" Anna pushed Sam away and lightly tapped the back of his hand.

Lottie shuddered and averted her eyes. The group had recently passed a motion censuring the use of smacking in childcare. Anna and Tessa had supported the motion, then glanced at each other and acknowledged their hypocrisy. "I bet Julia never lifts a hand to her children," Tessa had whispered. "Never," Anna had whispered back. "She simply reasons with them, I expect," Tessa had added with a snort.

"Bo!" retaliated Sam indignantly, slapping his mother back and pointing at Toby.

Anna took his point. Toby had sabotaged Sam's carefully laid out railway track. "Yes, he was bad." She put it back together again for him. "All the same, you shouldn't have pinched him," she murmured, kissing the top of his head. She picked up Toby. The wail had by now declined into a sleepy whimper. "Time for your bottle, old man." She switched on the kettle. "It's all right, Lottie. You can look now. It's over."

"I really do think, Anna . . . "

"It's different from the childcare books, you know."

"So it seems. I was only going to say that if you didn't slap Sam, perhaps he wouldn't pinch Toby."

Anna stared at her. "You're mad. Wait till . . . oh." She flushed and busied herself with Toby's bottle.

"As a matter of fact, Anna, though this is strictly confidential, I may be a mother myself soon."

Anna swung round in surprise, holding the bottle.

"Yes, we've put our names down for adoption. I'm not particularly fussed but Clara's always wanted a child."

"Adoption? Isn't that rather complicated? Aren't there easier ways? Why don't you find a man? I mean . . . "

"A man?" Lottie looked shocked. "I don't think either of us could bring ourselves to do *that*, Anna. It's all right if you like that kind of thing, I suppose. It's always sounded fairly horrible to me. Do you enjoy it, Anna?"

"I've forgotten," mumbled Anna, sticking the bottle in Toby's mouth. Sometimes Lottie was about as tactful as a steamroller. She hadn't made love since Toby was conceived. Caution all through pregnancy, sheer exhaustion afterwards and then it had been too late. Like most mothers of young children, she felt she was past all that kind of thing anyhow; the way she felt at the moment, it wouldn't bother her if she never had sex again in her life. "Sex?" Tessa had said once. "What's that? Oh yes, I remember. Bill and I used to do it three times a week. Now I feel about sex the way I feel about full employment – a nice idea but it won't happen in my lifetime. As Victoria Wood says."

"Why are you smiling?" asked Lottie, suspiciously. "This is serious, Anna. What I have to tell you is extremely serious."

Anna shifted Toby onto her other knee, looked at Lottie with resignation and said, "All right, Lottie. What is it? Have you decided to go ahead with the appeal?"

Lottie set down her mug with an air of importance. "There will be no appeal, Anna. George Mitchell's been found dead. Murdered, they think."

Anna put down the bottle and reached out a hand to steady herself. She gripped the edge of the table and gazed down at her white knuckles in bewilderment.

"As soon as I heard the news I said, and Clara agreed with me, we're going to be in trouble over this, Anna will have to go up there this morning and take a look around."

"Up where?"

"The Beverley Westwood. That's where he was found. I say, are you all right, Anna? You're looking rather odd."

Anna glanced up briefly and nodded.

"Go on."

"There'll be crowds of people nosing about on the Westwood this morning. The plan is, you join them. See what's going on. Then report back to us this evening."

"Us?"

"The women's group. I mean me."

Anna stared at her blankly. "Why?"

"Because of course, we're going to be the chief suspects."

"We?" On her knee, Toby gave a whimper. Automatically, Anna picked up the bottle again and put it in his mouth.

"The women's group. Honestly, Anna, where are your wits this morning? Just think for a minute. George Mitchell was an important man around town. The police are going to come under pressure to solve this case quickly. What happens in such circumstances? The police look around for the nearest scapegoat. And that, bearing in mind the publicity that surrounded the case we took against him, will be us. You know what the cops are like about feminist groups – they're convinced we're hotbeds of subversion. Which, of course, in a way we are." She paused. "We expect to start getting visits from them very soon."

Anna listened in a rather dazed way to what Lottie was saying.

"Are you sure about this?"

"Yes."

"That he was murdered?"

"Yes."

"How do you know?"

"First item on Radio Humberside this morning. I must say, Anna, for someone who used to lecture on Revenge tragedy, you're being remarkably sceptical."

"That's fiction. Are you sure you've got the name right?"

"Yes! His body was found on the Beverley Westwood early this morning, by Black Mill. I must say, as I said to Clara, it's a warning to all employers that . . . "

Anna interrupted her. "What else did the report say?"

"Nothing much. The family's been informed . . . "

"The family?" echoed Anna faintly.

"Yes, he's left a widow and a son who works in the family business. He did have a daughter, apparently, but she died. Suicide. Sounded quite tragic, actually. Some kind of mental illness. I'm not surprised. Having old Mitchell for a father would be enough to drive anyone over the edge."

Anna clutched Toby close and tried to concentrate as Lottie rattled on.

"Clara and I only have each other as alibis. After the meeting

finished we went back home, washed our hair, and sat in front
of the television cutting out paper bunnies for Clara's class to
colour in. As I said to Clara, the police will never believe we
lead such boring lives. Where were you last night?"

"Here."

In her lap, Toby began to whimper. Anna set him down on
the carpet. He crawled away. Out of the corner of her eye, she
watched Sam go over and hand him a train. Sam the
peacemaker. Like his father . . .

"So you haven't an alibi either."

"The children – "

"They're hardly independent witnesses, are they? Besides,
Toby can't speak and Sam hardly does."

Anguish struck at Anna's heart. "I know," she muttered.
"Anyway, does it matter?" Her alibi, she meant, not Sam's
speech. That did matter to her, enormously.

"Anna! Of course it matters! I thought you read detective
stories! The police will be looking for anyone with a grudge
against George Mitchell."

"Oh." Anna was suddenly struck by what Lottie was saying.
"Oh . . . OK, I'll do it."

"Good. You're the obvious person. You're much the brainiest
of us – though you've given up using your mind recently – and
you've got contacts. Didn't you once have the Assistant Chief
Constable to dinner?"

Anna nodded. Richard had sat on the law and order
committee of Humberside police force. The contacts had been
his. Like most people Anna met these days, Lottie avoided
mentioning Richard's name directly. Probably they thought she'd
burst into tears. But she did all her crying at night. She looked
down at the carpet.

"The thing is – the children. I can't take them with me."

"We thought of that." Lottie looked smug. "Carol's on
afternoons this week. She'll have them for the morning."

Anna stared. How had that got itself arranged? So far as she
knew, Carol wasn't on the phone. This women's network had
spread its secret tentacles all through the city. What chance

would the police have against them? Lottie was surely worrying unnecessarily.

"Is that the time?" Lottie suddenly jerked out of her chair. "I'd better get a move on or I'll be late for work. This will be so good for you, Anna," she shouted over her shoulder as she clattered down the stairs. "Get those old brain cells functioning again. Before you know it, you'll be back at work."

Anna grunted and shut the door.

She went back into the kitchen. The children crawled up in tandem to hug her knees. She bent down to hug them back and then started to cry. He was dead. It didn't seem real. Nothing had changed for her. Nothing would change. It was a long time since George Mitchell had been part of her life.

She went on crying till she saw that her crying was starting to upset the children. She stood up, blew her nose and began gathering up their things. Nappies, bottles, changes of clothes, Sam's beaker. Moving anywhere nowadays was like packing up an expedition to the North Pole.

"Sam, how would you like to spend the morning with Carol?"

His eyes lit up. "Ky?" he said. "Ky?"

"Yes, I expect Kylie will be there."

He gave a shriek of delight, went over to his Pooh box and pulled out Richard's tie.

"You're not bringing that."

His face puckered.

"No, Sam!"

Always give your child reasons for your actions, the childcare books said. Even to herself she couldn't formulate a valid reason why Sam shouldn't bring the tie along. It was just that it didn't seem right and might involve her in awkward explanations with Carol.

Sam held out the tie. "Ky."

"Don't be silly. Kylie won't want that. Anyway, it might get lost or torn. Anyway, you're not bringing it."

Sam burst into tears.

"Oh, all *RIGHT*! You can bring it as far as the car."

Always be consistent, the childcare books said.

She made four trips down to the Volkswagen, carrying bags, toys, the car-seats, Toby. Her lower back and left leg began to ache. "Try not to lift or carry anything," the physiotherapist had told her. She'd roared with laughter and enquired whether he had children. He hadn't. Sometimes her leg just ached and ached, like a rotten tooth. When it got too bad, she stuck bags of frozen peas down her knickers as he'd told her. But she never had time to do his exercises and she'd missed her last two appointments. Probably she'd been struck off his list by now.

She installed Toby in the car and raced back upstairs to collect his brother. She found him dithering over his Duplo. "Ready, Sam?"

"Mm," he said, hopping from one foot to the other.

"I'm sure Kylie has Duplo."

"Mm."

She sighed. Fatal to hurry him. He'd only dig his heels in. "Shall we give your hair a brush?" she suggested, perceiving she'd omitted to do this yet.

"No!" His hands shot up to protect his head.

"Don't you want to look nice for Kylie?" Never bribe your children, the books said.

"No."

"Are you bringing the Duplo or not?" she said more sharply. She was getting anxious about Toby left alone down there in the car. It was a quiet street but child-snatching could happen anywhere. She broke out in a sweat.

"Sam, I'm off now. Bye, bye."

"Bye, bye," he said, sceptically.

"Come on!" She tugged at his arm. Never attempt to physically coerce a child, the books said. What kind of people wrote these books? "Toby's waiting for us."

Sam gave her a look, then gathered up his bucket of Duplo and shot past her down the stairs.

"Wait! Wait! There might be cars!"

She hurried downstairs, her left leg throbbing with pain.

In the street, she found Julia rocking her Silver Cross pram with one hand and holding Sam by the other. "Everything under control, Anna?" She smiled. "India and I were just keeping an eye on Toby – I knew you wouldn't be leaving him alone in the car *too* long – when out dashed Sam. I held on to him just in *case* a car came along."

Anna swallowed. Now she knew – people like Julia wrote those childcare books that made her feel so inadequate. "Thanks, Julia. Into the car now, Sam."

Julia beamed. "Going for a nice little family outing with Mummy, boys?"

No, actually, thought Anna. They're going to be dumped in a high-rise block on the other side of town while their Mummy goes to investigate a murder. She decided to mention none of this to Julia. Julia's ambition, she'd once explained to Anna, was to turn this into a neighbourhood of really nice middle-class families. Anna already felt she was letting the side down by being a one-parent family though not, as Julia was always quick to point out, what's normally meant by a single-parent family – "with all that that entails," she was apt to add, rather luridly.

Looking fresh and cool in a summer print frock, Julia waved them off on their family outing.

Carol's high-rise flat was in a group of sixties tower blocks planted outside the city in the Beverley direction. Following the instructions Lottie had given her, Anna eventually found the right block. Holding Sam by the hand, she staggered up the five flights of concrete stairs, carrying bags, toys and Toby and was let into the flat by Carol's mother. They found Carol in the kitchen making banners with Kylie. She waved a felt-tip pen at them. "Hi!"

Sam rushed up to the table and stood beside Kylie. She gave him a condescending pat on the head.

Anna dropped her bags, the toys, then Toby on the floor. "Protesting?" She restrained herself from adding "again?"

Carol looked cross. "You bet. You know what they've done now? Some of the people on the estate have got behind on their bills so they've started cutting off their water. They don't seem to realise that four out of five adults living round here are unemployed. It's always the same. We're always the ones to suffer. While you middle classes get rich buying up shares, it's us workers who have to pay the price." She glared at Anna.

"I didn't . . . " began Anna, shifted uncomfortably under Carol's gaze and fell silent. Useless to point out that she hadn't bought shares, that in fact she disapproved of all the various privatisations. She'd moved up from London. She spoke with a Southern accent. She'd been married to a barrister. Carol had slotted her into a class and that class was a definite black mark against her. To hide her discomfiture, Anna bent down to unbutton Toby's cardigan.

"You've heard, I suppose? I mean, you know why I'm here?"

Carol nodded. "George Mitchell. Lottie wants you to find out what the police are up to. I'm expecting a visit from them very soon. They'll be hardest on me, of course, living here, instead of in the nice houses you all have."

"Oh, I don't know . . . " Anna saw the look in Carol's eye and stopped. "I shan't be long," she said hurriedly. "Toby will need a bottle in about an hour's time. Will you be all right with the children?"

"Sure. We'll be all right, kids, won't we?"

This was the nice side of Carol. The warm homely everybody's-welcome side. She put down her felt pen and took Toby up in her arms. He began playing with the string of wooden beads round her neck. Sam, flirting madly with Kylie, hardly noticed his mother leave. So it will be, she thought, on the day he finds his first girlfriend. Feeling old and redundant, she tramped back down the concrete stairs, past the graffiti-covered walls and out into the hot sunshine.

The blue sky clashed incongruously with the grey and dusty grass. The grass was littered with cans, empty take-away cartons and other refuse. There was an evil smell. She noticed several packets scattered about on the grass under the windows. Her stomach turned. Prisoners did that too. The people here had lavatories but no water to flush them. So they tossed their excreta out of the window. There'd be cholera next. Angry, she got back into her car.

She drove out of the estate in the Beverley direction. The

road widened to a dual carriageway. Housing estates gave way to fields. She arrived on the Westwood, a large area of common pastureland on the outskirts of Beverley. Dotted here and there with copses, it was a place to walk the dog or have a picnic or make love on a sunny day. It had been a favourite spot of her father's. He'd often stopped off for a stroll on his way home from work. He'd even, once or twice, brought them up here as children to fly their kites or play football. She'd loved that. Her charming dark-haired father had cast a spell over the early part of her childhood. He'd been, within limits and for a Northern male, a good father; at least in the early days, before he'd got so busy.

Today, the Westwood was swarming with police officers. She parked her Volkswagen between two panda cars and started up the hill towards the squat brick tower known locally as Black Mill. An area around it had been cordoned off and a sort of tent affair had been erected. People in white coats and gloves were hurrying in and out of it. She shivered. Was his body still in there then? What were they doing to him? Why couldn't they let him rest in peace? Tears started in her eyes.

She reached the cordoned-off area. Officers had been posted to keep members of the public away. She wasn't going to get very far then. What would Lottie say if she returned without discovering anything? She stood amongst track-suited joggers, men with dogs, mothers with buggies, and stared along with the rest of them.

She was beginning to feel rather hopeless when she noticed that a friendly-looking constable standing just inside the cordoned-off area was nodding to her. She blinked, then recognised him to be the officer who'd taken them all for a ride in a police car on Sam's second birthday (Richard's idea).

"Hello. My son still remembers that ride. Have you given up traffic police then?"

He shook his head. "They've drafted in a lot of us extra today. Half Beverley police force is up here. Joy-riders and burglars will be having a field day."

"I suppose murder *is* a bit unusual in a place like Beverley."

She leaned forward and whispered confidentially. "Have they got any leads yet?"

He laughed. "If they have, they're not telling me."

Nor the general public either. Reading detective fiction was not the same as actually doing it yourself, she decided. She lacked the right touch. Miss Marple would never have been so crass.

A tall, short-haired woman in her early fifties strode briskly out of the tent. She frowned when she saw Anna standing so close to the cordoned-off area and started towards her. Halfway across the grass, her frown turned into a smile. This was the Assistant Chief Constable whom they'd once had to dinner. She'd had a high regard for Richard. She'd sent Anna just the right kind of letter of condolence. But then Anna imagined that the Assistant Chief Constable did most things just right.

"Anna! I didn't expect to see you up here amongst the ghoulish general public."

"I . . . I was passing." It sounded far too weak, so she added, "I knew the family."

"Did you?"

The Assistant Chief Constable gave her a sharp look, making Anna feel that ever since she'd come up here she'd gone about things the wrong way. If only she'd thought out her tactics a bit more carefully. Or, better still, not come here at all.

She gazed across the cordon. In the past, she'd found herself a little afraid of the Assistant Chief Constable. She'd had a brusque way of correcting Anna's opinions over dinner which Anna had found alarming. "Nonsense," Richard had said afterwards. "It's simply that she doesn't suffer fools gladly." Precisely, Anna had thought, drying a plate. She'd asked whether it was difficult being a woman in the police force and had been made to look silly. The Assistant Chief Constable was impatient of anything that smacked of feminist chit-chat. She had a job to do and she did it.

Luckily, at that moment, the Assistant Chief Constable's attention was distracted by the sight of a shortish man with a shock of curly grey hair coming up the hill towards them, limping slightly.

"Ah, McMahon. At last," she said, in a manner which reminded Anna very much of her old headmistress. "I've been expecting you for the past half-hour, Detective Superintendent."

McMahon looked sheepish. "Sergeant Bradley was unwell, ma'am. I drove her home."

Anna noticed with surprise that he spoke with an Irish accent, Southern Irish.

"Unwell?" queried the Assistant Chief Constable, sounding more like Anna's headmistress by the minute.

"She fainted."

The Assistant Chief Constable raised her eyebrows.

"It was her first body," McMahon explained. "And this is her first day back after her maternity leave. She was bound to feel a bit dodgy."

The Assistant Chief Constable made a gesture of impatience. Sergeant Bradley and her hormones were dismissed from the conversation. "Any news, Detective Superintendent?"

McMahon glanced at Anna. Anna shifted to one side and tried to make herself as inconspicuous as possible. He shook his head.

"The incident room's been set up and HOLMES has swung into operation. Force Support is doing a house-to-house on all the houses facing onto the Westwood. I'll be interviewing the widow myself, ma'am. Her son is with her. Also a member of Victim Liaison looked in, but she didn't seem needed."

"Good. Find out all you can about the women in the family. This is obviously a woman's job."

Anna's blood ran cold. Lottie had been right, then. They were going to be suspects.

McMahon looked doubtful. "There's the question of how the body got up here. Could a woman have . . . ?"

"You're out of date, Detective Superintendent." The Assistant Chief Constable cut across him. "I've been talking to the pathologist. The body wasn't dumped here. He died here. Out for an evening stroll, most probably, when he met someone he knew. Has to have been someone he knew for them to get so close. Looks like a woman's job to me. Such a very small knife.

59

We'll have the pathologist's report confirming this later today. Meanwhile, if I were you, I'd begin checking out the family pretty thoroughly. See if any of the women – his wife, sisters – had any sort of grudge against him. I'd check out that women's group too. They brought a case against him recently. These groups often harbour extremists. That's certainly one of the lines I'd investigate, Detective Superintendent, if I were in charge of this enquiry."

McMahon's expression was inscrutable. "Anything else you can think of, ma'am?"

"No, that's all. He did have a daughter but she died a few years ago. Look, Anna here knows the family. I'm sure she'd be glad to answer a few questions."

Thanks a bunch. Anna stared after the Assistant Chief Constable's retreating back. Very sisterly, as Lottie would have said.

"Er, well, I'll be off then," she muttered.

"Not so fast." McMahon grabbed hold of her arm. "Friend of the family then, are you?"

"I wouldn't say friend exactly. I used to know the daughter, Georgia. A long time ago. Very long." She bit her lip nervously.

He gave her a look. "You're not a member of this women's group by any chance, are you?"

"Er . . . "

"*I* see."

There was a short silence.

"What were you doing up here anyway?"

"I was just – er . . . um . . . " This never happened to Miss Marple.

"*I* see."

She wished he'd stop saying that. She glanced at the constable standing beside the cordon and saw by the expression on his face that she'd lost all credit with him. No more rides in police cars for Sam.

"I think you and I had better have a little talk." McMahon began to frog-march her down the hill.

She'd kill Lottie.

"You're not arresting me, are you? I've got children . . . lots . . . they'll be expecting me . . . "

"I've been known to arrest parents before now," replied McMahon grimly. "Of course I'm not arresting you. I thought we'd have coffee. I've been up half the night."

He released her arm. She bent down and rubbed her ankle.

"What's up?"

"Sciatica."

"Had a baby recently?"

She nodded. "How did you know?"

"My eldest sister had back trouble after her third. Don't worry. It goes away. Eventually. After three or four years."

"Four years!" she muttered. "I'm not cut out to be a woman."

Together, they limped down into Beverley. She wondered where he'd got his from. They turned in the direction of the North Bar.

"Jaysus, Mary and Joseph!" He gazed down at his foot in disgust.

"What's the matter?"

"Horse shit." He began scraping his shoe on the edge of the pavement. "Good God! How picturesque! The streets of rural Ireland are cleaner than this."

"There's a riding-school down the road, you see."

"That's no excuse," he growled. "Well," he straightened up and glared at her. "Know anywhere that does coffee?"

"Of course. There're a couple of hotels in the centre and dozens of cafés. Take your pick. Don't you know Beverley?"

"Give me a chance. I only came off the boat from Belfast a week ago."

"Belfast?" she said, puzzled. "You don't have a Northern accent. I thought you were from the Republic."

"That's right. I'm from Mayo. *'Tis a bitter change from those gay days that now I'm forced to go, And must leave my bones in Santa Cruz far from my own Mayo.'* Yeats."

"I know."

He looked at her with new respect. "For Santa Cruz read Hull."

"You're planning on leaving your bones here then?"

"Not if I can help it. I've been working in Belfast for the past eighteen years. If I can survive that, I can survive Hull. I suppose." He glanced at her. "You know Ireland then?"

"I lived there for six years before I got married. I worked in Trinity. English department."

"Like it?"

"Great fun – sorry – crack."

He nodded. "You add altogether."

"What?"

"Great crack altogether. Oh, never mind."

They turned into the Beverley Arms. McMahon glanced around the foyer. "Very English, isn't it?" The way he put it, it didn't sound like a compliment. He pointed to the sofa. "You take that. If I sit on it I'll fall asleep." Anna did as she was told. He sat down on a hard-back chair.

"Have you really been up all night? When did they find the – the body?"

He picked up the menu. "I don't think you've quite understood. I ask the questions." He signalled to a waitress. "A pot of your strongest coffee, please."

"Certainly, sir. Anything else I can get for you?"

"A pill to wake me up? No, it's all right. Coffee will do."

The waitress smiled and went away.

He had charm. She supposed. Anna leant back on the sofa and propped her leg up on a cushion.

"That bad, eh?" he commented, watching her arrive at this arrangement. "What are you doing for it?"

"Exercises. Frozen peas," she replied vaguely. "I'm not supposed to drink coffee. Caffeine is particularly bad for sciatica, apparently."

"It's particularly bad for most things. So how do you keep awake?"

"I drink coffee. Anyway, there's not much chance of sleep with the children about."

"I should think not. How many do you have?"

"Two."

"Good grief, is that all? The way you put it earlier I thought you had at least six."

"It feels like six sometimes, being on my own," she replied, bristling.

He glanced at her. "You're a single parent then? Divorced?"

"I – "

She was interrupted by the waitress bringing their coffee. McMahon poured it out with the feverish haste of an addict and drank half a cup straight off. "That's better. Good coffee. Just as I like it – strong enough to feel the tumours forming as I drink it." He sat back. "There're eight of us in our family."

"Eight!" She was scandalised – and surprised. He didn't look the type to force his wife to go on child-bearing. "Goodness! And did they all come over with you?"

He looked puzzled. "No, why would they? Aren't they happy enough in Mayo? With good jobs, too."

"Grown-up children?" Eight of them! He hardly looked old enough. Late forties, at most.

"Grown up? Of course they are. They've families of their own by now."

She perceived he was speaking about brothers and sisters. She'd forgotten how close-knit Irish families were. Even when you married, you didn't leave the nest. She'd had difficulty in Ireland explaining away the absence of relatives in her life.

"I thought you were talking about your children."

"My children? How could I be? I'm not even married." He drank another half cup. "Are you always this confused? How am I going to question you if you keep getting the wrong end of the stick the whole time?" He paused. "So you lived in Ireland. Marry an Irishman, did you? What good taste."

"He was English, actually. We got married in a registry office in London."

"That's lucky. There'd have been no chance of a divorce if you'd married in Dublin."

"I'm not divorced."

"What are you then? Separated?"

Now who was getting the wrong end of the stick? "I'm a

widow." For once she felt pleased to point this out. It sounded more respectable than being divorced, at least if you were being questioned by a police officer.

"Sorry." He had the grace to look abashed. "Don't meet many of those. Not your age, anyhow." There was a short silence. "So, you got married and moved to Hull?"

"No. In between we lived in London. I've been up here just over a year and a half."

"So you're a blow-in like myself." He sounded disappointed.

"That's right, Detective Superintendent." She crossed her fingers.

"What brought you to Hull?"

"My husband's job. Richard was offered a place in chambers up here. He has – had – quite a reputation in Hull legal circles." She wanted to make that absolutely clear.

He smiled, taking her point. "I'm not arresting you. So. You were a friend of Georgia Mitchell's, were you? Didn't she die rather violently?"

He'd been checking up on the family already then, had he?

"Georgia committed suicide," she replied carefully. "Madness. It runs – ran – in the family."

"And what about this son? Is he . . . ? Does he suffer too?"

"Is he mad, do you mean? I don't know. He works in the family business. Perhaps you have to be a little mad to want to do that." She smiled sweetly.

"Is that so? Why?"

"Haven't you heard about George Mitchell's reputation? He worked eighteen hours a day and expected everyone else to do the same."

"Hm. And did the daughter help run the family business too?"

"Hardly." That wasn't George Mitchell's style. Women – or girls, as he preferred to call them – were all right behind the counter. He reserved management jobs for men. "Georgia was an artist."

"Really?" He leaned foward eagerly. "What did she paint?"

"Oils mostly. She was becoming quite successful. Shortly

before her death she'd had an exhibition in the Ferens. It's a large gallery in the centre of Hull – "

"Yes, that's one place I have managed to get to. I – "

He was interrupted by a police constable appearing, as if by magic, at his elbow, waving a sheaf of papers.

"The pathologist's report, sir."

"Thank you, constable." The constable disappeared again. He glanced at her. "Before we go on, I'm going to take a minute to read through this, if you don't mind."

She shook her head. Her thoughts had suddenly been taken over by images from Georgia's paintings. Gaudy red and orange flowers (she'd begun to be compared to O'Keeffe). Moorland landscapes of North Yorkshire. The flat limestone plateau at Malham. Gordale Scar bleached white. The tarn, an isolated sheet of water surrounded by bracken and heather. The remotest, most barren landscapes, Georgia had sought them out to paint them. And Anna in London, reading about her in the arts pages, had been so proud of her, had even written her a note of congratulation, though there'd been no contact for years. Georgia had never replied.

He folded up the papers and stuffed them in his pocket. "Tell me more about this Georgia."

"She was brilliant. A genius perhaps. She was only starting to make a name for herself when she died."

"Painted every day, did she?"

"I don't know. I didn't know her that well, Detective Superintendent. We met in London, through mutual friends. She used to come down from time to time to sell her paintings."

Made up on the spur of the moment, did this sound convincing enough? Not really. The trouble about lying was that once you started you had to go on and on. She hadn't the imagination for it. She decided to go on the offensive.

"Anyway, how is this relevant to your investigation? Georgia can hardly be a suspect."

He smiled. "No. You see, I do a bit of painting myself. Watercolours, mostly. I'm only a Sunday-afternoon painter but I've always been interested in the ins and outs of professional painters' lives. What a tragedy to have killed herself when it sounds as if she had so much to live for . . . "

"Yes," she said shortly.

No one understood about madness. No one. Madness wasn't people tearing their hair out or flinging themselves about the room. Madness was Nana sitting perfectly still in a darkened room for days on end. Madness was extreme exhaustion, a running down of all the faculties. Madness was Georgia turning to her one day, her face shining with tiredness, and saying, "That thing Nana had, I've got it too. I know I have." And Anna, staring at Georgia's strained and tense face, at her eyes glaring with fatigue, had seen that it was true and there would be no way out. Nana, right as rain one day, bustling around, doing the housework and gossiping about old Mrs So-and-So down the road, the next day sitting motionless in their front room, a figure of tragedy staring into the jaws of hell. In the end, neither of them had been able to endure it.

"The mother – Mrs Mitchell – is all right though, isn't she? A charming woman, by all accounts."

"Mm."

It appeared she wasn't expected to expand on Mrs Mitchell for he went on, "Tell me about this women's group then."

"It's a sort of support group. We meet once a week. We support one another when we're in trouble."

"Like Angela Smith?"

"Yes. Why not?" she said defensively. "It was clearly a case of unfair dismissal."

"Certainly it was." He raised an eyebrow. "Why do you automatically suppose I'd be against your group?"

"Most men are."

"Listen, I've got six sisters. I've seen enough domestic violence, rape and assaults, not to mention discrimination within the force, to know women need all the support they can get."

"Oh." She felt the wind had been unfairly taken out of her sails.

"Mind you, I'm against the loonies."

"Who are they?" she enquired coldly.

"The politically correct mob. The ones who insist we call criminal behaviour 'ethically different' or shoplifters 'non-traditional shoppers' or who object to the phrase 'fat chance' on the grounds that it's size-ist."

She sniggered. "We're not like that. We're quite tame really."

"Well, Mrs er . . . "

She frowned. Men were never as feminist as they thought they were. "*Doctor* Vale."

He smiled. "Doctor Vale. I need detain you no longer."

She rose to go, feeling she'd been let off the hook.

"One more thing – where were you last night?"

She grimaced cynically to herself. Pop in the crucial question just as your victim's beginning to relax. Nice style, Detective Superintendent.

"Where I always am," she replied. "At home with the children."

"All night?"

"Yes. They can't be left. It's illegal, you know."

He looked unimpressed. "I'm not picking on you. You heard me get my orders. I'll be questioning every member of your group."

"In that case, Detective Superintendent, you'd better know that we were all at a meeting. It would have ended about nine. I left early."

"Why?"

"The children."

"And you went straight home?"

"Yes."

"So you were at home between the hours of midnight and two o'clock?"

"Yes!" She paused. "That was when he died, was it?"

He ignored this.

"Stabbed, did I hear the Assistant Chief Constable say?"

He looked at her. "Persistent little bugger, aren't you?"

What does that make you then? she wondered.

"Well, OK, it'll be plastered all over the evening papers anyway. According to the pathologist's report he was stabbed in the throat."

In the throat. Like Nana. Like Georgia.

"I suppose, in view of the case your group was pursuing against him, you'd call it a politically correct murder?" He grinned cosily.

She smelled a trap. "I don't regard any form of violence as politically correct. Good day, Detective Superintendent."

She flounced out of the hotel foyer (as far as anyone can flounce in leggings).

As she drove back to Carol's to pick up her children, the voices started up in her head. "What kind of a daughter were you?" "If you'd stayed, Georgia might have been saved." No, Georgia's madness was inherited. When a person has that in their blood there's nothing to be done for them. I had to go. They would have stifled me. I was right to go.

Nevertheless, the voices persisted all the way back to Hull and when she arrived at Carol's and heard Toby crying on the other side of the door, another was added, "What kind of a mother are you?"

"Don't worry," Carol reassured her. "He fell over and bumped his head, that's all. He was fine until now."

But Anna, taking Toby in her arms, seeing him howl at her beneath Richard's fair brows, felt she deserved to be punished.

The phone rang as she was giving the children lunch.

"Anna, it's Penelope. I've just this minute heard the news on the radio. I'm so sorry, my dear. It's quite dreadful for you."

"Yes." Anna rested Toby on her right hip, cradled the receiver against her left shoulder and with her left hand guided a spoon into Sam's mouth. "It was a shock." But not one she wanted to talk about. "Look, Pen, I'm in the middle of feeding the children. I'll have to go."

"All right, love," said Penelope, sounding terribly hurt. "Take care." She rang off.

Anna sighed, put down the phone, set Toby in his high chair and went on with the messy business of trying to coax mince and carrot and potatoes into Sam's increasingly reluctant mouth. Never force your child to eat, said the books. Leave him to come to the food himself. Left to himself the only food Sam would come to would be chocolate and crisps.

The phone rang again. It was Adam.

"Anna, what a terrible shock for you. Can I do anything? Shall I come round?"

"No. Thanks. I'm here with the children. I'm all right."

"How's your mother taking it?"

There was a silence.

"At a time like this . . . " he said gently.

There was another silence.

"I suppose you think I should go and see her?"

"Well . . . "

"I have to go now, Adam, I'm in the middle of giving the children lunch."

She put down the phone. Now she'd offended two people.

Sam stared at her miserably, his mouth smeared with carrot. She sighed. "All right, then. Get down."

He beamed and slid off his chair. She turned her attention to Toby. She couldn't face lunch herself. She was too churned up inside. Churned up and dizzy. Like the last stages of pregnancy when you walk around in a daze and the whole world seems unreal and rather remote, as if there's a pane of glass between you and it. And as you walk down the street you feel like some kind of a freak and think it would be a great service to everyone to take yourself and your swollen belly off the streets. And the baby gives an enormous heave and you imagine there's a giant frog inside you – or worse. A nightmarish time. She felt nightmarish now. Murder.

She came to a dead end in her thoughts and recognised they'd been only a diversion. There was no getting away from it. Adam was right. She had to go and see her mother.

CHAPTER THREE

THE ROAD WAS AS PITTED AND pot-holed as ever. Time had come to a halt here. Even in the village nothing had changed. Church on her left, post office and almshouses on her right. The pub had perhaps been painted? She drove past it and in through a gate hung with a sign saying *"Holme Park. Beware of the Bull"*. She wasn't taken in. There was no bull. There never had been a bull. The sign had been her mother's idea, to discourage casual visitors.

It was as if an embalmer had been at work, preserving everything exactly the way it had been all those years ago when she'd driven away, tears streaming down her face, her worldly possessions packed into the front of her Deux Chevaux, declaring she was going down to London and never coming back. Trees stood about in the fields heavy with memory, as in a dream. That oak where she'd hidden for a whole afternoon . . .

She remembered another homecoming . . .

As always when she'd been away visiting friends the frozen unnatural atmosphere of her home had struck her sharply. Large pieces of furniture arranged haphazardly in the vast entrance hall made it look like the scene of a shipwreck. When you buy a country house and lack ancestors, as her father had done, you have to fill it with whatever you can find. Some of their furniture had come from the old farmhouse at Rudston that had been in her mother's family for generations and sold after Nana's death, but most of it had been bought at auction. None of it went together particularly well. She used to think it was somehow symbolic of their whole family set-up.

She heard her mother's heels come tap-tap-tapping across

the stone floor of the entrance hall. The high-pitched, imperious tones.

"There you are, Anna."

The adolescent Anna shuffled a little.

"Hello, Mother."

She took a step forward. Might there be a kiss? Anna's mother took a step backwards, as if warding off something. Anna's kiss, presumably. Anna came to a halt.

"You've grown again."

"Dear me, have I? I must stop doing it." Anna grinned. In the endless guerilla war between herself and her mother, jokes were Anna's means of keeping her spirits up. She took after her father in that. He was always trying to turn uncomfortable things into a joke. She'd never known anyone who could spread so much gloom merely by being cheerful.

"Don't be frivolous, Anna. I only meant you'll be taller than most men if you go on like this. At sixteen, girls have usually stopped growing. I certainly had." Stella glanced down at her daughter's feet, already a healthy size six, and then, with complacency, at her own petite size fours encased in Italian leather. "You always have to be different, of course."

"Is that our daughter?" boomed her father, striding round the corner. His voice, echoing in the high-ceilinged hall, caused Anna's mother to flinch. Anna felt the roughness of his unshaven cheek, a smell of whiskey and tobacco as he enveloped her in a warm bear-hug. The old charmer. He always knew how to get her on his side. "Well, Annie." He held her at arm's length. "Enjoy your visit? Brought back the roses to your cheeks. Bit of a holiday, eh?" He gave her cheeks a nip.

"Holiday!" Her mother sniffed. "Why should she need a holiday? She should spend her holidays here, with us."

Her mother resented Anna's attachment to her friends, had forbidden her to bring them home for tea and disliked casual droppings-in after school or at the weekend. Not that there tended to be much of that. Her friends dropped by once, were treated to her mother's grandest manner and never came back.

Anna looked at her father. His expression was hard to

71

fathom. Sometimes he supported her, sometimes he didn't. He was unpredictable. Could reduce her to tears with a cutting remark about her dress or her intelligence, or make her feel like a million dollars just by giving her a hug. She swung from joy to despair a hundred times a day when he was around. She smiled at him.

"It was a good visit. Where's Georgia?"

"In bed." Her mother cut in drily. "We expected you hours ago. I could see she was getting overstrained, waiting up for you. So I sent her to bed."

"Oh." Anna felt the sharpness of a sister's betrayal. *She* would have sat up for Georgia if *she*'d been away a whole three weeks. But Georgia never went away. She was a dreamy solitary child. Mother said she'd never cope on her own, away from home.

"I hope you weren't expecting anything to eat? Cook's gone home."

"Well, I . . . "

"Didn't you eat on the train? Really, Anna, how thoughtless! Fancy turning up here at all hours, expecting food." Her mother glared.

Under the force of that glare, Anna's sense of humour deserted her. She began to stammer her excuses. "You see, I ran out of money. I had to pay for the taxi from Hull and . . . "

Her mother sighed. "I suppose I could make you a sandwich, if you're really hungry."

"Don't bother." Anna's growing unease made her tone sharper than she'd intended.

"It's no *bother*, Anna. However, I did think that, arriving at this time of the evening, you'd have had the sense to eat dinner on the way. And why have you run out of money? What have you been spending it on?"

"The girl's starving!" Her father cut cheerily through their cross-fire. "We can't have that on her first night home. Come on old thing," he slapped her on the back, "let's take a peek in the kitchen and see what we can rustle up, shall we?"

Most of Anna's childhood memories were like this. Other people intervening, a welcome defence, between her mother and herself.

The house in which these scenes had taken place was a plain three-storey Georgian mansion with two splendid curving wings. Anna drew up on the gravel in front of it. She got out of the car. Her battered Volkswagen looked incongruous beside the enormous oak front door.

She rang the bell. The distinctive peal hit her like a slap in the face. The door was opened by Bates, looking only slightly more wizened since her last visit. His expression was inscrutable.

"Good evening, Miss Anna," he said, as if she'd popped out for five minutes instead of eighteen years. "The family is in the library."

She followed Bates across the entrance hall, through another oak door and along a corridor. She tried out several conversational openings in her head. "How are you keeping, Bates?" "Isn't the weather hot?" "Have you missed me at all?" All of them foundered on the sight of that ramrod back.

He opened the library door.

"Miss Anna," he announced in tones which, in view of his age, should have been quavering but were not.

Anna stood by the door taking in the tableau. Her mother, dressed in unrelieved black, was seated stiffly upright in an armchair, clasping a lace handkerchief. Her face, with its thin lips, delicate nose and large dark eyes, was still, after all these years, dauntingly feminine. She'd kept her raven-black hair. Or was it dyed by now? Looking at her mother's dainty hands and dainty feet, Anna felt, as always, dishevelled.

Leaning against the mantelpiece, fiddling with an ornament, was Brian. A little shock ran through her. He'd become a middle-aged man. His pale brown hair was balding and he'd grown stout. If he'd passed her on the street, she wouldn't have recognised him. The ornament, a shepherdess, looked too fragile between his plump fingers. She checked an impulse to rush over and seize it from him before he dropped it and incurred their mother's wrath.

"So, Anna. You've come."

Her mother tucked her handkerchief away with a gesture of contempt. Her back became, if anything, more rigid. Anna could see there wasn't about to be a spontaneous outburst of emotion. Feelings, suppressed for years, were not about to come tumbling out. What had she expected?

"We were wondering whether you'd turn up."

"Were you?" Anna hovered uneasily in the middle of the room. "Then you knew I'd moved back?"

"I knew."

"Why didn't you . . . get in touch or – or something?"

Her mother stared straight at her. "Why didn't *you?*"

Anna's eyes dropped to the floor. "I thought you wouldn't want . . . "

"What? Speak up, Anna. I can't hear you. You always did mumble."

"Oh, Mother," said Anna wearily. "I didn't come here to quarrel. I came to say how sorry I am . . . "

"It's a bit late for that."

"I didn't mean about leaving. I meant about . . . " Anna faltered as her mother impatiently averted her eyes. She'd never been keen on pity.

Knowing she would not be invited to, Anna sat down in an armchair.

"How are you, Brian?"

"Mm?" Brian flushed and fumbled with the ornament. The sound of shattering china filled the room. He dropped to his knees and began frantically picking up the pieces.

"Brian has been trying to comfort me. Leave that." Stella waved a finger in his direction. "Bates will sweep it up later. I imagine it's beyond repair."

"Sorry," mumbled Brian, plunging from his knees onto the sofa.

"Are there going to be changes for you now, Brian?" asked Anna, in a bid to restore some of his confidence.

From the sofa he mumbled something ambiguous. She refrained from asking him to repeat it. He looked even more ill at ease. She'd obviously not chosen the right subject. But then, in this sort of atmosphere, what would be the right subject? Her relationship with Brian had always been marked by distance. Two years younger than herself, he'd been whipped off to prep school at the age of seven and then to Harrow. Their holidays, which had not always coincided, had never been long enough for them to establish a close relationship.

"No great changes." Their mother replied for him. Come to think of it, she'd always replied for him. "Brian will take over the business. We'll have to see how he gets on. He will, of course, continue to live here with me."

So Mother's life would hardly change.

Her mother continued to stare (or was it glare?) at her. Anna became conscious of her feet. As a consequence of her two pregnancies, they'd grown to size seven. She hastily tucked them under her chair and said, "Can I . . . ? Is there anything I can do to help?" Her words, echoing in the high-ceilinged room, seemed to drop into a bottomless pit.

"Help? You, Anna? I hardly think so."

Her mother laughed – though laughter was scarcely the right word for it. It sounded more like water being sucked down a drain, very slowly and surely, ending with a smart snap-to of the jaws. As a girl, Anna had always felt menaced by that mirthless laugh of her mother's. It had seemed a reminder to them all of how deeply unhappy she was. She found it no less menacing now.

The jaws snapped shut. "One way or another we've been seeing quite a lot of the family today, haven't we, Brian? There's your cousin Adam – hasn't been near the place for months and up he pops today. Called in to see if we were all right, he said. Sniffing around to see if he'd been left any money, more like. And if you're hoping for something out of all this – incidentally, is that why you're here? – let me tell you, there won't be anything."

"I say, Mother," mumbled Brian from the depths of his hideaway on the sofa. Brian was obtuse about personal relations, especially at the level of sophistication Anna and her mother played, but even he sensed, in this last interchange, some wielding of an unseen weapon.

"Perhaps it was a mistake to come?" she said quietly.

"Not a mistake. Hardly a help, though. But then, Anna, we never expect you to be that, do we, Brian? You abandoned your family once. We expect nothing more from you."

Anna stared at her mother. Be kind to me, Mummy. Don't punish me for going. I had to go.

Her mother returned her gaze thoughtfully. "I wonder how much of a blow this is to you, Anna?"

She was going to cry. She couldn't, not in front of her mother. She stood up abruptly. In the distance she heard the front door bell. "I – I have to go . . . the children . . . "

"You have children of your own now, Anna, do you?" Again the thoughtful scrutinising gaze. "Difficult to imagine you as a mother. It seems a role for which you are peculiarly unsuited. I wonder if I shall see my grandchildren some day?" The question was left dangling in the air.

No. No, no, no. Anna almost ran out of the library. I will never let you get your hands on my sons. For everything you touch shrivels to dust and bitterness. She walked rapidly down the corridor and was about to go into the entrance hall when a voice she recognised made her hang back. McMahon. Being shown in by Bates. She turned on her heel and went out through a side door.

Later that evening, when the boys were both in bed (the best time of day for mothers, Penelope always said), Anna stood in her cool rose-scented courtyard, a glass of whiskey in her hand.

Between herself and her mother it would never come right. Somewhere, a long while back, things had been said on both sides that were irrevocable. What they were had long been forgotten by both mother and daughter, but the dry dead feeling still existed. There was no impetus to overcome it. Things would never be right between them. She'd never be the kind of daughter her mother needed.

She leaned forward and filled her nostrils with perfume from the roses.

She'd failed to make her mother happy. Yet there must have

been a time, early on, before Brian was born, when we were all in all to each other. Or perhaps, even from the beginning, you never liked me very much? What was it? Did you resent having to give up your job for me? Or did you simply not like my personality? I wonder.

Now there were only women left – her mother, Richard's daughter . . . No, she could never take her on. Never. She wouldn't know what to do with her. She'd been such an unsuccessful daughter herself.

She plucked off a couple of dead heads, flung them into the wheelie-bin and wandered back into the house. The sitting-room, though tiny compared to the rooms she'd grown up in, felt empty and desolate tonight. The familiar pain stabbed at her. Richard, I need you. Why did you leave us like this? Didn't I make you happy either?

On her way up to bed, she stopped off to look at her sons. Sam was sleeping peacefully half-way down the bed, with his duvet thrown off. She covered him again. Toby was lying on his stomach in his cot, his bottom up in the air. My boys, she thought. You are all I have. Let me not devour you, or ruin you, or be cruel to you. Let me know how to let you go gently and easily, when the time comes.

The next day, Anna had a phone call from Lottie and a visit from Tessa.

"Well? What did you find out?" asked Lottie.

"He was stabbed."

"I know that. It was in the *Hull Daily Mail* this morning."

"They're going to interview all the members of our group."

"We guessed that. Anna, didn't you find out *anything* new?"

Anna lifted Toby onto her knee and began the tedious business of spooning yoghurt into his mouth. "The Assistant Chief Constable thinks it was a woman's job."

"Why?"

"The knife that was used was very small. Apparently, it's the kind of weapon a woman would use."

Lottie snorted. "Yes – and I suppose words like cunning and

underhand and sly were bandied about. Typical male chauvinist thinking."

"Actually, the Assistant Chief Constable's a woman." Anna shifted Toby into a more comfortable position on her knee.

"Oh. Well. That doesn't mean anything. Look at Thatcher. Now, what we have to do is find another line of enquiry from this sexist one the Assistant Chief Constable's pursuing."

"The Assistant Chief Constable's not in charge of the investigation, Lottie. Someone called McMahon is. He's a man."

"What's he like?"

"All right. I suppose. You have to be careful with him. He turns on the charm and when you're off your guard, he puts the boot in. He's Irish."

"Ah. You know, everything's pointing to you as the person to spearhead our investigation, Anna. You've got the brains. You read detective stories. You know how to deal with the Irish. We must draw up a list of suspects, marshal our defences . . . "

The sound of all this energy coming whizzing down the phone line at her made Anna feel suddenly very tired. She wiped Toby's mouth and set him down on the carpet to play. Lottie was the kind of person who really blossomed on the phone. Anna didn't. She liked to see people's faces when she was talking to them. It wasn't words which told you how a conversation was going, it was the expression in people's eyes.

"You'll have to go to the funeral of course."

"Why?"

"Why? Anna, I thought you read detective novels. It's a well-known fact that murderers attend their victims' funerals."

"Lottie, there's my children. I can't simply leave them and go haring off here there and everywhere. And I can hardly take them with me. Whoever heard of an investigator with a couple of infants in tow?"

"We'll work out a system of minders. Or you could put them into the crèche at the centre. It'll be back in operation next week."

"I don't want to leave them, Lottie. I don't like being away from them."

"Anna! Don't be so feeble! You've read the research. You

78

know the disadvantages for children of having mother hanging around them the whole time. Give them a break. A spot of detecting will be good practice for going back to work."

"I'm not going back to work."

"You'll have to some time, you know. The money won't last forever." This was true. "Or are you planning to bring them up on the dole? Anyway, Anna, I've got to go. We'll discuss this in more detail at the lecture."

"You're going ahead with it then?"

"Of course. We can't turn down Gloria West. Besides, the posters are plastered all round town. It's too late to cancel."

"You realise that with Angela's case cropping up in the newspapers again we'll probably get sightseers?"

"Let them come. It'll do them good. Who knows, we might even get some new members. See you Saturday then."

No chance of my not being there, I suppose? Anna put down the phone.

Then Tessa came to visit.

"Anna, I'm on my way to work." Tessa was a part-time social worker. "I want to know what's going on. Lottie was on the phone for half an hour last night muttering darkly about detectives and questionings. What's it all about?"

Anna recounted her latest conversation with Lottie.

Tessa shook her head. "Mad. Quite mad. Why doesn't she leave it to the police to sort out?" She sat down in a chair. "God! This feels great! I've been on my feet with the children all morning. Hungarian Nora's got them now, thank God." She pushed back her heavy mane of red hair. "People keep saying wait till you get to adolescence, then you'll really find out what parenting is all about, but nothing can be worse than this utter dependency and having to watch them the whole time."

"Perhaps people forget what it's like to have toddlers?"

"I'll never forget."

"Nor shall I. Time for a coffee?"

Tessa glanced at her watch. "No, but I'll have one anyway. Gosh, it's quiet in here. What have you done with the kids? Banged them on the head, or something?"

"Toby's having his afternoon nap and Sam's there, in the corner, playing with his trains."

Sam looked up at the sound of his name, gave a nod and went back to his trains.

"He is good, isn't he? My two never stop. They follow me around the house. When are we going to the playground, Mummy? I got ice lolly down my dress, didn't I, Mummy? I did wee-wee, didn't I, Mummy? It's a constant stream of not very elevated consciousness."

"Yes, but you see, Sam doesn't speak."

"You're lucky."

"No, I'm not." Anna handed her a mug of coffee.

"No, you're not. Sorry. Silly thing to say. What are you doing about it?"

"Nothing." Anna sat down at the table. "He'll speak when he's ready. I don't want to force him."

"We never force our children to do anything, do we? I wonder if we're doing the right thing. Or are we creating a generation of self-centred monsters?"

"Sometimes I dream of Sam speaking."

Tessa reached across the table and clasped Anna's hand. "He'll be all right, Anna, I'm sure he will. He's a bright kid."

"Lottie thinks it's bad for him having me around the whole time. She thinks I should go back to work."

Tessa looked surprised. "You don't want to? I took it for granted you would."

"I don't think I could bear it. Don't you hate having to leave your two?"

"God, no! When they behave like they did this morning, I can't wait to go out and shut the door on them. It's no wonder over half the people suffering from depression in this country are mothers of children under the age of five." She glanced down. "Well, I do miss them sometimes. But I'm glad of my job. It holds me together. Makes me remember how I used to be." She groaned and pushed back her hair. "We're on the treadmill now, aren't we? Child-minders, school run, those ghastly children's parties, music lessons, riding lessons, Brownies. I can see it stretching on and on into the future without a break, nothing for ourselves any more. I need to hang onto my job, it's something of my own. Besides, we've got a new team leader. She's great. I think I'm going to really enjoy working with her. You ought to go back, Anna."

Anna glanced over at Sam. "I want to help him speak. How will he survive in the world without language?" She paused. "How's Bill?"

"The same. Bill's always the same. Solid, dependable. Never changes."

Anna felt an ache inside her for Richard. But Richard hadn't been solid and dependable, or not as solid and dependable as she'd thought. He'd had a daughter.

"That's why I married him, of course. I knew Bill would make a good father. I just didn't think fatherhood would take him over to this extent. Well, I suppose I need talk. Last night when he put his arm round me and asked whether I loved him, all I could think was, 'Yes, yes, but not now, I've got to bath the baby.' I never thought motherhood would be like this."

"Neither did I."

"I nearly married a Greek," Tessa said regretfully, stirring her coffee.

"I nearly stayed single in Dublin."

They laughed.

"This is better," said Anna.

"Or worse. For Bill as well. He's given up his freedom. He never gets a game of golf in nowadays. Marriage is gruesome. Yet we go on doing it."

"Marriage's a gilded cage, as Socrates said. Those on the outside want to get in. Those on the inside want to get out."

"Poor Socrates. Tied to that ghastly Xanthippe."

"We haven't heard her side of the story," Anna reminded her. "It must be annoying to be married to someone who puts you in the wrong the whole time."

Tessa smiled. "It is."

A shadow crossed Anna's face.

"What is it?"

Anna stared at the ground.

"Anna! I'm sorry. What a fool I've been. What a tactless fool."

"I can't expect everybody to tiptoe around me for the rest of my life."

"It won't be for the rest of your life, Anna. You'll find someone else."

"No. I'm past all that, Tessa."

"No one's ever past it. An aunt of mine recently remarried at the grand old age of eighty-one."

"I – " She felt Sam tug at her sleeve. "What is it, Sam?"

Slowly he put his lips together. "Chush."

"Juice?"

He shook his head. He tried again " . . . ik."

"What?"

" . . . ik."

She stared at him and started to panic. They weren't going to have a scene, were they? Not in front of Tessa. She was, after all, a trained social worker. She might think Anna was handling Sam all wrong.

Sam's voice rose. " . . . ik! ik!"

She hazarded a guess. "Milk?"

He hesitated, then nodded.

She rose and went over to the fridge.

"Is it always like this, Anna?"

"Always."

"I don't know how you understand him."

"Sometimes I wonder whether I do." She handed Sam the beaker. "I'm not sure whether he really wanted milk, or something else he couldn't remember the name of. Sometimes I think I'm just putting words into his mouth."

She sat down at the table again. "Tessa, I've found out something about Richard."

"About Richard? Well it can't be too awful. Not tabloid stuff anyhow. Barristers aren't like that. In my experience, they're dreadfully dull and respectable. He can't have embezzled a bank or been married before."

"Close. He's got a daughter."

Tessa's jaw dropped. "Richard! A daughter! You're kidding."

"No."

"How old is she?"

"Ten. She used to live with her mother in London. Now she's been dumped on my mother-in-law. That's how I found out."

"But why did he never tell you about her?"

"That's what I want to know."

Tessa blinked. "Aren't men extraordinary? What does go on in their minds? Richard! I can hardly believe it."

"Nor can I. Except I've seen her."

"Does she look like Richard?"

"Yes. That's the bad part."

"What's the good part?"

"I'm never going to see her again."

CHAPTER FOUR

AT GEORGE MITCHELL'S FUNERAL THERE WAS such a crush in the crematorium's tiny ante-room that Anna had to wait outside. She glanced around at the other mourners. Businessmen in suits, one or two elegantly dressed women standing, like herself, on the edge of the crowd. Relatives? Colleagues? Or friends?

The previous funeral finished. People began moving forward. They filed through the ante-room, which resembled a doctor's waiting room, and into the small plain chapel. Anna took a seat in the second row from the back. Up at the front, on the right-hand side, stood the coffin. It looked lonely and sad and bare standing there. It ought to have been covered in flowers. It ought to have been in Holme church not in the crematorium. What had Mother been thinking of? Why all this drabness? She could see her mother clearly, sitting on the opposite side of the aisle in the front row, stiffly upright, staring straight ahead. Beside her sat Brian.

They all stood up as the vicar entered. He was dressed, not in vestments, but in an ordinary black suit. They sang, in a desultory fashion, and without benefit of organ, a couple of well-known hymns. Brian, looking harrassed and uncomfortable in his too-tight dark suit, stumbled his way through a reading. A few prayers were said. Anna had never been to anything so utterly soul-destroying in her life. Even the vicar looked depressed. Thank God Richard had been buried, not cremated. This was a million miles away from the short moving service conducted by Adam during which Penelope and she had alternately smiled and wept and clung to one another for comfort.

While the congregation stood to sing the final hymn, the

plush velvet curtains to the right swung apart and the coffin, driven by some unseen mechanical device, squeaked and ground its way along the rails to its final destination. Some sort of oven, she assumed. The crimson velvet curtains swung to again. He was gone from them for ever. Whilst the rest of the congregation knelt for a final prayer, Anna sat back on her chair, unable to pray.

Her mind had gone a complete blank. At the thought of his body going up in smoke, it had shied away in panic; just as it had when she'd stood beside Penelope and watched Richard's coffin being lowered, so agonisingly slowly, into the ground. The next day going back and seeing the mound of fresh soil where the gaping hole had been, she'd found it hard to believe Richard was lying down there. His dear lovely body, every inch of it known intimately to her. The cortisone scars across his back. His long white legs, which Toby had inherited. The mole on his left shoulder-blade. Her memories bore no relation to his body as it would be now. Nana, Georgia, Richard and now this. All those bodies, all that love, all gone.

She felt a tap on her shoulder. A voice behind her whispered, "You omitted to mention George Mitchell was your father, Doctor Vale. Rather a grave withholding of evidence, don't you think?"

"You pick your moments," she said bitterly, without turning round.

"Giving you something else to think about."

McMahon came and sat beside her. The mourners, now starting to file out, didn't give them a second glance.

"Who told you? Mother?"

He shook his head. "The computer threw it up. Eventually. I must say, they do funerals differently over here. When the Mammy died, the entire village turned out and the four of us, my brother and myself and two of my brothers-in-law, carried the coffin ourselves from the church over to the graveyard across the road. That kind of thing helps. In Ireland, they really know how to do a funeral."

"They're not all like this," she muttered. "Richard's wasn't."

She glanced up and saw that a man in a brown suit was staring at her as if he recognised her. For a moment she couldn't place him, then she remembered he was one of those protesters outside the women's centre. Hard to recognise him without his placard. He moved on and was lost in the crowd. She turned her attention back to McMahon.

"What are you going to do then? Arrest me?"

"You're very keen on that, aren't you? Don't rush me. If I'm going to arrest you, I'll do it in my own good time." He looked at her sternly. "But there is a pay-off. Take me to the lecture tomorrow."

"What lecture?"

"You know very well what lecture. Professor Gloria West is giving a talk to your women's group tomorrow evening."

"How did you find that out? Have you been questioning our members?"

"Not yet. I saw a poster. This Gloria must be well known, is she?"

"Yes, she's a radical. You wouldn't approve."

"Never mind about that, I want to be there."

"Why?"

He ignored this. She got the feeling he never answered a direct question if he could help it.

"So?"

"So what?"

"Will you take me?"

"You must be joking!" She could imagine Lottie's face if she turned up with a man, let alone a police officer, in tow.

"Look, I want to get a feel for what goes on there."

"Spy on us, you mean?"

"That's another way of putting it."

"Well you can't. Men aren't allowed. It's in the rule book."

"I wouldn't have thought you're a person who bothers much about rules, are you?"

She looked at him coldly. "Why don't you get one of your women officers to come along incognito? It would be far simpler."

"There probably will be one or two there. But I'm a hands-on man. I want to see for myself. And if you've really got nothing to hide why can't I come along? Otherwise I might start drawing comparisons with the Masons and other less desirable secret groups."

"Don't be silly. There's nothing funny about us."

"Well then?"

"No."

He sighed. "I could get a warrant and insist on searching the building."

"All right!" She threw up her hands in defeat. "Meet me outside Marks and Spencer's at eight."

"You think of the most glamorous places."

She grunted. "Found much glamour in Hull, have you?"

The chapel was empty. Brian and her mother must have walked past without her noticing. Anna and Detective Superintendent McMahon rose and tagged onto the end of the file of mourners. Outside another funeral party was already assembled, waiting to come in. A uniformed police officer came up to McMahon.

"Here's the list of mourners you requested, sir."

"Thank you, Sergeant Bradley." He glanced at the sheet of paper and pocketed it. "Right." He nodded at Anna. "See you tonight then."

They walked away. After a couple of seconds, Sergeant Bradley glanced back over her shoulder at Anna. An odd glance. He must have told Sergeant Bradley who she was then. George Mitchell's daughter. Left home at eighteen. Concealed her identity. How high up on the list of suspects was she? She mustn't let McMahon's Irish charm lull her into a false sense of security. Lottie was right. They all needed to keep tabs on this investigation. The time might soon come when she'd need a well-prepared defence. She read the newspapers. She knew all about entrapment and beatings down at the station. She must be prepared.

People were beginning to drift off. She watched Brian help her mother into a long black car. They were driven away. She lingered for a moment, looking at the wreaths laid out on a wall. A red one from her mother. *"To George from Stella."* Nothing more. Not even love. *"To Father from Brian."* She didn't blame him for missing out love.

She wandered along beside the wall. Most of the wreaths were from business associates. *"To George, with affectionate remembrance from all at BVP." "To George, with kindest regards from the staff of Rylands Associates." "To George, for many happy memories on the golf course and particularly on the nineteenth hole. From all at Holme Park golf club."* In amongst them somewhere was her own, quite a small, discreet one, *"Love from Anna and the boys."* The grandsons he'd never known. There would be no final reconciliation then. Strange. She must always, deep down, have expected them to meet up again, expected the old charmer to have found out her address and looked her up. Invited her out to dinner, perhaps. But he'd taken her mother's side to the last.

Her attention was caught by a large wreath with, in gold lettering, *"For George. All my love, Jacqueline."* A relative? She couldn't remember any with that name. A secretary? Yes, perhaps a secretary who'd harboured who knows what secret longings all these years? He'd been a handsome man, her tall dark-haired father. After his wedding day, fattened up by his wife, he'd turned into quite a catch. Some women might have envied her for being his daughter. The wealthy good-looking George Mitchell.

As she drove home, pictures tumbled confusedly around in her mind. Her father taking her ice skating, her father making her tea, her father defending her . . . All of it done clumsily, uncertainly, tiptoeing around her as if she might break. He hadn't known how to treat a daughter, had been on surer ground with Brian whom he'd bullied mercilessly, as he'd been bullied by his own father. It was the Northern way of raising male children.

At home, she was met at the kitchen door by Donna. The boys were sitting at the table eating their lunch.

"I don't approve of all this yoghurt."

"Pardon?"

"Have you read how much sugar they put in them?"

"I thought yoghurt was good for children?"

"Not every day. I've made them rice pudding."

"That is kind of you, Donna. I . . . "

"It all depends how much effort you're prepared to put into their diet," she muttered, turning back to the table. "Oh, Sam, that spoon's not very clean, is it? Mummy must have forgotten to wash it. I'll get you another one."

Anna crept sadly out of the kitchen and went upstairs to change. And I don't want to see you again in a hurry, she thought, hanging up the black suit she'd bought for dinner parties and worn to Richard's funeral and now her father's so that she'd never wear it to a party again. She struggled into jeans and T-shirt, swallowed, touched the chest of drawers three times for luck and went back down to face Donna.

"Thank you *so* much for looking after them this morning, Donna," she said, overdoing it. "Er, are you still all right for tomorrow evening?"

"Yes," replied Donna, her expression impassive.

Yes, I'll be delighted to, wondered Anna, or yes, but it's a dreadful chore. That ad for a new child-minder was going in the newsagent's shop window tomorrow. "Now, boys, shall we go for a walk? It's a lovely day," she added, trying to impress as a mother.

Toby glowered at her and Sam started to whine.

Donna, putting on her jacket, gave a snort. "Toby's practically falling asleep. He needs a nap. And Sam likes to watch *Playdays* after lunch."

"So he does," agreed Anna, thoroughly deflated. She picked Toby up and switched on the television. When she heard the front door slam, she leant over the banister to check Donna really had gone, then got Toby's bottle ready. Donna didn't approve of bottles at this time of day.

She put Toby to bed and came back down to the kitchen where Sam was sitting glued to *Playdays*.

"Good boy," she said. "You watch that for a moment. Mummy's busy."

He got up immediately and came to see what she was busy

at. He stood by her elbow as she took out pencil and paper and drew three columns down the page. Her father's life. The lines wavered slightly where Sam was leaning against her.

"Don't you want to watch *Playdays* any more?"

He shook his head.

She headed the columns. *Business. The Law Case. Personal.* The first column she left blank. She couldn't go snooping around his shops and she didn't have access to his papers. The law case – but to suspect any of the women's group of murdering him was simply daft, just the kind of thing the police would go for. Angela was shy as a mouse. It was true that Carol flew into rages and Lottie went over the top sometimes. But neither of them would have tried to murder him. Would they?

That left his personal life. The family. Most murders were committed by family members. She had the advantage over the police that she could rule herself out. Brian? Bullied once too often by their father, had he decided to get rid of him and run the business himself, having to answer to no one? She couldn't see it. Brian scarcely seemed to have changed from the clumsy, slightly slow little boy she'd known as a child. Unless it was all a brilliant camouflage? And what about Mother? Anna paused. Yes. Why shouldn't Mother be a suspect? She wrote down *Mother*. After all, it was only right that someone should keep an eye on her.

Sam nudged her and grunted.

"What is it, Sam? I'm still busy."

He made a writing gesture with his hand. She found him a crayon and a piece of paper. He sat down to draw. She returned to her list of suspects.Who else was there? Adam's father? Dead. Adam? Of course not. Friends? Members of the golf club (but did one murder someone over a game of golf?). Secretaries? Mistresses? Her father didn't have mistresses. He'd always been a man's man. Hard-working, spending his free time on the golf course or in the pub. The father she'd known would never have had time for a mistress.

Later that evening, after the boys had gone to bed, she phoned Holme Park. Bates answered the phone.

"Could I speak to Mr Brian Mitchell, please?" she asked, heavily disguising her voice, as all first-rate detectives learn to do.

"Certainly, Miss Anna. Just a moment."

Probably she wasn't going to make a first-rate detective.

"Brian. Hello. It's Anna."

"Who?"

"Anna. Your sister. I was wondering how mother was."

"I can't see why you're bothered all of a sudden. Till this week you hadn't seen her for years."

Anna clenched her teeth. "I know I haven't seen her for years but she's still my mother. It wasn't entirely my fault, you know."

"No. No, I suppose not."

"We should stick together, you and I. We'll be high on the list of suspects."

"Yeah, that McMahon chap's already given me a grilling. I felt awful afterwards."

"And Mother?"

"They didn't bother much with her. Once her alibi was established, they left her alone. She was here of course. As I was. Asleep. Dad had told us he had a business meeting and not to wait up. What he was doing walking over the Westwood at twelve o'clock at night, I can't imagine."

"He liked it up there."

"But at that time of night, even in June, it would have been pitch-dark."

"I know. Listen, Brian, do you have any idea who it could have been? Who was the person he was meeting to do business with that night?"

"No one knows. There's no record in his diary. And the police have checked all his usual hotels and restaurants. Nobody saw him dining that night."

"Can you think of anyone who had a grudge against him? Did he have any business enemies?"

Brian snorted.

"All right, stupid question. I meant, was there anyone in

91

particular? Anyone he might have sacked recently, for instance?" The red-faced man at that children's party. Pushing up to her, breathing whiskey all over her: "Remember me to your father." Later, she'd learned he'd been dismissed by her father.

"He's sacked a lot of people recently. He's always sacking people. He sacked me five times."

"Do you think you could get me a list of names? Going back, say, six months or a year?"

"I suppose so. Why are you interested?"

"I'm not interested. I'm a suspect. As you are. We've got to work together on this one, Brian. We both look as if we've got grudges against him. You were sacked by him and I'm a member of the women's group which took that case against him."

"Oh you are, are you?"

"Yes. Did you ever meet Angela Smith when she was working for Father?"

There was a short pause. "May have come across her once or twice," he mumbled.

He'd never given anything away, even as a child. Father's bullying had made him secretive and passive. He'd always need prodding into action because to act was to risk criticism. They were a hopeless family. Hopeless.

The following afternoon, Brian rang her.

"I've got news for you, Anna. He put you back in."

"Back in? Back in what?" Anna frowned with the effort of trying to hear her brother over the noise of Sam charging round the kitchen being a train.

"Father's will. He added a codicil three months ago. There's money for you and your children."

"But . . . " She was stunned. She didn't know what to say. Here was another message from beyond the grave. All these years then he'd not lost sight of her.

"He's left you twenty thousand."

"My God! What a lot of money."

"Thought you'd be pleased."

"What did Mother say?"

"Not much. Nothing, actually. It's no skin off her nose. She's more than enough to live on. Anyway, I thought I'd let you know. I'll ring you about the other thing in a couple of days."

"Thanks, Brian."

She put down the phone and burst into tears. Money for the boys. The grandsons he'd never seen. Or had he seen them? Had he found out their address and come secretly to watch them play? She put her head down on the table and wept. "Daddy, Daddy, forgive me."

Sam crept up and jogged her elbow. There was a worried look on his face.

"Da?"

"Yes. But not your Daddy. Mine," she explained, drawing him up onto her lap. "You never knew him and now he's dead. Poor boys, you do badly for grandparents." Never saw one set and now Penelope was cut off too, for they could never, never go back to that house.

Sam reached up and dabbed clumsily at the tears running down her face.

"It's all right, Sam," she said hastily, as his face began to pucker. "Shall we wake Toby and go out for a walk?"

He slid off her lap and went to fetch his new red shoes. He held them out to her with a look of encouragement.

"My boys," she murmured, as she bent down to fasten his buckles. "How would I survive without you?"

As they were going out of the house, they met Julia about to go into hers. She was wearing a brown and cream striped skirt and a cream jumper. Didn't India ever throw up, sneeze or crap over her? Anna had given up wearing pale colours the day Sam was born.

"Lovely day." Julia beamed.

"Yes," said Anna, shortly. It probably always was a lovely day in Julia's house. Lovely games, lovely furniture, lovely meals. She and Donna would get on like a house on fire.

"Hello, Sam."

Sam stared up at her dumbly.

93

"Still not speaking, is he? We must do something about that, mustn't we?" Julia bent down to him. "Sam, my name's Julia. Can you say Julia?"

Sam shook his head.

"Try."

Sam frowned.

"Try it, Sam, it's easy. J-u-l-i-a."

Sam stamped his foot.

"It's no use," Anna said hurriedly. "He clams up altogether if he's forced."

"Humph!" Julia straightened up. "If he was my child, I'd . . . oh Anna, I almost forgot, I've got a petition for you to sign. Wait a tick."

She disappeared inside and came out a few moments later waving a piece of paper. "Sign here," she said in her singing telegram voice.

Anna obediently took the pen. "What's it about?"

"That patch of grass over there." Julia waved a hand towards the wasteland opposite. "They want to knock down the old warehouse and build townhouses over our green space."

"People have got to live somewhere."

"Not opposite us, they haven't. I've got signatures from everyone in the road. You're not going to let us all down, are you, Anna?"

Meekly Anna signed, deeply despising what she was doing. After all, her house had been a field once. And that warehouse had lain disused for years.

"Thank you. I'm going to send it off today. We want to preserve the character of this neighbourhood. After what's happened in Beverley, one can't be too careful."

"What has happened in Beverley?"

"That murder – haven't you heard? George Mitchell, his name was. Important man Frank says. He did business with him once."

"Er, yes, I think I did hear something about it on the radio."

"A murder in Beverley of all places! Who'd have thought it? It just shows you can't be too careful. As I said to Frank, there must have been something odd about that Mitchell fellow to get himself murdered like that. Thank goodness we don't have people like that around here."

"Er, no."

Anna and her children crossed the dual carriageway and headed for the Marina. Toby sat up in his buggy looking out at everything with a mixture of curiosity and disdain. Sam pushed him. She helped him manoeuvre the buggy out of the way as three highly made-up young women in short skirts and thigh-high boots came prancing towards them. Off out for a night on the town. How it went on, the mating game. How glad she was to be finished with it all. They took no notice of her. Just another middle-aged woman with two snotty-nosed kids. They weren't going to end up like her.

Anna began telling the boys a long complicated story about boats which neither of them could possibly have followed, though Sam nodded his head sagely at decent intervals to encourage her. Telling this story and walking past the sleek highly polished boats bobbing on their moorings made Anna feel more cheerful.

Things deteriorated, however, on their return home.

Toby, released from his buggy, immediately burst into tears.

"Chush!" rapped out Sam, in his most military style.

"Hang on a moment, Sam. Let me change Toby's nappy."

"Chush! Chush!" He waved his beaker at her, narrowly missing her nose.

"All right!" She tucked a screaming flailing Toby under her arm and went to the fridge to get juice for Sam. "Now sit down at the table and drink it."

"Yut! Yut!"

"Yoghurts aren't good for you, Sam. Mummy doesn't like you eating so many." Or rather Donna doesn't.

"Yut!"

"Oh what the hell!" With her free hand, she reached into the fridge and took out a chocolate yoghurt. "Here you are." She opened it and thrust it at Sam. "Now will you let me change Toby?"

Grinning through a chocolate-smeared mouth, he nodded.

"Good of you," she muttered, bending down to change Toby roaring and kicking on the mat.

Would Julia hear? How thick were the walls? She never heard a thing from their side but perhaps that was more a tribute to their calm orderly life than to eighteenth-century building techniques?

"Ouch!"

Toby kicked her on the arm and then in the stomach. I am not here, she thought. I am not their mother. I am lying, bronzed and slim, on a beach in the South of France, with a good book beside me and a glass of something cool. Several promising-looking men are eyeing me up. I have never heard of children.

"More!" came the command from the table.

She reached into the fridge for another chocolate yoghurt. There wasn't one.

"Oooh, look what I've found! Lovely vanilla yoghurt! Lucky boy."

She thumped it down on the table.

"Yeuck!" He shot her an accusing look.

She felt grossly inadequate. "Look, Sam, there aren't any more chocolate ones. Make do with vanilla. OK?"

He pouted, grimaced, looked let down, then accepted the inevitable.

She bent down again to Toby, still roaring on the mat. I'm not their mother. I'm a New York film producer. I have an apartment on Fifth Avenue, a cook and a housekeeper all to myself. My life is made up of baseball matches and the movies, rabbis and jazz, analysts and acupuncture. Not a single nappy (diaper) – she tossed the stinking mess into the bin (trash can) – in sight.

She prepared some Milupa for Toby. At the approach of the spoon, his jaws snapped shut. If Donna asks what they've had for tea, I shall simply lie, she thought. She whipped them, protesting and whining, into their pyjamas, switched on the television and sat in a chair sunk in gloom while the children played around her feet. The great thing about television was that it didn't expect you to talk to it and it never answered back.

The doorbell rang. Donna. Anna heard her let herself in with her key. She can say what she damn well likes. Tomorrow I'm advertising for someone new.

Her short plump shape appeared in the doorway. The boys looked up, each with a plastic man dangling from his mouth. Donna's face broke into a smile.

"Don't they look sweet?"

"Well," said Anna cautiously, "they're hardly heading up to win the Einstein brain of the year competition . . . however – "

"They're lovely." Donna knelt on the floor to hug them.

Anna decided she'd reserve judgement on that ad.

"Er, Toby's not had his solids," she risked. "I tried, but . . . "

"Not want his solids? Oh, Toby!" Donna picked up the spoon. Toby opened his mouth like an angel.

Honestly, thought Anna, such hypocrisy and not yet one year old. I wonder if he's taking after Richard. She gathered up her bag and jacket.

"Thanks, Donna. I won't be late back."

She hoped. Or was she walking into a trap? Did McMahon have plans to haul her in for questioning after the lecture? She'd already looked up the number of a solicitor friend of Richard's. She shoved the scrap of paper into her bag. Just in case.

He was waiting for her outside a shut and deserted Marks and Spencer's. He was wearing the same grey suit he'd worn on their two previous meetings. Perhaps he possessed no other. He'd swapped the black tie he'd worn to the funeral for a navy silk affair with a cunning red stripe. She began to regret her jeans.

"What's the matter?" he asked, as she drew near. "You've got a hunted expression."

"Is it any wonder?" she growled. "With you following me around everywhere? I've had an awful evening so far. Toby wouldn't eat anything and Sam only wanted chocolate yoghurt."

He grinned. "You wait till you get on to puberty."

"Gee, thanks."

"Come on then."

She glanced at him. "It's not too late to back out. Are you really ready to face a roomful of women?"

"The rooms were always full of women where I was brought up. Six sisters, remember? I shall feel quite at home."

She hoped not.

They went down the deserted street and crossed the empty central square with its massive Victorian municipal buildings. It was like walking through a film set. Their footsteps echoed hollowly.

"I bet even Galway is livelier on an evening than this," she grumbled, picturing downtown Manhattan bustling with New Yorkers on their way to the movies or to dine in fancy restaurants.

"I like walking through empty city centres. And I happen to be fond of Victorian architecture."

"You should try the cemetery then. Very Victorian. Black marble. Women weeping. Angels praying. Usually deserted. And you'd have one up on its occupants that you're still alive."

"You are in a grump this evening. Don't you like living here?"

She shrugged. "When I left here I swore I'd never ever live in the North again. I came back because of Richard. Nothing happens in this town. It's stuck out on a limb, forgotten. No one interesting or the least bit famous lives here."

"Famous!" he sneered. "Who cares about that?"

"I do. I like places where famous people live. It's somehow heartening. That's what I liked about living in Dublin. You could walk down the street and say, so-and-so the painter lives here or, I saw so-and-so the poet in this café yesterday. They're here. They're successful. You say to yourself it is possible to live in this part of the world and lead an interesting life."

"Larkin lived in Hull."

"The whole point about Larkin is that he didn't lead a life that was interesting – not even to himself. He built a career out of it. Besides, he's dead. Doesn't count."

"His spirit lingers on in his library."

"Oh, please!"

"It's a very good library. I've been in it."

"So have I. I used to teach at the university."

He looked at her. "Did you? Why on earth did you give up a good job like that? Or were you sacked?"

"Certainly not. When Richard died, I decided the children needed me more than my students did. I took leave of absence. But I'm not going back."

"Hard decision to make. And unusual for a feminist."

"Is that so?"

They crossed the road in silence.

"Well, here we are."

"Er." He stood still. "Could you prepare me a little? I mean, what's the form?"

"You *are* getting cold feet. Well I'll tell you – we sit round in a circle and each of us in turn stands up and says, 'My name is so-and-so. I'm a woman. My first period was on such-and-such a date (we'll let you skip that bit). I ask the forgiveness of my lesbian sisters for any prejudice or wrong I may have done them in the past.' Then you sit down."

He looked bewildered. "But what's the point of it?"

"It's important that we all focus on our common identity as women. The date of our first menstrual period gives us a starting point. It has certain disadvantages of course. The older members amongst us had their first period, or the menarche, as we like to call it, much later than girls have them nowadays, consequently a shorter period of womanhood but – "

"What if you forget the date?"

She looked shocked. "A woman never forgets how old she was when she had her first period."

"I don't believe you. I don't believe this really goes on."

"No? But you nearly did, didn't you? You must think we're crazy. You're hardly approaching this investigation with an open mind, are you, Detective Superintendent?"

She led the way through the small knot of protesters standing on the pavement outside the centre.

"What was all that?" he asked, when they were safely inside the building.

"Take no notice. They're always there. They've somehow got it into their heads we're an abortion referral clinic."

"Pro-lifers, are they?" He took a look outside the building again. "There are other women's groups around. Why pick on yours particularly?"

She shrugged. "We fax lists of the telephone numbers of UK abortion clinics to places of work in the Irish Republic. To help our beleaguered sisters over there." She smirked.

He held up a hand. "OK, spare me."

"It was you who suggested coming to this meeting."

"I know. What possessed me? Was this faxing your idea, by the way?"

"Well, yes, actually. It's not illegal. We checked that. He seems to be the ringleader," she added, as the man in the brown suit joined the group of demonstrators. "He's unemployed, I think. Anyway, he seems to have a lot of time on his hands." Time to pop in to funerals, for instance. "They'll stay here till half eight, then they'll all troop off to the pub for a beer and a bit of a singsong."

"How do you know?"

"Lottie followed them once. It makes a nice evening out for them. When you think about it, we're doing them rather a service."

"Who's Lottie?"

"You'll see. Shall we go up?"

She led the way up the scuffed lino-covered stairs. Though she'd phoned in advance to warn Lottie, when she entered the room with McMahon in tow Anna could tell by the expression on Lottie's face that she thought Anna'd gone over to the enemy.

"A man? We can't have a man!" Lottie had wailed down the phone. "We've never had a man. Why can't they send a woman officer?"

"McMahon's the one in charge of the investigation. Honestly, Lottie, he's not that bad. As police officers go."

Lottie had sniffed, expressively.

"And if we don't let him in, he'll only get a warrant."

"Let him get one then."

"Um. Lottie. There's something else . . . "

"Yes?"

"I need to keep in his good books."

"We all do."

"No, it's different for me. You see, George Mitchell . . . " Was there a good way of putting this? There wasn't. "He was my father."

"Father!"

"Yes."

"That's impossible, Anna. Your family lives in the South. Guilford, I thought you said."

"Did I?"

"Yes, definitely. I remember you saying so. Anyway, you don't have a Northern accent."

"I left home at eighteen, Lottie. I never had any contact with him after that."

"Well! I can quite see why you'd want to keep that connection quiet! So the police suspect you of doing away with him, do they?"

"I'm high on their list of suspects."

"I can see the headlines – politically correct daughter murders racist, sexist, capitalist Dad. This could do wonders for the cause."

"But not for me. And McMahon is after me. You've got to help, Lottie."

"OK," Lottie had said, resigned. "Let him come to the meeting. Only see that he behaves. We can't have Gloria's lecture mucked about."

"Lottie, this is Detective Superintendent McMahon. Watch it, she's PC," she added, out of the side of her mouth.

Lottie held out her hand with a faint air of distaste.

McMahon shook it and beamed. "So you're in the force too?"

Lottie took a step backwards looking as if she'd never been so insulted in her life.

"There are other meanings of PC besides the one you're used

to," murmured Anna, giving McMahon a little shove in the direction of the back of the room. "Lottie's very, very politically correct. Try and get on our wavelength, will you?"

McMahon sat down meekly. Anna sat beside him. The room was crammed with women, many of whom Anna had never seen before. Nothing like a hint of scandal to bring the punters out. She waved to Tessa across the other side of the room. Tessa looked at McMahon and raised her eyebrows. Anna shrugged. Explanations would have to wait till later. Lottie was on her feet, introducing Professor West –

"Call me Gloria," interrupted the large blonde woman.

Lottie smiled.

"Gloria has come over from the University of the South Riding to speak to us this evening on the topic of 'Women and Writing.' Gloria will speak for approximately forty-five minutes. Then there'll be a coffee break and after that Gloria will take questions from the floor. There will be no other business. Is that understood?" She looked sternly at them all.

A small ripple of understanding ran round the room. There was to be no talk of the murder tonight, not with McMahon present. Who was it said the community of women is like a community of dolphins, communicating by secret signals? Anna, sitting next to McMahon, felt like a pariah.

Gloria began. She spoke without notes, standing up and addressing them in a strange, urgent, hypnotic manner.

"We must write our bodies. Women must write, paint and sing their bodies. We must write our love for women in our mothers' milk. In our writing, in our art, in our music, we're constantly brought back to our mothers."

Not, thought Anna, if the only thing of mother is a hostile, complaining voice in your head.

"Women's language is different from men's. It's circular and diffuse. Just as a woman's sexual pleasure is different from a man's." She paused, then threw out challengingly, "Women experience their greatest pleasure in auto-eroticism."

Anna avoided meeting McMahon's glance. Anyway, it's not true, she thought, remembering Richard touching her hair,

Richard kissing her neck, her breasts, coming inside her, waiting inside her. His soft, gentle touch. It's not true. I miss his body beside me. Nothing makes up for that loss. His body gave me Sam and Toby. His body made Beatrice. The unwelcome thought rose in her mind. Beatrice. She was afraid of this little girl. Gloria's voice floated in and out of her consciousness.

"Men's language is language used to put someone else in the wrong."

This was more promising. Anna almost gave McMahon a nudge. Ever since their first meeting, he'd been intent on putting her in the wrong.

"Men's language is language in a straight line, conforming language, the language of the phallocracy. Women's language dances and sings. For women are connected to the cosmic rhythms of the universe. Women's language is the language of the womb. It's not afraid of babbling."

Fine, thought Anna, but how will that improve our promotion prospects? Then she felt ashamed. Lottie would say she had a phallocentric mind.

Gloria was winding up.

"Women writers want total revolution. We want to displace the symbolic order where patriarchal language rules and the male logos is king. Women must write women. Never forget, sisters, a woman's sex is composed of two lips which embrace continually. Women have sex organs just about everywhere. We have an endless capacity for pleasure. What are we going to do about it?"

She sat down to rapturous applause. Anna glanced sideways at McMahon. His expression was a complete blank.

She smiled to herself. Good to see him nonplussed for once. He always seemed so much in control.

"Come on," she said. "Let's grab a coffee before it runs out."

They joined the queue.

"Well?" she asked. "What did you think of it?"

He put a hand up to his forehead and looked vaguely stunned.

"It's not usually like this," she added hastily. "I mean it isn't usually so – well – so . . . "

"No? No, I'm sure it's not," he filled in kindly, not believing her, she saw, for a moment.

With any luck he'd think they were all too bats to commit murder. Insanity's an effective disguise, as Hamlet well knew.

"What I found interesting," he went on, having apparently recovered himself a little, "is all this concentration on the body. I thought women wanted to get away from the old idea of being defined by their bodies?" He shot her a look. "Or have I got it wrong?"

"We do and we don't," replied Anna, hardly feeling equal, at this moment and in these surroundings, to explaining the intricacies of feminist theory. She glanced nervously over her shoulder. Not far behind them in the queue was Carol. She lowered her voice. "You see, on the one hand, women have a right to be treated on equal terms with men – equal pay, equal promotion prospects and so on." He nodded. "But on the other hand, we inhabit our bodies. Because of our gender, we've had a different social conditioning from men. It may mean we look at the world differently from men."

"Yes, I've always thought women did." He took the plastic cup of coffee handed to him rather sourly by Lottie. "And speaking of auto-eroticism, Fleur Adcock has rather a good poem about masturbation. Catches the rhythm just right."

Anna blushed and grabbed a coffee. What a subject to bring up in the presence of a widow!

"Fleur Adcock?" she gabbled. "Translates East European poets, doesn't she?" She glanced around rather wildly. "Oh, look. There's some of our group over there. I'll introduce you."

The regular members of the group – Clara, Carol, Jennifer, Tessa and Angela – were standing together in a little knot. By the way they eyed her when she came up, Anna realised Lottie had spread the news. Angela stared at her with particular interest, seeing her as the daughter of the man who'd sacked her, Anna supposed. She sighed quietly to herself. Were they going to ostracise her for being George Mitchell's daughter? She introduced Detective Superintendent McMahon to them and then stood back. Let him sink or swim by himself. *She* wasn't going to help him. Tessa moved over to join Anna on the outskirts of the group.

"You might have told me who your father was." She looked hurt.

"I've never told anyone, Tess. I left home when I was eighteen. The past, my childhood – it seemed like another world. I had no contact with them till all this happened."

"The past always catches up with you."

"I suppose it does." She thought of Richard.

"Why are you with him?" Tessa nodded towards McMahon.

"He practically blackmailed me into bringing him. I'm high on the list of suspects, Tess. Daughter leaves home. Comes back eighteen years later planning revenge. Are they going to cold-shoulder me, do you think?"

She shook her head. "There's quite a lot of sympathy for you, actually. Anyone would want to keep that family connection quiet."

"What did you think of the lecture?"

Tessa smiled ironically. "Gloria West's not my favourite person at the moment."

"Oh?"

"Tell you some other time. Too complicated to go into here."

They rejoined the group.

"I rent a couple of rooms over a pub in the Land of Green Ginger," McMahon was saying.

"Funny place to live," commented Carol. "It's full of offices and banks. I didn't know people could actually live there."

"Well I do."

"Whatever made you choose it?" enquired Clara.

He shrugged. "The name made me feel at home. Green Ginger. It seemed Irish somehow. You know – *The Gingerman*."

By the glances Carol and Clara exchanged, Anna could tell they hadn't the faintest idea what he was talking about. She foresaw a lot of trouble ahead for him in England if he persisted in behaving like this.

"It's a book," she explained. "By JP Donleavy. It's set in Trinity. Donleavy was a student there."

"Oh," said Carol, uninterested in books by men, especially men who'd been to university. "Well, Detective Superintendent, found any more clues yet?"

"We're working on it."

"I hear we're all to receive a visit tomorrow?"

"Yes. One of my officers will be calling round to your homes to take down a few details. I think you've all been notified in advance?"

Several heads nodded. Anna stared at him. This was the first she'd heard of any visit. Or wasn't she to have one? Was some other fate reserved for her? Questioning down at the station, for example? She looked very hard at McMahon. He appeared impervious.

"Such a pity they didn't put a woman in charge of this investigation." Lottie had abandoned her kettle and joined them.

"Why?" enquired McMahon in a tone Anna recognised as dangerous.

"Women have greater powers of empathy than men, Detective Superintendent. They can more easily think themselves into the mind of the murderer. Like Miss Marple."

McMahon shook his head. "A murder investigation isn't like an Agatha Christie novel or an Inspector Morse episode where one man, sorry, person, wanders around with all the facts inside his or her head. For one thing, it's much too risky. What if he or she suddenly dropped dead? No, nowadays everything's fed into a computer. In fact, it's often the computer that solves the crime for us. We call it HOLMES."

Jennifer smiled. "So there is some connection with fiction."

"Anyway," said Carol darkly, over the rim of her coffee cup, "I'm sure we all agree George Mitchell got what was coming to him. He's thrown his weight around this town for years."

There was an embarrassed silence.

After a few moments, Carol realised why. "Sorry, Anna. I keep forgetting he was your father." She looked thoughtfully at her. "So it turns out you're not really middle class at all, Anna. I knew there must be some reason why I liked you. I don't mind the upper classes – they've long been our allies."

Clara stared. "Is Anna upper class then?"

"Not really, I . . . " began Anna.

"Come on!" exclaimed Lottie. "Brought up on that huge estate, brother at – where was it?"

"Harrow," put in Angela shyly, then ducked her mousy head down again.

"There. You see. You're upper class if anyone is."

Anna felt her cheeks go red. She noticed McMahon grinning infuriatingly at her. "Yes, well, none of us chooses our family," she snapped.

"How's Kylie?" asked Jennifer, tactfully changing the subject. "Is Kylie unwell?"

"She's gone off her food," explained Carol. "But when we ask her if she feels sick, she says no. She's not really herself at the moment. She's lost all her bounce. If it goes on like this, my sister's going to take her to the doctor tomorrow."

Lottie glanced at her watch. "Time to start again. I wonder what Gloria's going to tell us in the second half?" She looked a little nervous.

"Didn't you like the lecture?" murmured Anna.

"Well it was a bit strong, wasn't it?" replied Lottie. "Not what our regulars are used to. Some of them were looking a tinge bewildered. Still, I expect it's good for us. Once in a while."

Anna smiled and they returned to their seats for the second part of the meeting.

A middle-aged woman, not one of their regulars, started the questions off by asking Gloria what political correctness meant.

Gloria smiled. "It means using language in such a way as not to offend or insult anyone. I'm sure all of us here would as soon call an Afro-American a negro as – as we'd slap our children."

Lottie glanced across at Anna who suddenly found something interesting by her feet.

"And it doesn't stop there," continued Gloria, getting into her stride. "Words like blacking, black mark, black sheep also have to be removed from the language. And what about the elderly, the blind, the mentally handicapped? We obviously can't go on calling them by those insulting labels, can we?"

The questioner looked puzzled. "So what should we call them instead?"

"The chronologically gifted, the visually or intellectually challenged."

"I see." The woman sat down looking not noticeably less puzzled.

"And if you're short and bald," whispered McMahon, "you're vertically and folicly challenged." He rubbed his hands in glee.

"Short people, for example," continued Gloria, "can be called vertically . . . "

Anna glared at McMahon. "Shall we go?" She hadn't brought him here to have a good laugh at their expense.

"Go? Not at all. I wouldn't miss this for the world."

This was what she'd been afraid of.

A few more questions were asked and then, to her horror, she saw that McMahon had got to his feet and was about to ask a question. She froze in her seat with embarrassment.

"Professor West, you've spoken a lot this evening about women's creativity and the need for them to get in touch with their bodies. What about men? Where does their creativity come from?"

Gloria looked at him kindly. "Men are permanently wounded by their separation from the mother. Unlike daughters, you see, a son can never return to his mother. It's from this wound that men get their creative energy. I can lend you some books on it if you like."

McMahon mumbled something non-committal and sat down.

Soon after this, to Anna's relief, the meeting broke up.

They walked back together as far as Prince's Quay. He was limping more than usual, she noticed.

"Those damned plastic chairs," he explained. "I wonder your sciatica isn't worse."

"In my case it's the children that make it worse. It's probably psychosomatic. Have you always limped, or did it suddenly come on?"

"It suddenly came on. Trying to rescue someone, I got too close to a bomb."

"Brave."

"Foolhardy. I was reprimanded for it."

"That doesn't seem fair."

"Life isn't, is it? Fair, I mean. That's where these politically correct people have gone wrong. They mean well, but you can't force life into a mould."

"I know." You couldn't plan, either. Life escaped your control. Richard . . .

"Still," he glanced at her, "you must be feeling pretty cheered up. I heard your father left you some money."

"Oh. You heard." She stared down into the inky still water. "Yes, well, it'll come in useful for the children's education."

"Your husband left you badly off then, did he?"

"He was young. He didn't expect to die."

She looked up suddenly, aware of a change in the atmosphere. Yes, she could tell by his eyes. What had been a friendly conversation had turned into an investigation. Once again, she'd been caught off-guard by that soft Irish voice. He'd worked it all out – impoverished widow in need of some ready cash does away with her wealthy father. Suddenly she disliked him intensely, this short slight man standing there so self-assured and in control.

"Good night, Detective Superintendent."

She turned abruptly on her heel and walked away. Thanks, Daddy. You meant well, but your generosity has landed me in it up to my neck.

CHAPTER FIVE

SHE WOKE WITH THE SAME THOUGHT going round in her head. Richard hadn't been truthful. Their happiness hadn't been happiness but a lie. She was doomed. Unhappy childhood, unhappy marriage. She hadn't broken free after all.

The telephone rang. She struggled downstairs to answer it.

"Oh. Brian."

"They've been here again questioning me. This time they wanted to know a lot of things about you."

"What sort of things?"

"How you got on with our parents. Why you left home."

Her heart sank. "What did you say?"

"That you left to do a course in London."

"Good."

"Then they asked why there hadn't been any contact for years. I said you and Mother didn't get on. They seemed interested in that."

"I bet. Who was it? McMahon?"

"No, some woman. Bradley, I think her name was."

"Well, thanks for letting me know. Have you got that list ready for me yet?"

"I'm working on it. I've a hell of a lot on at the office at the moment as you can imagine and these constant interruptions from the police don't help." He said it half-accusingly, as if it was somehow her fault she'd got herself suspected by the police.

"Sorry," she said humbly.

He rang off. Was it her imagination or did Brian sound stronger, less dithery this morning? Was he coming into his own now that Father had died?

She went back upstairs feeling confused and persecuted. The

children were crying to be got up. She felt shaky inside. No doubt there were still a few hormones left over from Toby's birth. No doubt that was why she felt so strange. Or did all new mothers feel like this? Torn to pieces, nerves shattered by their children's crying? Nana's madness had started after the birth of her first child. Was she going mad too? "Nonsense," said her mother's voice. "You always did exaggerate. You've a job to do. Get on and do it."

She got the children up and brought them both down to the kitchen. Toby had a dirty nappy. With a sigh, she laid him on the mat. That conversation with Cornelius Fry seemed a lifetime away. Her professional career was over. She was now simply a machine for changing nappies and pushing food into children's mouths.

She wrestled with Toby's flailing limbs. He kicked her on the arm and then on the breast. She gasped in pain. She felt no love for them this morning. She felt no love for anyone. Richard had lied to her. She'd never got close to anyone in her life. Never been loved, really loved, by another human being. Toby's foot caught the side of her cheek.

"Stop it, Toby!" she roared. "Stop it! Stop it! Stop it!" She slapped him on his plump right thigh. Hard.

For a moment there was dead silence in the room. Sam stopped playing with his trucks and stared at her. Toby stared at her, then opened his mouth and screamed. Sam rushed over and hammered on her arm.

"Bo! Bo! Bo!"

She dissolved into tears. "I know, Sam. I know. I shouldn't have hit him."

"Ma! Ma!" howled Toby.

She hauled him back onto the changing-mat. "I'm your Ma," she muttered through her tears, her hair brushing his naked tummy as she bent over him. "This is as good as you're going to get. And if I don't get it right now, you'll be messed up for the rest of your life. Or you'll spend the whole of your adulthood pitying yourself and trying to come to terms with my mistakes."

It was too much. She finally succeeded in substituting a dry clean nappy for his smelly one. When you thought about it, it was too much to ask of any one person. Her mother was not to blame for her unhappiness.

She gave Sam a tube of Smarties in reparation and sat down on a chair to give Toby his bottle. She pictured Donna walking through the door. "Why is Toby having a bottle at this time?" "Because it's the only way I know of shutting him up." Would that be grounds enough to have him taken into care?

The phone rang again. Keeping the bottle in Toby's mouth, she reached round and lifted the receiver.

"Hello, love. It's Penelope."

"Look, if you've rung about Beatrice, the answer's still no."

"I – "

Anna ploughed on. "I can hardly cope with the two I've got. How on earth do you expect me to take on another one?"

She slammed down the phone and sat for a moment, biting her lip. She'd quarrelled with Penelope, the last person on earth she'd ever thought she'd quarrel with.

She went upstairs and laid Toby, now sleeping peacefully, in his cot.

She went back down to the kitchen. Her head ached. Her leg ached. Her eyes were sore from crying. She longed to lay down her head on some motherly lap and cry like a child and be comforted like a child. She sat on the floor beside Sam and reached out to hug him. He pushed her away. He hadn't forgiven her. She felt he was in the right. She was a dreadful human being.

She watched him play silently with his trains. Donna had said, "He lives in his own little world. He's quite happy." Her words had struck terror into Anna's heart. He must learn to speak, he must, or how would he survive? We can't exist outside language. It's how we create our identity. He mustn't stay shut up in his own world. It's wrong.

The phone rang again.

"Hi. It's Lottie. What did he say?"

Anna put a hand up to her aching head. "Who?"

"The Detective Superintendent, of course. You were having quite a conversation with him."

Anna felt a tug at her skirt. Sam smiled up at her. She bent down and put an arm around him. It made her feel a bit happier.

"I can't remember what we talked about. We discussed political correctness, I think."

"But what did you find out about the case?"

"Well, nothing really."

"Anna! You're hopeless."

"I know," she said humbly. "I'm not cut out for this."

"Didn't you find out anything?"

"I got caught up with what Gloria was saying . . . but I can tell you one thing – I'm higher up the list of suspects than anyone else in the group. I wouldn't worry if I were you."

"I'm disappointed in you, Anna."

"Sorry. What about letting someone else take over? What about Carol?"

"I couldn't possibly ask Carol. She's out of her mind over Kylie."

"Kylie? Why? What's wrong?"

"Haven't you heard? She was off her food and behaving strangely so Carol's sister took her to the doctor's yesterday evening and he said Kylie was showing classic signs of having been interfered with."

"Interfered with?"

"Abused."

"No!" Anna's blood ran cold. "That's terrible."

"It's a nightmare."

"Do they know who it is?"

"She won't say. Too frightened probably. A social worker's examining her today. Carol's boyfriend's going spare, threatening to beat the living daylights out of whoever it is."

"Lottie, how dreadful." Anna's arm tightened around Sam. "You'll let me know what happens, won't you?"

She put down the phone and knelt beside Sam to give him a hug. That poor little girl, she thought.

All day she waited in for Lottie's phone call. It never came. In the evening, after the children had gone to bed, she phoned her instead.

"Oh. Anna," said Lottie, sounding rather strange.

"I'm ringing about Kylie. What's happening? How is she?"

"I can't talk to you, Anna. I've – there's someone with me." She rang off.

Ten minutes later Jennifer rang.

"Someone has to tell you, Anna, and no one else would. Kylie's named Sam."

"Named Sam? What do you mean?"

"Sam was the person who interfered with her."

"Sam!" exclaimed Anna, bewildered. "But . . . he's just a child. There must be some mistake. She's making a mistake."

"Anna, you shouldn't be on your own. Shall I come round?" She came round.

Anna ran down and opened the door the minute she heard the car pull up outside. "What's he been accused of doing?"

Jennifer stepped into the hall. "I don't know, exactly. Tessa will tell you."

"Tessa?"

"Yes." Jennifer followed Anna upstairs. "As soon as she heard, she moved quickly to take on your case. You're lucky."

Anna halted at the door of her kitchen. "Lucky!"

"Yes, Anna. Lucky. She'll stop the worst happening."

"What is the worst?"

Jennifer gazed at her.

"Oh God! You don't mean they want to take him away?" Anna felt her knees about to crumble. She sat down on a chair.

"Nothing like that will happen." Jennifer filled the kettle. "Tessa will see to that. Now I'm going to make you a cup of tea. You're in shock."

Anna clutched the edge of the table. "I don't want a cup of tea. I want to know what's going to happen to Sam."

"First of all, he'll have to be talked to. Here, in his own home. Don't worry, Tessa's trained in this kind of thing. She'll handle it sensitively."

"But Sam can't speak. He has no way of defending himself. This is a nightmare, Jennifer. An absolute nightmare."

She swallowed back the tears. Jennifer put an arm round her shoulder.

"I know, love, I know. You ought to have someone to talk to

about this. A professional, I mean. A thing like this affects the whole family. Here, I'll leave you the name of someone. I've not met him myself, but I've heard he's OK."

When Jennifer had gone, Anna paced up and down the kitchen. It was incredible. She refused to believe it. Sam knew nothing about sex, nothing. She tried to think back for any signs. In the bath. On the toilet. There was nothing. She went over to a drawer and pulled out a pile of his drawings. A three-year-old's typical scrawls. Round heads on sticks. Long narrow cylinders with wheels. His trains. She put them back in the drawer. What on earth was she doing? Sam was innocent. She'd prove it even if it broke every bone in her body.

She couldn't face this on her own. She glanced at the piece of paper on the table. Had they become then – what was it they called it? – a dysfunctional family? She fingered the bit of paper. Philip Lawrence. She looked him up in the book. She picked up the phone. Hesitated. Put it down again. What a ridiculous idea. She didn't need to talk to anyone. She'd work it out by herself.

A voice in her head, a voice from very far back in her childhood, Nana's voice, said, "Don't worry yourself. Everything will be all right." But she feared it wouldn't.

She switched on the television. The figures on the screen went up and down before her eyes. The words that came out of their mouths didn't seem to make sense. She picked up the receiver again, dialled and got an answering-machine.

"Philip Lawrence here. Either leave a message after the tone or give your phone number and I'll ring you back as soon as I can."

She put the phone down without waiting for the beep. She could never think what to say to answering-machines. It was a nice voice. Not too old, not too young. Warm and low and calming as he must surely have to be. People must ring him up in all kinds of states. She glanced at the television. Thank goodness she wasn't in a state. She listened to the news headlines. Then burst into tears.

"You look as if you haven't slept a wink," said Tessa.

"I haven't."

Neither of the women smiled. Anna felt that she'd never

smile again. She felt as if someone had stretched the skin so tightly across her face that any small movement would cause it to crack.

Tessa was wearing her work clothes – shortish skirt, navy jacket, clean white shirt. She plumped a file of papers down on the table, sat down and took out a pen. Their relationship had become professional.

Anna sat down opposite. She'd phoned Donna early that morning and asked her to take the children out. She wanted to get Tessa on her own first before she let her anywhere near Sam. Of course, she'd had to tell Donna the reason. Donna had exploded. "They want their heads examining, that lot. I've spent time with that child. I know him. He'd never do a thing like that. Honestly, social workers! They're a load of crackpots." Anna could have hugged her.

She looked at Tessa. "What exactly is Sam accused of doing?"

"Lifting her dress. Inappropriate touching."

"How do you know?"

"Kylie told us."

"And you believed her? A little girl of four?"

Tessa shook her head. "Children don't lie about things like this. They can't know about sexual behaviour unless someone has taught them."

"Precisely. Sam knows nothing about sex. She's lying."

Tessa hesitated. "I don't think so. Having told us this much, why would she make up the rest?"

"But Sam adores Kylie."

"I know."

"He'd never do anything to harm her."

"He's too young to realise what he was doing." She glanced down at the papers in front of her. "Anna, you do know – children who abuse have often been abused themselves."

"Sam hasn't been abused. I'd know. He'd have all sorts of emotional problems."

Tessa glanced at her. "He does have emotional problems, doesn't he? He can't speak."

"He's grieving for his father!"

"Anna, how well did you know Richard?"

116

Anna stared at her. "Very well. He was my husband."

"You didn't know he had a daughter."

Anna felt anger rise up in her. "That's a dirty trick, Tessa. I told you that in confidence, as a friend, and now you're using it against me."

Tessa leaned forward. "I'm trying to help you, Anna. It was lucky I was in yesterday. My team leader wanted to take the case on herself. If she had, she'd have come down like a ton of bricks on you. Perhaps even got Sam taken into care. She'd want to know why you haven't done anything about his speech."

Fear replaced the anger. "Sorry," she mumbled. "But why suspect Richard? What about me? I could have abused him."

"Yes, you could."

Tessa picked up a drawing of Sam's that was lying on the table and stared at it for several moments.

"It's a train, Tessa. A train going through a tunnel."

"Is it? Kylie's been drawing things too. A child's cry for help. I think I'll keep this for a while." She slipped the drawing in amongst her papers.

Anna clenched her hands. "Tessa, what's going to happen?"

"I'll have to speak to Sam. Not today. In cases like this it's usual to recommend he sees a child psychiatrist. And he'll obviously have to go for speech therapy."

He'd become a case. Their lives from now on would be out of their control. She felt hemmed in on all sides. The police, social workers, therapists. How would they be able to live as a family?

Tessa went. Alone in the empty house, Anna felt panicky and claustrophobic. The children weren't due back for another half-hour. This is no use, she thought, I'll have to get out.

She let herself out of the house, walked to the end of the narrow cobbled street and turned right. She passed Holy Trinity church where her parents had been married. She never went in it. The vicar was the kind who got his congregation to roll coconuts down the aisle as a way of illustrating his sermons. She preferred her theology unillustrated.

She passed the pub on the corner where Richard and she used to go on their weekly night out. She never went there either now.

She became conscious that she was hugging the wall as she walked, trying to slither past people unseen. She felt scarred, disfigured. Surely her shame must be written all over her face? She'd failed to protect her child. She'd not given him the weapons to defend himself. Instead she'd tried to smother him with love. They were now a family under suspicion. Even Richard was under suspicion. Could it be true? How well *had* she known him?

She reached the dual carriageway. The pedestrian crossing was a hundred yards away. She decided she couldn't be bothered with it and weaved in and out of the cars on the busy road, earning herself three "fucks" and one "silly old cunt."

No, she refused to believe it. Richard had been brought up by Penelope. And if, as Tessa said, there was a chain of abuse, could she imagine the extremely correct, extremely respectable Colonel Vale doing a thing like that to his sons?

The boats in the Marina rocked gently on their moorings. Raspberry Ripple, Queen of the Ocean, they came in all classes, large and small, weather-beaten and glossy. Who could she turn to for help? There was no one she could trust with this. Only, funnily enough, Richard. And he was gone.

She watched a solitary seagull search for scraps in a discarded fish-and-chip wrapper. That's what we do, she thought – root for comfort wherever we can find it. Should she phone Penelope? (Her mother pushing her teenage daughter away. "Don't bring your problems home, Anna. We don't want to hear about them.") No. Penelope had Beatrice to think about. She had enough on her plate.

Anna thrust her hands down into the pockets of her dark blue jacket and walked on. She felt stressed, confused, persecuted. She wanted to lie down and sleep for days till her leg stopped aching and this sore weary feeling disappeared. Till she felt able to cope again with all she'd have to do to defend Sam.

She arrived at the Estuary. The air slapped ozone at her. She leaned against the parapet and gazed across the flat wide waters of the Humber. A trawler chugged its solitary way out to sea. The pale June sun sent out a silver ray across the grey water. Seagulls swooped and dived in the wake of the trawler. She turned and began to walk back. It was too much to cope with on her own. This accusation against Sam. Her father's death. Beatrice. She had to talk to someone.

She went into a phone box and dialled the number again.

"Philip Lawrence here."

"Oh." She was caught off guard. She'd been expecting the answering-machine again. "I'm phoning because . . . because . . . "

"Yes?"

"I – um – need to talk to someone. That's what you do, isn't it?"

"Of course. Can you tell me what the problem is? Is it a relationship?"

His voice was low and calm, like warm water washing over her. She closed her eyes for a moment and rested her cheek against the receiver.

"Hullo?"

She pulled herself together.

"Is it a relationship?"

"Yes. Well, several, actually." Goodness, that was going to give him the wrong impression, wasn't it? "I mean everything's going wrong." She remembered his advert in the phone book. "I feel under a lot of pressure at the moment. I get angry."

"We can deal with that."

"Can you?"

"Yes. Would you like to make an appointment?"

"Yes."

"Let's see." There was a sound of pages flicking. "Tomorrow at two?"

"Fine."

"Can you tell me a bit more? Can you give me a name?"

"Anna," she replied, concealing her surname, out of a desire to protect – whom? Her family, presumably. Penelope's good name.

"All right, Anna. See you tomorrow then."

She put down the phone feeling that a burden had been lifted from her shoulders.

As she turned into her street she saw Donna and the children and Julia in a huddle outside her house. Damn.

"Hello," she said cautiously, as she walked up to them. She bent down to give Sam a kiss. Toby was asleep in his buggy.

Straightening up, she met Julia's eye.

"My dear. Donna's told me all about it. In confidence, of course. Naturally, I don't believe a word of it. We all know social workers have a bee in their bonnet about this kind of thing. Practically put confessions into children's mouths. I'm sure it happens a lot less than people think and *never* in families like ours."

Donna nodded. Anna opened her mouth. Then shut it again. These were Sam's defenders. She might need them as witnesses.

"Thanks, Julia," she said. She took the children into the house.

They stayed inside all the rest of the day. It was safest at home. Outside the door were people who might point accusing fingers at them. Inside, however, was the phone. Tessa rang to make an appointment to see Sam the next day at five. Thank God she'd be seeing Philip Lawrence before that. It would give her a breathing-space from this nightmare, a chance to talk things over.

Then McMahon phoned. "Would you say your parents had a happy marriage?"

"I suppose so." What was a happy marriage? Were there any? Richard had not told her the truth. "Why?"

"I ask the questions, remember? Your brother suggested there'd been some unhappiness. I wondered if your father had affairs?"

"Affairs? Don't be silly. He was much too busy. Anyway, he didn't like women much. He preferred drinking in clubs with male friends."

"Are you sure? Your brother sounded quite positive."

"So am I, Detective Superintendent. Quite positive. How's the investigation going?"

He rang off.

It was while she was lifting Sam onto the potty that she suddenly remembered the white wreath. *"All my love, Jacqueline."*

"Are you all right there, Sam?"

Settling him on the potty with a book, she rang Brian.

"Could you come round after work, Brian? There's something I want to ask you."

"No can do. I've promised to meet Angela."

"Angela? Not Angela Smith?"

"Yes. I want to get something sorted out about this case. Dad was mad to let things get this far. They're talking about an appeal. I'm going to offer her her old job back."

Something was definitely happening to Brian. After all these years his real personality was kicking its way out of its shell.

"Look, Brian, McMahon's just rung me. He seems to have got hold of the wrong end of the stick. He said you told him Father had affairs."

"That's right."

"But he didn't."

There was a pause.

"Did he?"

"Didn't you realise?"

"I . . . but . . . You're talking about recently – after I left home?"

"It's been going on, on and off, for years."

"You mean – all the time we were growing up?"

"Yes."

"Mother didn't know, of course."

"Yes, she did."

Anna put down the receiver and ran a hand across her face. Then she picked it up again.

"Let me get this straight, Brian. Mother knew and she put up with it?"

"Yes."

"Why? That's not like Mother."

"You don't know much about our mother, do you, Anna?"

"I – "

"Got to go. Someone's hammering on the door."

She put down the phone. He was beginning to sound exactly like their father. Important and overworked. She glanced over at Sam on the potty. "Finished, Sam?"

He nodded and stood up. She wiped his bottom and went to empty the potty. When she came back into the kitchen, Sam still had his trousers round his ankles and he was playing thoughtfully with his penis.

"Stop that at once!" she roared, full of fright. "Pull up your trousers, do you hear me?" She rushed across the room, slapped his hand away and whipped up his trousers. He burst into tears.

She reached out an arm. "Come here, Sam." She drew him towards her. "I'm sorry I shouted at you. I was frightened. I know I've never stopped you doing that before. But things are different now. You mustn't do it any more." Especially not in front of Tessa. "Hush now, hush. Mummy didn't mean to shout." Mummy didn't mean to suspect you. For in that split second on entering the room, she had suspected him.

She sat on the floor and rocked him in her arms. She could no longer trust her own judgement. She'd been wrong about everything. Absolutely wrong. Richard had a daughter and her father had affairs. And mother had known. They were alike in that, two women deceived by their husbands. The only difference was, her Mother hadn't been blind. She gazed down at the dark head nestling in her arms. No. Nothing would bring her to suspect her own child. She was his only defence.

She passed another sleepless night. No one from the women's group phoned. She was cut off from them now.

At twelve, Donna came round. She'd brought a present for Sam. A new train. Sam was thrilled.

"When are they going to question him?"

"This afternoon. Five o'clock."

Donna shook her head in disbelief.

"Thanks, Donna."

"What for?"

"For believing in Sam. It – it helps me so much." She left the room before she burst into tears.

Anna went to the lunchtime Mass in St Hilda's. She felt in need of the comfort. Also she wanted to take the first steps to protect her son. She got there a little late and entered the small side-chapel as Adam was reading the text for the day, an extract from Proverbs. She slid into a pew.

"A good wife who can find?" read Adam, standing behind the lectern in his green robes. "She is far more precious than jewels. The heart of her husband trusts in her, and he will have no lack of gain. She does him good, and not harm, all the days of her life. She seeks wool and flax, and works with willing hands. She is like the ships of the merchant – " Adam paused and sighed heavily. "I think we'll stop there." He closed up the book. "This may or may not be the Word of the Lord."

"Amen," responded the congregation, uncertainly.

Anna smiled and then shivered. It might be the middle of June and warm outside, but it was freezing in church. A lunchtime Mass in Latin never attracted a large congregation, certainly not enough to justify any heating. Two rows in front Adam's wife, Sue, was wearing her winter coat.

Anna wrapped her jacket around herself and let the familiar, centuries-old phrases wash over her. *"Salvator mundi, salva nos." "Miserere nobis." "Per omnia saecula saeculorum."* Adam's voice issuing from his tall bony frame was high-pitched and diffident and tinged with an East Yorkshire accent. Only when he sang did his diffidence vanish and his powerful splendid singing-voice filled the church. But there'd be no singing this morning.

She watched his calm steady movements in front of the altar. Pouring out the water, washing his hands, drying them on the white linen cloth. He'd been such a comfort to her in the first few days after Richard's death. To Penelope, too. Penelope, like her son, never normally went near a church. The sight of a priest irritated her, she said. But Adam hadn't irritated her.

Kneeling to pray, Anna was suddenly filled with a soft melancholy longing; for what she didn't know. That voice on the phone? Calm and soothing, it had reminded her of a long-forgotten lover. Tall, fair haired, loose limbed. She'd not thought of Dan for years. Richard had blotted out the past for her. She'd never wanted, never looked at, another man so long as he was there. And now she was past all that. Past lovers, past affairs, past sex . . . All she wanted was to protect her children.

She closed her eyes. A hand reached out where she knelt and loosened the bow tying back her hair. Just that. Nothing more. A touch, ever so gentle, on her head, a hand brushing against her cheek. Come to me, his voice said, and I will comfort you and make you whole. She remained, like a child, on her knees, wrapped up in her vision, soothed and comforted.

The man next to her gave a nudge.

"Mrs Vale!" he hissed.

Startled, she looked up and hurriedly scrambled to her feet. Adam permitted himself a small smile. He held up the wafer. *"Benedictus Deus in saecula."*

After the service she approached Sue. "Can I have a word with you, Sue?"

Sue jumped and looked startled beneath her long straggly brown fringe. "Oh it's you, Anna."

"I was wondering – would you be able to take Sam on for speech therapy?" If she made the first move, would that swing things in his favour with the social workers?

"Yes, of course. Ring the health centre any time and make an appointment. There's a waiting-list but I'll make room for him on my books."

Adam had come up to them. "I'm sure it's for the best," he said.

"Are you in for lunch, love?"

"Er, no. I won't be home." Adam avoided meeting his wife's eye. "I've got an appointment."

"An appointment?"

"At the bank."

He hurried off.

Sue stared after him. "That makes the third meeting he's had with the bank manager this month," she muttered. "If the manager was a woman, I'd be starting to get jealous." She tucked her arm into Anna's. "Come and keep me company. It'll only be a cheese sandwich, I'm afraid. I'm not up to cooking at the moment."

"How are you feeling?" asked Anna sympathetically as they walked out of the church and round the corner to the rectory.

"Terrible. I'm in the drifting phase. My legs feel like cotton wool and I can't seem to concentrate on anything. Still, there's one good thing," she said as she unlocked the door and led the way through to the kitchen. "The more pregnant I get, the less I feel like alcohol. I gather you saw this place at its worst?"

Anna gave a short, embarrassed laugh. "My kitchen gets in a state sometimes."

"Not as bad as this was, I imagine."

"Still, it's all right now," said Anna, looking around.

"Yes. I woke up suddenly one morning, snapped out of my depression and had a thorough clean-up. Took me the best part of a morning to get it right. Sit down, I'll make us a sandwich." She began cutting some bread. "What made you change your mind about speech therapy?"

Anna gazed down at the table. "I was more or less forced to. The social workers have been round."

"Not about Sam, surely?"

"Not about his speech. The thing is – oh, Sue, it's dreadful. He's been accused of interfering with another child."

Sue stopped cutting. "My God! Anna!"

"They're coming to question him later this afternoon."

"Anna, you need help, you need . . . shall I ask Adam to be there with you?"

Anna thought of Adam's worn and worried face. "It's all right, Sue. We'll manage."

"I'll send him round. You shouldn't have to go through this on your own. I don't believe a word of it and neither will Adam." Sue set a cheese sandwich and a mug of coffee in front of Anna, sat down herself, looked at her plate and exclaimed, "Christ! Not again!"

She dashed out. Anna heard vomiting coming from the bathroom overhead.

A few moments later, Sue came down. "I've forgotten how long this damned sickness lasts. Can you remember?"

"Fourteen weeks with Sam, eleven with Toby."

"If it lasts fourteen weeks I'll die, I really will." She pushed away her plate and took a sip of coffee. "You haven't eaten your sandwich either."

"No, I . . ." Anna burst into tears.

Sue came round the table and hugged her. "It'll be all right, Anna. It will. They'll find out it was a mistake."

"I hope so." She wiped her eyes.

"Have you someone to talk to?"

"Yes. Yes, I have."

"Good."

Only I'm paying him, she thought. Does that count?

He didn't have fair hair, but black. Very straight and thick and faintly streaked with grey. Nevertheless there was something about him that reminded her of Dan. The way he held his body, perhaps, light and flexible, not rigid and stiff like most men. Also his clothes. Striped shirt, loose beige trousers. Dan might have worn those. She felt very housewifey and dumpy in her old skirt and sweatshirt. Was that a food stain down her front?

Anyway, he seemed normal. She'd been half afraid – you read all kinds of stories these days. Added to which, standing on the doorstep waiting for him to answer the bell, those thick net curtains drawn across the front-room window had struck her as vaguely sinister. His bungalow was rather remote. It stood alone facing onto the Westwood in Beverley and set apart from the other houses by tall trees. Nonsense, she told herself, psychopaths don't advertise in yellow pages. And if he's in the habit of cutting up his patients and boiling their heads in a pan, surely the *Hull Daily Mail* would have told us by now?

He'd opened the door and smiled. "Hi. Come in." He had rather an ugly mouth.

For better or worse, she took the plunge and stepped inside.

He looked at her more closely, gave a curious sort of start and smiled again. Almost as if she'd surprised him. "It's this way." He turned and led her into a low-ceilinged room with dark red walls and a polished wooden floor. The room itself was rather empty. It contained an uncomfortable-looking kitchen chair and a dralon-covered sofa. "Take a seat. Sorry about all this." He flapped an arm around. "I'm in the process of organising a new consulting room. Tea, or coffee?"

"Tea, please."

He went into the kitchen and she heard him rattling various things. It sounded comforting and familiar. She forgot to worry about him being a psychopath.

"PG Tips or herbal?" he shouted through. "I'm having PG."

"That'll be fine."

From her seat on the grotesquely patterned sofa she stared across at the painting opposite. A harbour seen through an open window. A cat lay stretched out on the sill, its paws in the air, its mouth drawn back in a grimace. It had a sinister air about it, that cat. Was it dead? It gave her the horrors. She couldn't take her eyes off it.

"Here you are." He handed her a mug. "Sugar?"

"No. Thanks."

"Well." He installed himself on the hard wooden chair opposite. "Are you comfortable there?"

"Fine."

He smiled. He had a warm smile. Warm smile and a warm voice.

How could she begin to tell him everything? Her fingers fluttered nervously over the arm of the sofa. Something was wrong with his skin. Above the dark shadow of stubble on the lower part of his cheeks, his skin was unnaturally red. A car accident? Skin grafts? Knocked on the head, he'd turned slightly crazy and decided to make a career out of seeing other crazy people?

"You said on the phone you felt stressed and angry?" His gaze, fixed and steady, dwelt on her.

"Angry? Yes, I am angry. Nearly all the time."

He rubbed his cheeks. "And you said you were having problems with relationships?"

"Yes."

There was a silence. He continued to look at her.

"Oh dear." She sighed. "I wish you were a woman."

"You'd have preferred to speak to a woman? I'll try to be as feminine as possible."

Beneath the thick dark brows, his eyes were friendly, encouraging. She wondered whether he had a family and, if so, where it was. There'd been no trace of children, or bikes, or prams, or shoes in the hall. Nor could she hear any voices. In fact, the silence here, compared with home, was deafening. Perhaps he kept this bungalow for seeing clients? Perhaps his real life took place somewhere else, in one of those large untidy Victorian houses round the corner, for example? A slight movement on his part brought her out of her reverie. She realised she'd been silent for rather a long time. She stared blankly at him.

"I don't know what to say."

He grinned.

"We can sit in silence for twenty minutes, if you like. It's OK by me."

127

But expensive for her. She could do that at home, for free.

"You see . . ." She hesitated and took a sip of PG Tips for courage. "I have all this anger inside me."

"Has anything happened to make you angry?"

"It's my child, my elder son, Sam. He's been accused of abusing another child. I don't know how to handle it, how best to defend him. He can't speak. He stopped speaking when my husband died."

"When did that happen?"

"Six months ago. In a car crash."

"Do you believe these accusations?"

"Of course not!"

"And you live on your own now?"

"Yes."

"How do you feel about that?"

"I hate it."

He rubbed his red cheeks. "I get a lot of people coming here because their partner's died. Have you tried joining a bereavement group?"

"No."

"Why not? Don't you fancy the idea?"

"No."

"Was it a good marriage?"

"I thought so."

"Thought?"

"I've now discovered he'd been lying to me."

He raised his eyebrows and leaned forward. "Unfaithful, you mean?"

"No. He had a daughter he never told me about. It was before he met me."

"Oh." He sat back in his seat. "Well, you're bound to feel angry about that."

"It isn't only that. My father died last week. Maybe you read about it in the papers? His name was George Mitchell."

For a moment a look of blind panic appeared in his eyes. Did he think she'd committed the murder and come here to confess? He must get used to seeing all sorts, in his profession.

"I didn't do it, of course," she continued hastily. "Before last week I hadn't seen my family for years. But the police keep questioning me. It's . . . annoying. And rather frightening."

He nodded. He'd retrieved his balance. "There's been a lot going on in your life. No wonder you feel angry." He leaned forward again. "Tell me about your husband."

"My husband? He was a very orderly, precise, fair sort of person. He hated injustice of any kind. He was totally reliable. I trusted him." She faltered, feeling tears prick the corners of her eyes. She gripped the arm of the sofa. She mustn't break down. Not in front of a stranger.

"Were you in love with him?"

"Yes. Of course."

"Was it a passionate relationship? It doesn't sound very passionate, the way you've described it."

"Passion?" She stared at him. "You can't found a marriage on passion."

"Is that what you think?"

"Yes. Passion's always ephemeral."

"I disagree." He looked away for a moment, then back at her. "So it was more of a companionship?"

"Yes it was. What's wrong with that?"

"Nothing's wrong with it. As long as it made you happy. Did it make you happy? Did he – what was his name, by the way?"

"Richard."

"Did Richard meet your emotional needs?"

She glared at him. "Of course he did, he was my husband," she snapped, then grimaced because that sounded so ridiculous.

"Good. Because it can be very painful when your needs aren't being met."

("Mother, let me sit beside you and watch while you iron." "Don't always be hanging round me, Anna.")

"Can it?" she said coldly. "But that isn't the problem here." What was he doing to her? This wasn't the picture of her marriage she wanted to have.

"Good. Because you sound to me like someone who feels she hasn't met much love in her life."

She looked down for a moment, gripping the arm of the sofa

and letting her hair fall forward to hide her face. "You're trying to make out my marriage was a failure," she protested. "It wasn't." She ran a hand nervously up and down her neck.

"OK. I'm not saying these things for any – " he glanced away, "any cynical reason. But when I see you sitting there, so fragile and vulnerable, I want to help."

His warmth hit her like a wave. She gasped for breath. Be strong. This doesn't mean a thing.

(Once, at a conference dinner, she'd watched a colleague opposite her spend the whole meal chatting to the attractive curly-haired girl sitting beside him. She'd seen hope rise up in that girl's blue eyes. Be careful, she'd longed to lean across the table and say, he has two young children at home and the most stunningly beautiful pre-Raphaelite wife. Some time before the end of the meal, her colleague had risen, as Anna had known he would, and said to the girl, "You've got nice eyes," brushed her cheek with his hand and left. And Anna, sitting across the table from her, had felt that girl's pain).

"You know, when you smile, the corners of your mouth turn up. And when you're sad, they go right down." He sketched out a mouth in the air. "Like a clown's." He stared at her for a moment, then stood up. "Excuse me." He left the room.

He'd gone to give her time to recover. She would not cry. She would not. What a thing to say. Had Richard ever noticed her mouth? She clasped and unclasped her hands. Don't say those things to me. I will remember them in the dark watches of the night and want you. It's too soon after Richard. Don't speak to me like that.

He came back into the room.

"Do you miss your father?"

"I hadn't seen him for years. It was as if he'd died already."

"But you must have been affected by his death?"

She glanced down at her hands. "Yes. Yes, I was. It brought back a lot of memories. He was . . . kind to me; at the same time he could make me very unhappy. When he withdrew from me." He withdrew to have affairs, she thought. He abandoned me. He left me with Mother.

130

"Tell me about your childhood."

"My childhood?" She frowned. "What's that got to do with anything?"

"Well, if I knew something about your childhood, I might begin to understand what kind of a person you are."

"I'm not at all the same now as I was then."

He smiled.

"I know you psychologists are all very keen on delving into people's childhoods, but my problems are here and now. What am I going to do about Sam?"

He got up from his chair and started hopping about on one foot rubbing his leg. She gazed at him, faintly alarmed.

"It's all right," he said. "Cramp. I must get a different chair." He sat down again. "Tell me, are you happy with your children?"

"Oh yes! I always wanted to have children. Life would be – very empty without them. Someone to care for."

A curious expression flashed across his face. Pain, she would have said. He looked away. His face in profile seemed suddenly familiar. She wondered why.

"Someone to care for," he murmured.

They seemed to have come to a halt. She glanced at the clock.

"I must go. The social worker's coming to see Sam."

"Social worker?" he said, jolted out of his thoughts. "What's her name?"

"Tessa. She is – was – a friend of mine. I must go," she added.

He nodded. How patient he'd been, letting her babble on like some demented housewife let out of her cage for an hour. It was so peaceful in his house. She could have stayed here another hour. With an effort, she pulled herself up off the sofa and wrote out a cheque for fifteen pounds.

He led the way back down the hall. "I hope it isn't too gruesome for you with the social worker. Give me a call if you feel you want to."

He was so kind.

She wrenched herself away from the peace of his house,

bundled herself into the Volkswagen and drove home with the radio on very loud, killing thought.

At home she went straight upstairs and put her arms round Sam. "Sam, Tessa's going to come and see us. You remember Tessa? Shall we draw a picture for her?"

He made a gesture with his hands. "Sss. Sss."

"No, not a train. Perhaps a flower."

What could be more innocent? Settling Toby on her lap, she drew a large flower for Sam to colour in. She felt strong enough now to defend him. Philip had made her strong. But when the doorbell rang and it was Adam, she fell to pieces again. This visit of Tessa's wasn't something she'd made up. It was actually going to happen.

"Thanks for coming, Adam. I can't think what to do."

"Just act as normal. It's your best defence."

Together they sat and waited, two untouched mugs of tea between them. She kept her eyes fixed on the clock. Quarter to. Ten to. Her stomach started to turn somersaults. It got to five past.

"She's late." She stood up nervously and went over to the window. No sign of Tessa's car.

At quarter past the phone rang.

"Anna? Tessa here. You'll be glad to hear that we've uncovered the facts. It turns out it was Carol's boyfriend. Kylie was too scared to name him – he'd threatened her she'd be taken into care – so she picked on Sam knowing – "

"He couldn't defend himself?"

"Yes. Anyway Sam's in the clear."

"Thank God! Thank God!" The receiver fell from her hands. She burst into tears.

Adam put his arm round her shoulders. "It's all right, Anna. Everything's all right. What happened?"

She explained.

"Ring her back."

"Why?"

"You've got to get Sam's name taken off the records."

"But surely they'll do that automatically? Won't they?"

He shook his head. "Ring her back now. Believe me, I know how these things operate."

She dialled Tessa's number.

"Sorry. I – it was such a relief. What's going to happen now?"

"He'll be prosecuted."

"I meant about Kylie?"

"She's young. It only happened once. We caught him in time. The psychologist thinks she'll get over it. Eventually."

"Tessa, you will take Sam's name off the records?"

"I can't do that, Anna."

"But he's innocent. Kylie was making it up."

"Still, there has to be a full account of the case. I can't suppress anything. My team leader would never allow it."

"But you will put in that he's innocent, won't you?"

"I'll put in that he was never questioned and the charge was never substantiated."

"But . . . "

"Sorry, Anna. Got to go. I'll speak to you soon."

Anna put down the phone. That was that then. Somewhere in somebody's records there'd forever be a question mark hanging over Sam. There'd been no apology. Funny how entirely you could go off someone when you met them in their professional capacity.

"She's refused?" said Adam.

Anna nodded.

He sighed. "It happens all the time. Children Sam's age are too young to be prosecuted so they never get a chance to clear their name. Shall I stay with you this evening?"

"No. Thanks, Adam, we'll be all right now. It's been a shock. But it's over."

Sam turned to her, his face beaming. He thrust a bright blue flower under her nose. She bent down and hugged him. Her beautiful innocent child.

CHAPTER SIX

LYING IN BED THAT NIGHT, TRYING to sleep, she went over the scene again and again in her mind. The long low bungalow, the polished wooden floor, the ridiculous sofa, the painting of the cat. The way he moved his body. His dark eyes. His warm deep voice washing over her. "We can cure that. We can work on that."

He'd surprised her – and perhaps she'd surprised him. She shut her eyes, remembering that first moment when he'd smiled, then looked again more carefully, then given a sort of a start. She opened her eyes and stared at the ceiling. "Call if you want to," he'd said. He made her feel like a child.

In the morning Richard's toothbrush stared reproachfully at her from its mug. She took it out and threw it into the waste-paper basket. Then retrieved it from the basket and stuck it in a drawer, underneath his jumpers.

The children were screaming again. She took her hands out of the sink and watched them tug at a train, nearly pulling it to pieces between them. They had dozens of toys; there was something eerily predictable about the way they always seemed to want the same one at the same time. Anger and despair swept over her. I can't cope on my own. I can't do all the things that have to be done. You don't have to be a perfect mother, he'd said. No one can be that. She could have wept in relief. Wiping her hands on her skirt, she took a deep breath, moved across the room to her screaming, red-faced children, took away the train and bundled them into their outdoor clothes.

As soon as they were out of doors calm descended. She fastened Toby into his buggy and they set off. She could do it. She could cope. He would help her.

At the bottom of their street, they met Julia. She was dressed in pale cream culottes and carrying a wad of papers under her arm.

"How did it go with the social workers?"

"They made a mistake. It was nothing to do with Sam."

"Typical! And to think it's our money that pays these people's wages!" Julia rolled her eyes. "Well, must dash. Got a children's party to organise. I've got hold of this amazing man who does doves and rabbits. Of course the snag with them is there's always one child in the back row, isn't there, who shouts out 'It's in your back pocket.' Never mind, I'll give it a go." She waved her papers at them and disappeared into her house. Anna smiled to herself.

They crossed over the road and went down by the side of the parish church to the covered market where she did most of her shopping.

"Morning, Doctor Vale."

She came to a standstill and glowered at McMahon.

"What are you doing here?"

"I live here."

Of course. The Land of Green Ginger was less than five minutes walk away. This was his nearest shopping-place too. How awful if she was going to start bumping into him everywhere.

Her eyes narrowed. "How's the investigation going?" Why wasn't he at work?

"It's progressing. I've been hunched up over the computer all morning. Thought I'd pop out for a breath of fresh air." He was still wearing the grey suit but he'd abandoned his tie and his shirt was open casually at the neck. It was his most slovenly appearance yet. He glanced around. "This is a grand little market, isn't it? I always buy my vegetables here."

"So do I." Not any more.

"Great choice."

"It's not that good. Don't you have vegetables in Mayo?"

"Hardly any. They're all imported. Very difficult being a vegetarian there."

She felt taken aback. "You're a vegetarian?" Somehow she'd imagined all police officers daily tucking into beef steaks to keep their strength up and help them catch criminals. Perhaps

135

that was why this investigation was taking so long? "Have you got any leads?"

"One or two." His expression was inscrutable. He looked down. "So these are your children. Grand little chaps. Is that Sam?"

She frowned. "How do you know his name?"

"His case crossed my desk. Because of the connection with your father. I didn't take much notice. Usual social services cock-up. Hello, Sam."

Encouraged, Sam took a couple of steps towards him.

"Sam!" she shouted. "Come back here!" She gave him a little shake. "Don't wander off like that! There's some strange people on the streets." She glanced at McMahon.

He straightened up and returned her glance.

"Are you all right? You're looking a bit tense this morning."

She glared. "Is it any wonder with you shadowing me like this?"

"I'm not shadowing you. I'm buying vegetables."

"Well don't let me stop you, Detective Superintendent."

"Perhaps we could shop together?"

"We were just leaving."

"By the way, the computer did throw up something." He hesitated. "Ever heard of anyone called Beatrice?"

Oh dear, they *were* being thorough. "Yes, I have, as a matter of fact."

An expression of relief appeared on his face. "Good. I didn't want to be the one to have to break it to you."

"It's not a motive though, is it? Why should I kill my father because my husband was unfaithful to me?"

"Unfaithful?"

"What else would you call lying to me? Good day, Detective Superintendent."

Now she'd really got his back up. She couldn't afford that. She was on her own. No one would help her defend herself. She must learn to control her tongue with him.

When you're sad, your mouth turns right down, Philip had said. She hugged his words to her all the way through the morning (they had to walk miles to another vegetable shop and Sam began to whimper and moan). For a moment in his bungalow he'd made her feel she could cast off the odd distorting roles of mother and widow and become herself again, the young woman she used to be.

At home, she calmed Sam down, sat him in front of *Sesame Street* and put Toby into his cot. Then she rang Brian.

"Oh. Anna. Can't speak for long. I'm in a bit of a rush. Meeting Angela."

Again?

"Was it anything important?"

"Do you remember anyone called Jacqueline? She may have been one of Father's . . . friends."

"Jacqueline? Jacqueline? Doesn't ring a bell. He didn't mention that side of his life. I tended to find out by accident. Mind you, he was awfully careless. Kept booking into hotels as Mr and Mrs Mitchell and the women were always leaving things behind and they'd be sent back to Mother. She gathered quite a collection of odds and ends over the years – rings, watches, shoes . . . "

"How awful."

She put down the phone. How frightening grown-up life was.

Later that afternoon the doorbell rang. It was Penelope. She gave Anna a hug. "Let's not quarrel."

"No," agreed Anna, blinking back her tears. She led the way upstairs.

"Granny! Granny!" Sam ran into her arms shrieking with delight.

Anna smiled. "That's one word he's never forgotten."

Penelope, kneeling on the floor with Sam, looked up. "Have you thought any more about therapy?"

"Therapy?" Anna started. Penelope couldn't have found out about Philip, could she?

"Speech therapy for Sam."

"Oh." Anna turned away. "I'm making an appointment," she mumbled. "But he doesn't need therapy. He needs love." She switched on the kettle.

Penelope stood up. "How are you feeling? What have you been doing with yourself?"

Mismanaging my children, fighting off accusations of child abuse, spilling out my heart to a stranger. "I'm being investigated by the police."

Penelope stared. "They surely don't suspect you of murdering your father? You hadn't seen him for years."

"That's why they suspect me."

"How crazy!"

"It's unnerving." She handed Penelope a cup of coffee. "So I decided to do a bit of investigating myself. Father had affairs. Apparently."

Penelope gazed into her cup. "What a pity."

"Yes. For Mother."

"I meant – what a pity you had to find out."

Anna stared at her. "You knew. How? You've never met any of my family."

Penelope made a vague gesture. "One hears these things."

So it had been common knowledge in the town. Poor Mother.

The children began fighting again. Anna felt herself tense up inside.

"No." Penelope laid a hand on her arm. "Let me. You look all in. And this is what grandmothers are for." She sat down on the floor, took Toby onto her lap and rocked him. With her free hand she helped Sam rebuild his tower.

Anna leant back against the cupboards watching. How easily and simply Penelope did everything. How natural she made it all look. I can't do it any more. The shopping, the cooking, the mothering. I can't go on. She closed her eyes. He'll help me. He'll give me strength.

"Anna?"

She opened her eyes. Toby was asleep in Penelope's arms and Sam was playing quietly with his Duplo. "How did you do it?"

"I don't have to do it every day. Shall I put Toby in his cot?"

Anna nodded. As Penelope took Toby upstairs, Anna started on the washing-up. There were pots left over from the day before.

"It will get better you know." Penelope patted her arm and picked up a tea-towel.

Anna stared dumbly down into the soapy water. "I never knew it would be this hard. Did you find it hard?"

Penelope nodded. "It was hell. I remember once getting up in the middle of the night. Richard was screaming. He wouldn't stop. He must have been about six months. Teething, probably. I remember pacing up and down the sitting-room with him, howling for my mother. I was at the end of my tether. Henry was no help of course. Turned pale if I even so much asked him to change a nappy."

"What did you do?"

"Telephoned my mother. She came up on the next train and stayed for a fortnight. Took over everything. I spent most of the time in bed. By the end of it I felt like a different person." She glanced at Anna. "You're looking terribly pale, love. Can't I take the boys with me? Give you a break?"

"No. Thanks." She wasn't having them making friends with that girl. "She's still there, I suppose?"

Penelope glanced down at the plate in her hands. "Yes, she is. Anna, I'm sorry about that. I should never have asked you to take her on. It was crass and stupid of me. Goodness knows, you've enough to deal with at the moment."

"What are you going to do with her?"

"I'm not sure. But Anna, she's not your responsibility."

She made a barrier between them, though. Their paths had separated. Anna had her children. Penelope had to think of Richard's daughter, for Richard's sake. She'd made that difference between them. I have only him, she thought. He's the only one who can help me.

"I'm sorry. I couldn't help it. I had to phone."

"You need never apologise for phoning me."

"Oh."

His voice soothed and caressed her; his gentleness took her breath away. (Her mother, hard and cold on the phone: "Why ring us with your problems? Your life outside this house is nothing to do with us. We aren't interested." She'd grown up expecting a slap in the face when she asked for help).

"I . . . I don't know what to say."

"I've been thinking about you. About all the things you've been going through. Finding out about your husband like that.

Your father dying. Your child – "

"That's all right now. It's been cleared up."

"I'm glad."

He must like her a little bit, mustn't he, if he'd been thinking about her? Or did he say that to all his clients?

"How's the anger?"

"Still there."

"You know, people often get angry because they feel trapped. Do you feel trapped?"

"I suppose I do. Sometimes. I used to be a teacher, you see. Now I spend my days changing dirty nappies and warming bottles."

"And you don't like that?"

She could hear pages being turned. Had he written her up after their session and was checking his notes? Or was he looking up what was on at the cinema? "I don't know. I can't decide. I don't want to leave my children and go back to work, but . . . "

"Your needs aren't being met?"

Really she would burst into tears if he went on like this. Mothers weren't supposed to have needs, were they? "You see, I have these fantasies."

The pages stopped flicking. "Tell me about them."

"I want people to be my mother. I imagine becoming a child again and being mothered."

"How interesting. Are these fantasies sexual?" His tone altered slightly.

She froze. "No, nothing like that." She wouldn't care if she never made love again in her life.

"Warm and comforting?" he suggested.

"Yes."

"This is all good stuff coming out here. I'm glad you phoned."

"Can I see you again?" she asked, seized with panic that he'd put the phone down. "I mean, can I make another appointment?"

"Of course. If you want to. When?"

"No. You choose." She wanted him to be free.

"Hm." Pages turned again. "Say Monday? Nine thirty?"

"Fine."

All of Friday and then the weekend to get through. And if he didn't say something nice to her on Monday, she would die.

On Friday, Lottie phoned.

"Hello," said Anna coldly. She didn't feel too friendly towards any of the group now. They'd ganged up against her. They'd believed the worst possible things about her child.

"Are you angry with us? Don't be angry. We were all in a state over Kylie. We didn't really believe what she said about Sam."

"No?" Then why didn't you call round?

"You *are* angry."

"An apology would have been nice."

"I've written one into the agenda of the next meeting. A formal one. Will you be there?"

"I don't think so, Lottie. I feel too upset still. I went through hell for seventy-two hours."

"I know, Anna. I'm sorry."

"Is that why you're ringing?"

"Yes. No. We need your help."

"I haven't found out anything."

"We have. It came out in the course of Angela's interview – you know they've been interviewing all of us? Routine stuff. Where were we on the night of the murder etc." Lottie hesitated.

"Go on."

"It's about your father. I'm not sure I should tell you."

"Go *on*." Nothing would surprise her about her father.

"He had an affair with her."

"With Angela?" She was surprised after all. "She's half his age."

"I know. The thing is, she got pregnant and he persuaded her to have an abortion. After she'd had it, she went to pieces and he sacked her for bad work."

"Why on earth didn't she tell you this at the time?"

"Too scared. She knew what we thought of George Mitchell. She thought we wouldn't support her case if we knew all the circumstances. The police got it out of her. I don't know how. They were questioning her and it all suddenly came out."

"Sergeant Bradley?"

"No. That McMahon person."

Of course. It would be.

"So you see, in the eyes of the police, Angela now has a double motive for wanting to do away with George Mitchell."

"You don't think she did it, do you?" Even as she said it, it sounded absurd. Timid, frightened little Angela.

"No, no. Of course not." There was a short silence. "I'm practically certain she didn't. But it's creating rather a nasty atmosphere in the group. What with this and the Kylie episode, people are starting to feel a bit tense. Can't you think of something, Anna?"

"There's a woman called Jacqueline – if only I could discover her second name . . . "

"Help us, Anna. Please."

Soon after this she had a call from Brian.

"I've been looking up backlists of personnel. I came across a name – Jacqueline Dawson. Used to be supervisor in one of our shops. It's a long shot. It may be a coincidence."

"It's all I've got to go on. You don't have an address for her, do you?"

"Hang on. Yes, she lives in Beverley." He gave her the address. "She's a nice woman, apparently. I don't know her but Angela met her once."

"Um, Brian, what is going on between you and Angela?"

"We're together again. She used to be my girlfriend. Before father pinched her."

"Pinched her?"

"Yes. Did it on purpose, of course. To prove to himself he was still in the market for younger women. I can't really blame her. Who'd go out with the son when you could go out with the boss? Anyway, we've made it up now."

As she put down the phone, a tiny doubt surfaced in her mind. Didn't all this begin to make Brian look just a little bit suspect? Father's death had given him the job he wanted and his girlfriend back. Wasn't it all too convenient?

She sat and pondered those two phone calls. Time for a spot of detecting, she decided.

"How about a walk, boys?"

Sam stopped tugging at Toby and pulled a face.

"In Beverley. We could look at the shops."

His face brightened. He brought over one of his Thomas the Tank Engine books and pointed to a picture.

"All right. We'll see if we can find James the Red Engine."

He whizzed off to fetch his shoes.

Driving over the hill towards Beverley town centre, she glanced at Black Mill tower on her right. It was a different scene from the day she'd gone up there to find out about her father's murder. In place of the police and the tent, there were families and dogs and an ice-cream van. She looked to the left. Over there, behind that dark green clump of trees, was Philip's bungalow.

Beverley on a Saturday was always crowded with farmers flocking in from the outlying villages to do their shopping. She had to park her car quite a long way from the centre. She strapped Toby into his buggy and they set off. The main street was a nightmare of shoppers and toddlers and dogs. She trudged slowly along, pushing Toby with one hand, holding tightly onto Sam with the other, all the time keeping watch, out of the corner of her eye, for a dark-haired man with bad skin. Eventually they located a toy shop. Sam spent several moments hopping around the shop, unable to choose between James and Mavis.

"Let's have Mavis," she said, taking the train out of his hands.

That decided him. "No." He substituted James.

They paid for it and left the shop.

"Shall we walk on the Westwood?"

Sam pulled a face.

"There might be cows."

His face crumpled.

"And sheep."

He began to cry.

"Oh, Sam! You've got James. Why can't we do something I want for a change?"

He stopped crying and looked up at her. "Mas?" He pointed back to the shop.

"You're not having Mavis. One train is enough for today."

He started yelling again.

"Oh, all right! We'll go back and get Mavis. Then can we go on the Westwood?"

He nodded.

"Good of you."

She bundled him onto the back of the buggy. He stood there beaming, a train in each hand, as she manoeuvred the buggy along several side streets and up onto the Westwood. She let Sam off the buggy and he ran around picking dandelion clocks. Toby had fallen asleep.

There it was, his bungalow. She daren't go too near it. He might be there. He might see her. What did men do when they lived alone? Did they sit in their dressing-gowns reading the newspaper till it was time to go down to the pub for a lunch-time pint? Or did they wander around the room in underpants munching a slice of toast, half an eye on breakfast television? She could imagine him doing that. His relaxed, loose male body lounging about the place.

But perhaps he wasn't alone. Perhaps he had a wife. Yes, surely he had a wife. You'd need a bit of support in a job like his. Children too. They were probably all out shopping at the supermarket. Or perhaps he'd taken the children swimming. She gazed over at the clump of trees, suddenly bereft. I do not know a single thing about him. And I never will, for that is part of the process. He learns everything about me and I know nothing about him.

Sam tugged at her skirt. Guiltily, she turned her attention to him. They stayed for a while on the Westwood, playing. Then they went back into the centre and had lunch. There was no sign of Philip. She packed the children into the car and drove them past Jacqueline Dawson's house. It was a modern detached house on an estate on the outskirts of Beverley. Designer homes for middle-class professional people with the houses cleverly arranged at such an angle that no one could see directly into their neighbour's sitting-room. There were estates like this all over England. Tiny tidy front lawns. One or two shrubs. A border of petunias. People leading tiny tidy lives.

On impulse, she pulled up a few yards down from the house. Sam stared out with interest. He liked seeing new places.

Toby woke up and yawned.

"Hello. Can I help you? Are you lost?" A tall slim-looking woman in her early fifties stopped beside the car.

Anna wound the window down further. If this was a neighbour she might be able to find out something useful. "I'm looking for Jacqueline Dawson. Do you know her?"

The woman smiled. "I am Jacqueline Dawson."

"Oh." What should she do now? Wind the window up and make a quick getaway? She glanced at the woman again. She had short dark hair, just turning grey. She was dressed in a pair of well-cut navy trousers and a silk shirt.

"What was it you wanted?" she continued briskly. "Are you from church?"

"No, I . . . Look, my name's Anna Vale. Used to be Anna Mitchell. You worked for my father. I . . . "

"Anna." The woman gazed at her. She looked through the back window of the car. Her face softened. "And these are your children." All trace of briskness had disappeared. "Bring them in for a moment."

"I – "

"Just for a moment. I'd like to see them."

Anna unstrapped Toby and led Sam by the hand, wide-eyed with curiosity. Jacqueline Dawson unlocked the front door and led the way through the tiny hall into the tiny sitting-room. Anna's heart sank. There were delicate china ornaments everywhere and the carpet was cream and spotless.

"This sounds rude but could we – er, I mean – do you have a kitchen? You see the children might make a mess in here and break things."

"Oh. Yes."

She turned and led the way down the hall to the kitchen. It was small and bright. Painted entirely in white. White cupboards, white ceiling, a cork floor. The only splash of colour was some green frilly blinds at the window over the sink. The window looked out onto a tiny back garden and then onto fields.

Anna deposited Toby on the floor. He began to crawl towards the cupboards.

"I'm afraid he'll try opening the drawers."

"Oh, let him. There's nothing in here he can hurt. He's a lovely little fellow, isn't he?" She glanced down at Sam still clasping Anna's hand. "So. These are George's grandchildren." The depth of tenderness in her voice surprised Anna.

"He never saw them. Unfortunately."

Jacqueline Dawson glanced at her sharply. "Yes, he did. He saw them several times."

"What! Where?"

"Around town. With you."

She gasped. "But why did he never get in touch?"

"I'm not really sure. He was afraid of annoying your mother, I think. Or perhaps he thought you preferred to be left alone."

Daddy, Daddy. I loved you so much. Anna sat down on a stool. "How do you know all this?"

The older woman went over to the sink and filled the kettle. "I suppose you'd like a cup of tea?"

Anna glanced down at the floor where the boys were quietly playing with two plastic ladles. "If it's not too much trouble."

"I wouldn't offer it if it were. Why are you here, Anna? I suppose it wasn't coincidence that you were parked in my road?"

"No. I – I want to find out about my father's death."

"Why pick on me?"

"Because," she floundered, "because it's years since I saw him and I thought you might be able to tell me something about him because – because . . . "

"Because I was your father's mistress? Yes, I was. For fifteen years."

Anna looked down at her lap. "His death must have been an enormous shock to you, Mrs er – "

"Miss. Call me Jacqueline." She sat down on the other stool. "It is. A terrible readjustment. George has always been here." She glanced away. "I don't mean physically here. But always there for me even when we . . . when we couldn't be together."

"Why did you put up with it?" The question burst out of her.

Jacqueline looked at her as if she'd said something stupid. "Your father was a brilliant businessman. Charming. Warm. I'd never met anyone like him." She paused. "I wasn't a naïve young girl you know when I met him. I was thirty-eight. I knew what I was doing. I always knew I'd have to share him."

"He was afraid of the scandal if he left my mother?"

Jacqueline glanced away. "It was more complicated than that. He felt – he owed her a lot." She got off the stool, poured boiling water into a teapot, let it stand for a moment, then spooned in some tea-leaves. "I suppose it was the wreath that gave you the clue? I shouldn't have sent it, I know, but I couldn't help myself. I hoped no one would notice it among so many." She poured out the tea and handed a cup to Anna. "Would the children like juice?"

"I'm sure they would. I've got their beakers here in my bag."

Jacqueline poured out orange juice. "How did you get my address?"

"Brian."

"Oh yes. Poor Brian." She looked faintly amused. Anna felt indignant on her brother's behalf. "I wonder how he'll manage with the business?"

"You don't work there any more, do you?"

"No. I used to work in the Driffield store. I left shortly after I met your father. He wanted it that way. In fact, he wanted me to give up work altogether. It was always a sore point between us. I'm glad I didn't now. I work four mornings a week in a dress shop in the centre of Beverley. It's something to hang on to." She sat down again on the stool. "I really don't think I'm going to be any help to you, Anna. As I told the police, I don't know who'd have wanted to murder George. He had business enemies, of course, as any man in his position has."

"The police have been here?"

"Yes. A woman and a Detective Superintendent McMahon. Irish. They wanted to know where George was on the last night of his life."

"Do you know?"

"He was with me. Until eleven. Then he went away. It was our usual pattern. There was nothing out of the ordinary in his behaviour. He didn't tell me he was going to meet someone else." Her voice trembled only slightly at the end. Jacqueline Dawson was a woman who kept a tight rein on her emotions. She gave a slight smile. "Of course, as the Detective

Superintendent pointed out, I can't prove any of this. We might just as easily have both gone for a walk up on the Westwood. But the question is, did I have anything to gain from his death?"

"He left you nothing in the will?" No, Brian would have mentioned it.

"That was agreed between us long ago. We didn't want to embarrass your mother. Besides, he'd already bought this house. The mortgage's paid off and he paid some money into a pension fund for me. He was an extremely generous man, your father. He gave me everything I needed."

Except commitment. Anna gazed at her in silence. Why do women do it? Why do they let men get away with behaving like this?

"I've been over and over it in my mind, Anna. I can't think who'd want to do a thing like that." She glanced up. "If you find your father's murderer, I'll be a happier woman." She twisted her handkerchief into a little knot in her lap.

The children were beginning to get restless. Anna picked up Toby and took Sam by the hand. Jacqueline led the way back down the hall.

"You have your father's eyes," she said, as she opened the door. "I'm sorry things went wrong between you."

"So am I."

In the car, Anna discovered she'd left Sam's beaker behind. She walked back up the garden path. She was about to press the bell when she heard on the other side of the door the sound of weeping. She turned and tiptoed away. A tiny tidy house concealing raw human emotions.

"We'll get you another beaker, Sam."

Anna woke in the night, her head buzzing with questions. Who had her father gone to meet after leaving Jacqueline? Could she trust Jacqueline's account? And what about Mother? Did she know about all this? Might she not, after years of putting up with his infidelity, suddenly have decided she'd had enough and taken her revenge?

The next day it rained. Cooped up inside the house, the children whined and fought. She tried to get Sam to practise some words with her, but he made a face and wandered off halfway through to play with his trains. Only one more day, she thought, lifting Toby off his high chair. Only one more day of crying inside, of feeling lost and bewildered and unable to cope and then I will see him again.

Penelope rang.

"My dear. How are you?"

She hesitated. How could she begin to tell someone as calm and rational as Penelope how she really felt?

"Fine," she answered.

"It's an awful day. Would you like to bring the boys over and have a break?"

"No. Thanks." She glanced guiltily down at Sam. Her fear of meeting Beatrice was denying him a treat. "Sam would like to speak to you though."

Sam "speaking" on the phone involved a lot of listening rather than speaking. At intervals he nodded his head sagely. Penelope was used to this, she was well able to handle it, but what would happen when Sam grew up and he couldn't do something as simple as use the phone? Anna took the receiver back from him.

"His speech hasn't improved, as you can see."

"Don't worry, Anna. It will come right, I'm sure it will. Give him time. It's only six months since his father died."

"What if he never speaks? What if he never learns to read or write? How will he get on in life?"

"Of course he'll speak. When he's ready to, when he can face the world without his father in it."

Anna glanced down. Sam was smiling up at her. Have a little faith, she told herself. Have a little confidence in him.

That evening she sat for hours in the sitting-room, the curtains drawn, Toby asleep on her shoulder, thinking of nothing. Worn out by the day, she'd drunk two glasses of wine. A warm animal peace invaded her. Dear sensible Penelope, I love her. Even Beatrice can't alter that. But I can't tell her how I'm feeling. It wouldn't sound rational. She ran a hand up and down her neck. When you're breaking up only the best can help – or the worst. Only he could help her.

CHAPTER SEVEN

SHE DROVE OVER THE WESTWOOD. ON her right was the Minster, on her left, St Mary's church. He said my mouth was beautiful. He said when I smile it turns up and when I'm sad it goes down, like a clown's. She'd changed her clothes three times that morning, thinking that each change might herald a change of personality (she was now wearing a long cotton skirt, black T-shirt and a loose cotton jacket). One hour. She clenched the steering wheel till the blood drained from her knuckles. One hour for him to give her some comfort; and if he didn't, she didn't know how she'd ever be able to leave his house.

Like last time, he opened the door, smiled and said, "Well. Come in."

He was wearing beige trousers again, with a round-neck black pullover. He was taller than she'd remembered. She raised her eyes to his and his face became a sort of blur in front of her. She hardly dared look at him.

"A different place this time. I've got my consulting room organised."

He led the way down a narrow corridor to a room at the back. It was painted pale yellow. In the centre stood a low square coffee table. There were green plants in the corner. A window running across the whole of one wall looked out onto a narrow lawn and some tall trees. She stood still in the middle of the room.

"What are you thinking about?"

"I was watching the sunlight fall through your trees. Your house catches the light. I hadn't realised how dark mine is."

"Is it an old house?"

"Georgian. Four storeys. Tall, dark and inconvenient."

He smiled and rubbed his cheeks. They looked red and sore. She decided it wasn't skin grafts but a bad case of eczema.

"Sit down." He pointed to an enormous, grotesque-looking red leather armchair. Doctor Freud and his patients.

She sat down gingerly. It was rather like sitting on a throne. She felt foolish and uncomfortable. The dralon sofa had vanished but the hard wooden chair was still in evidence on the other side of the table. That was no use. After quarter of an hour, he'd be hopping about with cramp again. Would it sound presumptious and officious to offer to swap places? Yes, it would. She sat tight, waiting for him to take the lead.

"Sorry about that chair. I'm waiting for a new sofa to arrive." He paused. "My wife left home recently."

Her heart gave a lurch. His wife had left him. No, not him. Home. Perhaps that only meant she'd got a job somewhere else.

"I seem to spend half my time apologising to clients about the furniture."

Would she have taken her furniture if she'd only moved jobs?

He sat down opposite her on the hard wooden chair. "Well. Here we are again."

"Yes."

There was a lengthy silence. He was looking at her, waiting for her to begin. She glanced down at the floor, up at the ceiling, over at the curtains.

"I like your curtains." She covered her face with her hands. "What an awful thing to say! I sound like a dreary housewife."

"No you don't. I'm glad you like my curtains. They're new." He got up to finger the material. His face in profile looked desperately familiar. "That kind of thing's important to me. I like my clients to feel comfortable. Besides, they were bloody expensive." He glanced sideways at her and smiled. She noticed again how ugly his mouth was. It formed a sort of rectangle. His teeth looked uncared for. "I'm getting the sofa done in the same material." It was dark green with narrow dull gold stripes. She loved it.

"We got our sofa from MFI. My mother always said I had no taste." ("Anna, you're not going out dressed like that, are you?")

He dropped the curtain and looked across at her. "Yes, we haven't talked about your mother, have we?"

She glanced down at the pale grey carpet. "Much better not to."

"Oh?"

She tightened her lips.

"PG Tips again?" he enquired, clearly feeling she was going to need jollying along this morning.

"Fine." Anything, even PG Tips, was welcome if it got them off the subject of her mother.

He went away to rattle things in the kitchen. She took off her jacket and curled up in the enormous armchair. It wasn't as uncomfortable as it looked. Opposite hung a large studio portrait of Philip in hood and gown holding a scroll. She found it odd and rather touching that he should have put up such a photo of himself. At any rate, it beat spending the hour staring at a painting of a dead cat. She glanced at her watch. Fifteen minutes of that hour had already gone by.

"Milk. Two sugars. See, I remembered."

He looked so pleased with himself she hadn't the heart to say she never took sugar. She smiled as he handed her the mug.

"So," he sat down again. "We've talked about your children, your husband and your father. Now tell me about your mother."

"There's nothing to tell. We never meet."

She took a gulp of tea, set the mug down on the carpet in preference to the polished table and crouched further into the armchair, like a sulky child.

"She isn't my real mother. My real mother was Nana. My grandmother." She stopped.

"Go on."

"Nana loved me. She never asked or demanded anything of me. She loved me as I was. She died when I was twelve." Something caught at her throat. "She was mad, basically. When she was well, she was on the go the whole time, cleaning, baking, sewing, going to whist drives and Mothers' Union meetings. Every five weeks or so, she'd crack up and sit very quietly for days in a darkened room."

"At home?"

"At our home. She always came to us when she was ill. They tried hospital once. She screamed the place down. She was terrified of doctors. They'd given her ECT a couple of times. Then they stopped that and she lived on pills. Red ones for breakfast, yellow ones for dinner, red and blue ones for tea. Every five weeks the system would break down and N – Nana would . . . " Tears trickled down her face. "Every time I'm sad, I come back to my grandmother. I hear voices in my head and I think I'm going mad, like her – like my sister."

"Christ!' he muttered, in his flat London voice. "You're bloody beautiful."

Bloody beautiful, beautiful mouth. She looked up angrily. "Why do you say things like that? It doesn't help."

There was silence. She crouched in her chair watching her hand run up and down the arm.

Nana at fifteen (that black and white studio portrait that had stood for years on the sideboard at home), wearing a white dress and white shoes, with a white bow in her long thick dark hair. Starting up out of her chair, lips parted, eyes shining, eager to get on with life. Nana at thirty, widowed and so lonely that she'd get dressed up and go into town and have her photograph taken, because she had no one to dress up for, now her husband was gone. Nana at forty, suffering bouts of depression, from time to time undergoing ECT which left her numb and panicky and confused in her mind. Nana at sixty, dead. Her death had torn a hole through Anna's teenage years. Things had never been the same again. She knew now that adults lied about life. She knew things about life it might otherwise have taken her years to learn. But what a price to pay, she thought, shaking with tears. What a price to pay.

"Here, have this."

He was standing beside her, holding out a handkerchief. She hadn't even noticed him get up and cross the room. She looked at the handkerchief. If she moved now, her whole world would turn upside down.

"Go on, have it. It's clean."

She reached out for the handkerchief and found his hand instead. For a moment he stood quite still.

Then he was down on his knees, with his arms around her, and the world had become a different place.

She laid her head down on his shoulder and sobbed. He knelt and rocked her in his arms and everything in the world fell away till there was only her and him and rocking back and forth in his arms.

Presently, he smoothed back her damp hair and whispered, "The professional relationship has broken down. I'm your friend."

She continued to sob, pouring out her heart for Nana, for her father, for Richard, for Sam who wouldn't speak.

He tilted her face towards him. "Did you hear what I said?"

She nodded.

He cradled her in his arms again, soothing her with meaningless phrases, as one soothes a troubled child. She felt raw and tender and open. Like those first few days after giving birth when your sensitivity matches that of your new-born baby and everyone else seems hard and coarse and brutal and all you want is to lie quietly in a room beside your sleeping child.

In gratitude she kissed his hand, not lightly, but greedily, frenziedly almost, like a child seeking comfort from its mother. She thought, I have kissed another man. I have betrayed Richard's memory. Shocked, she pulled away and fumbled for his handkerchief. "I don't know whether I can cope." She rubbed her eyes rather ferociously. "With a friend, I mean."

He took his arms away and sat back on his heels. "We can be as close or as distant as you want." To prove his point, he went back and sat on the chair. "It's up to you."

"I know nothing about you," she muttered through his handkerchief. "I've told you all those things and I know nothing about you."

He spread out his hands. "What do you want to know? I was born in Grimsby. My Dad was a fisherman. The work dried up so we moved down to Peckham when I was five – "

"I thought you were a Londoner. You talk like Michael Caine."

154

"Michael Caine?" He gave a pleased sort of wriggle. "My Dad set up a catering business down there. When that went bust we moved back up here. Mum never liked living in London. I went to school in Hull. Since then, I've worked all over the world – the States, Australia, all sorts of places. Six years ago I moved back here and set up practice."

All this told her nothing. What kind of man was he? What did he think? What did he feel? She hesitated, then said tentatively, "And you're married?"

He glanced away, out of the window at the trees. "We got married eighteen months ago. Eleven weeks and two days later, my wife said she was leaving me." He stared down at his knees in silence. "Excuse me, can I have my handkerchief back? Your tears seem to be catching." He reached across the table, took the handkerchief from her, wiped his eyes and stood up. "Can I hold you again?"

They stood by the window, he with his back to the garden, she leaning against him, looking out at his trees and the sunlight tumbling through them.

"When I first met my wife, she was married to somebody else."

A doubt crept into her mind. "She wasn't a client of yours, was she?"

"What? God, no! I met her at a party. She was . . . unhappy, I think, in her marriage." He paused. "At least that's the impression she gave. We slept together. She got pregnant, had an abortion and moved in with me. Left me. Bought a house of her own. Two months later, she came back to me, got pregnant, sold her house and we married. Eleven weeks and two days later, she moved out, had an abortion and bought another house."

He related all this to her in his flat expressionless South London voice as he stood leaning against the window, holding her in his arms.

She felt a nightmare beginning to take her over. She stared at him. "You're kidding me, surely? People don't behave like that. Do they?"

"Look at me."

"What?"

"Look at me." He pointed to his eyes. They were filled with tears. "Do I look as if I was joking?"

"But then," she said slowly, "it's the most horrible thing I've ever heard."

He nodded. "Good. I'm glad you think that. I thought so too. I thought, this isn't normal behaviour. Or is it me who's mad?"

She brushed a hand across her face. "I don't understand. Did she want a child or not?"

"She kept saying she did. She kept saying, next time it'll be different, marry me and it'll be different. I loved her, I trusted her, so I did and it wasn't."

"But did you want her to have the abortions?" What kind of a man was he?

He stared at her. "They were wanted, those babies. Both of them. She killed them." He glanced behind him, out of the window. "I probably won't be able to have any more. The specialist said my sperm count's a disaster. The last child was a kind of miracle. She killed it all the same."

She thought of her two miscarriages, those two babies who'd died very early in her womb. They had somehow got fused in her mind with Sam, as if those two half-lives had gone into making him the kind of child he was. She had two live children, thank God. He had nothing. Shaken with pity, she reached out a hand and touched his cheek where it was red, above the faint shadow of stubble.

"I've wanted to do that since the moment I first saw you."

He took her hand and kissed it, then turned and kissed her on the mouth, long and deep, till she thought that she would drown.

In the bible, adultery ranked with theft and murder. Did a kiss count as adultery? She drove away from his house over the Westwood. Did it count if one's husband was dead?

The flat fields spread all around her in the golden sunlight, a thousand shades of green and brown. By the side of the road a tractor was ploughing. Seagulls swooped and dived after it, white against the dark earth. The June sun shone through the trees onto her windscreen. The whole landscape was lit up, shot through with radiance. She drove and drove, till she came over the brow of a hill and saw the broad sweep of the Humber shining silver in the sunlight and the bridge flying like a bird across it. She was alive. For the first time in months she was a person again. Not a widow or a mother. Simply Anna. Herself.

She parked the car and went into a café. "Christ! You're bloody beautiful," he'd said. And she'd wept and kissed his hand.

"Excuse me, madam, do you want to order?"

The waitress stood by her table, pen poised. Anna opened her mouth to ask for a sandwich and found herself bursting into laughter instead. The waitress half smiled in response. Then looked firm. It had been a busy morning.

"Sorry." Anna stifled her laughter. "I'll have a coffee and a cheese sandwich, please."

The waitress went away.

We hugged and rocked and hugged and kissed. And I cried. And he didn't mind. "You need a mother," he said. "I'll be your mother."

"And what will I be for you?"

He glanced away. "You fill a gap. Since Ginny left, I've been dead. You give me feelings. Feelings are always good, whatever kind they are. I like to be close to people."

"Do you think you could be close to me?"

"Yes."

And he'd told her about returning from Cottingham, where his father lived, to find his wife's half of the wardrobe empty. Later that evening, when he was nearly frantic with worry, she'd phoned.

"Philip Lawrence," he'd said, picking up the phone and walking with it into the back room. Yes, she could picture him so well, sitting on the wooden chair, looking out at his garden.

Silence on the other end.

"Hello?" he'd said, more sharply.

Silence.

Christ! he'd thought. Not another crackpot. Not another mother who fancies her daughter, or that Spaniard who keeps beating up his wife.

"Phil? It's me."

"Ginny! Where the fucking hell are you? I've been going out of my mind here."

"At home. I mean, with my parents."

"Marvellous! Bloody marvellous! Would you mind filling me in on what's going on?"

"I – I needed a break. To put some distance between us. It's all happened so fast – the wedding and . . . and everything."

"Couldn't we have discussed this at all? Talked it over? Instead of me arriving back from Cottingham this evening to find your clothes gone?"

"Talk, talk, talk. That's your answer to everything, isn't it? Well I'm sick of bloody talking."

"It's the only way I know how to live."

"Look Phil . . . I still love you. I just needed some time off."

"How long is it going to last this time? I thought we were going to see this pregnancy through together. You're carrying my baby. I want to watch it grow inside you. I want to take care of you both."

Silence.

It was then he'd begun to panic.

"Ginny? Speak to me."

Silence.

He felt the waters closing over his head.

"You've killed it, haven't you?"

"I couldn't help it, Phil. I – "

"You bastard! You fucking bastard! You promised!"

The receiver fell out of his hand. He rolled on the floor clutching his stomach and groaning out loud. His last child – his miracle baby – gone. Killed.

He'd picked up the receiver again.

"Fuck you!" he'd roared down it. "Fuck you to hell!"

"I couldn't go through with it, Phil. I felt trapped. Look at Mum, with the three of us. We wore her out."

"It doesn't have to be like that."

"You don't understand." On the other end of the phone she'd begun to weep.

"You're a nutcase, do you know that? You should be bloody sectioned!"

He'd slammed down the phone, flung himself on the floor and screamed in pain. He'd lost his wife, he'd lost his child. There was no future for him.

"That's my story," he'd said.

And she'd wept again – for him, for herself, for all the misery of the past months. They'd held each other carefully, two bruised souls finding comfort in each other.

"Come back soon," he'd said. In the hall, he'd swung her round so that her back was against the wall and pressed his lips against hers. "Will you?"

"Yes,' she answered, forgetting her children, forgetting Richard, forgetting everything but the feel of his lips against hers.

"Cheese sandwich, love." The waitress smiled. "Enjoy your lunch."

"Sitting there calmly eating lunch." Her mother's voice echoed in her head. "You should be ashamed of yourself." Anna bit into her sandwich. "You deserve to be punished, going on like this." She clutched at her throat. What if something had happened to her children while she'd been out?

She half rose from her chair in panic and looked around for a phone. There wasn't one. She sat down again and forced herself to take several deep breaths. Because she'd kissed a man, it didn't mean her children would die. She bolted down her coffee, left her sandwich half eaten, thrust some coins at the startled waitress (she'd never be able to come here again) and ran out into the street to look for a phone box.

"Everything's fine," said Donna. "Toby's asleep and Sam's playing with his trains. Don't worry. They're fine."

She leant back against the phone booth, damp with relief. She'd got away with it. This time.

There was a tap on the glass. She turned round. It was McMahon. Angrily, she wrenched open the door of the booth.

159

"Are you following me? You are, aren't you?"

He grinned. "Not at all. Just passing by. Where are the children?"

"At home." She glared at him. "I need some time off, you know."

"Sure you do. I'm all for mothers having time off. Come for a coffee?"

"I've just had one."

"Have another."

"No. Thanks."

"I'll be on my way then. Incidentally, nifty piece of detective work, picking up on Miss Jacqueline Dawson."

"You are following me!"

He shook his head. "We're keeping a watch on her house. We're keeping a watch on several houses, as a matter of fact."

"Mine too?"

"Not as yet. It depends how you behave. I'd leave the detective work to us in future."

Was that a threat? He moved off and was lost in the crowds of shoppers. She started to shake. Then she remembered she had Philip. It would be all right. He'd be there for her. Everything was going to be all right.

She rang him the next morning. Early.

"Hello. It's Anna."

"Oh. Anna."

"Yes."

"So you are real. I was beginning to think I'd dreamed you up."

"Have you missed me?"

"Yes."

"Have you really?"

"Yes. Missed you, missed you, missed you. How are you today?"

"All right. Had a rotten night. Toby's got a cold. I'll have to take him to the doctor. I won't be able to see you today."

"Never mind. We'll see each other soon."

"Will you miss me?"

"Yes, my dream girl."

She put down the phone. He hadn't, after all, *suggested* they meet today. She leaned back against the kitchen cupboards. She ached inside for him, didn't feel safe without him. He was a soft warm space where she was free to be herself. How would she get through the day without him? She went downstairs, bundled a screaming, wet-nosed Toby into his outdoor clothes and pushed him along to the surgery.

He was off colour all day. Wouldn't eat his solids, wouldn't go down for his afternoon rest. Sam whined too, not getting enough attention. He tugged at her jeans.

"Er, er, er," he said, pointing at the fridge.

Exhausted she snapped, "Sam, I don't understand what er, er means! Can't you speak properly?"

He burst into tears.

Horrified at what she'd done, she knelt down and put her arms around him. "Is it juice?"

He shook his head.

"Milk?"

He shook his head.

"Yoghurt?"

He nodded.

Oh, to lay my head down on his shoulder again and be comforted, she thought, reaching into the fridge.

At six o'clock, as she was surrounded by the children's toys and debris from their tea, Lottie called round.

"Have you found out about this Jacqueline woman?"

"Yes, as a matter of fact, I have." Anna kicked a mound of dirty washing out of the way and went to put the kettle on.

"And?"

"She was my father's mistress for fifteen years."

"Aha!" said Lottie.

"Is that a motive for murder though?"

"She might have found out he'd been unfaithful to her. There was Angela," Lottie reminded her.

"Yes. I'd forgotten that." Anna set a mug of tea down on the table. "I rather liked her."

Toby sneezed, scattering a shower of snot over the floor. Anna knelt to wipe it up. Then he whimpered to be picked up. She sat down on a chair with him on her knee. "The police are having Jacqueline's house watched."

"And Angela's."

"I think they're following me too. At least I keep bumping into that McMahon fellow all over the place."

Lottie put her hands round her mug. "What are we going to do? The group's falling apart. Accusation and counter-accusation. Can't you do something, Anna?"

Anna stared. "What can I do?" She swept a hand round her kitchen. It looked as though a bomb had recently fallen on it. "You see how it is. Toby's ill. I can't do anything at the moment." And I've met a man. She kept quiet about that. Lottie wouldn't approve.

Lottie stared at the mess in Anna's kitchen. "You know, I think I'm going off the idea of children." Toby sneezed again, scattering another spray of snot. "Definitely."

The next day, she waited and waited for him to ring. Hardly dared move out of the kitchen in case she missed hearing the phone. At lunchtime, desperate to hear his voice, she rang him.

"This is Philip Lawrence. I'm not in at the moment, but if you'd like to leave – "

Where was he? She put down the receiver feeling panicky. She knew nothing about his life. Did he have lots of clients? What hours did he work? What did he do when he wasn't working? She didn't leave a message. She must keep a bit of pride.

She waited in all day, sweating and shivering. If this was love, then love was a disease. Several times when she was out of the kitchen, fetching something from Toby's room or watching a *Peter Rabbit* video with Sam in the sitting-room, she was certain she heard the phone ringing and dashed back upstairs only to find a silent and empty kitchen.

Finally, at five, as she was finishing giving the children their tea, the phone rang. Holding a piece of eggy toast in one hand, she grabbed the receiver with the other.

"Yes? Hello?"

"It's Brian. You sound rather frantic, Anna. Are you all right?"

"Oh. Brian." Her stomach gave a plunge. "Yes, I'm all right. I wasn't expecting you to call."

"I've got the list you wanted."

"What list?"

"Dad's business enemies – remember?"

She made an effort. "Oh, yes." She handed the piece of toast to Sam. "Anything interesting?"

"There's a chap called David Chappell who was sacked for alcoholism and a Barry Russell who was 'persuaded' into early retirement. Incompetent, apparently. As far as enemies outside the business go, three months ago Father took over Whittaker's, an ailing family firm, and turned it around. I shouldn't think they'd bear him a grudge though, they did quite nicely out of the sale. There's also a small retailer with a couple of outlets in the centre of Hull. Eric Finch he's called. Father bailed him out just as his business was about to go bust and took it over. That's all so far."

"Thanks, Brian."

"They're all still in the area, as far as I know, apart from Chappell. He moved away down south after he was sacked, rumour has it."

"I'll have to leave him out then. Anyway he'd hardly come all the way back up here, would he? I'll start with that Russell chap. He sounds the most promising. Where does he live?"

"In Cottingham." He gave her the address. "You will follow this up soon, won't you, Anna? Angela's getting nervous with the police camped on her doorstep."

"She's not the only one. I can hardly set a foot out of doors without bumping into Detective Superintendent McMahon."

"Beastly man. I wish he'd leave us alone."

"I suppose he's got a job to do."

"Well I wish he'd go and do it somewhere else." He rang off.

She put down the phone. Brian sounded rattled. Why? Did he have a guilty conscience? Was he sending her on a wild-goose chase after Barry Russell in order to throw suspicion off himself? And where did Angela fit into all this?

She must keep her wits about her. She must remain alert. She looked down at her children. Sam had thrown his egg cup on the floor and Toby had smeared butter all over his face. Was this the sort of atmosphere in which great detective work could be done?

At eleven, when she'd finished her wine and given up hope, he rang.

"Philip here. Is it all right to phone this late?"

"Yes, of course," she replied, the blood pounding in her ears. "Of course it's all right. I'm always here on my own with the boys in the evenings." Did this sound just a little bit desperate? "I do go out sometimes," she added. "To the cinema and – and so on." Where *did* people go out to? "The pub," she said, thickly.

"Have you been drinking?"

"No. Yes. I had a glass of wine." And another. And another.

He made a whistling noise down the phone. "Bad that, drinking on your own."

"I know." Why didn't you ring earlier then?

"I've been getting powerful feelings about you, Anna. Love feelings."

Thank God. Thank God. She leaned back in her chair and closed her eyes.

"Say something to me, Anna."

"I don't know what to say – I . . . " The misery and tension of the day washed over her. She burst into tears.

"It's all right, Anna. It's all right, sweetheart. I'm here. I'm holding you. It's all right. My Anna, I want to take care of you. Come here and I'll nurse you. I will make you whole again."

"I c-can't – the children . . . "

"Let my house be a sanctuary for you then. A place where you come to whenever you can and find a bit of peace. I live alone here in the woods with the squirrels and the birds. Let my house be a refuge for you."

She closed her eyes again and rested her head on the receiver. "You *are* being my mother, aren't you?"

"I'll be anything you want."

"Oh, Philip." She felt shaken by desire for him. "When shall we see each other again?"

"Soon, my darling. Soon. Sleep well, sweetheart. Dream of me."

The next day Toby's cold had improved. She decided she could risk taking him out for a walk. She wanted to call on Barry Russell. She rifled through a cupboard and found a few Animal Rights leaflets left over from a recent women's meeting. They would serve as an excuse.

She got the children dressed in their outdoor clothes. The weather had turned windy and cold. Sam didn't want to wear his long trousers. He didn't want to wear his shoes. And he certainly didn't want to wear his anorak. She sighed. It was a far cry from Poirot cultivating his little grey cells in the peace and quiet of his apartment. By the time the children were grown up, she doubted whether she'd have any little grey cells left to cultivate.

Barry Russell's house was in a quiet cul-de-sac off the centre of Cottingham village. It was a road that had come into existence at different stages. There were a couple of Victorian redbrick houses, an Edwardian terrace, houses dating from the thirties and houses built in the seventies. All jumbled up without order or planning. Barry Russell's was one of the modern ones. A semi-detached glass box, two up, two down. There was something very odd-looking about it. From where she was standing it seemed definitely lopsided. She checked the number again. Yes, that was the one.

"Come on." She pushed the buggy with one hand and pulled Sam with the other. He trudged gloomily along in a manner which suggested trousers and anorak weren't the clothes he'd have chosen if he'd had any say in the matter. "Don't be so vain," she hissed. "Here, hold these." She thrust a pile of leaflets into his hand and rang the bell. It played some sort of tune. Good King Wenceslas, she thought. Sam began to hum along, untunefully. She nudged him.

"Yes? What do you want?"

A tall lanky fair-haired man opened the door. For a second, he reminded her of Richard. He held a nappy in one hand, a bottle in the other and looked harrassed.

Anna recognised the symptoms. "Sorry to disturb you," she said, meaning it. "I . . . We're campaigning for Animal Rights."

The man frowned and wiped his chin with the bottle. "Hang on. I'll see if we've got any change."

"We don't want money." She grabbed a leaflet from Sam and thrust it at him.

Since he had no hand free to take it, the leaflet fell to the floor. A little girl of about three squeezed between his legs and picked it up. Sam and she stared at one another as if they hardly inhabited the same planet. Sam looked sadly down at his unexciting long trousers. In a room in the back of the house a baby roared. Anna began to feel more and more guilty.

"I won't keep you. I just wondered whether you could spare a few moments while I tell you about our campaign?" She'd rehearsed this bit that morning in the kitchen while giving the children breakfast.

"I'm sorry. Any other time. Laura, go and keep an eye on your sister for a second. And take this." He handed her the nappy. "But you see how it is. The baby needs her bottle. I've had the police here half the morning. Some obnoxious Irishman. My head's spinning. Sandy – that's my wife – has been away on business for two weeks. I'm trying to pack up. We're moving next week. The house is subsiding. You may have noticed. Only we would buy a house built over a medieval rubbish dump. We have to get out till the builders put it right. What I'd really like to do right now is lie down in a darkened room for a month."

"I know the feeling. All that and the police as well!" she added, disingenuously.

"They came about this Mitchell case." He leant against the door-frame and seemed disposed to talk. No wonder, she thought, if his wife's been away for two weeks he must be screaming for some adult conversation. "You must have heard about it. It was all over the newspapers."

"Yes. Yes, I think I did read about it."

"I used to work for the bastard. The police came round and gave me a right grilling. Wondered whether I'd planned some sort of revenge attack. Quite the opposite, I told them. It was a relief when I got my notice. I was glad to be out of that sweatshop. Meetings called at all hours of the day and night. No consideration for people with young children and a wife who works. Anyway, now the children have some stability in their lives. I'm a house-husband. I study accountancy in my spare time. When I have any spare time. The police couldn't believe I'm actually happy doing this."

The baby roared again.

"Look, got to go. I'll read your leaflet, I promise." He shut the door.

No, he couldn't possibly have done it. Where would he have got the energy or time to plan a thing like that? Besides, he'd seemed nice. She was all in favour of house-husbands. She could do with one herself.

She looked up and down the street. No sign of any police car. Perhaps there wasn't one. Difficult to watch a cul-de-sac without being noticed. She'd got away with her detecting this time. McMahon would never find out. She let Sam drop a few leaflets through letterboxes, to cover themselves, and then they went home.

As she was giving Toby a bottle, Penelope rang.

"I'm worried about you, Anna. You must have some time off. Go to the cinema or something. I'll come round and babysit tomorrow evening. I'm not taking no for an answer."

Anna cradled Toby in her arms and stared at the floor. When Penelope had said have time off, she'd had a sudden vision of holding Philip again. It was so sudden and so violent that she couldn't say anything, just stare at the floor.

"Anna?"

"Thanks. Yes. Thanks very much, Pen."

She rang Philip.

"Are you missing me?"

"Yes, darling."

"I could see you tomorrow evening."

"Smashing, darling. Come round here. I'm not doing anything."

At six the next evening, when she was in the middle of feeding Toby, he rang.

"It's Philip."

"Philip!' She cast a nervous glance towards the door. Penelope was down in the sitting-room, playing with Sam. "Why are you ringing?"

"I'm in a fix," he mumbled, sounding strangled. "A client's turned up on the doorstep. Bit desperate."

"Oh."

"I'll phone you tomorrow." He put down the phone.

Her world fell to pieces.

"Anyone interesting?" asked Penelope, coming into the kitchen at that moment, leading Sam by the hand.

"No. Nothing. Wrong number. Toby! Stop crying! I've got your spoon, you silly baby."

"I'll feed him," offered Penelope, settling Sam into his chair.

"It's all right. I can manage," she snapped, ungraciously. "Sorry, Pen," she said, after a few minutes. "Didn't mean to bite your head off."

Penelope looked at her in concern. "It'll do you all the good in the world to have an evening off."

Yes, it would have done. She'd have to go out now anyway, or Penelope would think it odd. She'd told her she was going for a drink with friends.

At half past six, he rang again. "It's OK. I can see you. I'll meet you outside the Beverley Arms in an hour."

"I thought you had a client?"

"They've gone."

She put the phone down, shaken. It didn't add up. Not at all. First he had a client. A desperate client. That should have meant anything up to two hours. Then suddenly the client had gone. Had he dashed out to throw himself off the Humber Bridge? It didn't make sense.

She went downstairs to find Penelope. "I'm going over to Beverley. I'm meeting friends there for a drink."

"All right, love. Drive carefully."

Anna bent down to wipe Toby's nose. "You will be all right?"

"Don't worry about us. We'll be fine, won't we, boys?"

Sam, sitting on his grandmother's knee eating a Milky Way, beamed from ear to ear. No need to worry about *him*.

But as she drove away from the house and saw the three of them, Sam, Toby and Penelope, standing at the downstairs window, waving her off, she felt like a traitor. The three people she loved best in the world and she'd lied to them, trampled over them, to get to this man.

She loitered on the steps of the Beverley Arms. She caught sight of him several yards away. He started to walk towards her, hesitated, then glanced away. Had he forgotten what she looked like? It had been – what? – four days. She'd thought of nothing else but him and he didn't even recognise her. She felt her face redden. She grimaced at him. Sure now, he hurried towards her.

He was wearing jeans and a black cord shirt. He was smaller than she'd remembered. She'd carried him around with her for four days and suddenly he seemed like a stranger. For a moment the structure shook. Then he took her hand, said, "Hello, girl," and everything was all right again.

"You didn't recognise me," she accused him.

He let go of her hand and smiled sheepishly. "It's those clothes. You look about eighteen."

She glanced down at her short blue skirt and bare legs and smiled at him. "That'll do for an excuse."

He took her by the arm and led her up a side street.

"Where are we going?"

"I thought we'd have a walk on the Westwood. It's a lovely night."

They walked in silence past rows of middle-class terraced houses. She glanced in at the windows. In the front rooms, toys lay scattered around. Newspapers were tossed over chairs. There were books, records. An evening in with the family. And she was outside all that. She felt a sudden rush of relief. For a brief moment she'd escaped the structures that pinned down her hours with such terrifying precision. She was with this man. She was free. No, not quite free. There were things to be cleared up.

She disentangled her arm from his. "You'll have to think up a better story. How could you have a client who came and went so quickly?"

He shrugged. "These things happen."

"I don't believe you."

There was a silence. He kept his eyes fixed on the pavement ahead.

"OK, I'll tell you," he said finally. "My wife turned up."

"Your wife?" Her world rocked a little. "I thought she'd left."

He gazed down at his feet. "She has. Only she was in the area working, suddenly felt weepy and sentimental and turned up at my house."

"Brilliant timing, I must say."

She felt cross and hurt and confused.

He stopped walking, turned and looked into her face. "I think that," he hesitated, "she suspects something. 'You've met someone else,' she said. 'I can see it in your eyes.' "

A pang went through Anna. Did Ginny know him that well then? Of course she did, she was his wife.

"I couldn't turn her away, could I? I had to be kind to her."

"But why did you lie to me? Why couldn't you have said, 'My wife's here.' Why lie? It makes me feel such a fool."

"I couldn't tell you something like that over the phone, Anna. I was afraid."

He looked so dark and masculine. But he lied like a woman. Sneakily, fearfully, so as to avoid hurting the other person's feelings. And what did "being kind" mean? She was afraid to ask.

"Don't ever lie to me again."

"I won't."

Like hell he wouldn't.

They wandered amongst the thickets on the Westwood, on the other side of the road from Black Mill where her father's body had been found. In the distance she could hear the

Minster bells calling worshippers to evensong. She'd been there once with Richard. Now she was betraying him with another man. And I go on about Philip, she thought. I'm just as bad. I lied to Penelope.

She turned and studied him for a moment, his dark-fringed eyes, his thick black brows and thick black hair, his ugly-beautiful mouth, that strangely comforting profile.

"Are you pleased to see me?"

"Yes."

"You waited for me to ring."

"I've had a lot on. Anyway, I never know whether you'll be busy with the children or whether there'll be someone around. I presume you don't want people to know about us yet?"

"I suppose not." She thought of Penelope. Coming so soon after Beatrice . . . "I suppose it would be a bit of a shock."

"That's why I don't phone very often."

She would have to be the one to do the running then.

They walked on for a bit. It was starting to get chilly. The sky overhead looked thundery. Shapes loomed up at them in the grey half light. Bushes. Trees. Once a cow that had strayed too far from her companions. The ground was uneven. Once or twice Anna stumbled. By now, the common was almost deserted. I am up here in the dark, she thought, miles from anywhere, with a man I hardly know.

"Come here." He took her by the hand and twirled her around. Together in the darkness their bodies circled round each other. "We're dancing, darling. Dancing without music." He kissed her hair and pressed her to him.

A shudder of longing ran down her body. She buried her head in his chest. "I ache for you," she murmured.

"That's my good girl." He kissed her, his tongue arching gently into her mouth.

She felt herself go limp in his arms. Then a thought struck her. She broke away from him. "What's this about your wife? Are you getting back together again?"

"No." He shook his head and gazed down at the ground. "I loved her. She's the only woman I've ever . . . Christ! I even married her. I gave up my freedom for her. There were times with that woman when I got down on my hands and knees and begged her not to leave. I'll never do that again. I don't trust her. She killed my babies."

"Are you going to see her again?"

He hesitated. "She – she was my wife. There's a lot of feeling left between us."

So – she was going to have to take his wife into account. She'd left him but they were still married. They'd been married for eighteen months. She had no right to interfere between them.

"Look at me. Look at me!" He put his arms round her and lifted her up so he could see her face. "What are you thinking?"

"How stupid I've been." She was thinking, this story can't have a happy ending. It hasn't even had a happy beginning. I deserved this. He can never be mine. He still belongs to her. "I needed to see you so much." She kissed the top of his head. "But I can never mean what she does to you."

He set her down. "Come and live with me."

She thought of those three faces at the window. "I can't."

"You see? It's the same. You ask if my wife is coming back. I say no. I ask you to come and live with me. You say no. Are you afraid of what people would think?"

She looked away over his shoulder at the sky darkening over the common.

"It's not that. It's the children. I can't uproot them from their home so soon after Richard's death."

"I understand that. So. We'll have an affair."

She flinched.

"What's the matter?"

"Horrible to put a label on it."

"Well that's what it is. Better to face up to these things. Come on, sweetheart, let's dance again."

Round and round they went in the dark, their bodies moving together to music they only heard in their heads. What is being in love, she thought, but an act of the imagination? A willed suspension of disbelief. I know nothing about his mind, nor

172

even what kind of person he is. After that phone call this evening I shall hardly trust him any more. But I know his body. I know what his body is going to do before he does it.

"Beautiful, darling." He held her at arm's length. "Are we going to fall in love, do you think?"

"You . . . " she hesitated, "bring me back to life. You bring warmth and comfort back into my life."

He pressed her close to him. "Good, darling, I'm glad."

He turned her round and stood behind her. She leant her head back and he ran his fingers up and down her neck, in the gesture of someone about to strangle her. And though the common was dark and she hardly knew him, she felt she trusted him absolutely. She could have died then and there, leaning back against his broad warm chest. Liberated. Death no more than a gentle haemorrhaging.

"I'm reading your body with my fingers," he whispered into her hair.

What did it matter that he didn't recognise her at first, when they had all this? She felt like saying, I love you, Philip. But it was too soon. "I'll have to go. My mother-in-law's babysitting. I don't want to keep her out late."

"Of course, darling."

He walked her back to her car. She tore herself away from his side, like a child forced to abandon its mother. This was their third meeting and each time they parted, she wondered whether she'd ever see him again. In the rear-view mirror, she watched him turn and walk down the street, his hands thrust into the pockets of his jeans. She watched and watched till she could see him no longer. Then she started the engine.

She glanced at the clock on the dashboard. Ten o'clock. On the dual carriageway between Beverley and Hull she put her foot down.

He loved his wife, he said, and he may come to love me, but he doesn't yet. Oh God, did I grab at you, darling? You said: when you're sad your mouth turns down at the corners and when you smile it turns up. And I thought, I have to have him. I will die if I cannot have him. You looked like someone out of my dreams. No one thinks of kindness or duty when there's something they must have.

At home Penelope, always anxious about women alone at night in cars, looked relieved to see her. Anna took off her jacket and hugged her. There'll always be guilt, she thought. But in order to see him, I can bear anything. Only keep my little ones safe.

In bed that night she tried to pray, as she always did, to Mary to guard and watch over her children. Something blocked her words. When she finally got a prayer out, she had no confidence in it. She glanced at the empty space beside her. She was on her own now. Without Richard who'd always given her such sensible advice. Without God.

In the middle of the night, she woke up in a cold sweat. Why had he insisted on meeting her at the Beverley Arms instead of at his house? Rather odd, wasn't it? No, it was easily explained. All the time they'd been up on the Westwood, his wife had been waiting for him back home. "I've got a client," he would have said to her. "Bit desperate. I said I'd go and see him." He would have said "him." "Wait here. I won't be long." She grabbed hold of the duvet for comfort. She had to get this man out of her life. She'd never be able to trust him.

From the room next door, a wail started up. She lay there a few moments, willing Toby to go back to sleep. The wailing continued. She dragged herself out of bed to give him a bottle. She sat in the kitchen while Toby, oblivious to the fact that it was the middle of the night, played and chattered happily at her feet. I need him, she thought. I don't trust him. But I need him.

CHAPTER EIGHT

"PUT TEDDY ON THE TRAIN," SAID SUE.

With an air of humouring her, Sam put the teddy on the train.

"Put teddy under the train."

Sam put the teddy under the train.

"Now put the train on teddy."

Sam stared at her in amazement.

"I'm testing his passive vocabulary," Sue explained. "He's not very certain about prepositions, is he?"

"He doesn't think it's logical, you see," said Anna, "to put the train on top of the teddy."

Sue looked patient. "No, no, if he understood it, he'd do it." She marked something down in her file. In the face of such certainty, Anna felt helpless.

"Now, Sam, make teddy jump."

Sam made teddy jump.

"Make him dance."

Sam made him dance.

"Make him sit down."

Sam made him sit down. He found a cup and gave teddy some tea.

"Now make him jump again."

Sam was absorbed in giving teddy tea.

"Make teddy jump, Sam."

Sam ignored her.

"He's used to making up his own games," Anna said. "He has a terrific imagination."

Sue glanced at her. "Has he?" She wrote something more

175

down in her file, then took the teddy and the tea cup from Sam and put them on the floor. Sam looked gloomy, but resigned.

"Now, let's do colours again. Look at this picture. What colour is the tree, Sam?"

Sam frowned. "Bown."

"What colour is the train?"

Sam wriggled in his chair. "Geen."

"What colour is the sky?"

Sam slipped sideways in his chair. "Blue."

"What colour is the cow?"

"Blue."

"What colour is the grass?"

"Blue." Sam fell off his chair.

"He's not very sure about colours either, is he?"

"I think he might be getting a bit bored," suggested Anna, stifling a yawn. She picked Sam up off the floor.

"Nonsense. Children his age don't get bored. His powers of concentration are lacking." Sue made some more notes in her file. "We'll stop there for today. Same time next week?"

"And this will help him to speak, will it?"

Sue glanced at her. "Trust me, Anna. I'm a professional. I know what I'm doing."

Anna decided she didn't much like Sue in her professional capacity. She switched to the personal instead. "How are you feeling?"

"Nauseous. I'm worried about Adam too, which doesn't help."

"Why? Is he ill?"

"No, but he's been acting strangely lately. Goes on and on about how tight we're going to be financially when this child comes along. I say, I've given up the alcohol. And I'll be carrying on working as I've always done. I think he's worrying unnecessarily. I know he's paid peanuts and the salary of a speech therapist isn't exactly glorious, either. But we'll manage somehow. I just wish he'd feel a little bit excited about this child," she added dolefully. "He was about the other two."

Anna and Sam walked back home through Queens Dock Gardens. The roses were out. The flower-beds were full. She decided to put the speech therapy session behind her. She was wondering about Adam acting strangely and whether that might be because he had a guilty conscience (but Adam would never murder anyone, would he?), when a voice behind her said, "Hello, Sam."

She turned round. McMahon was smiling down at Sam. Sam glowered back.

"What's the matter, little chap?"

"Speech therapy. He hates it. So do I. Are you following me again?"

He straightened up and gave her a severe look. "It's a sunny day. I suppose I'm allowed to walk from my rooms to the office?" He pointed across the Gardens to the flimsy-looking glass building that was the headquarters of Humberside Police Force. "But since I have run into you, it gives me a chance to give you a good telling-off."

"What for?"

"You ignored my warning. You went to see Barry Russell."

"Oh. You found out."

"I found out. This isn't a game. Keep out of it and let the professionals get on with it."

Professionals – professional police officers, professional speech therapists, professional social workers – her life was dogged by them.

"Are you about to make an arrest, then?"

"We're working on it. I mean it, Anna. Keep away. It's dangerous. One of these days you might come face to face with the murderer."

"So you don't think Russell did it?"

"I've eliminated no one from my enquiries, Anna. No one." He moved off.

She grimaced after his smug Irish back. Since when had he taken to calling her Anna? Sam stared at her, fascinated, then tried out the face on several passers-by.

"Don't do that, Sam, it's very rude." Then, deciding he'd had a raw deal from grown ups so far that day, she added, "Would you like an ice-cream?"

Here she was, ironing her children's clothes, in tears because he hadn't rung for two days. The evening before, she'd phoned him several times but his answering-machine had always been on. Her last call had been at half past midnight. He's gone back to his wife, she thought. Ginny is bone of his bone, flesh of his flesh. What right have I to complain? She folded Sam's shirt and laid it on a chair.

The phone rang. She reached out and grabbed the receiver.

"Hello. Oh. Lottie."

"Yes. Who were you expecting? Never mind. How's the detecting going?"

"I'm working on his business enemies. I've eliminated one suspect so far."

"Good."

"Yes, but I seem always to be one step behind the police."

"Do your best, Anna. We're relying on you."

"You sound down. What's the matter?"

"I'm thinking of giving up the group."

"What! Why?"

"All these suspicions floating around, it's not the same any more. We need some of the old crowd. Won't you come back, Anna?" Lottie sounded most un-Lottieish. Quite weary, in fact. "Carol never comes. She never goes anywhere nowadays, apparently. Sits at home with Kylie, watching over her like a hawk. It can't be good for the child. Jennifer's tied up with her preparations for ordination. And Angela's been banned."

"Why?"

"For going out with your brother."

"That's a bit extreme, isn't it?'

"He's a Mitchell. He's tainted."

"There's not much point me turning up at a meeting then, is there?"

"They're not angry with you. They know you're on our side. You're a suspect too."

"Thanks for reminding me."

"The thing is, Anna, the group's being infiltrated."

"Infiltrated?" This sounded more like the old Lottie. "Who by? The police do you mean?"

"No. Gloria West's supporters. It seems she has quite a following in Hull. I wish I'd never invited her to give that talk."

"What's wrong with them? They're feminists too. You were saying we needed more members."

"Not like these."

"Why not?"

"It's the atmosphere they create. It's difficult to explain. Anna, won't you come and see for yourself? I need some of the old crowd for moral support."

"OK, Lottie, let me know when the next meeting is. I'll come if I can."

She put the phone down. It rang almost immediately.

"Yep?"

"It's Philip."

She switched off the iron. "Hello," she said coldly.

"It's a long time since we've spoken."

"You noticed."

"Don't be sarcastic, Anna. It doesn't suit you."

"Yes it does. It suits me very much. It cheers me up."

"Anna, what's the matter? I thought we were going to be there for each other. I thought that was the deal? I've had a hell of a day. One client cancelled at the last minute. Another began making sexual suggestions down the phone."

"That must have been nice for you."

"Come on, Anna. What is this?"

"Tell me something. When you left me on Thursday evening, did you go back to your wife? Was she waiting for you at home?"

"No! I told you – she left before I did. Went back to her parents' place in Grimsby."

"You didn't tell me."

"Well I'm telling you now. Christ! Anna! What kind of a man do you think I am? She fucked up my life and now she's going to fuck us up too. I can't bear it!" His voice started to tremble. The line went dead.

She sighed. Just like a woman. He behaved just like a woman. She waited a moment, then dialled his number. It was engaged. Cut off from him, she began to panic. She tried again. Engaged. Obviously he'd taken the phone off the hook. That was that then. She was to have nothing nice in her life. She picked up a pair of Sam's jeans, sprinkled them with water and resumed her ironing. Two minutes later, the phone rang.

"Who were you on the phone to?" he snarled. "Another man?"

She smiled for the first time that day. "Don't be silly, I was trying to phone you." What a lot of energy we waste when we're in love. She twisted the phone-cord round her finger. Or half in love.

"I'm going into Hull this afternoon to do some shopping. Shall we meet?"

To save her life she couldn't have said no.

"I'll get Donna in."

"See you in the Ferens Gallery at three."

Waiting inside the gallery she watched him cross the road and come towards her. His black hair, slightly too long, was swept back in the wind. My God, he was gorgeous.

"Hello, darling! Have you been here long? Stop chewing your nails."

He put an arm on her shoulder and pirouetted her around in a circle. An elderly woman standing nearby smiled at them. He whizzed her through three rooms (she caught a glimpse of her sister's painting hanging on a wall, between two portraits). They arrived back at the front entrance.

"Well? Did you like your brief tour of the gallery?" He put his head on one side and gave her a cocky smile. She suddenly saw what he must have been like as a young man. Cheeky, endlessly charming, everyone's favourite nephew. Till Ginny knocked a hole in his confidence. "Why are you laughing?"

"I'm so pleased to see you."

He squeezed her arm. "I just went up to heaven when you said that." He rubbed his cheeks. "Come on, darling. Things to do. I want to get this jacket fixed."

She noticed he was carrying a plastic bag. He led her out of the gallery into the department store nearby, up three flights of stairs and stopped outside an unmarked door. He knocked and went in. Inside were two plump middle-aged women seated at sewing machines and surrounded by scraps of material, needles, pins, threads.

Philip went up to one of them. "How was that holiday, Mrs Beeson?' he asked cheerily, filling the small feminine room with his male presence. "Can you do me a jacket?"

Mrs Beeson removed some pins from her mouth, winked at her companion and said, "We can always fit you in, Mr Lawrence, can't we, Rose?"

Rose nodded.

The two women came fussing around him, taking the dark blue jacket out of his bag and holding it up against him. Anna leaned against the wall, watching. Naturally he was good at getting on with people. It was his job. All the same she felt a little pang of resentment. She had to lend him to these women for a moment and their moments together were so few.

She watched as he tried on the jacket so that they could take measurements. He strutted a little in front of the mirror. Stooping with tape-measures, the two women exchanged glances of amusement, noticed Anna watching and smiled at her too. The male bird in his pride, puffing out his feathers.

He turned round.

"Hey! You're laughing at me!"

Anna grinned. "It's affectionate."

The middle-aged women smiled in understanding. Was it so obvious then that she was enthralled by him? Did they think her foolish? His hand brushed accidentally against her arm. Something exploded all the way down her body. She gazed hungrily at the place where his jacket-sleeve was rolled back. She noticed the dark hairs on his arm, his square clean fingernails. She glanced at the women again. Was there pity in their smiles? Did they see her rushing headlong into disaster?

"That'll be a quick job, Mr Lawrence. We'll have it ready for you by next week."

"Smashing!" he said, taking off the jacket. Smashing. He'd said that to her once when she'd rung him up unexpectedly. "Oh, Anna. Smashing." It hadn't meant a thing, then.

They went back out into the street. "Now, darling, shall we go for a drink?" He took her arm. She flinched. "What's the matter?"

It was a small town. She didn't want Penelope to find out. Not that way. "Someone might see us."

He let go of her arm. "OK, I can be discreet." He led her down a side-street into a shabby working-man's pub. She glanced round at the juke box and the group of men huddled at the bar. She was safe here. Neither Penelope nor any of her friends would set foot in a place like this in a million years.

He bought her a drink. Men stared as they made their way to a table in the corner. One man stared with particular interest.

"Damn!"

"What's the matter?"

"Someone I didn't want to see. A detective who's working on my father's case. I've an idea he's following me."

She glared over at the opposite side of the room where McMahon was sitting on his own, nursing half a pint of beer. He nodded curtly in response to her glare, finished off his beer, stood up and went out, avoiding looking over again in her direction.

"We've seen him off," remarked Philip, with an air of satisfaction.

"Yes."

But what would he think of her? Abandoning her two young children to go off drinking in squalid pubs in the middle of the afternoon with strange men. He might think she picked up men for a living, as a way of keeping herself and her children in clothes. She wondered how much prostitutes earned. She stared into her lager. Had Richard's death sent her moral standards spiralling downwards?

"Are you still here?"

"What? Oh, sorry. I was thinking."

"Tell me about it."

"I was thinking how funny this is."

"What is?"

"Us doing something as ordinary as shopping. We're starting to behave like a couple."

He laughed. "We've had a therapy session, we've kissed and hugged, we've danced on the Westwood in the dark and now we've gone shopping together. Isn't that nice?" He put an arm round her. She let it stay there. The pub was dark and anyway, the damage had been done.

"It doesn't seem to fit, you and I doing ordinary things."

He glanced at her. "Doesn't it? But that's what I want. An ordinary life. A wife. A family." His voice faltered a little. He paused. She saw there were tears in his eyes. "I'm a simple man. I live on the Westwood, surrounded by squirrels and trees. My dancing days are over. Ginny killed all my desire for excitement." He was silent for a moment. "You've a bonny face," he said.

Bonny. Strange, old-fashioned word to use. It was one of Nana's words. It made her feel safe. She gazed at him over her pint. Who was he really? She loved the way he'd related to those two women in the shop, so simply and naturally. But she loved him in a state of panic because she didn't know who he was. He was still a stranger to her. It hadn't been like that with Richard.

She took a sip of her lager. She had to find out something about him.

"I phoned you one evening this week, but every time I tried getting through to you you had the answering-machine on."

"I was probably visiting my mother.' He glanced away. "She's in a nursing home in Cottingham. I go over once or twice a week to see her. I hold her hand and tell her what I've been doing since my last visit." His voice went flat and expressionless the way it'd done when he'd told her about Ginny. "She doesn't recognise me. She has advanced Alzheimer's. A lot of people would say it was a waste of time going to see her, but I know my visits give her something. A warmth. She remembers I was someone close to her. She resists me leaving."

She'd been wrong. He was a good man. He cared for his mother, he cared for his clients, he grieved for his wife and his two dead babies. "Does she speak to you?"

"Nothing that makes much sense. She calls for her mother. She died more than forty years ago."

"If I were old and sick, it's not my mother I'd call for," she said. "I'd want my grandmother."

"Ah, yes. Your grandmother." His hand tightened on her shoulder.

"I had a dream last night."

"Yes?"

She shook her head . . . I woke up and you held me in your arms and I told you all about Nana dying like that and all she'd meant to me. And when I came to the part about the stabbing, you held me in your arms and cradled me like a child and for a while you became Nana and all she'd meant to me. And I, who have children, became a child again.

"Anna, will you come to my house again? Will you come now?"

"I can't. The children . . . "

"Will you come soon, then?"

She hesitated, shut her eyes and asked, "Are you getting back with your wife?"

"No."

Relief flooded over her. She opened her eyes. "Ring me this evening."

She walked home along Prince's Quay. Did she believe what he'd said about Ginny never coming back? They'd lived together as husband and wife for eleven weeks and two days. Twice Ginny had left him and come back. She was unstable as water. She'd killed his babies. I'm never going to be able to compete with that kind of madness. I met him too soon. They may still get back together again. Unhappiness descended on her like a shroud.

At home the children rushed across the room to hug her. She swung Toby up into her arms. Why do I need a lover, she thought, when I have all this?

"They've been as good as gold," said Donna, smiling. The crisis over Sam seemed to have brought out the best in Donna. It was as if she now saw it as her role to protect all three of them from the hostile outside world.

The moment Donna left, Toby started to cry. He wanted his bottle. Anna moved around the kitchen, filling the kettle, getting the changing-mat out, comforting Sam who'd started to whimper because he wanted her to play with him and she had to feed Toby first. A picture came into her mind of dancing with Philip on the Westwood, their bodies curving in towards each other, a perfect fit.

She changed Toby who was kicking and screaming by now. She sat at the table feeding him and aching for Philip. The Greeks had a word for it, she remembered: *pothos* – the desire for the absent being. It hurts when you've been dead, to come alive. And she'd been dead for so many months.

She laid Toby upstairs in his cot and came back down to find Sam sulking in a corner.

"Shall we have some tea, Sam? Would you like fish fingers?"

"No."

"An egg?"

"No."

"Toast?"

"No."

"Yoghurt?"

He scowled.

Her standards collapsed. "Jelly and ice-cream? A nice chocolate biscuit?"

"No!"

He kicked her, went over to his Pooh box and pulled out Richard's tie. He sat on the floor playing with it. She supposed he was punishing her for leaving him all afternoon with Donna. She began to feel panicky. Her family was falling apart and she was powerless to stop it. The doorbell rang. She ran down to answer it. For one wild moment she thought it might be Philip come to rescue her.

"Oh. It's you."

"The computer's on the blink," said McMahon. "I thought I'd drop by and see you."

"Did you?"

She stood blocking the door.

"Can I come in for a minute?"

She glared at him. "Are you planning on questioning me? I think I should ring a solicitor."

"No, no, don't be so defensive."

A wail started up in the kitchen.

"Oh hell! Come in if you want!"

She let go of the door and bounded back up the stairs two at a time. Behind her, she heard the front door close. McMahon followed her up the stairs.

Sam was standing in the middle of the kitchen holding out Richard's tie and howling. "Da! Da!"

"I know, love, I know."

She caught him up in her arms and sat down on the floor covering his small, rigid, grief-stricken body with hers. She rocked him to and fro. Little by little the sobbing ceased. He lay back limp in her arms.

She looked up. McMahon was standing in the doorway, an expression of concern on his face.

"Does he often do this?"

"From time to time." She brushed back the damp hair from Sam's forehead. "It's only natural. He misses his father. Would you like some juice now, darling?"

Sam nodded.

She rose to get the Ribena out of the fridge. When she turned round, she found McMahon sitting on the floor with Sam in his lap. She was not certain that she liked this turn of events much. She poured some juice into a beaker.

"Here, Sam. Come and drink it at the table."

"Sure, we're grand down here aren't we, little fellow?"

Sam nodded and buried his head in McMahon's jacket. To try and disentangle him might provoke another scene. She handed him the beaker. McMahon's shoulder was the last place she would personally choose to cry on; however, Sam seemed quite comfortable, settling back into the crook of his arm and drinking his juice. It must be all those Irish nephews and nieces.

"He doesn't see many men," she said coldly. "That must account for it."

McMahon looked up. "Doesn't he?" he said and she knew he was referring to Philip.

She flushed angrily and turned away, busying herself at the sink.

"I don't bring men home, Detective Superintendent. I'm a widow. I'm mourning my husband. To have strange men in the house so soon after Richard's death would only upset the children further," she added, meaningfully.

"It depends on the man, I would have thought," he said softly. "I'm sure in some cases you're right not to."

She glared at him, then turned back to the sink, picked up the Vim and began scrubbing rather ferociously. So he hadn't liked the look of Philip and was letting her know was he. Bloody cheek!

"Why have you come round?"

"If you'd just stop scrubbing for a moment – is your sink really that dirty? – I'll tell you. I can't communicate with your angry back."

She flung the sponge into the sink, turned round, folded her arms and leant against the cupboards. "I'm listening."

"Your cousin Adam's been arrested. I thought it best to let you know personally. I – "

She stared at him, thunderstruck. "Adam? Adam! He couldn't have done it."

"He's admitted it, I'm afraid."

"That means nothing. I know your methods. I read the newspapers. I expect you beat a confession out of him. Adam could never commit murder, I'd stake my life on it."

"So would I." He stroked Sam's hair. "I'm not talking about murder. If you'd let me finish I could have explained. You're not a very patient person, are you?"

She stamped her foot. "You're so . . . ! Tell me then."

"He's been arrested for possessing a stolen credit card."

"What!"

"Strictly speaking, he didn't steal it. The owner rather carelessly dropped it out of her purse. Your cousin found it in the street and apparently couldn't resist the temptation to use it."

She remembered all those bills on his desk. Oh, Adam, however could you have got yourself into such a state? She looked down and found that her hands were trembling. "What – what will happen to him?"

"He'll be let out on bail. The Bishop's standing surety for him."

"You won't charge him, will you?"

"I'm afraid we're going to have to."

"But he'll lose his job. He's another baby coming. Think of what it will do to him."

He shook his head. "I'm sorry. It's out of my hands. There's nothing I can do." He moved Sam into a more comfortable position on his lap. "Another thing I wanted to ask about your family – this thing between your brother and Angela Smith, how serious is it?"

"How should I know?"

"I mean, will they be getting married do you think?"

"Hardly. Mother would never allow it. Don't tell me you suspect them of plotting together to do away with my father? Come to think of it, why not include Mother in the plot as well? She had reasons to take her revenge."

"She has a cast-iron alibi. Bates was there."

"That must let out my brother too."

"Not really. You see, Bates was up watching a late-night film, heard a noise in the house and looked in on your mother, thinking she'd called. She was sleeping soundly. He didn't check on your brother, so we have only his word for it that he was asleep all night."

"So Brian's a suspect?"

"Everyone's a suspect." He set Sam gently on his feet and stood up. "Well, must get back and see if the computer's got its act together yet. Time for your supper, little man, I expect. What do you like to eat?"

"He doesn't speak," she interposed swiftly. "At least not since his father died. He used to."

McMahon hesitated, straightened his tie and said, "You know, sometimes it helps them speak if they're with other children, in a nursery or something. It worked with a nephew of mine who was slow in speaking."

"Sam doesn't need to be with other people, Detective Superintendent. He needs to be with me. He needs love."

McMahon looked unconvinced.

He's my child, she thought angrily.

"Fish fingers," said Sam very clearly.

They stared at him.

"Little dote," said McMahon softly.

Anna was too moved to speak. What had made Sam suddenly come out with that?

She followed McMahon down the stairs to make absolutely certain he left the house. At the door, he turned and said, "Shall we drop this Detective Superintendent business? You could call me Mike."

She stared stonily at him. "Why?"

"It's my name. Well, bye for now." He gave her a cheery wave and was gone. She went back upstairs.

"Horrible man!" she exclaimed, placing two fish fingers under the grill. "Wasn't he horrible, Sam?"

Sam shook his head. She felt cornered.

While Sam was eating his tea, she phoned Sue.

"Sue, I'm so sorry about Adam."

"How did you hear?"

"McMahon came round."

"Oh." Sue sounded relieved. "For a moment I thought you might have heard it on the news. We're trying to keep it out of the papers. The media would have a field-day, as you can imagine."

"What's going to happen to Adam?"

"The Bishop's stepped in, put up bail and whisked Adam away to a place in the country."

"He's not going to punish him, is he?" For a moment she had a vision of Adam being forced into a solitary cell somewhere, made to fast and pray seven times a day on his knees.

"No, nothing like that. The Bishop's been very understanding – as he would have been if Adam had gone to him in the first place. It's a rest home they have for exhausted clergy. The Bishop reckons he's on the verge of cracking up. Two weeks there and he'll be all right. They have saunas, a swimming pool and television in every bedroom. I must say I wouldn't mind it myself."

"What's going to happen about his job?"

"Apart from the police, hardly anyone knows about it. If the media don't get hold of the story, the Bishop thinks we can weather it. Don't breathe a word, will you?"

"I won't . . . Sue, Sam said 'fish fingers' this evening, ever so clearly."

"See? It does work."

Anna put down the phone, relieved. Adam had been rescued. Upstairs, Toby started to wail. An ache spread across her back and down her leg. *Pothos.* Desire for the absent being. Even the sound of the word was like a lament. She was about to go upstairs when the phone rang. She snatched it up.

"It's Lottie. There's going to be a meeting of the women's group tomorrow evening. Can you come?"

"I'll try. I've got to go now – Toby's howling," she replied, too disappointed that Lottie wasn't Philip to prolong the conversation further.

When she'd finally got both children to bed, she dialled Penelope's number. A child answered. A girl. Beatrice. For a moment Anna froze. She was about to hang up when Penelope came on the line.

"Anna, sorry about that." Penelope sounded flustered. "How are you?"

"All right. Look I hate to ask you this, but could you babysit tomorrow evening? Donna's already engaged."

"Of course. I'd love to. You only have to ask. I'm pleased to see you're having a social life again."

Social life – was that a good description of the women's group?

Anna put down the phone and glanced at the clock on the cooker. Half past ten. Why hadn't he rung? She picked up the receiver. No, he might be out. No, she didn't want to know. She replaced the receiver and went to bed. She lay awake till midnight but he didn't call.

Pothos.

CHAPTER NINE

SHE GLANCED DOWN BRIAN'S LIST. SHE rejected Whittaker's. It would take months to infiltrate a company and anyway Brian had said the takeover had been friendly. She'd leave that one to McMahon. She looked at the next name on the list. Eric Finch. What had Brian said? His ailing business had been bailed out by their father and taken over. Would he have borne him a grudge for that? She looked up Finch in the phone book. There were four E Finchs living in Hull. She rang Brian.

"Didn't I say? He lives in the Avenues. By the way, you'll have to congratulate me. Angela and I got engaged last night."

So McMahon had been right. How galling.

"Congratulations," she said feebly. "How's Mother taking it?"

"Badly. But it's none of her business, is it? She'll have to get on with Angela or move out. Can't speak any longer. I'm in the middle of a meeting." He rang off.

Really, she thought, Father couldn't have bettered that. She felt almost sorry for their mother. Brian couldn't, surely, be proposing to turn her out of her own home, could he? Then she remembered that under the terms of George Mitchell's will, Brian was now the legal owner of the family home. The black cloud of suspicion hanging over Angela and her brother in her mind expanded another inch. Was all this business about Finch a wild-goose chase?

She bundled the children into the Volkswagen and drove over to the part of Hull known as the Avenues: broad, leafy streets of Victorian family houses with elaborate fountains in the centre and roundabouts that had once served as turning areas for horses and carriages. Most of the houses had been converted into flats and bedsits. There were always gangs of students

191

about, and on warm summer evenings the Avenues resounded with conversation and music. She liked the area for its scruffy, down-at-heel charm. It was an odd choice for a businessman though.

She located Eric Finch's house. It was painted dark brown and didn't appear yet to have been divided into flats. She drove up and down the street a couple of times till the children got bored and started to whine. She stopped the car and took them to play on the swings in Pearson Park. If she was to call on him, she must do it without the children. Perhaps she'd try this evening, after the women's meeting?

Toby fretted all the way home. He'd started teething again. He always seemed to be teething. How many teeth did a child need? She rubbed Bonjela on his fiery gums and walked up and down the kitchen with him in her arms, trying to soothe him. By the time Penelope arrived, her back ached, there was a band of pain round her forehead and they'd both been in tears.

"What's the matter?" Penelope flung her bag down on a chair and took Toby in her arms. "You shouldn't be carrying him, Anna. It's bad for your back."

"He's teething. Won't eat anything. Won't even take his bottle. I think I'd better stay."

Penelope looked at her sharply. "You'll do no such thing. I'm quite capable of managing a teething baby."

"I feel guilty."

"Guilt comes with the job, Anna, love. Now you've got children you're going to spend the rest of your life feeling guilty over something or other. You'd better get used to it. Never let it stop you from leading your own life. Now scram. Go and have a relaxing bath and put on that nice silk shirt you were wearing the other day."

Anna stared at her. "I'm only going to a women's meeting. I hardly need to change out of jeans for that."

"Oh. Yes. I'd forgotten Tuesday's their night." Penelope sounded vaguely disappointed. Anna wondered what she'd thought she was going to do.

She stumbled along the street feeling old and sick and tired.

On impulse, she pushed open the door of a phone booth and dialled his number. Her palms began to sweat. Her heart beat faster.

"Hello. Philip Lawrence."

For a moment, she couldn't speak. She leant back against the glass, overwhelmed by a rush of longing and desire.

"Hello?"

"It's me. Anna."

"Anna, speak to me. Are you missing me, Anna?"

Everything – the children, the meeting, the case – dropped away. She rested the receiver on her shoulder and let his voice wash over her, caressing and soothing her, as a mother soothes her child. She'd fallen in love with his voice over the phone offering her comfort, and it was still his voice on the phone that comforted her most. "I don't feel so good. I've been walking up and down with Toby all afternoon. He's teething."

"Tell me about it. Come here and I will nurse you. I will make you whole again and give you strength for your children."

She put a hand to her forehead and groaned.

"What's the matter?"

"I can't. I've got a meeting. I promised I'd be there."

"Let's talk on the phone then. Would you like to be with me now?"

"Yes."

"Would you like me to be holding you?"

"Yes."

"Kissing you?" His voice purred in her ear, soft and low.

"Yes."

"We're lying on my bed and I'm rocking you in my arms. Oh, baby. Oh, Anna. Can you feel the heat between us? I'm getting hard for you. I'm pushing my way inside you. Are you going to let me in? Everything is pulsating around us. It's warm inside you. All tender and warm and sensitive. Now, I'm plunging inside you. I can feel you closing around me like a glove. I'm rocking to the rhythm of your body. I want to fuck my way into your soul, baby."

"Stop! Stop!"

He reverted to his everyday voice. "What's the matter? Don't you like it?"

"I – I'm not sure."

He laughed. "Poor Anna! Has no one ever made love to you on the phone before? Didn't Richard?"

"No."

"Where are you?"

"In the centre of Hull."

"Good God! We'll have brought the entire city to a standstill." She giggled. "I'm in a booth."

"That's a relief. You know, I like it when you laugh, Anna. You've a nice warm laugh. Feeling better?"

"Yes."

"Good. Come round tomorrow."

She hung up and leaned back against the glass wall. How was it he always knew exactly what to say to cheer her up? Was it because he was a therapist? Had she become a sort of extended case study for him?

She started to walk across the square to the women's centre. She wondered what Lottie would have made of that phone call. The heterosexual woman in thrall to the heterosexual male? She quickened her step. One thing was for sure, Ginny couldn't be a feminist. Philip wasn't the sort of man a feminist should love. She wished she could meet Ginny, see this woman he'd fallen in love with and married and had wanted to have children with. Then she'd know what she was up against.

She pushed her way through the little knot of protesters – the man in the brown suit almost cut off her nose with his placard – and raced up the stairs, for she was going to be late.

The room was full – but not of women she knew. She looked round for a familiar face and saw Tessa waving to her. She hesitated, then went over and sat down beside her.

"I been leaving you alone. I supposed you weren't very pleased with me."

"I wasn't."

"I'm sorry, Anna. It was my job. I had to act in my capacity as a professional."

Anna thought that if she heard the word "professional" once more, she'd scream.

"Besides," Tessa went on, "my team manager was breathing down my neck. She has a special thing about abuse."

"Has she?"

"Yes, she's a survivor of abuse herself. She's a wonderful woman. You'd like her, Anna. She's here tonight, as a matter of fact. Over there, talking to Gloria."

Anna looked and saw a long-legged woman with a blonde plait down to her waist and a very short skirt, listening with a fixed expression to what Gloria was telling her.

"Lovely-looking, isn't she?"

"Yes. How's Kylie?"

"Still having nightmares, poor kid. But she'll get over it, I think. Anna, it is all right between us, isn't it?"

"It's all right," she replied, in cowardly fashion. Things would never quite be the same between Tessa and herself. She'd never quite be able to forgive her for what she'd almost done to Sam.

Lottie came and sat beside them. "See what I mean? All the old gang gone. Jennifer, Angela, Carol . . . "

"Who's speaking tonight?"

"Someone called Sandra. I don't know her. Gloria invited her. That's her."

A large woman in a blue tracksuit stood up to speak. She looked both homely and efficient, as if she was a staff nurse or the matron of a residential home. She turned out to be a professor of gender studies at the University of the South Riding.

"Tonight I'm going to talk about DWEMs." She smiled round at them. "Dead White European Males, for those of you not in the know. Why do they still figure so largely on our literature syllabuses in schools and colleges and universities? Why are we still studying them?"

"That's it," whispered Anna. "Let's have a good clear-out – Shakespeare, Donne, Milton, Eliot, Joyce. Get rid of them all."

"Ssh!" Lottie nudged her.

"The answer lies in our patriarchal society where the female is constantly denigrated and – "

A glum-looking woman sitting beside her with notebook and pencil interrupted. "I think, Sandra, you'll want to rephrase that last sentence." She wrote down a word in her book.

"Who's that?" whispered Anna.

"The monitor. She checks for racist, sexist or any other discriminatory terms."

Sandra nodded and started again. "The answer lies in our patriarchal society where females are constantly put down and – "

"What was wrong with denigrated?" whispered Anna.

"Think about it," murmured Lottie.

Anna thought about it.

"I still can't see."

"*Denigrate.* Very offensive."

"But the word derives from niger, the Latin for black, not from – "

"Ssh!" said Lottie. "If you go on like this you'll be lynched."

"Why is the female systematically den – put down? After all, we now know that all embryos are anatomically female during the first six weeks of embryonic life. Our society seems blind to the fact . . . "

The monitor coughed.

Sandra flushed.

"Our society chooses to ignore the fact that the penis develops as a result of suppressing the growth of ovaries. The penis is nothing but an exaggerated clitoris."

Anna wondered what Philip would make of that.

Sandra distributed photocopies of a poem by TS Eliot. The woman with the blonde plait studied her copy with an intensity Anna recognised. She'd read poetry like that herself once upon a time, thinking that each new poem might change her way of life. Now she knew it wasn't books that changed people's lives – it was all the things that happened to them. Deaths and births and misunderstandings. Feeling like this, how could she possibly go back to teaching literature?

"I want us to undress this text," Sandra was saying. "Engage in intercourse with it. Show it up for what it is – an assumption of superiority – sexist, racist and imperialist – by a DWEM."

"Excuse me," muttered Anna.

She slid past Lottie and made for the door. She could think of better ways of spending the evening than engaged in intercourse with a text.

She got into her car and drove west across the city to the Avenues. She pulled up opposite Eric Finch's house. His windows were dark. Should she creep round the back and see if he was at home? But then she might miss him coming in at the front and she wanted to see what kind of a man he might be. She understood now why the police worked in pairs. You couldn't be everywhere at once.

She switched off the engine, wound down the window and waited. And waited. She wished she'd thought to bring a flask of coffee. She wished she still smoked. She hunted in the glove-compartment for a bar of chocolate or even some of the children's biscuits, but all she found was a spare nappy of Toby's. She drummed her fingers impatiently on the steering wheel. Perhaps she wasn't cut out to be a detective.

Then she saw a man come down the street, open the gate and go up the garden path. She leaned forward and gave a start of surprise. By the light of the streetlamp, she saw that the person letting himself into Eric Finch's house was none other than the man in the brown suit who'd nearly taken her nose off with his placard earlier that evening outside the women's centre and who had, she now remembered, attended her father's funeral.

She started up the car. She'd seen enough for one evening. She didn't want to be noticed by Finch. In all probability he knew exactly who she was and if he thought she suspected him . . . It was an eerie thought. He'd killed once, after all. McMahon was right. This was getting too dangerous for her. She'd phone him tomorrow, tell him her suspicions about Finch and let him do the rest.

It never happens like this in detective stories, she thought sadly, pulling up outside her house. The sleuth is always in at the arrest. But then, according to McMahon, detective stories had nothing to do with real life. Let him put Eric Finch through his computer and see what he turned up with.

"You're back early," said Penelope.

"The meeting was a wash-out."

"Why don't you join a nice mixed club? Have you thought about tennis?"

"Tennis!"

"It was only a suggestion."

When she phoned McMahon early the next morning he was surprisingly non-committal.

"We've already investigated Finch. We found nothing against him."

"Don't you think it was a bit odd, though, turning up at my father's funeral?"

"Not at all. He was a business associate of your father's. Most of the mourners were people who'd done business with George Mitchell."

"But Eric Finch had been done *out* of business by my father."

"A lot of people were. It was what your father was good at – buying out small businesses and making them profitable. The owners didn't go round murdering him."

"Perhaps they did. Perhaps they all ganged together to put a stop to him?"

"Flying this morning, aren't we? Why don't you stick to fiction and let us professionals get on with the job?"

She screamed.

"What on earth's the matter?"

"I swore I'd scream if I heard that word again."

"What word?"

"Professional."

"You know, Sergeant Bradley did remark that you came from an odd family and some of it was bound to rub off. I'm starting to believe her."

So he'd been discussing her, had he? She rang off.

She drove along the dual carriageway, beside the Humber Estuary, past the warehouses and disused railway carriages. She turned off right and drove along country lanes squeezed between fields. The fields were already harvested, their dull gold stubble waiting to be ploughed. She parked her car and stood for a moment looking out over the Westwood, at the cows grazing on the sun-ripened grass, at the butterflies and dragonflies fluttering amongst the daisies and buttercups.

"I was watching you from the window. What on earth were you doing?" He put out a hand and pulled her over his doorstep.

"Reviving my spirits. I live in the city centre, remember. This seems like the country to me."

"I will revive your spirits."

Swiftly he pulled her towards him, bent her head back and kissed her harshly on her mouth, her neck, her shoulders. She felt his rough stubble start up a rash on her skin. In one rapid movement, he put a hand inside her shirt and touched her breasts, then pushed up her skirt and put his hand inside her knickers. He gently felt for her cunt with his finger and moved it up and down inside her. Leaning back against the wall in his hallway she felt herself begin to open, like a petal, to his touch. Then he stood back and looked at her.

"Well, darling. How did you like your welcome?" He gave her a sidelong smile. "You see, with me, you never know what's going to happen next."

She laughed nervously. On the whole, she preferred the other Philip, the warm tender Philip who brought her comfort.

Then he took her by the hand, led her through into the kitchen, sat her down on a stool, said, "Coffee, darling?" and he became her Philip again.

"Did you like your phone call yesterday, darling?"

She looked down at her knees. "Yes."

"Made you feel soft and warm and cosy inside?"

"Yes."

"Good." He handed her a mug. "How did your meeting go?"

She described it to him.

He shook his head. "I was always telling Ginny – you can fight for equality in the workplace, but you can't fight the male's primitive instinct for domination. It used to make her furious."

"Your wife's a feminist?" she said, in surprise.

He nodded.

So she'd misjudged Ginny. Somehow it made her feel more, not less, of a rival. In Anna's view, all intelligent women were feminists, though not all feminists (remembering last night's meeting) were intelligent.

He took a mouthful of coffee. "It was just one more thing to row about," he said sadly. "She belongs to a radical women's group at work. They're out to get men. They've a particular thing about male bosses. When she lived here, women were always ringing her up. She's sort of their leader. She's got power, has Ginny. They look up to her."

"You didn't like that?" She was struck by his tone. He sounded almost angry.

He rubbed his cheeks. "Well, it was hard to. Mostly they went on about how she should leave me."

"Why?" she asked, suddenly uneasy.

"I've no idea." He slid back her long skirt. "Your lovely, lovely legs. Why aren't you wearing stockings?"

"Stockings?" She was genuinely appalled. "You mean, stockings and suspender belts?"

"Yes, darling. Women wear them to please their lovers. Hint, hint."

"Does that sort of thing really turn you on?"

"Yes, darling."

Had Ginny worn stockings?

"But it's bondage. Slavery," she protested. Richard had said once, "It's your body that turns me on, not the clothes you wear." She'd thought it was a perfect thing to say.

He groaned. "You're the same as Ginny! All those qualifications and you know nothing."

Perhaps his wife hadn't worn stockings then?

He took his hands off her legs and leant back against the washing-machine, drinking his coffee. "When I first met Ginny, she wore schoolgirl knickers and her hair was going grey at the front. I got her to dye it and grow it out."

"Is her hair long?"

"Down to her waist."

She felt a pang of jealousy. He wasn't being very motherly this morning.

"Look on my liking for stockings as a weakness, darling. A hangover from primeval man." He leered at her.

"For goodness' sake!" She laughed and gave him a little push.

He took her mug from her hands, set it down on the counter and kissed her again, slowly and gently this time, exploring every inch of her mouth with his tongue. Her body took over from her mind. She stopped feeling uncertain about him.

"Come to bed," he said. He lifted her up and carried her through into his bedroom. He drew the curtains and switched on the light above his bed. The room was lined with dark fitted wardrobes. The curtains were dark red and navy. The sheets were dark brown. She felt safe and warm and protected in here. There was no one making demands on her. She lay very still and let him undress her.

"Gorgeous knickers, darling. What did you think – give old Philip a treat, eh?"

They were new. The first piece of underwear she'd bought since Richard died. "Make up for the lack of suspenders, do they?"

He gave her a look. "Almost."

"Ho! Ho!" She lightly cuffed the side of his head.

"Come here!" He pulled her down beneath him. "Your gorgeous breasts. Two beauties. My girl! Is this what your cunt wants?" His fingers worked their way inside her.

"Yes!"

She took his cock in her hands. It was still soft. She started to panic. He didn't fancy her enough. She wasn't his type.

He gently pushed her hand away. "It's not you," he said. "It's all the things I've been through with Ginny."

She half believed him.

He licked and sucked her breasts. He moved his finger inside her. She started to come. "My girl! My Anna!" With his other hand he began touching his cock. His eyes were closed. She wondered what he was thinking of. She wondered if he was thinking of her. She felt his cock harden against her. He turned her over and pushed inside her.

"Oh! Beautiful, Anna! I want to fuck my way into your soul. Take my cock into your soul. Take me up to the stars." He nibbled her ear. "I'm going to flood you with my spunk," he murmured. "Do you want me to?"

"Yes," she replied, forgetting about babies, forgetting about AIDS.

"Oh, girl! My beautiful girl!" He roared as he came inside her.

She'd had all this. Anna lay back on the bed beside him. Her eyes filled with tears. His wife had had all this richness and she'd left him. She was conscious of him lying beside her, one arm curved above his head, breathing deeply, half dozing. She was afraid to look at him now, afraid to see what it was she'd desired so much. His strong shoulders and narrow hips. His small tight buttocks that gave him the sexiest walk of any man she'd known. The knot of dark hair across his chest. The dark hair lower down where his penis lay curled. It was just a body. A middle-aged, slightly overweight male body. Nothing out of the ordinary. But she desired it more than anything else in the world. How could Ginny have left him?

He looked across and smiled at her. "Happy, darling?"

"Yes."

He squeezed her hand. "Good."

She got up to go to the bathroom. She looked in the full-length mirror at her flushed puffy face. Her body had altered out of all recognition since the birth of her two children. There were extra inches on her hips, her stomach muscles sagged and her breasts had developed into fat round apples. You're fat, she told herself. Fat. She splashed cold water on her face and looked round for a towel. His bathroom was spotless. At home she was used to plastic ducks and boats and baby baths. She noticed, with relief, that there was only one toothbrush in the mug.

When she got back to the bedroom, he was already dressed.

"Got a client coming in half an hour," he explained.

"I see. Timed everything just right then, didn't you?"

He looked at her.

"Sweetheart, I can cancel the client. I thought you said you had to get back for the children."

"I do. Sorry." Why was she always suspecting him?

She looked at her clothes lying about on the floor. Who was it had said the worst thing about sex was the sight afterwards of used underclothes strewn around the bedroom? Chekhov perhaps. Embarrassed, she grabbed her knickers.

"I'll go and put the kettle on."

Seated at his breakfast-counter again, drinking coffee, she glanced round at his neat bright kitchen. The shiny cooker, gleaming dishwasher, spotless white microwave seemed hardly used. The whole bungalow seemed hardly used. Whereas at home the furniture she and Richard had brought up from London was already battered and scuffed from the children. The paintwork was scratched, her carpets and sofas spotted with food stains.

"Do you really live here? It seems so bare."

It was all an elaborate pretence. A set for his clients where he could observe how they reacted in a home environment (some of them he took to bed). His real life went on somewhere else.

"Yes, I live here." He glanced away. "It's bare because when my wife finally left she took half the things with her."

"Oh." She looked at the empty picture hooks, the gaps on the shelves, the bare boards where rugs should be. "I see. I thought she moved out over a year ago, eleven weeks after you were married, you said."

He nodded. "She did. Only she kept coming back. Backwards and forwards between here and Grimsby. I never knew where I was with her."

"But she's gone now?"

"Yes."

"For good?"

"Yes."

"Did she . . . When did she move out? Finally, I mean?" Why ask? The whole business of their separation had been more recent than she'd thought, than he'd led her to believe.

"April."

Two months ago. He'd lasted on his own for two months. Was that the sort of man she could trust?

"Where's she now?"

"I told you. Back in Grimsby. With her parents. She always ran back to them when she was in trouble. They adore her. Before she met me she was married to Duncan, her childhood sweetheart. He's the son of friends of her parents. All very cosy. At weekends they all went hill-walking together. Till she met me, Ginny'd never put a foot wrong as far as her parents were concerned. Meeting me changed her life. They couldn't understand what she was up to. They've always refused to meet me. I'm not even sure she told them we were married." He glanced out of the kitchen window at the trees. "She knew nothing about men before she met me. Had never been really close to anyone before. Now she hangs round with this gang of women at work. For all I know they may be having some kind of lesbian love-in. In the evenings, she dresses in high heels and incredibly short skirts and goes off to nightclubs. I taught her how to be attractive to men and she's buggered off and used it on other men."

Anna sat in silence looking down at her knees. This woman had power over both their lives. He was never going to let her into his life while Ginny was around. Her madness, if madness it was, was controlling them both. Nothing was going to replace her for him. She'd left him hungry, had Ginny, so that all his life would be hunger and searching for what was lost as soon as he'd found it – love, marriage, children.

He rested his elbows on her knees. "What are you thinking about?"

"High heels, short skirts, long hair, night clubs, lesbianism. She sounds absolutely fascinating." She slid off the stool and went to survey herself in the mirror in the hall. "More exciting than me, anyway. I feel old. Dumpy. A housewife."

He came and stood behind her. "You've a beautiful body."

She sighed. "It's never got back to what it was before Sam was born." Ginny'd be all right of course. She'd never had children.

204

He lifted her up in the air. "You're my beautiful, beautiful Anna."

She looked down at the top of his head. "Are you planning on seeing your wife again?"

He set her down. "No, I'm not. I don't trust her. I love her, but she's so bloody unstable. I can't take any more of her coming and going."

She could hear the note of longing in his voice. *He's never said he loves me. I'm for sleeping with and talking with and playing games with. I'm a diversion. As long as there's a chance she'll come back, he'll never let himself go with me. She has all the power whether she cares about that or not.*

Besides, what have I to give him? There's the children. They'll always come first. They have to. Before anything I might be feeling. I can't make them go through any more changes. She gazed at Philip. Then reached out a hand and touched his cheek. *I'd give him my life if he asked me to.*

At home, she spent hours playing with her children, watching them laugh and giggle as they played hide-and-seek with each other behind the sofa. *Her beautiful, beautiful life. He'd created a warm space for her, a place where she could breathe. I was starved before, starved of love. I heard nothing but angry, nagging voices inside my head. I had nothing to give my children. Now I can give and give to them from my secret store of happiness. He has done all this for me, with his sanctuary in the woods.*

Penelope rang.

"My goodness, Anna, you sound happy."

"I am quite happy today – or at least calmer."

"I'm glad. Anna, I phoned to say I'm sending Beatrice away for a bit. So if you want to bring the boys round any time – "

"Yes, they'll love that." Vainly she tried to stifle a tiny twinge of guilt. "Where's she going?"

"To a holiday camp. It will do her good to be with other children. Quite frankly she's getting too much for Nanny and me. Besides, it's a pretty unnatural life for her, stuck with a

205

couple of grown-ups in a house that hasn't had children in it for years. Will you bring the boys round soon, Anna?"

"I will," she promised.

She put down the phone and glanced at the photo of Richard on the shelf above the cooker.

"What do you expect me to do?" she burst out. "She's not my problem. She's not my daughter. She's yours. You should have taken better care of her. I can't look after her. I can't. I might harm her. A girl's adolescence is a terrible time. I can't take the risk."

The photo stared back unmoved. On impulse, she took it down and thrust it into a drawer. Then she went upstairs, opened the wardrobe and began sorting through Richard's clothes. It was time she did something about them. His suits she'd give to Penelope for Douglas. The rest could go to Oxfam. It was time.

She was halfway through this task when the doorbell rang.

"You again."

"May I come in?" asked McMahon.

"I suppose so."

"Don't worry. You're off the hook."

She paused on her way back upstairs. "Why? What do you mean?"

"Your hunch was right. We arrested Eric Finch last night."

"Has he admitted it?"

"Not yet. But we've got enough circumstantial evidence to bring him to court. I went back over your father's papers and discovered something that had slipped Sergeant Bradley's attention – a threatening letter from Finch to your father."

"Threatening? In what way?"

She lifted Toby up off the floor and sat down in a chair, holding him close to her. The shakes had come on again. Her legs felt as though they were about to give way.

"Finch somehow found out about your father's relationship with Angela Smith." McMahon pulled out a chair and sat down. Sam came and leant against him. "He was still sore about the buy-out. So he threatened to expose your father. You know how strongly Finch feels about abortion."

"But not, apparently, about murder. How ironic." She shifted Toby on her knee. He was beginning to fall asleep. "And will this be enough to convict him?"

"I think so."

"So we're all in the clear. That's a relief. Thanks for letting me know, Detective Superintendent."

"I really came to thank you for giving me the hint. I was getting bogged down in HOLMES and going round in circles. Sometimes the old-fashioned ways are best."

She waited for him to go. But he remained in his chair, absent-mindedly stroking Sam's hair. He seemed drained this afternoon. The case over, the adrenalin gone, he'd lost all his sparkiness.

"What will you do now, Detective Superintendent?"

"What?" He looked up at her and blinked.

"Now the case is finished?"

"Oh, take three days off and sleep. I've been working round the clock since the case began. We all have. The team have been living like a family. Now they'll go back to their real families and life will return to normal."

"And after you've slept?"

"I'll take some time to get to know Hull. Also, I want to start painting again. Ever since I got here I've had my eye on catching the light over the Humber."

"You won't be going over to visit your family in Ireland then?"

"Ireland." He brushed a hand across his eyes. "In Mayo now the fuschia will be out. The light will be playing across the white stones on the beach near my home."

"You miss it, don't you?"

"Ireland's a wound buried deep. It's there every day – a lack behind everything I do."

Anna glanced at him. He looked older this afternoon, unshaven, vulnerable somehow. His words reminded her of Richard. How odd, though, to feel like that about a place.

Sensing her puzzlement, he tried to explain. "Ireland's more than a country to me. It's an attitude. A way of life, a way of thinking and being."

"Why don't you go back?"

"I won't go back. This," he pointed to his leg, "provoked a crisis of identity on my part. What was I doing, an Irish Catholic, setting myself up to be targeted by my own people? It's described in the report as a breakdown. I can't go back to work there. Besides, Hull's growing on me. It's not quite England, stuck out as it is, halfway to the Continent. If you look in the phone book, every other surname is foreign. Would you go back to Dublin?"

"No. There's no going back. Everyone I knew there will have moved on. Besides, Dublin's no city to bring up kids. Too much traffic. Too many drugs. And the kind of things I liked doing there are no longer possible."

He looked at her. "You miss the single life?"

"I am single, Detective Superintendent. It's just I have children."

"Thought any more about going back to work?"

"No."

"Pity. I approve of mothers working. All my sisters do."

"I know. You told me."

He glanced at her and stood up. "Sorry for babbling on like this. I feel light-headed this afternoon. It must be lack of sleep. What I really came to say was this," he hesitated, "if you're at a loose end, ever, perhaps you'd like to come out for a jar with me? Here's my number." He pushed a piece of paper across the table. He must have written it out before he came.

"Thanks."

She folded it up and put it in the back pocket of her jeans. She didn't think she'd ever be at that much of a loose end.

He hesitated again. What *was* the matter with him today? He reached out and lightly touched the top of Sam's head. "You've a couple of grand boys."

"I know. I'm lucky."

Was he ever going to go?

He went.

At the front door, he said, "You told me your sister was a painter. Is it possible to see any of her pictures?"

"There's one hanging in the Ferens. The rest are stored in my mother's house. I think. I keep meaning to do something about them. Good day, Detective Superintendent."

He looked after her rather pathetically. "Won't you call me Mike?"

She shut the door and went back upstairs. His talk about Ireland, the quality of his feeling about the country, had somehow brought Richard back. She stood in the middle of the kitchen hesitating.

"Sam, shall we visit Daddy's grave?"

Sam rearranged Thomas and James. "Why?"

"Well, er . . . " She was wrong-footed by surprise. Usually he loved coming with her. "We could take him some flowers."

"Why?'

"Because it's a nice thing to do. It's nice to remember."

Sam hooked Claribel onto Thomas. "Da not coming back," he murmured.

It was the longest sentence he'd uttered since Richard's death. She stood stock-still and stared at him.

When they got to the cemetery they found that someone – Penelope probably – had visited recently and tidied up and placed fresh flowers on his grave. Had she brought Beatrice with her? Anna stood staring down at the plain white cross. It was longer than usual since she'd come here. She felt she wanted to explain her absence, tell Richard about Philip. *I needed some comfort. It's not always easy on my own with the children. He makes me feel . . . I've never felt this before, such longing for another body . . .* The words tailed away. They suddenly sounded cheap and shoddy. Richard had been her husband, the father of her children. She felt ashamed saying these things to him. She turned away.

"Come on, boys. Let's go across the road and walk in the old cemetery."

So they crossed the road and wandered under the trees. She pushed Toby in his buggy while Sam scampered in and out of the statues of weeping women and praying angels.

That evening she took a sheaf of cuttings and letters from the desk in the sitting-room. A glass of wine in her hand, she sat down in the armchair where Richard used always to sit and read through the letters. *"The makings of a fine barrister,"* colleagues had written. *"Would have been a QC." "A tremendous loss to the profession."* She wept again as she read them. Yet she couldn't help feeling, as she put them back in the drawer of the desk that had been Richard's and was now hers, that something had changed since she'd last looked at them. She was no longer the person she had been, no longer Richard's wife. She'd changed. Was it time, or Philip, that had changed her? But Philip was married to Ginny.

"What am I?" she said aloud. "What am I if I'm no longer Richard's wife?"

Her memories were becoming blurred. She couldn't remember any more the precise tone of his voice. Looked for it and failed to find it in Penelope. Packing up his clothes that afternoon, she'd noticed his smell had almost entirely faded from them.

Later in the bath she discovered two small bruises on her upper arm and one large one on the inside of her left thigh. A sort of lost yearning came over her for Richard's gentle love-making. Tears rolled down her face and into the water. To make love with Richard again, slowly, gently, without roughness or urgency, to make love as two old friends, in innocence, honouring one another's bodies – that would be like coming home.

She stepped out of the bath, wrapped a towel around herself and went downstairs to the kitchen to put Richard's photograph back on the shelf.

CHAPTER TEN

"PHILIP LAWRENCE HERE."

As always, the sound of his voice on the phone, gentle and low, the voice of the professional, stunned her into silence.

"Who is it?"

His voice grew sharper. She knew what he was thinking. Some lunatic on the other end. He got lots of calls from jokers. Office girls ringing him up for a dare.

"Philip?"

"Yes?"

"It's Anna." Suddenly she felt humiliated. Why did he never recognise her voice? Did he get so many calls from women?

"Anna."

"I managed to get away earlier than I thought. Can I see you now?"

"If you like. Where are you?"

"In the hotel beside the Marina. Will you come here? We could go for a drink."

There was a silence. Her blood ran cold. "What's the matter?" She started to shake.

"There's this client. Said they might be turning up."

"But we arranged to meet this evening. I thought you'd be pleased I got away early."

"I am, but . . . "

"We can spend more time together."

There was a long silence.

"Bloody hell!" she said at last. "Your wife's there."

"She just turned up."

"Christ! Philip! If I suggest a time and it doesn't suit you, tell me. Say 'My wife's coming round. I can't see you.' Only don't lie to me. I'm worth more than that. There's no future for us if we can't be honest with each other."

"I'll come as quickly as I can."

"Don't bother!" she replied, breaking up inside.

"Anna! Calm down. I'll be there in half an hour."

In the bar, surrounded by parties of businesspeople, she sat sipping her drink and looking out at the Marina where darkness was folding in around the boats. She thought: because he noticed more about the way I spoke and understood more of what I felt than anyone I'd ever met, I expected him to act like a mother to me. But he's not my mother. He can never be my mother. He's my lover. And he lied to me. The relationship with Ginny hasn't ended. It's going on and on.

Something touched her toe. She looked up. It was him, smiling down sheepishly at her, looking gorgeous, damn him, in dark trousers and a black silk shirt.

"Rather chi-chi this place, darling. Shall we go for a walk?"

She picked up her jacket and followed him out of the hotel. As they went through the swing doors, the cold night air hit them in the face. He shivered and buttoned up his shirt.

"I didn't plan to come into Hull tonight. I thought we were going to meet at my place."

"Your wife's there."

"She's gone now," he said, almost bitterly.

She glanced at his face turned away from her. He looked sombre and grim. Somewhere deep inside her, a memory stirred. Who did he remind her of? "You wanted to stay with her, didn't you? When I rang, you thought, oh God, not her again, I want to stay with my wife."

"No, Anna." He half turned back to her. "I'm always glad when you ring. Only she was feeling tearful and lonely. It was a time to be kind to her, not a time to rush off."

"Lonely? Ginny? I thought you said she had loads of friends."

"She does. But we've been married eighteen months. You can't just let go. I worry about her. She said this evening that she's lonely. I don't think she's found anyone else yet. I thought she had – she's always off at nightclubs with those friends of hers." His voice sounded full of tears.

He hasn't stopped loving her. I'm not enough for him.

They walked on in silence beside the dark lapping water and the boats rocking to and fro in the wind.

"What did you tell her?"

"That I had to come out to see a client."

He lied so easily.

"What did you tell Donna?"

"That there was a women's meeting."

And so did she. They were both liars, God help them. She thrust her hands into her pockets.

"She's like Pavlov's dog," she said, in despair. "She seems to have some kind of homing instinct. She always turns up just when you're about to meet me."

"Perhaps she does have some kind of intuition." He fingered his chin. "She's sensitive. Like you."

Sensitive. Long hair. Long legs. Anna stiffened her shoulders and walked on quickly.

"Come here!" He grabbed her arm. "What's the matter with you?"

"I thought you were going to be my mother," she muttered into his shoulder, feeling suddenly lost. "But a mother doesn't act evasive when her child rings up, she doesn't grumble at having to come into town to meet her, she doesn't put other people first."

He stood back and looked at her. "OK then. Come and live with me."

"I can't. The children. I can't uproot them like that."

He shrugged. "If you're unhappy . . . Some people would argue that what a child needs most is to be brought up by a mother who's happy."

She bit her lip. "I don't show them I'm unhappy – at least . . . "

"Don't you think they sense it?"

Somewhere a boat clanked on its moorings. She looked away from him, out to sea. "I don't know." Tears began to run down her cheeks. "I never thought my children would have an unhappy life. They've got no father. Their mother's in a mess. It's terrible. I can't bear it for them. I can't!"

He took her in his arms. "Come on, darling, don't cry. Don't cry, Anna. My Anna. My girl in pain. Let me take on your pain and share it. Like that animal in the bible – what's it called?"

"A scapegoat."

"A scapegoat. I'll be your scapegoat, darling and share your pain."

He was good at comforting. He was skilled at it. Had plenty of practice. Take this evening. Two weeping women. Herself and Ginny. It was more than he deserved. She pulled away from him and blew her nose.

"Come on, darling, give me a kiss. That's a good girl. That's my Anna."

Arm in arm, they walked round the Marina, then crossed over the dual carriageway and went in the direction of the city centre. They turned down a narrow dimly lit back street. On a patch of wasteland to their left several cars were parked. Young men sat inside them in darkness, watching every movement on the street.

"Pimps," muttered Philip.

Pale girls with unhealthy complexions shivered on the pavement in their too-thin clothes. Some of them were barelegged. They stood in a row, not talking to one another.

Anna stopped and looked down at her short denim skirt.

"I could do that," she said. "Shall I join them? You don't want me this evening. You'd rather be with your wife. Shall I offer my body for sale?"

He took her arm and hurried her on. "Darling, if you went and stood there, I'd knock you unconscious and drag you away."

She began to feel happier.

Hull throbbed with its usual night-life. Scantily dressed girls paraded arm in arm from pub to disco. Gangs of young males wandered the streets, their shirts open to the waist, their hair cropped short, whistling after them. Squaddies on the loose for the night. They picked their way over broken glass and went into the first hotel they came across. It was bare, modern, nondescript. Elderly couples sat around at low tables sipping their drinks.

"Why are they all staring?" she asked, flopping into a chair.

He grinned. "It's that skirt of yours. They probably think I've brought you in off the streets."

214

"I'd be good at it too."

"All right." He took out his wallet. "What do I get for twenty quid?"

"Nothing. I'm very expensive."

"Fifty?"

"A blow-job."

He started, then smiled and put away his wallet. He went to get the drinks.

So he thought she was too much of a lady to know words like that, did he? What was she then? His bit of posh? While his wife was the genuine article. Northern working class, born and raised in Grimsby. Who said the class system was dead? It operated even in love. She felt middle class and naïve.

He came back with the drinks. "What are you staring at?"

"You. The way you move your body."

He looked smug. "You like the way I move, do you?" He sat down with a swagger.

"It's strange. I feel I know everything about your body, but nothing at all about you."

"What do you want to know? I was born in Grimsby. We moved down to London – "

"No, not that. That's only facts. I mean, what kind of a childhood did you have?"

He brushed a hand across his face. "My father bullied me. He wanted me to get on, to go to university as he never had. He thought I was . . . slow. In the end, I ran away. Roamed around the States for years, driving trucks, working on ranches and building sites. One day, I met this American psychologist who took an interest in me. He persuaded me to study for a degree. Then my mother got ill and I wanted to be near her, so I came back here and set up practice." He glanced at her. "Ginny doesn't approve of my work. Thinks I've sold out to the middle classes. She used to poke fun at the women who park their Range Rovers and BMWs in my drive and spend hours spilling out their hearts to me. She used to say she looked after people with real problems. Not the fake sort dreamed up by middle-class women with too much time on their hands."

"What does she do?"

"Didn't I say? She's a social worker."

"Where does she work? In Grimsby?"

"No, she's attached to Humberside Social Services. Her patch is East Hull."

Nearer than she'd thought. Perhaps Tessa knew her, even.

"Do you meet her after work? Do you have lunch with her sometimes?"

"I never see her when she's working. She's never liked me to come to her workplace. I think she pretends she's single."

"Why?"

"In the circles she moves in it's not politically correct to be married. Especially to someone like me." He was silent for a moment. "Ginny knocked a hole in my confidence about my work. When she criticises what I do, I can't care for my clients as I should. I don't think they're fake. Everyone needs someone to talk to. Some of these women are suicidal. It's not trivial."

"Are you going back to her?"

He shook his head.

"I feel that you will."

"She killed my babies. I can never trust her again."

"I know." It was her turn to look away. "But there's no reason in love. You love her. Trusting doesn't come into it." Her throat ached. In another moment she would weep.

He pulled her towards him. "I'm not leaving you, darling." He sat looking at her.

"What's the matter?"

"I want to sleep with you," he said, too loudly.

The elderly matrons clinked their glasses in disgust and turned their backs on them.

"Come with me now, Anna. I need you. You're my lifeline."

At his house he took her by the hand and led her through into the bedroom. The curtains were already drawn. She looked down at the duvet and wondered whether his wife had been in here earlier. But the duvet was pulled straight and the pillows were arranged above it in orderly fashion. She must not go on suspecting him like this.

They lay down on the bed fully clothed.

He looked up at the ceiling. "I try to be a good person, to

care for my mother and look after my clients. But I need taking care of too."

She reached out and touched his cheek. "I will take care of you."

If wanting to comfort someone isn't love, what is? He was hers. Not Ginny's. His tears dropping onto her breast told her that. All of a sudden she felt tremendously strong. All these people depending on her – the children, Philip. She had so much to give. She felt strong and free. He'd done that for her.

"Ginny doesn't care for me. I don't know why." He began to unbutton her shirt. "She cared for her first husband. She cares for her clients. But she can't seem to care for me. I was always the one who did the cooking when we lived together. I did the housework, waited up for her, worried about her driving alone late at night." He buried his head between her breasts. "My Anna. My beautiful Anna."

They tore off their clothes. She was waiting for him, all warm and soft and wet inside. But when he tried to make love to her, he couldn't.

"I'm sorry." He lay back, his head on her shoulders. "I'm fucked up this evening. I shouldn't have asked you to come back with me."

"Yes, you should." She stroked his thick dark hair. "I don't only want you for that."

He moved restlessly on the bed. "It's Ginny's fault I'm like this. She killed my babies. I can't get a proper erection any more."

"It doesn't matter."

She lay back as his fingers moved inside her. They plunged inside her. She came and came. He touched his penis. She watched it grow hard between his fingers. He caught hold of her hair.

"Come here, fuckface," he whispered. "Are you going to behave? Are you going to be my woman?"

For a second, she wondered who he was talking to. Then his cock was inside her and she forgot about everything except the feel of it moving there.

She spent the morning playing with the children. She entered their safe innocent world and felt soothed. Her love for Philip was a pistol-shot through this world. She sensed an edge of violence in him. It was there in his love-making, there in the way he'd grabbed her hair, in the way he'd run his fingers down her neck. Something terrible was going to happen. Only last week a wife had shot her husband's mistress. It had been in the papers. Ginny was mad enough for anything. She clasped Toby to her, suddenly seized with panic. God, please keep my children safe. Let these little innocent ones not come to any harm.

By the afternoon, her feelings towards him had become calmer. I am with you, he'd said. When you're in the kitchen or playing with the children, I'm with you. Nobody was as comforting with words as he was. He gave her soft warm feelings, like Nana. Her life was a closed circle and he was the opening onto the outside world. He let in the fresh air. She thought over what he'd said, about his wife not caring for him. This was to be her role then – she was to care for him because his wife, whom he loved, didn't.

In the evening the phone rang. Thinking it would be Philip, she tore across the room to answer it. It was Brian.

"Just ringing to tell you the case is cleared up. The police have charged that Finch fellow."

"I know."

"So you're off the hook."

"*I'm* off the hook!" What about you?

"Angela and I want invite you to our party. To celebrate our engagement. Will you come?"

"Will I be welcome? I mean, there's Mother."

"Not her sort of do. Besides, she's moving out."

"Moving out?"

"Into the lodge. We're having it done up. She's giving the house over to Angela and me. Says the place is too big for her now Father's gone. Not that he was here very much."

"Brian, are Georgia's paintings still in the house?"

"Yes, they're up on the second floor."

"Can I come round and see them sometime?"

"I suppose so. Why?"

"Someone was talking about them the other day. I've never

seen them. Perhaps we should do something with them? Donate them to a gallery or something."

"Mother was always dead set against that."

"Why?"

"Haven't a clue." Brian had lost interest. "Look, got to go. Angela's arrived. So you'll come to the party?"

"All right."

Could she bring Philip? No, she couldn't. Much too public for a widow.

She was to leave the children with Penelope whilst she went to look at Georgia's paintings. It was two days since they'd made love and Philip still hadn't rung. They were supposed to be meeting later this morning. Four times, in the middle of packing up the children's things, the bottles, the nappies, the spare sets of clothes, she went over to the phone with churning stomach and clammy hands, determined to call him. Pride held her back. At the last moment, when everything was packed up and Sam had his shoes on and was ready to go, the phone rang. It had to be him. It had to. Heart in her mouth, she ran to answer it.

"Hi! It's me. I've got my coat on and I'm off over to Cottingham to bring the old man to visit my mother. I thought, I must give Anna a ring before I go."

"Oh."

He'd forgotten, then, about their meeting. She glanced out of the window. Down in the courtyard the wind was battering the roses. Soon the blooms would all be gone.

"How did the day go yesterday, Anna?"

"Better. The thought of you gave me energy. I enjoyed being with the children."

"Good. I'm glad."

"What have you been doing?" Why didn't you phone? Rather odd, isn't it, to make love to someone and not phone them the next day?

"This and that."

She laughed nervously. "This and that? It doesn't tell me much. Did you see any clients?"

"One or two. I need to get more. I've been thinking of going on a course. I'll get more clients if I have more qualifications."

He went on outlining his plans. There was something different about his voice this morning. He sounded stronger somehow. Had something happened to him?

"Well, I'm off to Cottingham. Give you a ring tomorrow."

"Right."

She put down the phone and pressed her fingers to her temples. So now she had the whole morning free. She could linger over Georgia's paintings without having to dash across to Beverley to see him. It was more freedom than she wanted. She looked down at Sam, waiting there patiently, holding his Winnie-the-Pooh lunch-box packed with juice and biscuits and crisps.

"Come on then, boys, let's go." Her voice in her ears sounded funereal.

They took the dual carriageway out to Swanland. The Humber Estuary lay flat and grey and lifeless, mirroring the sky above. It was wretched weather for July. And all the time she drove she kept thinking, what has happened to him? I left him so weak and now he sounds so strong. At the back of her mind another question was framing itself but it remained buried. For some reason, she couldn't get it up to the surface.

At Penelope's she noticed that a photograph of Richard had gained new prominence on the mantelpiece. For Beatrice's sake, no doubt. Though the girl was absent, Anna couldn't help feeling her presence haunted the house. After a few minutes, she was glad to be able to escape from it.

She drove inland, along narrow winding country lanes empty of traffic. Fields spread out on either side of the road. Green corn. Yellow rape. Barley rippling like water. As she turned into the village and drove past the post office and the almshouses, the unformulated question that had been battering at her brain since he'd rung, rose to the surface. Have you seen your wife again? Yes, that was it, that's what she'd wanted to ask him. Now she'd have to wait a whole twenty-four hours for his answer.

She turned left through the five-bar gate and up the winding driveway to the house. She pulled up on the gravel in front of the oak door. But he doesn't trust Ginny. He said so. He said she'd killed his babies and he'd never trust her again. No, it isn't his wife. It's someone else. Someone new. The tears started in her eyes. He'd found someone else to care for him, someone who didn't have children, someone who could be with him all the time. Her heart ached at the picture this conjured up. The two of them walking down to the pub or curled up in bed watching a late-night film together. She got out of the Volkswagen. What had she expected? He was lonely. He needed someone to be with him all the time. It served her right. Their story couldn't have a happy ending.

She rang the bell. Bates came to the door.

"Good morning, Miss Anna."

"Hello, Bates, I've come to see some paintings. Mother's left, I suppose?"

"In the process, Miss Anna. She's in the library now, packing up odds and ends to take with her. Shall I tell her you're here?"

"No, it's all right, Bates. I'll find the way myself." She hadn't foreseen this. She'd been counting on her mother having already moved out.

She found her on her knees in the library, surrounded by cardboard boxes and tissue-paper and old newspapers.

"Well, Anna. This is a surprise. What brings you here?" Her mother hardly paused in her packing. She'd left off her mourning outfit and was wearing a navy blue suit. Very smart, very well cut, it suited her neat trim figure.

"I – er – Brian said about . . . I've come to look at Georgia's paintings."

Her mother's busy fingers paused. She stared across the cardboard boxes at her daughter. "Why on earth would you want to do that?"

"I thought . . . I've never seen them," she replied, lamely.

For a split second her mother seemed to hesitate, then she shrugged and returned to her packing. "Look at them if you like, Anna. Only be prepared for a shock. Your sister's paintings weren't all pretty flower-paintings like the one in the Ferens."

"I know." She remembered those gashed landscapes, those barren moorland scenes.

Her mother went on packing.

Anna fingered a china shepherd, the pair of the one Brian

had broken. "Um – will you be all right in the lodge, Mother? Will you be comfortable? I mean, you've lived here so long."

Her mother glanced up at her. "Naturally, I will be all right. Brian is having it redecorated for me and central heating put in. I shall be very snug. I'm not a martyr, you know."

"Have you lots of things to pack?"

"There won't be room for lots of things, Anna. I'm taking my books and a few ornaments. The furniture will stay here. This is where it was bought for. This is where it belongs." She turned back to her packing.

Anna sighed. "I'll go and look at the paintings then."

Her mother didn't bother to look up. "You'll let yourself out when you're finished, won't you? No need to come in and say goodbye." She turned away. Her attitude clearly told her daughter: you made your decision to leave years ago, don't expect to be able to walk in here and make it all right again. She was a mother betrayed.

Anna walked up the wide curving staircase to the first floor. She'd last walked up here eighteen years ago. In between, she'd married, had children and become a widow. Like Mother. That, if anything, should have created a bond between the two of them. But it hadn't. She glanced up at the huge domed skylight. The landing was unchanged since she was a child. Wedgwood-blue walls and intricate white plasterwork. She'd never seen anywhere half so pretty. But beautiful surroundings don't make up for a wretched childhood. And she had been wretched here. Always fighting off her mother's suppressed rage. Always yearning for her absent father.

The doors along the landing were firmly closed. She felt no temptation to take a look behind any of them. Her bedroom had been at the end of the corridor. She and Georgia had shared the bathroom next door to it. A privileged childhood. She smiled wryly.

She walked along the landing and found the small door on the right that led to the second floor. She groped her way up the bare wooden stairs. There was no electricity here. The second floor had remained undecorated and unoccupied for as long as she could remember. Plaster peeled from the walls. Cobwebs dangled in front of her. She brushed them away. There were four or five rooms on this upper storey – she could never remember exactly how many. In Victorian times it had been, probably, the children's quarters. A day-room, a night-nursery and rooms for the nanny or nannies. In her time they'd only ever used one room, to store things. She found her way to it and unfastened the string which served instead of a door-handle. The door swung open to reveal a large octagonal-shaped room with a bay window. She looked around. There was Brian's old school trunk. Suitcases. Her father's golf clubs. Her hockey stick. She picked it up and examined the white tape where she'd mended the handle. She put it down again. She'd detested hockey.

The canvases were propped up against a wall, their backs to her. She picked them up one by one and carried them over to the window seat. She leant them against the window. Open red flowers. The dales. The peat lakes. The heather. The bracken. All of their childhood was there. She squatted back on her heels looking at them. Her sister had been fourteen when Anna had left home. What a shame there'd never been an opportunity to get to know her. Mother had seen to that. She hadn't wanted her elder daughter's hunger for independence to infect her youngest child. She'd kept them apart. Anna's letters to her sister had gone unanswered. Very soon she'd stopped writing. Either Georgia shared their mother's view of her, or the letters were being intercepted. All the same, she thought, looking at the pictures, we could have been friends.

In a corner were more canvases, covered by an old piece of curtain. She went over to them, removed the curtain and turned the first one round. She gasped and leapt back in horror. It was a painting of a Medusa head dripping in snakes. The Medusa held out a knife. She stared out of the canvas with eyes that were deadly. Anna covered her face. She'd recognised those eyes. They were her mother's.

She looked at the painting again. Yes, it was Mother all right. Frantically she searched through the rest of the pictures. They were unlike any of Georgia's she'd ever seen. Half-finished self-portraits. Georgia in a white party dress with short puffed sleeves, her hair tied back in a bow. Little-girl clothes, but her face was lined and tense. She glanced at the date, 1990, the year before her death. Georgia would have been twenty-six. What on earth was she doing wearing clothes like these?

There were more Medusa heads, green and purple and black. Sometimes the face was her mother's, sometimes it was Georgia's. Mother and daughter had become interchangeable.

Anna sat back on her heels. They were crazy pictures – done, it was easy to see, in tremendous haste. The paintings of her sister's madness. She looked at the pictures and thought, this is the real Georgia, my sister, violent, subversive and terribly angry. And this is the mother of her inner myth. We share the same mother. I haven't been wrong all these years. There's something in Mother that turns us against her. Georgia heard her voice in her head too. That's why she killed herself. That's what madness means – hearing voices. She clasped her hands together. I need Philip. Only he understands about the voices. She'd get into her car and drive over to see him. Then she remembered he was visiting his mother in hospital and she didn't know how to get in touch with him.

She replaced the canvases one by one, turning their faces to the wall. On the back of one of them Georgia had scribbled, *"Mother hates me," "Mother hates me,"* over and over again. She had been mad – Anna felt she'd never really believed it till now. No wonder her mother didn't want these pictures exhibited. They were crazy pictures. She covered them up with the curtain again and crept back downstairs. She didn't want to meet anyone. Had Mother, knowing what was up there, known how she would feel? Anna sighed. Say what you like, they were emotional survivors, her mother and herself, tough as old boots. Georgia wasn't. She'd been gentle, like Nana. Crazy, like Nana.

She opened and closed the front door softly behind her. She had only one thought. To get back to her children as quickly as possible.

"What on earth's the matter?" asked Penelope, the moment she walked through the door.

"Those paintings of Georgia's. They were like a mad woman's. Shocking. I can't explain."

"Sit down. I'll get you a cup of tea."

Anna sat down on the carpet beside Sam. He was absorbed

in constructing a tower out of Duplo. She felt grateful that Penelope wasn't the sort of person who asked intrusive questions. There was no one she wanted to talk to about this, except Philip.

Penelope came back with the tea. The two women sat and watched Sam build up his tower.

"He's getting good at that," remarked Anna proudly.

"Yes, he is." Penelope hesitated, then said, rather quickly, "Don't you think, love, he'd benefit from being with children of his own age a bit more? I know he's got Toby, but Toby's too young yet to be a very challenging playmate."

Something closed up in Anna's heart. Why were people always trying to separate her from her children? They were all she had left. All that was safe and secure in the world. Without them, she'd be lost.

"What are you suggesting?" she asked dully.

"There must be a playgroup near you. Or what about nursery school for a couple of mornings a week?"

"He's too young. He'd be lost. He can't speak."

"He might learn to speak. Children learn more from their peers than from adults."

"He won't join in with other children. We left gym club because of that. I can't put him through it again. It just makes him miserable." And me.

Penelope smiled. "All right, Anna, love. I won't go on. You're his mother. You know what's best for him."

Anna gazed across at her son lost in the small world he was creating with his hands. Was it true she knew what was best for him? Or was she simply repeating old patterns by keeping him tied so closely to her? Would he grow up to hate her?

From upstairs came the sound of Toby crying.

"I'll go." She leapt to her feet, glad of something practical to do.

She picked her younger son out of the cot – Richard's old cot – and hugged him close. "My baby." His damp sweaty hair, matted from sleep, smelled warm and comforting, like a dog's. She burrowed her face into his body, smelling his warm baby smells. His innocent childhood world. It would save her from disintegration if anything could.

She waited in all the next morning for him to call, eyeing the phone as if it was her enemy, willing it to ring. It got to twelve and he still hadn't rung. Her hands were damp with fear. She couldn't stand the suspense a moment longer. Swallowing her pride, she dialled his number.

"Anna! Hello."

Was that surprise in his voice?

"You were supposed to ring," she reminded him.

"I hadn't forgotten. Just doing a spot of housework. I've been thinking of you. What we could do to get rid of your voices."

She'd gone back to being his client.

"Philip, what's the matter?"

"Nothing's the matter."

She could make neither head nor tail of him this morning. "Are we going to see each other today? I've booked Donna to come at two."

"I've got this housework to finish and some shopping to do and a client's coming later this afternoon . . . "

"Tomorrow then?"

"I may be going to visit my mother again."

"Philip, have you met someone?"

"What do you mean?"

"Have you met someone new? A new woman. You sound different."

"In what way?"

"Stronger. Not so lonely." Not so much in need of me. Not in need of me at all.

There was a pause. She gripped the receiver till her knuckles went white. Oh God, she'd been right. Oh God, she couldn't bear it.

"You know me so well," he said at last. "How come you know me so well?"

"I c-care about you." Her insides were doing peculiar things.

"All right. I've been holding back on you."

"I knew it!"

"Calm down, Anna. It's only this – I'm going to York for the day tomorrow with Ginny." The words came out in a rush.

"I see."

All of a sudden she felt tremendously dizzy and had to hang on to the edge of the kitchen table. She sat down. It wasn't someone new. It was his wife. Funny how convinced she'd been that it wouldn't be his wife. Funny how she'd trusted him.

"I feel I've let you down."

"No. You haven't."

"You see, I've been lonely."

"I know. I can't give you – "

"And when she spoke on the phone and said she missed me and cried, all my love for her came back."

Love. He's never said he loved me.

"I know. I understand. You don't need me any more."

"I do need you, Anna. I don't trust her. When I'm with her, half the time I feel love, but the other half is distrust. She's got to make me trust her again if anything's going to come of it."

"Meanwhile you'll go shopping with her in York."

She could picture it. The two of them walking round, hand in hand. A striking-looking couple, he so very dark, she with her long legs and long hair. People would stare after them. Together, they'd look in shop windows. Discuss materials, prices, laugh together, drawing on memories of their few weeks of married life.

"Is she moving back in with you?"

"No. I don't trust her."

"Yet."

"Ginny gets through to me. She touches me. I don't know why. I'm sorry, Anna, have I let you down?"

"No."

"Anna, you're crying!"

"No, I'm not."

"Yes, you are. Anna, darling, this may bring us closer together. You know the sex between us hasn't been very good. You've been good in bed but I haven't. This may make us closer."

"How can it? If she moves back, I'll never be able to ring you again."

"We'll find somewhere else to be."

"Will you tell her about me?"

"No. She couldn't cope."

"Why not?" Why shouldn't she know about me? I know about her. Why do I always have to be the strong one? "There's nothing for her to get jealous about, is there? You can tell her I was someone who would have cared for you but you didn't love me like you love her and you didn't find me a sexual turn-on. I should think any wife could live with that, don't you?"

"Anna, I do find you a turn-on. I want to make love to you now. We will make love again, very soon."

Will we? Or will your voice on the phone next time I ring tell me you've gone back, body and soul, to her? She thought of her life, trapped in domesticity. The slow slide into middle age without a man. The end of youth. The end of love.

"Goodbye, Philip."

She put down the phone.

She peeled and boiled potatoes for the children's lunch, got Toby out of his cot, changed him, fed him, all on automatic pilot. Tomorrow he was going to York with Ginny. Today he couldn't see her because later this afternoon a client was turning up. Suddenly something clicked in her brain. She dialled his number again.

"Is Ginny there?"

"Not yet," he replied, giving himself away.

"You're a bastard."

"Why?"

"You're sleeping with Ginny. It's not a client, it's Ginny who's turning up this afternoon. You're getting the house clean for her."

"Anna, darling, she's my wife. She's not coming back for good. This is just finishing off something. It's you I want. I want you to be my lover for the rest of your life. We'll sign a contract."

She laughed harshly.

"Anna, I love you. I'm going to miss you tonight."

She put down the phone. He'd said it finally. The word love. As he was about to sleep with his wife. She rested her head in her hands. But all his love, all his capacity for tenderness, would be focused on somebody else tonight.

The doorbell rang. It was Donna. Now that she wouldn't be

seeing Philip, Anna wondered whether to send her away again.
No. She had to get out of the house for an hour. Walk
somewhere, anywhere. Get away from that picture of Philip
making love to his wife.

"They've had lunch and Toby's had a sleep. I won't be long,"
she said wearily.

Donna glanced at her. "Are you all right?"

"Fine."

She walked down the narrow cobbled street and turned
right, towards the Marina where they'd walked together three
nights ago. His wife. It had always been his wife. Right from the
start she'd only been a stop-gap. A shoulder to cry on while he
waited for his wife to come back to him. Ginny held all the
cards, always had. She'd been there from the beginning,
controlling their relationship. A word from her and he'd drop
everything and rush back to her.

Anna leaned against a railing looking out over the Humber
Estuary and imagined all the different ways of beating him up.
Why shouldn't she drive round to his house now and make a
scene? Walk in through the door and slap him in the face?
Punch him in the stomach? Grind her heels in his groin?

Her anger ebbed away. She'd thought Philip was going to be
her happiness. He'd made her feel safe. And all the time she'd
been walking on the edge of a precipice and hadn't known it.
Well it was over. There'd be no more lying. No more hurried
phone calls. No more tears. No more love.

The sex between them hadn't been good, he'd said. Her
mouth twisted in pain. She'd thought it had been marvellous.
Was Ginny better in bed then? Or was it simply that they'd
known each other longer? He says it will be the same, but it
won't. There won't be room for me any more in his life. No
more going to his little bungalow in the woods. No more safety.
No more language of love. These feelings were terrible and
she'd felt them all before, years ago. But when?

She became aware of someone watching her. She turned
round. McMahon was seated on a bench, holding a paintbrush
in his hand. In front of him stood an easel with a painting on it.

"Are you all right?"

229

"Fine."

"You don't look all right."

Her mouth smiled at him. "You're painting," she said, stating the obvious. The obvious was about all she felt up to at the moment.

"Just finished," he replied, whipping the painting away before she had time to look at it. He shut his paintbox, folded his easel and stood up. "I deserve a coffee. What about you?"

"OK."

Anything to take her mind off Philip.

They walked across the road to the floating shopping centre. McMahon grimaced.

"Masturbatory music."

"I beg your pardon?"

"Masturbatory music. Masturbates the emotions, arouses them for no purpose and always ends in disappointment. And lethargy." He turned to her. "Or perhaps I'm not doing it right?"

"Do we have to have this conversation?"

He grinned. "Let's go to Herbie's. It's a recent discovery of mine."

They walked through the streets in silence.

"You're looking banjaxed."

"It's the children. Toby's teething." And my lover's gone back to his wife. She felt her eyes fill with tears. "What about you?" she said hastily. "Still missing Ireland?"

"Yes."

"But after all what's the difference between the two countries? We speak the same language."

"No." He stared into a shop window for a moment. "We use the same words but they mean different things over there." He walked on. "Ireland's a perfume, a scent. The air smells different over there."

"You're a romantic, McMahon."

He gazed at her. "Have you only just realised it?"

They went into Herbie's café, got their coffees and sat down. He looked around. "Nice place. Crap pictures."

She glanced at the pale coloured pictures on the walls. "Did you ever go to see my sister's painting in the Ferens?"

"I did and I was jealous. A very talented artist. Tragedy she died so young."

She wondered what he'd say if he saw the Medusa pictures. "What's your favourite kind of art, Detective Superintendent?"

"Irish, of course."

"I didn't know there was any."

McMahon looked thundery. "You'll have heard of Yeats?"

"Of course I've heard of him." She paused. "I didn't know he painted as well."

McMahon raised his eyebrows to the ceiling. "You're thinking of WB. I'm talking about JB, his brother. Not to be confused with JB his father, the portrait painter."

"This is sounding more Irish by the minute."

He stirred his coffee with more vigour than was strictly necessary. He didn't look pleased. "I never know what people mean when they say that."

"It's just a thing one says, isn't it?"

"No."

"What does it mean? Crazy? Unnecessarily complicated?"

"A country which has a Civil Service like the English Civil Service is in no position to call another country crazy. Or complicated."

"Point taken." She smiled. "So what do you like about Yeats?"

"His sea paintings. The Dublin dockyards. The quays of Sligo and Galway."

"So you're going to paint the quays and docklands of Hull?"

"That's the idea. A very second rate imitator. What do you do in your spare time?"

"I don't have any."

"That's a pity. Couldn't you make more use of that girl – what's-her-name?"

"Donna? I don't want to. I want to keep my children with me."

She bent low over her coffee. He's gone. He's with his wife.

"You miss your husband?" he said softly.

She nodded, hypocrite that she was! Yet it was true in a way. She did miss Richard. He'd have comforted her now. Given her good advice. He'd been her best friend. She lifted her head.

"Tell me, Detective Superintendent, what do you think love is?"

"Love?" He looked into his coffee, as though the answer might be found there. "Tenderness. Compassion. Respect for one another's bodies. Forgiveness. Companionship. Sorry about the clichés. No one can ever say anything new about love." He looked across at her. She'd never noticed before that his eyes were grey. "I make it sound terribly tame, don't I? Ten years ago, five years ago, even, I'd have gone on about passion. But now I've come to believe that passion is always simply sexual passion and it always dies. I didn't like what I . . . " He was silent for a moment. "Passion's the reason I left Mayo. Followed a girl to Belfast and got a job there."

"What happened?"

"It didn't last."

"You've never been married then?"

"No. For a lot of the time I don't seem to mind. I have my work, my painting. We have grand times whenever I get back to Mayo. The oul' fella's still alive, God be praised. I have sisters and a brother, nephews and nieces. All the family I need." He paused. "And yet, I'd be sorry to miss out on the adventure of love. I've made it sound tame, but it isn't. It can take a whole lifetime to learn to love one person well, with enough distance and enough humility."

"I think you make too little of passion," she objected.

"Do I? I wonder. In passion you never get to know the other person. Not really. It's only sex and emotion. You're blinded."

He's wrong, she thought, I know Philip. Deep down, I've always known he'd go back to his wife.

"Why?" His eyes rested on her. "Was passion what you had with your husband?"

"No. It was more like you described. Friendship."

"You had the best then. No wonder you miss him."

Philip wouldn't call it the best. He believes in passion. He feels passionate about Ginny. She stood up.

"I've got to go. The children."

"Dotes, the pair of them."

She looked at him. "They're all I have."

CHAPTER ELEVEN

SHE WAS SHOWN INTO THE BALLROOM by Bates. The first thing she noticed was the huge crowd. She hadn't realised her brother knew so many people. Or were they Angela's friends? Shy little Angela? Unlikely.

She hovered by the drinks table, glass of wine in hand, wondering how best to make the plunge.

"Hello, Anna, fancy seeing you here!"

She turned round. It was Julia, managing to look both sexy and respectable in a short black evening dress. At any rate, she didn't look as if she was the mother of three children under five. In her long skirt and jacket, Anna felt seriously dowdy. Why did Julia always do this to her?

"Hello, Julia. What are you doing here?"

"Frank's been doing business with Brian. What about you?"

"I – I'm a relation. Sort of."

"Relation!" For the first time in their acquaintance, Julia looked impressed. "Gosh! I didn't realise you were so well connected. I've been dying to see inside this house for ages." Her eyes narrowed. "If you've this sort of background, Anna, I can't think why you're so much against private schools for your children."

"I went to one. I know what they're like." She was relieved to see Brian and Angela approaching. "Excuse me, Julia."

They stood before her, holding hands. Brian was in evening dress. Angela, tall and slender in a pale pink frock, suddenly looked strangely familiar. She'd lost weight and her hair, which had gone blonde, was cut in a different way, showing off her face instead of hiding it. Being engaged to Brian obviously suited her.

"I suppose I should say congratulations." It was a cliché, but then so was being engaged. "Loads of people. Who are they all?"

"Mainly business," admitted Brian. "No point giving a party if it doesn't also oil the works."

Anna blinked. He was becoming a carbon copy of their father.

"Is Mother here?"

"No. She moved down to the lodge this morning.

"There're plenty of people you know, Anna," put in Angela. "There's a whole crowd from the women's group."

Anna glanced over to where Angela was pointing and saw Lottie, Clara, Jennifer and Tessa standing together in a corner. Carol was with them.

"Shall we go over?"

"Um. I'm not sure."

"Come on, Anna, don't be silly. You have to meet Carol some time. I'll take you over. They're quite understanding, you know. I myself took the plunge and patched things up with them last week."

Angela took her by the arm and guided her decisively through the crowds. She certainly seemed to have blossomed into a different person since being with Brian.

"Here's Anna," she announced and then went off, making Anna feel like a parcel which had been dumped unceremoniously on somebody's doorstep.

"Odd place to meet, isn't it?" said Lottie. "As I said to Clara as we were setting out, celebrating heterosexual union isn't quite our style. Still, olive branches and all that."

"Besides," added Clara. "I wanted to see inside the house."

Carol said. "Can I have a word?"

Anna jumped and stepped backwards. This was what she'd been dreading.

"I've been feeling awfully guilty about you, Anna," Carol went on.

"Guilty? Why?"

"We must have put you through hell for a while. I didn't

think about it at the time, I was so caught up with Kylie. But I realise it now. I'm sorry."

"Oh, Carol." Anna felt like hugging her. "I'm just so relieved it all got sorted out. How's Kylie?"

"All right, I think. Of course you can never really tell what's going on in a child's mind but she's come out of her shell and she's playing normally again with other children. My sister's still devastated. Well, so am I. This is the first time I've been out since it happened. We can't understand how neither of us realised what kind of man he was. We should have seen."

"Abusers come in all shapes and sizes, classes and ages, Carol," Jennifer put in. "It's not written across their foreheads, you know."

"Still . . . "

"Virginia, my team leader, says you were marvellous to spot it so soon, Carol," said Tessa. "She regards the case as a major *coup* for our department."

Anna thought she didn't much like the sound of Virginia.

"You must come to our next meeting," Tessa added, turning to Anna. "Virginia's going to be there again. I'll introduce you to her this time. She's wonderful."

Anna mumbled something non-committal. "How's the group going?" she asked.

"Worse and worse." Lottie frowned. "Gloria's people seem intent on taking it over and making it so radical they'll alienate the ordinary women of Hull. And it was for them it was started in the first place."

"Oh, they're not so bad," said Tessa.

There was a silence. Anna became aware of a division in the group. Tessa had aligned herself with Gloria's lot. She wondered why.

Clara changed the subject. "Doesn't Angela look smashing? She's really leading the life of a lady these days."

"Oh yeah." Carol sniffed. "She's modelling herself on Princess Di."

So that's it, thought Anna. No wonder she looks familiar.

Carol raised her eyebrows. "She goes to exercise classes

twice a week. She's joined a tennis club and has fortnightly colonic irrigation sessions. Getting engaged to your brother, Anna, has gone right to her head. I can't think how you turned out so normal. So far this evening, I've met her chiropractor, her homeopathist, her astrologer and her therapist. She says her acupuncturist is somewhere about, too."

Anna felt a hand on her shoulder. She turned round. It was Adam. "Hello!" Hastily, she led him away, out of earshot of the group.

"How are you?"

"All right."

She looked at him.

He smiled. "Really. I'm all right. Two weeks on the Bishop's health farm has straightened me out."

"Where's Sue?"

"At home. In bed. Tired out with the baby coming. The doctor's told her to rest in the evenings from now on. I wouldn't have come tonight but your brother was insistent. He's asked me to marry them. An act of loyalty for which I'm very grateful. I'm not much in demand at the moment, as you may imagine. So I felt I had to look in."

"Adam, I am sorry about what happened. Are they going to prosecute?"

"They may not. The Bishop's arguing my case behind the scenes. He wanted to move me to a quiet rural parish, but I think I've persuaded him to let me stay. There's so much to be done where I am."

"Take care, Adam." She reached up and kissed his cheek.

"Bless you, Anna. I've been missing you. Come to church again soon." He hurried off.

Angela came up to her again. "Come on, Anna, you can't spend all evening talking to people you know. Come and meet some new people." She led her across the room. "This is Patricia – she gives me acupuncture once a week for my migraine. This is Steven, my homeopathist. He cured my insomnia. And this is Philip, my therapist."

Anna shut her eyes. She didn't dare look. Would Ginny be

hanging onto his arm? She opened her eyes. She wasn't. But Philip was looking nervous. As well he might, she thought, with a sudden rush of anger.

"What did you say you did? I didn't quite catch."

"I'm a therapist," he replied, uncertainly.

"A therapist! How interesting! You must meet all sorts in your line of business."

"Y – yes."

His eyes held a warning. Ginny must be somewhere around, then. Anger went on welling up in her.

"Real nutters," she persisted, waving her empty glass about.

"Philip doesn't like to think of them as that," put in Angela. "Is your glass empty, Anna? Let me go and fill it for you."

"I bet your clients tell you all sorts of interesting things though, don't they?" She ploughed recklessly on. She was enjoying herself. "What's the most shocking thing you've ever been told?"

Out of the corner of her eye, she saw the acupuncturist and the homeopathist beat a tactical retreat.

"What are you trying to do? Ruin my practice?" he muttered.

"I'd love to."

"Don't you think you've had enough?" he added, as Angela popped a wine glass into Anna's hand, murmured, "So glad you two are getting on," and dashed off.

"Not nearly enough." She downed half a glass. "Where's your fucking wife?" she hissed.

"My fucking wife isn't here," he hissed back. "She's fucked off back to fucking Grimsby."

"I thought she'd moved in with you?"

"Not yet she hasn't. I don't trust her."

She put down her glass and pressed her fingers to her temples. She was on a roller-coaster with this man. He was leading her a dance. She gazed at him for a moment, seeing a door open onto emptiness, blackened walls, windows gaping to the cold sky. A burnt-out house. Then she blinked and the vision disappeared.

"You bastard!" she whispered. "I spent two sleepless nights because of you."

"Anna, listen. I married the woman. I've never been married before. It meant a lot to me, giving up my freedom. I thought it was going to be for life. I thought we were going to have children and grow old together. It takes a while to get these things out of your system."

"I know."

He looked gorgeous, damn him, in his black silk shirt and black trousers. It wasn't fair. He smelled of after-shave. Had he come out looking for a woman?

"I've missed you, Anna. All the time I was with Ginny, it was you I was thinking of. I feel very close to you, Anna. You're my double, my soul mate."

I know, I know. When I look into your eyes which are the same colour as mine, I get the feeling I'm seeing myself. You're so familiar to me. You were familiar from the first moment I saw you.

"It's uncanny, Anna. I feel if I were to die and you were still alive, I'd go on living in you."

Don't do this to me, not here, not now. Don't awaken all those feelings again. All those childish feelings.

"What are you doing here, anyway?"

"Angela was a client of mine. I helped her through her abortion. She was really fucked up."

"Did you sleep with her?"

His eyes widened. "Of course not. What do you take me for? I don't sleep with clients."

"You slept with me."

"That was different. Look, I came here tonight for business. I thought I might get some new clients. I was about to go. Then you turned up."

She glanced around. "We can't talk about this, Philip. Not here. Not now. It's too public. There are too many people here who know me."

"All right, but before I go, look at me, Anna. Do you want me to make love to you?"

"You made love to your wife," she muttered.

"It wasn't very good."

"I dreamt of beating you up."

"Then you do care."

She hung her head.

"I want to be inside you now, Anna. Do you want me inside you?"

"Yes." She bit her lip.

"That's all I need to know. I'll phone you tomorrow. Good night, sweet Anna."

She watched as he went out of the door. Her heart leapt with longing for him. Then she turned round and saw McMahon staring at her from across the other side of the room. Damnation! What was he doing here? He hadn't suddenly become a friend of the family, had he? She turned her back on him and found Tessa and Angela bearing down on her from opposite directions.

Tessa reached her first. "I saw you talking to Philip. Steer clear of that man, Anna. He's bad news."

"How do you . . . ?"

"Anna, can you come and help in the kitchen? I'm in a bit of a mess and Bates says he won't have anyone else in but you."

"Of course." She set down her glass and followed Angela out of the room.

In the kitchen she spent the next quarter of an hour dealing with sausage rolls and cocktail sticks. Angela had underestimated the amount of food that would be needed. Perhaps she hadn't entirely got to grips with her role yet.

To think Mother did this sort of thing twice a month for years, Anna thought, pressing a stuffed olive onto a stick. After a while, there was a lull in the proceedings. She leant back against the Aga, sipping the wine Bates had filled for her from a special bottle. From the taste of it, it must be very special indeed. Brian would be furious. She gazed around the kitchen. It had hardly changed since she'd last been in it. The same yellow tiles on the floor. The same dark green cupboards. The same row of knives and ladles and whisks hanging above the Aga.

"Quite like old times, Miss Anna. Seeing you here."

"Is it Bates? I was trying to remember the last time I was at a party here."

He rubbed his chin. "I reckon it would have been back in 1976, the year you left home. Your father gave that big party to celebrate his twenty years in business."

"No, Bates. I never went to that. I left home in 1975."

"Did you, Miss Anna? I could have sworn it was 1976. Eh, I'm getting real bad these days at remembering dates. Good job I've your mother to set me right. Nothing wrong with *her* memory."

Anna stared at him, wondering why his words had suddenly sent shivers down her spine. What did it matter that Bates's memory wasn't as good as it had been? It did matter, though. She couldn't lay her finger on why. She arranged a few more sandwiches on a plate.

"Crisis over." Angela came through the swing doors carrying an empty tray in her hands. "Thanks for the help, Anna. I came quite unstuck for a moment." She touched her arm. "Anna, I wanted to say, this is your home as well, you know. Your mother didn't want to stay with us. I can understand that." A shadow passed over her face. "But I want you to feel you can come here whenever you like. Bring the children."

"Thanks, Angela. I don't have altogether happy memories of this place but I might bring the children here. In time."

"Lovely lass, isn't she?" said Bates, watching Angela go out of the room. "Your father would have been proud to have had her as his daughter-in-law." She winced. "She's going to bring some life back into the old place. It needs it."

God knew, it did.

Bates's special wine must have been stronger than she'd realised for when she went back into the ballroom, the noise and the smoke made her feel quite dizzy. She sat down on a chair and listened to the small jazz band playing at the far end of the room.

"Hello there."

"What are you doing here?"

"I was asked."

McMahon looked up at the ceiling. The plasterwork spread out into white fans in the four corners of the room. In the centre was an enormous, very delicate, Tudor rose.

"Magnificent room."

"When we moved in it was in ruins. My father wanted to use it as his office but my mother persuaded him to restore it to a ballroom."

"Quite right. It's what it's made for. Who's your friend?"

"I beg your pardon?" She could hardly believe her ears.

"Haven't I seen you with him before?"

The cheek of it!

"I thought, Detective Superintendent, the case was closed. Why are you still spying on me?"

"Not spying on you. I suppose I can't help noticing things. It's part of my job. Difficult to switch off."

"Doesn't painting help you relax?"

"Not really. You need to notice things for that too. Though in a different way."

She looked at him. "Come on," she said, "I have something to show you."

She led the way into the main hall and up the curving staircase. (Why was she doing this? Was she drunker than she'd thought?) Halfway up, McMahon stopped to examine a couple of portraits hanging on the wall.

"Come on." She tugged at his arm. "Those are a job-lot my father picked up at an auction. He had no ancestors so he borrowed other people's. I've got something better to show you."

She led him down the corridor, through the small door in the wall and up to the second floor.

"Careful on the stairs."

Arriving at the top, she felt along a ledge and found a torch. She switched it on and undid the door.

"You were asking about my sister's paintings, Detective Superintendent. Come and see them."

She swung the torch round till it lit on the canvases stacked in the corner. The room seemed in rather a mess. Someone had been up since she'd last been here. Mother, presumably, to get suitcases for the move to the lodge. Papers were scattered around the floor. A trunk stood open. She handed McMahon the torch. "Here. Go and look at them."

She stood watching as he crouched down on his heels and ran his torch carefully over the pictures.

"These are good," he murmured. "They ought to be put in an exhibition."

"I know. But what about these?" She whipped off the curtain and showed him the portraits.

He stepped back, visibly shocked. "They're horrible. Ghastly."

"Yes." She suddenly found herself incredibly relieved that he thought so too. She hadn't been exaggerating things then. They were horrible. "She was mad."

He shook his head. "Your poor mother, seeing these pictures."

"She was used to living with madness. My grandmother was mad too."

He glanced at her. "Madness isn't hereditary."

"Isn't it?"

"No."

"That's not what I've read. Georgia stabbed herself. Like Nana. They found her wrapped up in an old coat of Nana's. I think she was trying to get back to her." To the warmth and comfort of Nana.

"You shouldn't dwell on these things, Anna. It isn't healthy, especially for a woman living on her own." Gently he replaced the curtain. "She was unbalanced, your sister. You can see it in the brushstrokes. But you're not. You're one of the most stable people I've ever met."

"How do you know? How can you tell what goes on in another person's mind?"

"I can tell. In my job . . . " He stood gazing at her, head on one side. "Is he good for you, Anna?"

"Who?"

"This friend of yours – the one I've seen you with twice now."

"Oh, him." She tossed her head. "I hardly know him. He's Angela's therapist."

"I suppose you're going to tell me next that it's none of my business? OK." He sighed. "McMahon, you're making a right eejit of yourself." He walked out of the room.

As she turned to follow him something rustled by her foot. She bent down to look. A bundle of letters. Her mother must have intended taking them with her to the lodge. She shone her torch on the top one and recognised Nana's small neat print. She stuffed the bundle into her pocket and caught up with McMahon at the top of the stairs.

At five the next morning she woke in a cold sweat. She saw herself standing again in the kitchen, saw the array of knives above the Aga, heard Bates say again, "I've no memory any more for dates. It's a good thing there's your mother to put me right."

She imagined the scene. Her mother saying, "Oh no, Bates. You've got it quite wrong. It was the night of the 16th that you heard a noise and came up to check on me." What did this do to her mother's alibi?

All those stabbings – Nana, Georgia, Father. No, it was too horrible to contemplate. And anyway, Eric Finch had confessed. Or if not confessed, at least he'd been charged and was being held in prison awaiting trial. It was all quite clear. Nana and Georgia had taken their lives whilst the balance of their minds were disturbed, and Father had been murdered by Finch out of revenge.

The letters. The letters might provide a clue. She pushed back the duvet, switched on the light and fumbled for her dressing-gown. She found the bundle of letters still stuffed into the pocket of her jacket and tiptoed downstairs to the kitchen. She laid the letters down on the table and made herself a cup of herbal tea. Then she took two Anadin. All that wine had given her a headache.

She picked up the first letter. It was from Nana to her father.

Summerhouse Farm
Rudston
20th of May, 1955

Dear George,

I am afraid you will think I have been a long time
answering your letter, but it's such a very serious matter that
I felt I must have a little time to think about it. Also, I have
been ill and today is the first day I have felt strong enough
to pick up my pen and write to you.

I expect dear Mabel has told you about my little
illnesses. They're nothing to be alarmed about, but if you
are to become a member of our family it's as well that we
start straightaway by being honest with one another. Dear
Mabel is such a comfort to me at these times and I know
she will want to go on being so, after she is married.

I see that in a roundabout way I have already told you of
my decision. All I want in life, George, now that Arthur is
dead, is my daughter's happiness. If you make Mabel happy,
then I will be happy too. I would have preferred you to
delay the wedding for one year until Mabel finished her
teacher training course but I understand your impatience to
be married and since your parents are agreeable, I'll not be
the one to stand in your way.

The best I have to offer you both is that you may be as
happy in your love for one another as Arthur and I were in
ours. More than this I cannot say,

Yours sincerely,
Muriel Holden.

Anna blinked back the tears. It was a stiff old-fashioned letter.
Nana had never been a great letter writer. But it was her voice
all right. Anna heard it coming down the years to her.

The next letter was from her father.

Cottingham Rd
Hull
May 21 '55

Dear Mrs Holden,

Thank you so much for your kind letter. I feel in a sort
of a panic as I write this. I'm starting a new chapter in my
life, the chapter with Stella – I hope you don't mind me
calling her that to you? It's the name I've chosen for her. Oh,
Mrs Holden, in entrusting your daughter to me, you've made
me so happy. I hope I will be able to live up to your trust
and give Stella the happiness you'd wish for your only child.
Best wishes,
George Mitchell.
PS I hope you're now quite recovered from your illness.

The charm was there. But how young he sounded. Anna laid
the letter aside. Surely Nana must have felt nervous, entrusting
her daughter to such a callow young man?

The next letter was dated January 1965, three months after
Georgia's birth.

Norwood
Beverley
January 6 '65

Dear Mrs Holden,

I'm not going to attempt to justify myself. There are two
sides to every story and surely "desertion" is rather a strong
word? Stella has the house and an income of her own.

I'm sorry about the baby, but it's hardly my fault if she
wakes up every two hours. Stella will cope. She always has.

I remain your affectionate son-in-law,
George.

Anna stared at this for several minutes. Across the bottom
someone (Nana?) had scrawled *"My poor, poor baby."* Keeping
the letter in her hand, she picked up her father's first letter again

and laid them side by side on the table. How to get from one to the other in the space of ten years? She must have been about seven at the time. She remembered nothing of this. What had been going on? Why had her father moved out?

The next letter from George was dated 1955.

Cottingham Rd
Hull
May 22 '55

My darling,

It's all out in the open now. Our families both know. Oh my love, my Stella, I hope you're as happy as you've made me. How did I live before we met? Now that your mother's better, hurry back from Rudston. I can't wait to see you.

All my love,
George.

Pinned to it – someone (her mother?) must have arranged these letters – was one dated April 1965.

Norwood
Beverley
April 4 '65

Dear Stella,

When I mentioned about the furniture, I didn't of course mean that I expected to take all of it. What I meant was, is there anything you can spare? The furniture from the guest room, for instance? I know your mother is staying with you at present, but there is presumably nothing permanent in this arrangement?

I hope you and the children are keeping well. I have a cold. I think it's because I don't have enough bedding. I really don't think there's any point in us meeting till we are both calmer,

George.

Next was a fragment from a letter dated 1956. It had been torn off and stuck to a letter from 1965. They were both from George to Stella.

The first quoted part of the marriage service. *"It was ordained for the mutual society, help and comfort, that the one ought to have of the other."* George had written, "This is what we will have, my darling."

The one from 1965 said, "Nothing can be legislated for. Any sort of demand on feelings is impossible. One can't prevent these things, they just happen. The heart is very mysterious."

"Rubbish!" muttered Anna and poured herself another herbal tea. Then she thought, that's the kind of thing Philip would say. But when he says it, I believe it.

South Street
Cottingham
April 12 1965

Dearest George,

I do not know, because you seem unable to tell me, what it was made you decide married life was no longer for you. I can't believe it's simply Janice. She's only the catalyst. Somewhere, deep down and very early on, you must have found something deeply unsatisfactory in our marriage. I keep going over and over in my mind what it could be. What did I do wrong? Could I have done things differently? Was I too taken up with the children? With Mother? (She's a little better by the way. She was able to get dressed and come downstairs today). The trouble is I'm so run off my feet with looking after the children I hardly have time to sit down and think. That's the problem. I'm just not thinking clearly. Please write and explain things to me in a way I will understand, my love. I can't bear this silence between us. You act as if talking would tear you to bits. I'm not your enemy, George. I could never be your enemy. Let's not act as if we were strangers,

All my love,
Stella.

South Street
Cottingham
April 20 1965

My Dear George,

It's no use you telling me to pull myself together. You might as well tell a paralytic to take up his bed and walk. Of course someone once did. However, although I love you with all my heart, darling, I know you aren't God. You cannot put me together again in a flash. You could, though, make a start by explaining to me just what is going on. Forgive me. I don't mean to sound desperate. It's just that I'm so tired, what with looking after Mother and getting up four or five times in the night to feed Georgia. Oh, my dear, you seem like part of myself that I've left somewhere.

All my love,
Stella.

Norwood
Beverley
May 3 '65

Dear Stella,

Your last letters were rather alarming. I don't think there's any point in us meeting until we are both able to take a more detached view of things. Perhaps it would help if you got a job? Some outside occupation might stop you brooding so much. What a pity you never finished that teaching course.

Tom will call round to collect the bed, desk and other furniture from the guest room, as arranged. If there are any other matters outstanding, please let me know.

George.

Anna rustled the letter irritably. Here was a woman writing for her life and he kept on about the furniture. She hardly recognised her mother in these hurting vulnerable letters.

248

Norwood
Beverley
July 18 '65

Dear Stella,

I suppose it *was* necessary to redecorate the living-room? The bill seems very large. Next time you're planning on having work done in the house, send me the estimate first. You did get an estimate, did you? It might stop these fellows taking you for a ride if they knew there was a man on the scene.

Yes, we'd better meet to discuss the arrangements about Anna's school. Is it really necessary to send her to a private school? And such an expensive one? I'll meet you in the cemetery at two. I presume your mother can look after the kids?

George.

Anna pored over this letter with something like glee. Mother was beginning to get her own back. Spending his money like water. Good for her. It was the first time in her life she'd consciously sided with her mother against her father.

There was one more letter.

Norwood
Beverley
October 10 '65

My dear Stella,

I was sorry to hear that your mother has been taken ill again. No, I'm certain she would never take her own life. All the same, you were right to do as the doctor said and hide her pills.

Coincidentally, *my* mother has just fallen ill – a heart attack. Very mild, but a nuisance all the same. Janice is away on a course at the moment, so she's no help. Anyway she tends to be unsympathetic as far as illness is concerned. I expect it's because she's so young.

You can imagine what hell it is for me, dashing into work each morning the minute the nurse arrives, dashing back in the evening to take over. There is, unfortunately, a two-hour gap between the departure of the day-nurse and the arrival of the night-nurse. It seems these things can't be synchronised. I'm worn out.

How marvellous it would be to have someone to oversee the smooth running of the household. What a weight off my mind that would be!

Dear Stella, look after yourself and don't brood too much over your mother. I'm sure you've done all you can and from what you say she's well on the road to recovery again,

Love,

George.

Attached was the rough draft of a telegram. *"Arriving tomorrow. 6 p.m. train from Hull. Stella.'"*

Anna laid down the letters. She'd got him back. For a while. But it was to go on and on. Janice was only the first. How had her mother borne it all those years? Why had she borne it?

With the letters was a black notebook. On the flyleaf was scribbled the date 1965. She flicked through it. Her mother's handwriting. So she'd kept a diary of that terrible time. From upstairs came the sound of Toby crying. Wearily, Anna pushed the notebook aside and stood up. She felt, for the first time in her life, her mother's daughter.

At ten the next morning he phoned.

"Are you going to come round?" His voice was heavy with unshed tears.

"What's the matter? What's happened?"

"Nothing. I need to know you care for me, that's all. I feel so empty." He was crying now. "She killed all my babies. I have no future."

"I care. Of course I care for you. Don't cry now. Don't cry on the phone when I can't be with you and hold you."

"It helps to cry. I need you, Anna. You're my lifeline. Without you, I'd go under."

250

"I'll come round this afternoon."

She put down the phone. McMahon was wrong. Passion was everything in life. Everything. It was worth risking everything for. No wonder her mother had stayed with her father all those years. She gazed at the sunlight dancing in the courtyard below.

"Shall we go out for a walk, boys?"

In the park they met Julia and the twins.

"They've just broken up from school. That's another advantage of going private. The holidays are longer. They've made such progress this term. Julian can talk about relativity. And Dorian can say hippopotamus. Say hippopotamus, Dorian."

Behind his round blue-framed glasses, Dorian looked earnestly up at his mother. "Who to?"

Julia flushed slightly. "Never mind, Dorian. Go and play on the swings."

Anna noticed Sam gaze longingly after them.

"Do you want to go too?"

He nodded.

She took him by the hand and led him over to where the twins were sitting on the roundabout.

"Can Sam play with you?"

Julian and Dorian looked at each other, then nodded. They made room for him on the roundabout. Sam hesitated, glanced at his mother, saw she was smiling at him and climbed on.

While she chatted to Julia, Anna kept her eye on Sam. He was playing quite well with the twins. More children joined them. It didn't seem to matter that Sam couldn't speak. He was doing his communicating through gestures, copying the actions of the other children.

When it was time to go, he dragged his heels and kept looking back over his shoulder at the other children till they were out of sight.

"Did you enjoy that, Sam?"

He nodded. "Sam like it," he said, very distinctly.

Penelope had been right then. Playing with other children took him out of himself. He might forget about the empty space where his father had been. He might even start to speak again. She must learn to let him go. It was his right.

He opened the door. He was unshaven and there were tears in his eyes.

She touched his cheek. "Oh, Philip," she said.

He pulled her inside and kissed her, soft tender kisses all over her neck and face. "Baby, I need you. Do you need me, Anna?"

"Yes." She buried her face in his chest. "I don't want anyone else to have your body or anyone else to be in your thoughts. I want you to love me. Only me."

"I do love you, Anna."

She lifted her head. "What happened with Ginny?" She felt confident enough, now, to ask.

He groaned. "We had a row."

"Tell me about it."

"Not here." He lifted her up and carried her into his bedroom. They lay down on the bed. He lay on his back looking up at the ceiling. "I bought her this dress."

Anna felt a stab of envy.

"I like buying her clothes. She has such a beautiful body. It was red silk. Absolutely gorgeous. Anyway, then we had a row. I asked her to cook dinner. I said if she wanted to move back that was one of the things she'd have to do more of. To prove she cared. She said she felt trapped. The old excuse. I said what kind of a marriage was it going to be if she wouldn't cook for me or have my children? She went for me then. Punched me in the stomach a couple of times. I pinned her to the floor. And then, I don't know, we ended up having sex. It was good sex. Pretty wild, I guess. Anyway, I got up then and went to the bathroom. When I got back, she'd taken a knife from the kitchen and slashed the dress to shreds. Said she was sick of me controlling her life. Then she buggered off back to Grimsby. She's mad, I tell you, mad."

She thought, I must seem dreadfully tame after Ginny. She touched his forehead. He turned and kissed her on the mouth, biting her lips, her neck, taking her breasts by turn into his mouth.

"That's better, that's my good girl," he murmured. "This is

252

what you want, isn't it? Hide yourself in my arms, my mad girl, show me what you like."

He tore off his shirt and unbuttoned his jeans. She undid her skirt.

"Do you love me, Philip?"

"Let's just fuck."

He rolled over. She was moving on top of him.

"Go, girl, go. Take my cock into you. That's it, that's better." He rolled back on top of her and lifted her legs up so high against his shoulders that she gasped in pain. "Shut up!"

She struggled. "Let me go!"

He grabbed her ankle. "You're not going anywhere, darling. You're staying right here."

He reached into a drawer and took out some cream. He turned her over and then she felt him thrusting into her. She screamed in pain.

"Shut up!"

Blackness swept over her. For a moment she thought she was losing consciousness.

"Lovely, darling. Your lovely arsehole." He slipped out of her and went into the bathroom to clean himself up.

She lay back dazed on the bed. She was hardly aware that he'd come back to bed and was gently touching her clitoris.

"That was great sex, wasn't it, darling? You're mine now, aren't you? My woman. This cunt belongs to me. No one else."

"Yes," she said, feeling his fingers inside her. But as she said it she seemed to see herself step out of bed, walk across the room and out of the door, leaving only a shadow lying on the bed beside him. His cock was inside her. His body was a drug. She couldn't get enough of it. At the same time, her mind was saying, "This has nothing to do with me. This is not what I am." He came inside her.

"Well now, darling." He lay on his side looking at her. "Would you like a bath?"

"Yes."

He ran the water for her and sat on the side gently massaging her shoulders. She closed her eyes. She was coming back to herself, finding the self that had got lost during their love-making. And he was back again – her Philip, the caring gentle Philip.

"Why can't it always be like this?" she asked, meaning, why can't you always be like this?

He handed her a towel. "Didn't you like the sex?"

"I – I'm not sure." She stood up in the bath and wrapped the towel round her.

"You seemed to enjoy it. You had plenty of orgasms."

"That's not the point."

He chuckled. "Isn't it? I thought it was!" He put his arms round her. "Sex is a primitive instinct, my love. It can't be socialised. Man is a primitive beast. He wants to dominate. I know you go to these feminist meetings, like Ginny does, and you both lap it all up. I believe in equality myself. But not in bed. In bed the primitive male instinct comes out. There are, always will be, crucial differences between men and women. Men are physically stronger. They have muscles. Women have subcutaneous fat."

"Thanks." She finished drying herself.

"Men are better at spatial tasks. Women at tasks that involve dexterity. It's well documented." He lifted her out of the bath and planted a row of kisses on her mouth. "I measure women's mouths by the number of kisses I can get across them."

"What's the average?"

"Eight."

"What's mine?"

"Ten," he said very quickly.

She laughed. She wondered whether men's cocks could be measured in the same way. She decided not to mention it. She went into the bedroom and began to dress. He sat on the edge of the bed, watching.

"Shall I show you a photograph of her?"

"Who?"

"Ginny."

"No. Yes. I don't know." She was afraid to see this woman who had such a hold over him. Afraid, yet curious. Curiosity won.

She shut her eyes as he placed the photo in her hands.

254

"Go on! Open your eyes, silly girl!"

She opened them. Her first reaction was one of disappointment. Was this Ginny then? What on earth had he been making all the fuss about? Her second thought was – she'd seen that face somewhere before.

"Well? What do you think?" He stood back, his head on one side.

"She's um," she struggled to find something flattering to say. "She's got nice legs."

She was showing a great deal of them too. She was wearing an extremely skimpy blue dress. Her hair was frizzed out in a perm. Her nose was slightly crooked.

"I thought you said she had long hair?"

"She does, usually. We were experimenting. Do you like the dress? I bought it for her. She never wore short skirts till she met me. Hadn't a clue how to dress. She was very naïve. I really made something of her." He took the photo back and studied it. "Funny, when I first met her, I thought she was bloody ugly. Then, I don't know, she grew on me somehow. She touched me, got through to me, like no one else ever had – till I met you."

"You added that just in time." Anna pulled on her skirt and fastened her watch-strap.

"Where are you going?"

She stared at him. "Back to my children, of course. Where did you think?"

"How come I never get to see your children? Are you hiding something from me? Have you got another man living with you?"

"Don't be silly. I live alone. Come round one evening. See for yourself."

He rubbed his cheeks. "Sorry. Living with Ginny, I've got used to being suspicious." He touched her face. "Give me time, Anna, to get her out of my system."

She kissed his forehead. "We have all the time in the world, my love."

CHAPTER TWELVE

THAT EVENING, AS SHE WAS PUTTING Sam to bed, the phone rang. It was Penelope.

"Anna, you haven't got Beatrice with you, have you?"

"Beatrice! No, of course I haven't."

"She's run away from the holiday camp. I'm frantic about her. The police are combing the area but I suddenly thought she might have come to you. She was always terribly interested in you and the boys."

"Was she?" Anna felt a stab of guilt.

"She felt – feels – she's got no real family. Even at her age she can see that her mother's never going to be there for her. Sorry for bothering you, Anna. It's not your problem. I'll just have to sit it out. She'll probably turn up in the morning."

"I . . . "

But Penelope had rung off.

Anna put down the phone and gazed at Sam. His half-sister. That little bit of Richard, wandering about lonely and confused, lost in some city. How long could a ten-year-old girl survive on her own? Pray God, she hadn't gone down to London. Some man would get hold of her and that would be the end of her.

She suddenly felt terribly guilty. She should have done more for her. She shouldn't have let Penelope shoulder the burden by herself. She should have taken an interest in her, invited her round to play with the boys. If Beatrice was found strangled, dumped naked in some ditch, it would be partly her fault. She'd been so afraid of her, so taken up with Philip.

She finished putting Sam to bed, then dialled Penelope's number.

"You will ring me, won't you, Pen, the minute she turns up?"

"Of course. Don't worry about this, Anna. It's not your problem."

"It's becoming mine."

She put down the receiver, poured herself a glass of wine and prowled restlessly around the kitchen for quarter of an hour. Then she kicked off her shoes and sat down at the table. She reached for her mother's diary and began leafing through it.

"November 6 1964 – George brought his new assistant home for dinner. I think she'll do very well for him. She's young, bright, extremely pretty and seems efficient. Her name is Janice.

December 29 1964 – George was in the strangest mood all day. Wasn't interested in what I was saying and kept gazing over my shoulder. I thought he was coming down with a cold, but it turns out he is in love. He told me this evening. Or rather, he left me a note. I feel quite, quite numb. Dread, like a mist, lies over everything. There will be no one, now, to turn to.

January 2 1965 – The senseless, senseless cruelty of leaving me a note. Why couldn't he have told me to my face? My Anna crept up to me this afternoon and asked when Daddy was coming back. I had to say I didn't know. How could he do this to the children? I feel as if I've stumbled over the edge of a precipice and haven't yet hit the ground."

How well she describes it. Anna twisted the stem of her wine glass. That sense of abandonment.

"January 8 1965 – I remember one thing. About a month after our wedding, George suddenly turned to me and said, 'It used to be just the two of us. Now I get the feeling there's always a third person sitting down at the table with us – our marriage.'" So he must have felt it, even then.

"January 30 – My mind bends on its unhappiness, round and round, like the spirals on those shells Mother and I used to collect on our holidays in Whitby. I was happy then. God! I sound like ninety-nine instead of twenty-nine."

Younger than me, thought Anna.

"February 16 – George was the ground of my being. I didn't know it was possible to feel so much pain.

February 18 – I'm so tired. I look in the mirror and hardly recognise the white-faced old hag who stares back. No wonder he went for someone younger. Cradle snatched, as mother puts it. She's so young it's hardly legal. Probably my lawyer will say it isn't legal. But that's not the point. Lawyers rarely see the point, I find. I don't want to bleed George dry. I don't want to prevent him seeing the children (quite the contrary, I wish he'd take more interest in them). I simply want him back. That's what no one understands. 'How can you?' they say. 'After all he's done.' But I do."

There are men we'd go through fire for. I've forgiven him Ginny. I'll go on forgiving him. I know I will. I know I'll have to. He's got used to sleeping with different women. He's forty-five. He'll not change now.

"March 13 – I can't get over the fact that my body is nothing to him now when once it was so much. Mother ill again.

March 14 – People keep saying, 'Poor Stella.' It makes me want to hit them.

March 27 – After Anna was born he wrote to me 'You're the fixed centre of my life.' He's swopped the richness of our life together for an affair with an immature young girl. The multi-layered text of our marriage for a blank page. Perhaps that's what he wanted, though, to escape from responsibility. A lot of men do. Is it the way we bring them up, I wonder, that makes them think they can get away with behaving so badly? Oh, I suppose I can understand it. When the children all have colds and I've been up half the night with Georgia, I can't help thinking why not leave the three of them out on the grass all night and have done with it? This business of child-rearing is more difficult than they let on."

Anna got up to pour herself another glass of wine. What a help she could have been to me. What a pity.

"April 5 – George sent me another of his business letters. Has Janice made him unkind? Or is this the real George? No. No one thinks of kindness when there's something they must have. Mother better.

April 6 – I suppose Janice thinks, if she thinks at all in that fluffy little head of hers, that I'm a possessive old cow. Stretched old stomach, sagging old breasts, one or two varicose veins. I fit the picture perfectly – deserted wife with three kids. I bet Janice doesn't snore or blow her nose in a vulgar way. No wonder he left me."

Anna drew up another chair and rested her feet on it. I like the writer of this diary. She could have been my friend.

"April 17 – People are strange. Emily wittered on about gardening for almost the entire letter, then right at the end told me not to be bitter. People keep saying this. What can they mean? I'm not bitter. I just want him to come home. Joan wrote that she wasn't surprised, she'd never liked George, then went on to list (for two whole pages) precisely what it was she disliked about him. I tore the letter up. Harold wrote that no two people should be expected to live together for more than three years and that I should take a kindly view of George and his aberration. Quite a good name for Janice, I think. The Aberration. How's your Aberration feeling today, dear? Oh, God, I feel awful!

May 15 – Mother ill again.

259

May 18 – Tom dropped by to pick up the furniture. He seemed frightfully interested in the situation and kept me chatting for over an hour, though I had Mother to see to. How boring he is! I'm beginning to wonder whether he spies something in the situation for himself? Naturally, I enjoyed talking about myself for an hour. Who wouldn't?

May 20 – Anna's pining for her father. My precious Anna, she's such a comfort to me these days. Yesterday, she said, 'You look tired, Mummy. Sit down and let me brush your hair.' What would I do without her?

May 26 – Left the children with Mrs Fox while Mother and I went over to Leeds for the day. We browsed round the shops and had lunch in quite a posh Italian restaurant. The little jaunt did both of us good. What would George have said though to me gallivanting about the country like this? I couldn't help feeling a bit guilty at the end of the day. Anna was glad to see me back, bless her.

May 28 – Why should I feel guilty? After all, he's off having his fun. I've made a decision. I will do something every day to please myself. Even if it's only buying a bar of chocolate.

June 10 – I've been going about things in the wrong way. I've been too open in my letters. Pretend a little. What does George want? A comfortable home, freedom to build up his business and have flings on the side. Or aberrations, as Harold would call them. Could I live with this? I don't know. Anna's missing her father. She's begun to have nightmares."

I can remember nothing of this. I've blotted it all out. I owe her such a lot and I thought I owed her nothing.

"June 17 – Have decided to redecorate the living-room (a present to myself).

July 19 – George has agreed to a meeting!

July 21 – We met in the cemetery. My heart lifted to see him standing under the trees (naturally it was raining). He looked thinner. Said he'd been working hard lately. He's bought a new shop. After he'd told me this, he shut up. I was so nervous I jabbered away for the rest of the hour, trying to establish some sort of contact between us. George hardly said two words. One of them was 'fab.' I hadn't heard it before. Perhaps it's one of Janice's? 'You mustn't feel guilty,' I told him. 'I don't,' he replied. Can this be true? I wonder whether Janice is looking after him as well as she might?"

Anna glanced at her watch. Twelve o'clock. Penelope wouldn't phone now. She shivered and pulled her cardigan around herself. It was chilly for July. Outside, it had begun to rain. Where was Beatrice? She flicked through a few more pages.

"September 28 – Mother ill.

October 2 – Mother still ill.

October 11 – What staying with George means – i) never asking him to be with me when he wants to be somewhere else; ii) not promising not to be hurt, but promising to conceal the hurt; iii) remembering that, despite everything, he needs and depends on me; iv) remembering that, because of everything, my George, the tender, kind George of our early happiness, has died. The George I loved was not the same as the real George; v) keep this constantly in mind: it will always be like this, he will always want other women.

October 12 – Can I bear it? I must, for the sake of my love and the sake of my children. No. Georgia is too young and Brian is frightened of him. It's Anna who needs him. My poor Anna loves him so. I will do this for my daughter. I will give her back her father."

The notebook ended. The rest of the pages were blank. Anna lifted her head. Too late. Too late to say don't do it. Too late to say this decision will poison your life; no one, not even your own daughter (especially your own daughter) is worth that amount of sacrifice. She did it for me and it all turned out wrong. Every step I took away from her, every tiny act of independence, must have seemed like a betrayal of all she'd sacrificed for me. And so she built around herself a hard protective shell and pretended to hate me. And now it's become so much part of her personality that she really does hate me. Too late to say, I'll never forgive him. Too late to say, forgive me, Mother, I never knew.

Pasted onto the inside of the back page of the notebook was a letter. Anna unfolded it and read,

Cottingham Rd
Hull
June 26th '54

Dear Miss Holden,
Since we were introduced to each other on the top of that bus, I haven't been able to get you out of my mind. This is just to say – may I come round to tea on Sunday?
George Mitchell.

And so it had all begun. So we all began. She shut up the notebook. It was half past one. Even if Beatrice was found, Penelope would never ring at this hour. She filled a kettle in case Toby woke up wanting a bottle. She thought she heard a sound down in the courtyard. She looked out. She could see nothing. Julia's cat probably. Nevertheless, she went down and put the chain on the door.

She went to bed and fell into a troubled sleep, passed the night in a curious state, half awake, half dozing, her thoughts alternating between the diary and Beatrice.

At nine the next morning, she phoned Penelope. Beatrice had still not been found.

At ten, she had a visitor.

"You again!"

"Work, I'm afraid." He was back in the grey suit. "May I come inside for a moment?"

She opened the door an inch wider. "I thought Finch had been committed for trial?"

"He has. There've been complications. He's out on bail. That's not what I've come about. I'm looking for a girl. A relative of yours."

"Not of mine, Detective Superintendent." She led the way back upstairs to the kitchen. "She was my husband's daughter."

"But you knew her?"

He stepped into the kitchen. Sam abandoned his trains and rushed up to hug his knees. Anna watched in amazement, then frowned. Since when had the two of them become so chummy? This was the last time she'd invite him into her house. From now on, he could conduct his business on the doorstep.

"I don't know her," she replied coldly. "I met her once briefly at my mother-in-law's."

"There's been no sign of her here then?" He glanced around the kitchen, as if he expected to find Beatrice hiding in a cupboard.

"No. She wouldn't come here, Detective Superintendent. Why would she?"

"To see her half-brothers. May I sit down?"

"If you must."

"Thanks. My leg's killing me this morning."

"So's mine." She sat down behind her half drunk coffee. She was blowed if she was going to offer him any. Snooping about like this. "You can be sure, Detective Superintendent, that if that girl came here, I'd let you know rightaway and send her straight back to my mother-in-law. Sam, get down."

Sam was clambering onto McMahon's knee.

"Ah sure, leave him be. He's grand here."

Sam poked a train in his face. McMahon gently took it from him. "Is that Mavis? Where's her trucks?"

Sam slid off his knee and went to fetch them.

Anna shot him a hostile look. "How come you're so up on Thomas the Tank Engine?"

McMahon grinned. "I've five nephews and eight nieces back in Ireland. They keep me informed." He gazed over at Sam. "He's a grand little fellow. How's his speech coming along?"

Anna glanced down at the table. "I'm thinking of sending him to a playgroup. People seem to think he'll speak more if he mixes with other children."

"I'm sure that's right. And you'll be happier if you mix more with grown ups." He shot her a penetrating look. "Have you thought any more about going back to work?"

"Yes and no. Yes, I've thought about it and the answer's no. I want to be with my children."

"Pity. You don't come across a good job like that every day."

"No, you don't, Detective Superintendent. But my children come first." I sound like Mother, she thought.

He stood up. "Well I'll go now. Without the coffee. If Beatrice does happen to turn up here, you'll let us know at once, won't you?"

"Yes, Detective Superintendent. But it's highly unlikely. Come on, Sam, stop it now." For Sam had hold of McMahon's hand and was dragging him back towards his trains. "It's because you're a man," she explained. "He doesn't see many men."

"Doesn't he? What about your friend?"

"He's never met them."

"Good. You're protective of them. Very wise. It can be confusing for children having people coming and going the whole time."

What kind of a life did he think she led? "The only person who comes and goes here," she said, prising Sam's hand away, "is yourself."

"Is that true?" He glanced over his shoulder as he went out of the room. "Perhaps you ought to take that job then? Get you out of the house a bit. Stop you brooding."

"I don't brood, Detective Superintendent," she yelled after him. "I have two small children. I don't have time to brood."

She heard the front door close.

"And don't come back," she muttered.

Sam kicked her.

"Sam!"

He pummelled her leg with his fists.

"Sam, stop it! What's the matter with you?"

"My friend. My friend play with Sam. I hate you, Mummy!"
He burst into tears.

"Sam, Sam." She sat down on the floor and took his stiff
resisting body onto her lap. "Sam, listen to me. Would you like
to join a playgroup? Play with other children in the mornings?"
His eyes shone. There was no doubt about his feelings on the
subject. She was silent for a moment. "And I have another
friend. A nicer friend. Shall we invite him to come round and
play this evening?"

He nodded.

So she rang Philip and he said he would come round about
seven, after seeing a client.

"You're sure you want your children to see me? I could come
later, after they've gone to bed."

"No, I want them to see you. I want you to be part of our
lives."

"Beautiful, Anna. I'll be there."

He sounded better this morning. Stronger. She did him some
good, then. If she'd done nothing else right in her life, she'd at
least given someone else strength.

She went off happily with the children to the shops. She had
no idea what Philip liked to eat. They'd never done anything so
ordinary as eat a meal together. In the end she chose smoked
salmon. It was simple to make scrambled eggs to go with it and
people always liked it. "I'll live on bread and water for the rest
of the week," she told Sam.

On the way home she began to feel they were being
followed. She kept glancing over her shoulder, convinced
someone was watching her. Had McMahon set his spies on her?
Did he suspect her of secretly kidnapping Beatrice? His words
came back to her. "Finch's out on bail." She shivered in fear and
hurried the children home.

Safe inside the front door, she lost her fear. The day began to feel like a celebration. The boys caught some of her excitement. Sam followed her around with his little dustpan and brush. Together, they swept and polished and dusted ready for Philip's visit. Toby crawled around after them. She felt so excited she could hardly stay still all day. Philip would be with her, in her house, he would meet her children. He would be let into the heart of her life. It would be like having Richard back again. Almost.

What would they talk about? She stood by the sink, a half-peeled courgette in her hand. They wouldn't talk. They never really talked, discussed books or politics, like she used to with Richard. They didn't have to, that wasn't what their relationship was about. They'd put on some music and sit in companionable silence. They'd comfort each other. She finished peeling the courgette. We'll have the whole night together. Our first night. Oh my love.

Towards seven o'clock, she began to have doubts. She was letting him into the most sacred part of her life. If he came here as a lover, kissing her in front of the children, it would be a disaster. She took the children upstairs with her as she went to change her clothes for the second time. Look casual but not too sexy. She exchanged her leggings for jeans. Sam, watching her hesitate in front of the mirror, picked out some wooden beads for her to wear. He dabbed perfume on her cheeks and then on his own.

The doorbell rang.

Inwardly shivering, she ran downstairs to answer it. He was standing on the doorstep looking clean and handsome. He'd shaved, dressed up a little in beige trousers and striped shirt. Suddenly shy, she could hardly bring herself to look at him.

"Come upstairs. The children are in the kitchen." She led the way. "This is Toby." She picked him up. He stared solemnly out of her arms at the stranger. "And this is Sam." She placed a protective hand on his shoulder.

Philip took Toby's hand and gently stroked it. Anna held her breath. Toby stared at him, shifted slightly in her arms but didn't, as she'd feared, start to cry.

"And how's Sam?" He sat down on the floor beside him and picked up a train.

Anna leaned back against the cupboards in relief. It was going to be all right. He was being just what she'd hoped he would be. He'd made no attempt to kiss her.

"Coffee?" she offered, holding onto Toby in case he cried.

He looked up. "Lovely, darling."

She put on the kettle and got things ready for Toby's bottle. Philip was playing with the teddies now, inventing funny voices for them all. The children stared at him in wonderment.

"Your children don't get enough fun."

"What do you mean?"

"Do you play games with them?"

"Of course I do. But there're other things to be done as well. Shopping, cleaning, cooking."

She handed him the coffee. Something seemed to change in the atmosphere. Sam wandered off to look at a book and wouldn't be enticed back. In the end she took him downstairs and set him in front of a Thomas the Tank Engine video while she put Toby to bed. Then she put Sam to bed. Then she went back into the kitchen where he was sitting reading a newspaper.

"Would you like to eat something?"

"Yes, darling. I'm starving. Do you always eat this late?"

"Yes."

She turned her back on him and started scrambling eggs. "Do you want a drink?"

"Only if you're having one."

"I am."

"You drink too much."

"That's what children do to you. It helps me unwind."

"Come here and I'll help you unwind."

"I thought you were starving. I've got to cook."

"Stand there then." He came up behind her and began gently massaging her shoulders.

She leant back against him for a moment and closed her eyes. "That feels wonderful."

"Good. Food ready yet?"

"Coming up."

They took their plates downstairs and sat side by side on the sofa to eat.

"This is delicious, darling."

"It's the first time we've eaten together, isn't it?"

"Is it, darling?"

"Yes. Is Ginny a good cook?"

"No. I did the cooking. She didn't take much interest. Too busy with her career."

"Is she good at her work?"

"Yes. She's a team leader. The women who work under her, they all adore her."

Something clicked in her mind. "Didn't you say she was a social worker?"

"That's right, darling."

"I think I've seen her. I think she works with a friend of mine." Virginia, Tessa's team leader, the girl with the long golden plait. The photograph hadn't done her justice. "I saw her at a women's meeting. She was sitting next to Gloria West."

He groaned. "That awful woman. She's got some kind of a hold over Ginny. I don't know why. I think Gloria's psycho myself. Aren't you eating your food, darling?"

Anna gazed meditatively down at her salmon. All of a sudden she didn't feel like eating it. She was too tired. It was ages since she'd cooked in the evening. Not since Richard's death, in fact. Usually she had a slice of toast with the children and a glass of wine and some biscuits after they'd gone to bed. She put down her fork. "I'm exhausted."

"It's those children. Running around after them all day. I don't know how you do it."

"People think I should go back to work."

"Rubbish! You stay with your children. Young children need their mothers at home."

"That's what I say. I'm glad you agree."

She pushed her plate away and lay beside him on the sofa watching the news. He stroked her hair, then reached for her hand. He gently played with her fingers, weaving them in and out of his. The sight of his square strong fingers entwined with hers moved her almost to tears.

"You're being gentle with me. You're not usually this gentle."

"Aren't I, darling? Are you watching this?"

"Not really."

"Let's go to bed."

Her shyness returned as she led him upstairs to her bedroom. She went into the bathroom. When she returned he was already undressed and in bed. She switched off the light and started to undress.

"Why did you do that?" he asked, aggrieved, from the bed.

"I'm fat," she muttered, climbing into bed beside him. "I've had two children. My body's not what it used to be." Ginny's stomach was probably still beautifully taut. She didn't want him making comparisons.

"Come here. Mm. Your breasts are wonderful. Ginny's as flat as a pancake."

Good.

He worked his fingers into her cunt. She felt her senses take over again, drowning out her worries and doubts.

"Philip, my love," she whispered. She felt for his cock. It was soft.

"Take it into your mouth."

She bent down and kissed it. "I love your cock."

"Do you, darling? Good."

She sucked and kissed till it grew hard. He thrust inside her and came without warning. She was a bit disappointed. This wasn't quite how she'd imagined it would be. After all, they had the whole night in front of them.

He lay on his back and closed his eyes. She lay beside him, watching him doze. All of a sudden a shock of recognition went through her. She'd realised who Philip reminded her of. Her father. The same nose, the same strong cheekbones, the same dark-fringed eyes. She should have realised. She'd always avoided dark-haired men before. No wonder Philip made her feel like a child again. No wonder she'd wanted him to need her, as her father never had; to depend on her, as her father never had. No wonder she was in thrall to him. In loving you, my sweet, I have been my father's dutiful daughter. I dress up for you, I cook for you, I submit to you. I do everything fathers like.

She began to weep.

"What's the matter?" he asked, feeling her tears on his chest.

"Nothing. I can't explain."

She dried her eyes. In some deep part of herself, she suddenly felt enormously liberated. She had the explanation now. Philip reminded her of her father. No wonder she'd behaved like a child with him.

He put an arm round her. "Go to sleep now."

Exhausted with cooking, cleaning and emotion, she dozed off. When she next awoke, he'd taken his arm away and was staring wide awake at the ceiling.

"What's wrong?" She glanced at her watch. Two o'clock.

He rubbed his eyes. "I can't sleep here, Anna. It's this bed. It's too soft. And I keep hearing noises. I think it must be your pipes. I'll have to go."

"All right."

She watched sleepily as he got dressed.

"Don't come down. I'll let myself out." He went out of the bedroom door, came back in again, hesitated and said, "You're all right, Anna, aren't you?"

"Yes, I'm all right. I love you."

He went out of the room without answering.

She was so sleepy she forgot to panic.

All next morning she waited in. When he'd still not phoned by lunch-time, panic seized hold of her. He'd not stayed with her. He'd left her.

He was like her father. Her charming, dark-haired father whom she'd loved absolutely and completely, in a way that she would never love anyone again. And who at some point in her childhood (when he'd met Janice?) had withdrawn his love from her so that, forever after, she'd avoided the love of dark-haired men. Until now. Philip had awakened those old feelings in her;

all those childish feelings of hunger and yearning and dependency. What could she do? If she suppressed them she'd become like mother. I don't want to be bitter. I have to face them and live through them.

By half past three she was shivering in alarm. She couldn't keep the children in any longer. It was a sunny day. They should be out playing in the park.

She dialled his number.

"Oh. Anna."

This was horrible. It couldn't be happening. He didn't want to speak to her, she could tell by his voice.

"I thought you would have phoned me. After last night. Leaving like that. I've been waiting in for you to call."

"I've – er – had things to sort out. I'll give you a ring in a day or two."

"What!?" He might just as well have hit her. "Philip! What's the matter? I thought we were going to start being together. I thought you were going to start coming here in the evenings. I thought that's what you wanted."

"I've things to do here first. I'll see you again soon."

"Philip! What's going on here? Are you leaving me?"

"No. I said I'd be your friend for as long as you want."

"Friend?"

"Yes. Or you can be my client again, if you prefer."

"Oh God!"

"What's the matter?"

"Your wife's come back."

"She hasn't come back."

"But she's going to. I can feel it. So can you. That's why you're leaving me. I can't bear it!" She began to cry.

"Anna! Grow up! You're not a child. You're a mother. You've got your children to think about. Ginny's got no one."

"So you felt guilty about making love to me last night, is that it?"

I'm not enough for him. I've never been enough.

"Ginny's on her own." His voice began to break.

"I thought you said she went to nightclubs and picked up men?"

271

"I . . . I may have been wrong."

"Why? How do you know? Have you seen her again?"

"I – I've been following her."

"What?!"

"These last couple of days I've been following her in my car. I go to where she works and waits till she leaves. Then I follow her. She visits her friends, then she goes back to her parents' house. I'm pretty sure she's on her own. Last night her car stayed parked outside her home in Grimsby."

"Last night? You mean after you left here, you drove down to Grimsby to check where she was?" Anna found herself speaking extremely slowly, as if in a nightmare.

"I have to know whether I can trust her again."

Anna shivered and drew her cardigan more closely around herself. It had all been an illusion. He had no comfort to give her, not now, not in the future, not ever. It had been Ginny's face he'd seen as he'd lain beside her in the dark last night. Ginny he'd been thinking of, Ginny he'd made love to.

"I'll see you in a couple of days, Anna."

"Yes."

She put down the phone and stared blankly out of the window. It had always been Ginny. She, Anna, had hardly existed for him. So this was what being grown up meant. When she cried there'd be no one there to comfort her. Like Mother, she had nothing.

Out of the corner of her eye she saw a flash of red in the courtyard. There was someone down there. She remembered the noises Philip had said he'd heard last night. She remembered the noise she'd heard the night before. She opened the window.

"Hey! You there!"

She ran downstairs and hunted all round the courtyard. No sign of anyone. If it was Finch she should call the police; she and the children might need protection. No, she was being melodramatic, it couldn't be Finch. How would he know where she lived? It was probably some tramp, rooting in her dustbins. It wouldn't be the first time it had happened. That's what came of living so close to the city centre.

As she got the boys ready for their walk, a plan formed in her head. She'd call Donna, ask her to come over and babysit and go down to Grimsby herself this evening. Find out what was going on.

When they got back from their walk, she looked up V Lawrence in the phone book, failed to find her and rang Tessa.

"You know your team leader – Virginia something?"

"Virginia Ward," supplied Tessa, conveniently.

"Ward, yes." Anna wrote down the name. "She's married to that guy I was talking to at Angela's party, isn't she? Philip Lawrence."

"Was married. It's over now."

That's not what I've heard, thought Anna.

"Seriously, Anna, that man's bad news. I don't know what your relationship is with him – "

"Oh, I hardly know – "

" – but keep away from him. He abused Virginia. We have to protect her from him."

She felt an icy shiver run down her back. "What do you mean, abused?"

"He seduced her, kept her trapped in that house of his, wouldn't let her see her friends. She'd say she was leaving, then he'd phone her up at work, crying and pleading with her to come back. She's so soft-hearted she couldn't say no. We've got to protect her from him."

"Who's we?"

"Gloria, Sandra, the rest of the gang."

"Can't she protect herself? Isn't she a grown woman?"

"She's vulnerable. In many ways Virginia's an extraordinary woman, but she's also very fragile. He knows how to play on her emotions." There was a pause. "Since you've rung, I may as well tell you now, Anna. I'm leaving Bill."

"Oh no! Why?"

"Gloria's bought a house. We're going to set up a women-only commune. Virginia's going to be part of it."

"But what about your children?"

"I need to get my head clear, Anna. The kids will stay with

Bill and I'll visit them from time to time till I sort myself out. I can't go on like this. I feel trapped. I never knew motherhood would be like this. I feel like a non-person. I haven't fallen out with Bill. Not really. But he's a man. He can't understand. Anyway, now you know. We'd ask you to join us, but we're not having children around and I suppose there's no one you can leave yours with?"

"No one."

She put down the phone and held her aching head. Was she nuts or was it everybody else?

She drove over the bridge to Grimsby, a road map open on the seat beside her. She'd never been to Grimsby before. She drove through the tiny town centre, got lost down at the docks and finally found herself in the middle of a network of terraced streets.

The road where Virginia lived with her parents was dingier than she'd expected. There was litter in the front gardens. One or two of the houses had their windows boarded up. Virginia's parents' house was neater than the rest – it had been recently painted and the net curtains hanging at the windows were clean. She parked her car a little way down the street and switched off the engine. What now? She looked at her watch. It was nine o'clock. There were two cars parked outside Virginia's house, a battered Ford Escort and a smart red Metro (Virginia's?). Presumably she'd come home from work, had her tea and was spending the evening in, watching television or washing her hair.

Anna felt a sense of disappointment. What had she come all this way for? To spy on her rival? Find proof of her infidelity to present to Philip? Should she ring the bell and demand to speak to her, find out once and for all if she wanted Philip back?

She was debating all this when another car drove up and stopped outside the house. Recognising Philip's Renault, she slid down in her seat and watched as he got out of the car and rang the bell. He was dressed in his black silk shirt and dark trousers. Had he a date with her then?

The door opened. Someone said something sharply and then the door banged shut again. Philip stood for a moment on the doorstep, deep in thought, then turned and walked onto the patch of brown grass that was the front lawn. He began to shout.

"Ginny! Ginny! Speak to me!"

Shivers ran down Anna's spine. The longing and desperation in his voice were awful to hear.

A bedroom window opened. A young woman stuck her head out. Anna recognised her at once. The long plait, the slightly crooked nose, the eyes set too close together. But what the photograph hadn't captured was that it was a face full of life. At this moment, it was blazing with anger.

"Go away, Phil! Just fucking go away!"

She calls him Phil. A pang went through Anna. She's been closer to him than I'll ever be.

"Ginny! Let me speak to you. Please! I miss you. I love you."

"Sodding hell!"

The window banged shut. Moments later, the front door opened. Philip went inside.

Anna started up the engine. She'd seen all she'd wanted to. He'd never been hers. She'd been living in a fool's paradise. She headed out of Grimsby, losing her way several times in the maze of working-class streets. He'd made love to her till she was drunk on it, till she couldn't do without it. And all the time, he'd been thinking of his wife, wanting Ginny, fucking Ginny.

She drove back over the bridge, flinging accusations at him. I let you come close to the most precious things in my life, my children, and you threw it all back in my face. Why did I allow you into my life? You showed me no love. You were never tender with me. You were thirsty for me, you wanted me. But that isn't love. It's your wife you love. Your bloody, unstable, uncaring wife.

God it hurt. She parked the car and rested her head for a moment on the wheel. I had a dream of you as my mother and, losing that, I've lost myself. Come to me, you said. I can cure you. That soft teasing voice, holding out hope. Well, there was no hope, no mother. She was back where she'd started. Without him. She raised her head in panic. What if the voices came back? Who would help her now?

She opened the side door into the courtyard and heard a noise to her left where the coal-shed was. What used to be the coal-shed. Since Richard's death she hadn't bothered with fires. She used it now for storing odds and ends of gardening equipment. Had some tramp made his home there? Or was Finch lying in wait for her with a knife in his hand?

Her heart in her mouth, she wrenched open the door and peered into the darkness. Two frightened eyes stared back at her.

"Beatrice!"

The child started to whimper. It was a terrible sound. Like some small frightened animal.

"Stop that!" roared Anna, her nerves unhinged by the evening's events. "And come out of there. What on earth are you doing?"

The girl crawled out. Her long hair was filthy. Her face was streaked with tears and grime. There was a hole in her red jumper. She was shivering.

"What are you doing here?" Anna repeated.

"I wanted . . . I wanted . . . "

Beatrice broke into sobs.

A light went on in the courtyard next door. Julia's head popped over the wall.

"Everything all right? I thought I heard a noise. Good gracious! What's that?"

"A – a relative of mine. It's all right, Julia. We were just going inside. Sorry to have disturbed you."

She put an arm round Beatrice's thin shoulders and guided her into the house. She switched on the light in the hall. The girl looked like a skeleton. What had she been living on these past few days? Anna pushed her into the sitting-room.

"Stay there," she ordered.

She went upstairs to pay Donna.

"Did I hear voices?"

"It's nothing. A relative – distant relative – of mine's turned up."

On her way out, Donna peeked into the sitting-room, raised her eyebrows in astonishment and disapproval and left.

"Right. Bath first. Then food. Then we can talk. Dump your clothes outside the bathroom door. I'm going to burn them. You can borrow something of mine."

"Can I? Can I really?" Beatrice's eyes lit up. She looked around the sitting-room. "So this is what it looks like inside. Did my father live here?"

"Yes."

"It's like something out of a dream. Can I see the boys?"

"Maybe. Tomorrow. We'll see."

She left Beatrice in the bath and went to phone Penelope.

"Your sixth sense was right. Beatrice's turned up here."

"Thank God!" exclaimed Penelope, her voice cracking with relief. "How is she?"

"Filthy. Starving. As you'd expect. It's too late to bring her over. I'll keep her with me tonight and then we'll see what to do with her tomorrow."

"Thank you, Anna. More than I can say."

Beatrice came down to the kitchen rosy and shining from her bath and wrapped in Anna's dressing-gown. Her hair streamed wetly down her back. She smelled of Anna's perfume, Anna noted.

"I'll get you a hair-dryer."

"No thanks. Makes split ends."

"Considering how you've been living these past few days, split ends seem a minor consideration. Will sausages and chips do you?" she added, trying to think herself into a pre-adolescent frame of mind.

"I'm vegetarian. And chips give me spots."

"Cheese on toast? Or are you vegan?"

"Cheese on toast's fine."

"Oh good."

Any irony in Anna's tone was lost on Beatrice. She wandered around the room touching things.

"I've liked the look of this house from the moment I first saw it. It looks like a home. A proper home. Not like the places Mum and I used to live."

"Oh yes? And how did you find out where I lived?"

Beatrice glanced at her with a touch of pity. "I looked you up in the phone book." She went over to inspect the boys' toys heaped up in boxes in the corner. "All these toys. Aren't they lucky?" She fingered one or two. Anna reflected that Sam would be furious if he saw her. "Have you any photographs of my father?"

"Of course." She hesitated. "There's one up here." She reached up and took it down from the shelf.

Beatrice studied it a moment. "Granny says I look a lot like him."

"Granny's right," replied Anna noting, and resenting, the switch from Mrs Vale. Why had Penelope allowed that? It was Sam and Toby's name for her. "Now eat up. I've made you soup as well."

"Thanks."

Beatrice set the photograph down in front of her on the table and started to eat as if there was no tomorrow. She ate a whole can of Heinz tomato soup, four slices of cheese on toast, a banana and a yoghurt.

"Don't eat any more or you'll be sick. What have you been living on all this time?"

"Odds and ends. The first two days I still had money left that Granny'd given me."

"Did she say you could call her Granny?"

"Yes. Kind of. She's nice, isn't she?"

"Yes, she is. You gave her a dreadful shock, running away like that. She's been terribly worried about you."

"I thought she might be." Beatrice looked down at her plate and bit her lip. "I'm sorry about that."

"Why did you do it?"

Beatrice's honest open eyes met hers. For a second, Anna saw Richard.

"I wanted to be near you. You and the boys. They're my brothers."

"Half-brothers." A thought struck her. "Have you been following us?"

Beatrice reddened. "I like watching you going out shopping and stuff with the kids. That holiday camp was crap and Granny's very kind, but living with her isn't like living in a family."

"I see. You want to be with a family, is that it? I'm sure that could be arr – "

Richard's eyes looked at her.

"I want to live here with you."

Anna stood up. "I'm afraid that's entirely out of the question." She began clearing away the plates.

"Why?"

"There isn't room. It might upset the boys." It would definitely upset me. "A hundred different reasons."

"I could help with the boys. I like little children."

"I don't need help," snapped Anna. "Now, shall we see about a bed for you?"

She made up the bed in the small attic room on the third floor.

Beatrice looked around. "This is lovely."

"But temporary. I need this room."

"Why? Who sleeps here normally?"

"Visitors."

"Do you have lots of visitors then?"

"No. Yes. Do you always ask this many questions? Go to sleep now. Tomorrow Granny will come round and we'll discuss what's to be done with you."

Richard's eyes peeked over the top of the duvet. "Do I have any say in the matter?"

"No," replied Anna firmly, switching off the light.

As she got ready for bed, the thought struck her that she ought to have phoned the police. She peered at the clock in the darkness. It was past midnight. McMahon would hardly be out looking for Beatrice at this time of night. Let him stew till morning.

As she lay in the dark, thoughts of Philip came flooding

back. Was he sick? Was he obsessed with Ginny to the point of madness? Or was he simply a man who'd got hurt for the first time in his life? Who, after years of knocking around the world, had finally risked a relationship and got his fingers burned? Was the Philip she loved the same as the real Philip?

It was five before she fell asleep. When she woke up, the clock told her it was half past nine. "My God!" She clutched her head and groaned. The house was ominously quiet. Normally both children would be howling in their beds by now. She reached out for her dressing-gown, remembered she'd lent it to Beatrice, dashed next door into Toby's room, saw his cot was empty and rushed downstairs in a panic. Had Beatrice absconded taking the children with her?

In the kitchen she found Sam sitting up at the table eating Coco Pops whilst Toby rolled around on his activity-mat squeaking his cow under Beatrice's watchful eye.

"They were beginning to cry so I got them up and brought them down here so you could have a lie-in," she explained.

"A lie-in?" She hadn't had a lie-in since before Toby was born. This was Richard's child all right. She was torn between irritation and gratitude. "Thanks," she managed to get out.

"I made myself breakfast. I hope you don't mind? I was starving."

"No, that's all right. Has Toby had anything to eat?"

"I gave him some milk."

"Oh. But I hadn't sterilised any bottles."

"I gave it to him in a beaker."

"Did he take it?" she asked in surprise. She'd been trying for weeks to get Toby to use a cup.

"Yes."

She looked at Toby. Little traitor.

"Beatrice slept here," Sam informed her.

"I know."

"She's our sister."

"Half-sister."

They were all traitors, all in league against her.

"I'm going to get dressed," she growled. She went upstairs,

pulled on leggings and a sweatshirt and grabbed some clothes for Beatrice.

"Here," she threw them into her lap. "You can borrow these."

"Thanks." She disappeared upstairs to get dressed.

"Beatrice stay with us a very long time?" asked Sam as she began changing him out of his pyjamas.

"No. Very short time. In fact she'll be going this morning. With any luck."

He pouted his lips. "Sam like Beatrice. Sam wants her to stay and play."

"Yes, well, Mummy doesn't."

The doorbell rang. It was Penelope.

"Granny! Granny! Look who's here." Sam flung himself at her.

Penelope glanced at Anna. "He's talking?"

"He's beginning to. We've had people about recently. It seems to be having an effect on him. I'm taking your advice and sending him to a playgroup."

"That's marvellous! Clever boy." Penelope gave her grandson a kiss. "How's Beatrice?" She followed Anna up the stairs, holding Sam by the hand.

"Fine. She's had a bath and enormous amounts to eat."

"Beatrice got me up this morning."

"All right, Sam." Anna gave him a nudge.

Penelope glanced at her daughter-in-law. "This is very good of you, Anna. I'll take her home with me now."

"No. Sam play with Beatrice."

They went into the kitchen. Toby was sitting on Beatrice's lap, their heads bent together over a book. Anna noticed their hair was an identical shade of reddish blonde. Sam went over to join them. Beatrice glanced up sheepishly at her grandmother.

"Granny, I – "

She was interrupted by the doorbell.

Anna went to answer it. It was McMahon.

"Your mother-in-law rang us this morning. Performing her duty as a responsible citizen."

"I was going to ring. I've only just got up," muttered Anna.

"Can I have a word with the girl?"

"Have as many words as you like, Detective Superintendent. She's not my responsibility." She showed him into the sitting-room.

The words McMahon had with Beatrice resulted in her emerging chastened but hopeful from the sitting-room. Anna wondered what he'd said to her.

"Gather up your things now, Beatrice," said Penelope when McMahon brought her back upstairs to the kitchen. "We must be going."

"No! Beatrice stay!" Sam rushed over and tugged at her hand.

Anna felt McMahon's eyes on her. She shrugged. "Oh, all right. She can stay a bit longer."

Beatrice's face lit up.

"Are you sure?" Penelope looked doubtful.

Anna nodded.

"Well, I'll be off then if everything's sorted out." McMahon rubbed his hands in satisfaction.

"Everything's far from sorted out," said Anna, following him down the stairs. "What are we going to do with her?"

"I know what would happen in Ireland." His hand on the latch, he turned to face her.

"You think I should take her in? Another person to mother? I can't do it."

"You never know, she might be a help to you. She seemed to be getting on grand with your little ones."

"I don't need help! Why does everyone think I need help?" snapped Anna, the tears starting in her eyes.

McMahon looked concerned. "Are you all right?"

My lover's gone. Richard's daughter's here. I have to try to be civilised about these things when all I want to do is curl up somewhere in a corner and die.

"Yes, I'm all right."

"Sure?"

"Sure."

She shut the door.

"Nice man," commented Penelope when she came back upstairs.

"Do you think so?"

The phone rang. It was Philip. He sounded dreadful.

"Just a minute. Pen, I'll take this in my bedroom. Can you put the receiver down?"

His voice faltered. "I feel so weak and needy this morning, Anna. I've missed you. Can't you come round?"

"No, Beatrice's turned up. Besides, I know where you were last night," she snarled. "You went to see your wife."

"Only for a couple of minutes. Then she threw me out. How do you know, anyway?"

"I saw you."

"Did you follow me?"

"No, I followed her. I wanted to find out about her. Is she seeing someone else?"

"She says she isn't. She says she just wants to be free. She says she felt trapped with me. I don't understand it. I let her come and go as she pleased. She was always off visiting her women friends. I never complained. How could she feel trapped?"

I could tell you, she thought, it's the way you make love. Come here, fuckface, are you going to behave? You make us feel our bodies aren't our own. You're a trap, my love. You sweet-talk women into bed with your gentle soft voice and then you turn primitive on them. She ran away from you. I know how she felt. And she kept coming back. I know about that, too. Always in the hope that this time it will be different, this time you won't use those words, leave marks on my body; that this time you'll be as gentle in bed as you are out of it. It was your body that trapped her. McMahon was right. Passion's a con. It's about power.

"I need a friend, Anna. I can do without the sex but I need a friend or I'll go under. You're my lifeline."

"I'll be your friend, Philip. Of course I'll be your friend. I'll come round as soon as I can. Perhaps tomorrow."

And when I come round friendship will end up in bed, if not tomorrow, then pretty soon after, because I'm like Ginny: I hope against hope that this time it will be different. This time you'll value my body. But I'll never entirely trust you again, my love. Not body and soul. You cannot be my mother.

She went back down to the kitchen. Penelope glanced at her, hesitated, seemed about to say something, then went back to playing with her grandchildren. All her grandchildren, thought Anna, leaning against a cupboard, watching them.

They played several games of snakes and ladders all of which Sam, cheating like mad, won. Anna glanced at Beatrice. There was one thing to be said for her – she was a good sport. But then so had Richard been. Anna contemplated her. In many ways, of the three children, it was Beatrice who resembled Richard the most.

Penelope stayed to lunch. They agreed that Beatrice would stay one more day with Anna.

"I'll ring you tomorrow and arrange a time to collect her," said Penelope, following Anna downstairs. At the door, she suddenly turned and said quickly, "I know it's none of my business, love. But over the past few weeks I've seen you get more and more unhappy. No man's worth that. You deserve someone good to take care of you."

"I . . . " began Anna.

But Penelope was already halfway down the street. Anna was left standing on the doorstep looking after her, thunderstruck.

CHAPTER THIRTEEN

THE NEXT MORNING THEY WENT OUT to the playground. Sam held Beatrice's hand all the way there and all the way back. Anna began to feel redundant.

When they got home, Lottie rang.

"I'm winding up the group."

"Lottie! Why?"

"It's not the same any more since Gloria's lot started taking it over. I wanted it to be a cosy friendly place where everyone could air their views. Now people are afraid to speak in case they get pounced on." She sounded close to tears. "There's a final meeting tonight. Will you come?"

"Of course I will."

Anna put down the phone and looked at Beatrice. "I'll ask Donna to babysit and I'll run you home to your grandmother's before the meeting starts."

"Beatrice stay here! Beatrice sleep here again!" roared Sam. "Don't want Donna! Want Beatrice!"

Beatrice knelt down and put her arms round him. "Don't cry, Sam. Beatrice will come and play with you another day."

"Beatrice sleep here!" shrieked Sam, red in the face.

Beatrice glanced across at Anna. "It isn't possible, Sam. This isn't my home."

Anna watched Sam's face. "All right, Sam, Beatrice can stay one more night. Just one, mind. Tomorrow she goes back to Granny's."

"Hooray! Hooray!" Sam clapped his hands, stood on his head and attempted a forward roll.

"I'll see if Granny wants to come over and spend the evening with you all."

She rang Penelope. She'd be delighted to come.

"But shouldn't I take her home with me?"

"I said she could stay one more night. Sam wanted her to."

"Sure that's all right with you?"

"Yes." Practically sure.

She rang Philip. "I'm going to a meeting. I could drop by later."

"Lovely, darling. I'll be waiting."

When Penelope arrived to babysit, Anna gathered up her mother's letters and notebook. Before she went to the women's meeting, she had a call to make.

She drove round to the back entrance of the estate and stopped her car outside the small neat lodge. She knocked on the door.

"Well, Anna. This is a surprise." Her mother, declining to elaborate on whether the surprise was a pleasant one or not, opened the door an inch wider. "I suppose you want to come in?"

"For a moment. Please. I'm on my way to a meeting."

Her mother led the way down the narrow passage into the tiny sitting-room comfortably furnished with a couple of sofas, a desk and a low coffee table.

"I came to bring you these." Anna held out the bundle of letters. "I found them when I went up to look at Georgia's paintings. You must have dropped them when you were packing. I thought you'd want them."

Her mother eyed the letters with indifference. "Those old things. I meant to throw them out." She took the letters and began tearing them up. "I ought to have done this years ago. I suppose you read them."

"Mother, I . . . "

"Yes, Anna?"

The light died in Anna's eyes. "I'm sorry, Mother. You must have suffered terribly."

"Not really, Anna. Not after the first few years. Life has a way of anaesthetising you. I'll put these in the bin." She took away the torn up letters and the notebook.

Anna looked around the room. She recognised a couple of the ornaments. There were no family photographs. Not a single one. They'd all – Nana, Father, Georgia, Brian, herself – in their different ways let her mother down. Her mother had cared for Nana all her life and Nana had thrown that love away when she'd killed herself. She'd loved Father with the sort of piercing passionate love that Anna had begun to recognise and he'd been unfaithful. She'd clung to Georgia and she, too, had taken her own life in a frenzy of mad hatred against her. Brian had disappointed her. He'd not been the heroic manly son she'd hoped for. Anna, rebellious and sulky, had drifted away years ago. Poor Mother, she thought.

Again came the nagging doubts. All those deaths, were they just coincidences?

Her mother came back into the sitting-room with an air of being surprised to find Anna still there.

Anna tried again. "Mother, life's been hard for you. You must be lonely here," she added, glancing round at the neat bare room. "Would you – would you like to come over and visit us some time? See your grandchildren?"

Her mother's sharp eyes fixed on her daughter. For a moment the two women stood facing one another. Anna was the first to look away.

"It's too late for this, Anna. You cut yourself off years ago. It was your decision. You must live with it." She made a movement towards the door. It was an unmistakeable gesture of dismissal. Anna followed her out into the hall.

"There may be grandchildren here soon. I gather Brian and his fiancée intend to start a family as soon as they're married." She stood with her hand on the latch. "So you see, I won't be alone. I'm sorry if you're lonely, Anna. It's hard being the mother of young children, but we all have to go through it. I never had any help, why should you?"

She shut the door.

Anna got into her car and started the engine. Something had gone wrong long ago between her mother and herself. At some crucial point in her childhood, she'd failed her mother. Failed to give her mother the love she needed; failed to make up to her for her father's infidelities; had betrayed her, even, by loving her father more. Things would never come right now. There would forever be a great rift across the early part of her life.

She drove out of the estate and back towards the city centre.

What if she was to raise a daughter of her own? Wouldn't that help heal the wounds? Especially a daughter of Richard's. Should she take her to live with them? This little girl, with Richard's hair and Richard's eyes and Richard's sense of justice? It would be a way of keeping him alive a bit longer. He'd never quite be gone so long as Beatrice was around.

She had the sensation of something shifting in her mind. A decision was being taken almost without her knowing it, one of those big decisions that affect the rest of your life. It was momentous. She wanted to share it with someone. She glanced at her watch. Yes, she just had time. She did a detour and turned off towards Beverley. She would bring him news of her decision, he'd be the first to know, and she'd cheer him up. Perhaps she wouldn't even go to the women's meeting. It would mean letting Lottie down. But after all, Philip needed her.

His bungalow was shrouded in darkness. She was disappointed. Then a little hurt. He'd said he was going to wait in for her. He'd said he needed her. She looked at her watch. Resigned, she drove on towards Hull.

The first thing she saw when she entered the room was Gloria West standing with her arm around Virginia.

Ignoring a beckoning wave from Lottie, Anna went up to them.

"Hello, you don't know me. I'm a . . . a friend of Philip's," she said nervously. "I know you've seen him recently. Can I talk to you about him?"

Virginia stared at her. Gloria's arm went down.

"You little whore! You fucking bitch on heat!" she shouted at Ginny. "So that's where you've been when I've been trying to phone you. In bed fucking your damn psycho husband."

Ginny flushed. "I haven't. I've seen him once or twice

288

because he pleaded with me." She sighed and looked over Gloria's shoulder. "I want to be free, Gloria. You're beginning to be as much of a trap as he was. I got married the first time round when I was eighteen. I went straight from that into marriage with Philip. I've never lived. I want to live."

Gloria frowned. A cold hard expression appeared in her eyes. "You know your trouble, you bitch? You can't keep away from men. You're not really one of us, are you, Virginia?"

Ginny twisted her long plait in her hands. "No, I don't think I am. But I'm not Philip's wife any longer, either. I don't know what I am. I have to find out."

Anna caught her arm as she went out of the room. "Then you don't mind if I go on seeing Philip?"

Ginny stared at her. "Mind? Why should I mind? Anything that keeps him out of my hair is fine by me." She looked Anna up and down. "You do realise what you're taking on, don't you? Don't be fooled by that soft sweet voice of his. It's just a trick to get you into bed. Therapy's given him the opportunity to hone his seduction techniques. And it's very convenient for him since he's always the one in control in the relationship." She clattered down the stairs.

Anna stared after her. Was Ginny telling the truth? Had what to her been an extraordinary event – not love-at-first-sight (she wasn't that stupid), but something passionate at any rate – been for Philip an everyday experience; his usual way of relating to females? His only way of relating to females? Was he as unreliable as her father had been?

She shook her head. Why trust Ginny? She was unstable, she was hard, she'd got rid of her babies. She just wanted to make Philip unhappy, to make him pay, perhaps, for the way she'd let him dominate her life, dressed her in sexy clothes, made her submit to him in bed. She wasn't going to listen to another woman tell her about Philip. She'd make up her own mind.

Tessa came up to her. "What was that little scene about?"

"Ginny's ex-husband. Philip's a friend of mine." From now on she was going to be open about their relationship. She was going to come clean – even to Penelope.

"I told you, Anna, keep away from him."

"What have you got against him?"

"I've heard enough from Virginia about that man to make your hair stand on end. Fucks his way through his twenties and thirties as if there was no tomorrow. Dumps women when it suits him, lies, cheats, abuses their trust. Children? No fear, darling, have an abortion, I'll go halves. Turns forty. Sees all his contemporaries comfortably settled with wife and kids. Suddenly gets sick of recounting his life story for the hundredth time to a stranger he's not going to want to see in the morning. Thinks there may be something in it after all. Goes out, grabs a woman, expects her to play the wife and mother role and is aggrieved when she doesn't immediately fall in with his plans."

"Philip's not like that. He's a homemaker, a carer. He visits his mother in hospital. He wants children."

Tessa snorted. "Don't you believe it! It's a part he's playing. He'll never change. Men at forty! They make me sick!"

Anna looked at her. "Why are you so bitter?"

Tessa closed her eyes. "I thought you realised," she murmured. "I love Virginia."

"Oh."

"For weeks I've been fighting Gloria for her. But it's no use, for either of us. The last thing Virginia wants is another lover in her life. She was married to Duncan for fourteen years, then Philip caught her. Now she wants to be free. Of all of us."

"So she's not moving in with you?"

Tessa shook her head sadly. "I don't know. I don't know what she wants. I risked my marriage and my children for her. It's all gone horribly wrong." Tears started to run down her cheeks. "Sorry, Anna." She hurried out of the room.

Passion, thought Anna. McMahon was wrong. It's a risk, an adventure. It's the only thing that makes life worth living. I shall ask Philip to come and live with us. There's room. He can keep on his bungalow in Beverley for seeing clients and move in with us. The three children and us. And if he doesn't earn enough money with his clients, I'll go back to work and keep us all.

Feeling happier than she had done for weeks, she pulled out a chair and sat down.

Lottie stood up. "I'm going to talk to you tonight about sex and the male identity. Call it my swan-song." She smiled ruefully. "Contrary to all the propaganda flying around, sexuality isn't a natural force. It's shaped by our culture. What goes on in the bedroom is as much a product of our culture as what goes on in the boardroom. Males identify with sexual activity in our society and feel their identity threatened when they can't perform. Women don't. Male sexuality therefore seems driven rather than liberated because it's the source of their identity. Women get their identity from a multiplicity of roles – mother, daughter, friend, lover." She glanced at Clara. "Our sexuality is less frantic. In the past, it's been too easily assumed that the male pattern of sexuality is the norm, but it's not the number of orgasms we have that matters, but the way our sexuality is integrated into our personality. Our sexuality is too often the product of our sexist conditioning rather than a true expression of our individuality. One way to escape this conditioning," she smiled at Clara, "is to love a woman. Lesbian love is creative, it is wild, it is free . . . "

In loving you, Anna thought, I have been my father's true daughter. Sex with you is orgasmic, pornographic, but it leaves my mind untouched. It's what you do afterwards that touches me, like running my bathwater or sorting out my underclothes, or telling me to drive home carefully. It isn't sex I want with you, it's all the things round it. We've been going about it the wrong way. We must make a fresh start. You'll come and live with us and we'll start doing ordinary things together, the things Richard and I used to do.

She joined in the applause as Lottie sat down. When the meeting ended she went over and gave Lottie a hug. "I'm sorry it's ended like this."

"So am I. We were going to do such great things . . . " She sighed. "Oh well. Clara and I are going for a drink to drown our sorrows. Come with us."

"Sorry, Lottie. I – I can't."

Lottie smiled at Clara. "Anna has a secret life of her own now."

Anna bit her lip. "It's not secret. Not really. I have a friend."

Clara looked interested. Lottie gave a groan. "The heterosexual woman! A man, do you mean? Yes, of course you mean a man. Anyone we know? Not that we know many men."

"He's called Philip. Philip Lawrence."

Lottie shook her head. "Never heard of him. Oh, wait a minute. Lawrence. Isn't that Virginia's ex?"

"That's right." Anna held her breath.

But Lottie only shrugged and said, "I've been steering clear of that lot. Their love lives seem awfully complicated. Don't you get tangled up with them, Anna. Look what's happened to Tessa."

"She's left her children," added Clara, tears starting in her eyes. "I don't know how she could. When so many people haven't . . . "

Lottie put her arm round her. "We've been turned down for adoption," she explained to Anna.

"Oh, I'm sorry." Anna touched Clara's head where it lay on Lottie's shoulder.

"It's hit Clara pretty hard. She spends her life with children. You'd think she'd be just the kind of person agencies would be looking for, wouldn't you?" Lottie kissed the top of Clara's head. "Come on, love, let's go and have that drink. Sure you won't join us?"

Anna shook her head. "I'll see you both soon. Take care."

"And you, Anna."

His bungalow was still in darkness when she drew up outside it. She started to panic. Where was he? Was he following Virginia again? She sat in the car. She'd wait all night if necessary. No, she couldn't wait all night. The children. Penelope. She switched on the radio, then switched it off again. Headlights flashed in her rearview mirror. He pulled up beside her and wound down the window.

"Sorry, sweetheart. Got held up. Coming in?"

"Where were you?" she shouted through her window. Apparently he hadn't heard. He'd wound up his window again. She got out of the car and followed him into the bungalow.

"I can't stay long." She stood in the hall facing him. She took a deep breath. Everything depended on his reaction. "I just came to say, if you want to move in with us, that's all right."

He squeezed her arm. "Smashing, darling. When?" His phone rang. "Damn. Just a minute." He went into the bedroom. There was a pause. Then "Oh, hi! It's you." With his free hand, he reached round behind him and shut the door.

She stood for a moment in the hallway. Her hands had started to tremble. She'd recognised that tone. Not intimate enough for Ginny, it was the one he'd used in the first stages with herself. Cheerful, half-excited, it projected the image of an open, friendly guy. It was only when you got to know him better that the barriers started going up; and you started noticing the lies. She gave herself a little shake. How silly she was being. It was probably an old friend of his on the phone. Or a cousin. It might even be a man . . . though when had Philip ever mentioned a male friend?

She wandered into the kitchen, trying not to read the scraps of paper lying about on the kitchen units (mainly bills), trying not to notice the dates marked on the calendar hanging on his wall (the day after tomorrow was ringed in red – why?). Her eye lit on a note that began *"Dear Ginny, You want to be careful behaving like this. What will the neighbours think? What will your family say? They won't be too pleased, will they? If you don't watch your step I'll be round to your house to give you a slap on that tight little arse of yours . . . "*

"Darling!" He swung her round and kissed her hard on the mouth. "How pleased I am to see you. You don't know how lonely I've been. Am I really moving in with you?"

"You did say you wanted to."

He stepped back and rubbed his cheeks. He smiled. "I do, I do. Listen, have you time for a coffee?" He moved over to switch on the kettle.

Out of the corner of her eye she noticed the note had gone.

She fingered a newspaper. "Who was that on the phone?" she said, as lightly as possible.

"Someone I bumped into in a pub a couple of days ago. They wanted the name of those dressmakers you and I visited once." He spooned coffee into two mugs with a jaunty air. She stared dumbly at him. He looked up. "What's the matter, darling? Can't I have friends?"

"Of course you can," she said miserably.

"Come here." He pulled her towards him. "You're my soul mate. The love of my life." He kissed her again and touched her breasts. She made a slight movement. "What's the matter, sweetheart?"

"I . . . Can't we just talk?"

"Don't you want to make love to me?"

"Yes, but . . . No. Oh, I don't know. I'm muddled. Everything's happened so quickly. I saw your wife tonight."

He started. "Ginny? Where?"

"At the women's meeting."

An expression of blind relief passed over his face. "So that's where . . . " Then he looked anxious. "You didn't talk to her, did you?"

He looked so worried she felt she had to lie. "No, I . . . she left shortly after I arrived."

"Good. Come here, darling. No, it's all right. We won't go to bed. You've got to get back to your children. Just give me a kiss and we'll talk soon on the phone. Make some arrangements about moving in."

"Philip." She hesitated. "I couldn't help seeing . . . " She gestured at the bills.

He looked away. "I am a bit in debt. The practice isn't going too well at the moment. I haven't been able to give it my full attention what with one thing and another. Living with you will help bring a bit of stability back into my life. Give me a chance to get myself together."

"If you're stuck for money I could go back to work." She looked at him. "Yes, I will."

She was so happy the car seemed to sail home by itself.

The house was silent when she let herself in. She went into the sitting-room where Penelope was reading Sara Paretsky. She looked up as Anna came in. "Good evening?" she enquired, closing her book.

"Yes." Anna sat down by her feet and took a deep breath. "Pen," she said, looking straight ahead. "You were right. I have met somebody. A man. I went to see him this evening."

Pen stood up and walked round so that she could see Anna's face. She looked down at her. "Does he make you happy?"

"He does. He really does. You see, he needs me. I've never known anyone need me so much."

There was a silence.

"Well," said Penelope, at last. "I hope he gives you something in return."

"What do you mean?"

"Never mind. I don't know him. I've no right to . . . Will I be meeting him?"

"Of course. He's going to be part of our lives. But we want to take it slowly. There's the children . . . And Pen, I've been thinking, let Beatrice stay with us another couple of nights."

"Are you sure?"

"Sure."

The next day, she rang Cornelius. "I've decided. If the job's still open. I'll take it."

"Splendid, Anna. Come in and see me in a couple of weeks' time and we'll divide up the teaching for next year. I can't tell you how glad I am about this. Thank God you've saved me from some politically correct maniac."

As she put the phone down, it rang again. "Yes?" she said, thinking Cornelius had forgotten something.

"Anna? It's Philip. I've, er, been thinking. About me moving in – when were you thinking of exactly?"

"Well, not straightaway, of course. For one thing, there's the children – I'll have to get them used to the idea, especially Sam."

"The thing is – I was wondering – can we put it off for a bit?"

She was silent a moment. Then she said flatly, "You're getting cold feet."

"No, darling. It's just that I've never lived in a family set up before. It rather gives me the shivers. At home with Mum and Dad there were always rows. It's a big step for me to go back into the family thing. I've lived with women of course. But before Ginny, it was always temporary. I always knew I'd be moving on."

"Look, you don't have to move in. I thought that's what you wanted. You said once . . . "

"Calm down, Anna. I do want it. I'm lonely. Give me a little while to get used to the idea."

"Of course. Take as long as you like." She put down the phone.

Ten minutes later he rang again. "Darling, you're not cross?"

She didn't say anything.

"I love you, you silly girl. You're good for me. You care for me. Not like Ginny. She . . . "

"Can we stop talking about her?"

"Sorry, sweetheart. She's taking a while to get out of my system. But with you around to help me straighten out my life, I'll soon be able to forget her. Are we seeing each other tonight?"

She remembered the ringed date on the calendar. She set him a test. Would he break his engagement, whatever it was, for her? "Not this evening. What about tomorrow?"

His hesitation, if hesitation it was, could only have been a fraction of a second. "All right. Tomorrow evening. I'll come round to your house, shall I? Start getting the children used to me."

"You're serious then about moving in?"

"Of course I am. It'll be wonderful, marvellous. To see my lovely Anna every day."

She spent the evening playing Postman Pat snap with Sam and Beatrice. Watching Sam laugh and shout and cheat with abandon, she saw how happy he was, happier than he'd been for months. Beatrice was smiling too. And I shall be happy, when Philip is here, she thought. We shall be complete then. A new family. I'll make it work. I'll make us all come together. I will.

The next day she took Beatrice shopping for new clothes. As they walked home, she said casually,

"A friend of mine is coming round this evening. You remember Philip, Sam?"

He looked pretty blank.

"Well anyway, he's coming round again tonight. That will be nice, won't it?"

They tidied up the sitting-room. She put on a long skirt in his honour. Beatrice wore one of the new T-shirts they'd bought that afternoon. Sam was in his best pyjamas. Anna's nervousness affected the children. They fidgeted around the room, unable to decide what game to play. At half past eight, she said embarrassed, "He must have been delayed." She took Sam up to bed. Beatrice settled down to watch *Two Point Four Children*.

Anna rang Philip's number. There was no reply. Not even the answering-machine. He must be on his way. At nine Beatrice went to bed. At quarter past nine Anna tried ringing him again. At half past nine she switched on the radio for company. At ten she heard the news come over the radio. "Fire in a house in Grimsby. A man and a woman feared dead." Her heart stood still in fear. She phoned Donna and waited by the front door, keys in hand, till she arrived. Then she got into her car and headed for the Humber Bridge. And all the time she was thinking, no, it can't be, don't let it be. Please don't let it be. We were going to start a new life together.

She turned into Ginny's street and saw the fire engines.

She tore out of the car. Frantically, she began grabbing at bystanders. "What happened? Who is it? Tell me, please!"

An old man answered her. "They found two bodies. Young girl and some bloke. Took them away in an ambulance."

"To the hospital? Where? I must see them."

He shook his head. "No use you following them, love. The doctor couldn't do nothing for them. Lovely girl that one. I used

297

to watch her go off to work every morning, swinging her plait as if she hadn't a care in the world. "

"It was her husband started the fire, they say," a woman put in. "Some crazy fucking idiot to go and do a thing like that."

Anna went up closer and stared at the burnt-out ruin. Her eyes filled with tears, her head began to spin from the smoke and the stench. She sank to the ground. She was conscious of someone bending over her and someone else, whose voice she recognised, clearing people out of the way.

"Stand back, all of you. It's all right, Sergeant Bradley, I know her. I'll look after her."

McMahon held a cup of water to her lips. "Drink this."

She opened her eyes. "You. Again."

"Criminal investigation. It's thought the fire was started deliberately."

She closed her eyes. Her head had started to spin again.

"It was your friend, wasn't it?" he said gently.

"How did you know?"

"I recognised something he was wearing. Nothing much else to recognise."

She turned her head to the side and threw up.

"Jaysus! I'm sorry. What a brute I am. We old pros get hardened. Here, come and sit in my car for a bit."

He helped her up and guided her down the street to where his car was parked. They sat in silence looking at the burnt-out house. From time to time, officers came up to the car and handed McMahon notes.

"Reminds me of Belfast," he said once, breaking the silence.

She said nothing. She was thinking, I never knew him. He was sicker than I thought. If someone's wife has two abortions and starts to act in an unstable way, you have to ask yourself what kind of a man her husband is. I never asked that question. I blamed her straightaway.

"Want a coffee?" he asked.

"Mm?"

She looked up. The fire engines had gone. The crowds had drifted away. How long had they been sitting there?

298

"I can't do anything more here. Forensic will go over the site in the morning. If you don't want a coffee, I'll drive you straight home. Sergeant Bradley can take your car back."

"But – "

"Your hands are shaking. You're in no fit state to drive." He got out and had a word with the policewoman.

"Coffee?"

She nodded. They drove round till they found an all-night café down by the docks. It was full of workmen. The atmosphere was smoky and warm.

They sat down at a table.

"The children! I must ring Donna." She began to scrabble in her bag for coins.

"I'll do it. You look as if you'd hardly be able to dial the number."

"Ask her to stay the night. She can sleep in my bed. I'll use the sofa or something."

He came back a few moments later. "All under control."

"Thanks." She put her hands round her coffee-mug to warm them.

"I suppose you can tell me the background to this?" he said gently.

She gazed down at the plastic cover on the table. It was covered with cigarette-holes and spots of congealed tomato sauce.

"I can. But not tonight."

"No, not tonight. I'm not such a brute as that."

She made an effort. Talk, talk, anything to cover this dreadful dead feeling. "One way or another, I seem to have been helping with your enquiries rather a lot lately, Detective Superintendent, haven't I? First Finch, now this. I hope this means you'll soon be getting promotion?"

He shook his head. "We've had to let Finch go. Not enough evidence. Another unsolved murder on the books. The Assistant Chief Constable's not pleased."

Anna's hands froze round her mug. The knives, the

299

stabbings, a woman swallowing her bitterness for years. Should she tell him? No, it was wild, outrageous. Who'd believe her?

She'd do this one thing for her mother – the only thing, probably, she'd ever be able to do for her. She'd let her live out the rest of her life in peace. If peace was what she'd found. She said nothing.

"Were you very much in love with him?" he asked softly.

On the plastic cloth, she traced figures of eight with her finger. "I thought I was. I was certainly in love with something. A dream, perhaps. Meeting Philip was explosive. There were days when I did nothing but ache for him and now I feel he was a stranger to me. He got closer to me than Richard ever did and now he feels further away than Richard does." She looked up. "How is that possible, Detective Superintendent?"

He shook his head. "I've no answers for you, Anna." He reached across the filthy table and took her hand.

"I'd started relying on him, you see. Oh, not entirely, I wasn't that stupid. Only I always thought he'd be there for me if I needed him. And now he's gone."

She began to weep. He came and sat beside her and held her as she wept.

"Poor Ginny as well. She wanted to live and all she found was death. She didn't deserve it. None of us deserves it."

She fumbled for a handkerchief. He took one out of his pocket and handed it to her.

"Thanks." She wiped her eyes. "How come you're always around when something happens to me?"

He looked at her. "It's no coincidence, Anna. I – care for you."

"Do you?" she said in surprise. "Why?"

"I recognise a brave woman when I see one."

"Brave? I'm not brave. I can hardly cope on my own."

"Most people can hardly cope on their own. You do better than most."

"I had him."

"Was he all that much of a help to you?"

"I . . . " She looked down at his handkerchief. "No, I don't suppose he was. But you don't love people because you think they can help you."

McMahon looked away. "That's what I was afraid of."

Her finger went on tracing figures of eight. In all her time with Philip she'd been imagining something that didn't exist. One part of it only had been real – Philip had awakened in her something that had lain dormant for years. It was unhealthy, it was obsessive, it was maybe even slightly childish but she was forced to recognise that unresolved childish part as her own, a thing she'd have to take into account from now on. Her finger stopped moving. She looked up.

"Can we go home? I want to be with my children."

"Of course."

He drove her back over the Bridge and dropped her outside her house. At the door, she hesitated,

"Will you . . . be around for the next while?"

"If you want me to be."

"I think I do."

"Then I'll be around."

"Thanks . . . Mike."

He smiled.

She went into the house where her children and Richard's daughter lay sleeping. This was her treasure, her life's blood. Anything else, if there were to be anything else, would be extra.

She leant her cheek against the mantelpiece in the sitting-room. But I could do with a friend. Everyone needs friends. She made up a bed on the sofa. Yes, Mike McMahon had grown to be a friend. Gently, almost without her realising it, he'd got himself involved in her life. He was kind, he was safe . . . She lay down under the duvet and slept.

At five she woke with Richard's name on her lips. Her cheeks were wet with tears. Richard, I miss him. I miss his touch, his smell, the feel of his arms around me. Richard, I need you here to help me get through this.

She flung an arm across the vast empty sofa. It's a myth that there'll always be someone there to comfort you, she thought.

It's a story somebody once made up and we all fell for it. I have to learn to care for myself. There is no one else to do it.

Then, very clearly, she heard Richard's voice say, "Nothing of love is ever lost, Anna. Nothing."

And she thought of the girl sleeping upstairs. Richard's daughter. His last gift to her.